3 9082 14518 9729

W9-BJZ-771

AUBURN HILLS PUBLIC LIBRARY 50
3400 EAST SEYBURN DRIVE
AUBURN HILLS, MI 48326
248-370-9466

Again, Rachel

Again, Rachel

MARIAN KEYES

Doubleday Canada

AUBURN HILLS PUBLIC LIBRARY 50
3400 EAST SEYBURN DRIVE
AUBURN HILLS, MI 48326
248-370-9466

Copyright © 2022 Marian Keyes

Blossom tree illustration copyright © 2022 Gemma Correll

All rights reserved. The use of any part of this publication, reproduced, transmitted in any form or by any means electronic, mechanical, photocopying, recording or otherwise, or stored in a retrieval system without the prior written consent of the publisher—or in the case of photocopying or other reprographic copying, license from the Canadian Copyright Licensing Agency—is an infringement of the copyright law.

Doubleday Canada and colophon are registered trademarks of Penguin Random House Canada Limited

Library and Archives Canada Cataloguing in Publication

Title: Again, Rachel / Marian Keyes.
Names: Keyes, Marian, author.
Identifiers: Canadiana (print) 20210370262 | Canadiana (ebook) 20210370289 |
    ISBN 9780385675741 (hardcover) | ISBN 9780385675376 (softcover) |
    ISBN 9780385675383 (EPUB)
Classification: LCC PR6061.E93 A72 2022 | DDC 823/.914—dc23

This book is a work of fiction. Names, characters, places and incidents are products of the author's imagination or are used fictitiously. Any resemblance to actual events or locales or persons, living or dead, is entirely coincidental.

Emoticons wink and smile by Simon Mettler from the Noun Project

Cover illustration: Gemma Correll

Printed in Canada

Published in Canada by Doubleday Canada,
a division of Penguin Random House Canada Limited

www.penguinrandomhouse.ca

10 9 8 7 6 5 4 3 2 1

Penguin
Random House
DOUBLEDAY CANADA

For my mother,
with gratitude and love

The Truth must dazzle gradually,
Or every man be blind—

Emily Dickinson

Forgive yourself for the many ways you
hurt yourself, when all you were doing
was trying to survive.

Anonymous

I

The touch of his hand, lightly circling my belly button, woke me. Still half-asleep, I enjoyed the feel of his fingers tracing lower.

But before we could go any further, I needed to know the time.

'Ten past seven.' His voice was thick.

The relief of sleeping through a whole night! I smiled straight into his face. '*Now* you have my full attention.'

Afterwards, we lay together in a rosy glow. But time was passing. 'I've to go, sweetie.'

'Already?'

'Have to drop in home, feed Crunchie, pick up a couple of things before work.'

'Uh.' There was that meaningful little pause. 'Okay.'

We weren't going there, not now. 'Have a great trip.'

He kissed me. 'I'll call when I can. But it's unpredictable.'

'Don't worry.' I slid from the bed. 'I hope it goes well. See you Sunday.'

He held my wrist. 'I'll miss you.'

'I'll miss you too.'

In the kitchen, I gulped a quick glass of water.

Finley wandered in, scratching his head. 'Hey, Rachel.'

'Hey. I'm off now. See you Sunday?'

'Nah, I'll be with Mum.'

'Say hi from me. And if you felt like doing an act of kindness, I'm guessing your dad'—I pointed a finger to the ceiling—'would kill for a coffee.'

Finley looked doubtful and I had to laugh. 'Go on, you lazy brat.'

'Okaaay.'

I gave him a quick hug, then darted away into the bright spring morning.

*

As soon as I pushed my front door open, Crunchie hurled herself at me in ecstatic welcome. I dropped to my knees, rubbed her ears and spoke in my special Crunchie voice. 'Hello, you good girl, hello!'

'That you, Rachel?' Kate stuck her head over the banister, strands of wet hair tumbling down. A round brush and a hairdryer were in her hands.

I dashed up the stairs and into the bathroom. 'I ran out of contact lenses.' I rooted around in the drawer.

'How's Quin?' she asked.

'Grand. Off to New Mexico until Sunday.'

'Lucky him!'

Kate was my niece, the daughter of my eldest sister Claire. She'd been living with me for the past few months because the brutal commute from Claire's house in West Dublin to her job in a care home in Wicklow was breaking her. These days, she spent a scant twelve minutes travelling to work instead of the two-and-a-half-hour round trip which had been the norm.

I was mad about her. She was serious, sweet, she walked Crunchie when I couldn't and she was (very much *not* a Walsh family trait) a clean freak. Obviously that came from her dad's side and while I was no fan of his, only a fool would complain about a housemate who was forever pulling a mop from the utility room and saying, 'I'll just give the floor a quick wash.'

Her 'real' job was acting. But the universe drip-dripped work for her, in exquisitely calibrated amounts, keeping her forever on a knife-edge of uncertainty. Every time she was on the verge of giving up, she got thrown a small part, just enough to resuscitate her hope.

'Why are you up?' I'd just remembered she wasn't rostered to work today. (Every week, she messaged me her schedule so I'd know if I needed to commandeer my neighbours Benigno and Jasline to walk Crunchie.) With a burst of hope, I gasped, 'You've an audition?'

'Today? No. Bit of work for Helen.'

My youngest sister, Helen, ran a small private detective agency. Recently, she'd been inveigling Kate to help out, especially on the unpleasant jobs, which usually involved lying in a muddy ditch for long spells of time, stealthily taking photos. It was the kind of work Helen herself used to take great pride in but lately she'd been saying, with increasing frequency, 'Rural surveillance is a young woman's game.'

Her stated opinion was that, aged twenty-three, Kate was the perfect person for such hardship. 'Twenty-somethings don't get cold, don't get wet and have no sense of smell.' Helen *insisted* that this was scientific fact. She was a defiantly contrary person with the strongest will I had ever bumped up against.

'Let me guess,' I asked Kate. 'She has you spying on some trickster who runs the smelliest pig farm in County Cavan?'

'Haha. Nothing so bad. Townie surveillance, an insurance claim. A man who says he can't walk because of his bad back.'

'God, it's twenty past eight!' I gave her a quick squeeze and jumped under the shower. No time to blow-dry my hair, I'd just have to let it dry naturally and accept the accompanying wayward misery.

To counteract the bad hair, I put on my denim jumpsuit, which made me look like I worked at a carwash. I wore it so often that my colleagues 'joked' that I had no other clothes. But something about the stride-y freedom it gave me, especially when paired with sneakers, made me feel mildly powerful.

Meanwhile, Crunchie was watching, her expression sorrowful.

'I *have* to work,' I told her woebegone face. 'But I'll be back this evening. It's a lovely day out there. Run around the back garden and bark at birds, you'll be fine!'

Despite my little house being only fifteen minutes' drive from work, I was still late for the morning meeting.

I hurried up the steps of the Cloisters and through the hallway, almost tripping over Harlie Clarke, one of my charges, who was hoovering the carpet with furious resentment. A 29-year-old alcoholic, with a devotion to her appearance that almost counted as a second addiction, she looked great—up at six thirty every morning to do the full works—intricate contouring, lustrous lashes and long blonde hair, Airwrapped into sleek obedience.

Like nearly everyone, she'd come to the Cloisters convinced she was fine. But I'd chipped away until her shell of denial had shattered. Now she couldn't not see that she was an alcoholic and she was *raging*.

'Morning, Harlie,' I said.

With a bile-filled glance, she drove the hoover towards my ankle. You know, she really had the most *amazing* eyebrows. Microbladed, of course, but very natural-looking. Undoubtedly done by an expert and not some chancer who'd learnt from YouTube. There were times when I *itched* for us to discuss beauty stuff.

But maybe not now. I skipped away before she maimed me.

In the meeting room, five of the seven therapists were at the table, plus three facilitators, Nurse Moze and Ted, our big boss—who glanced at his phone, shook his head and muttered, 'Tut-tut.'

I mouthed, *Sorry*, slid into a chair and twisted my damp hair into a messy bun to get it off my face.

Moze was reading her report on the previous night. 'Busy shift. Trassa Higgins—one of yours, Rachel? Didn't sleep. Came down to the desk at about three a.m. We chatted, did a crossword, she went back to bed around five, but when I looked in at six, she was still awake.'

This told me that Trassa would be vulnerable today. Which was both good and bad. Bad because vulnerable meant, like, *vulnerable*. Not great in a 68-year-old grandmother addicted to gambling. But good in that she might be too exhausted to maintain her shield of denial. She'd been here for well over a week and was proving to be a tough nut to crack. Today might be the day.

'Simon and Prissie,' Moze said to a chorus of sighs around the table. 'Yep. At it again. Waldemar caught them on his one a.m. check. Behind the sofa in the rec room, this time.'

'So?' Ted looked at me, then Carey-Jane, who were respectively Simon and Prissie's assigned therapists. 'What now?'

Full of regret, I shook my head. 'Simon has to leave. He's already had one warning. He's not ready for recovery. He doesn't care.'

'I want Prissie to stay.' Carey-Jane was just as resolute. 'But we add sex and love to her list of addictions. All part of the bigger picture.'

'But if Simon leaves and Prissie stays, what message does that send?' Yasmine asked.

Ted shrugged. 'Who cares? We make the rules.'

Ted could be a worry. A competent administrator and a (periodically) inspiring boss, a gleaming streak of 'Unopposed Despot' ran through him.

'Two newbies already arriving this morning,' Ted said. 'And with Simon going, we can take another one tomorrow or Friday.'

Addiction was big business. There was a waiting list—*always*—for the Cloisters.

Next, each therapist gave a round-table update on their various charges, so that we all knew precisely how every single patient was doing—who was extra-vulnerable right now, who was pushing back hard—then it was time to leave for group.

Ted caught me at the door. 'Not like you to be late.'

'Aaaahhh . . .' I could hardly say, 'My boyfriend is off to Taos for four days and we needed some together time.'

'. . . Rachel?'

'Traffic,' I said. 'Sorry. Won't happen again.'

Then I left to hoick Simon out of breakfast and tell him to pack his bags.

2

When people ask how I met Quin then notice my hesitation, they usually say, 'Tinder? Hey. No shame in that.'

But it was worse than Tinder. Almost two years ago, in 2016, Quin and I had met at a meditation retreat, a silent one, held in a big old house in the middle of nowhere. I'd gone because I was a Failed Meditator. In all my years of trying, despite the hundreds of candle flames I'd stared into, I'd never been able to stop my thoughts. *Fifteen minutes really isn't that long, I just need to empty my mind empty empty empty thinking of absolutely nothing. Hey, look, I'm actually meditating. Except if I notice that I'm doing it, does that mean that I'm actually not? God, I never cancelled that appointment with the physio, I'll do it now, well not now now but as soon as I finish my meditation . . .*

By seven o'clock on that Friday evening in late March, about thirty of us were sitting cross-legged on yoga mats, slyly trying to check each other out without getting caught. We were just this mass of nervous, hopeful people. More women than men—always the way—ranging in age from twenties to sixties.

I'd have *loved* to know everyone's reason for attending, but we were literally forbidden from speaking. Also banned were alcohol, coffee, phones, electronics, books and magazines.

Our instructors were a kind and deliciously lithe young woman (yoga, of course) and three well-meaning young men, all a bit *lentilly*—rough brown clothing, pale faces with sparse, whiskery beards, their hairlines already in retreat.

Over the forty-eight hours, we did oodles of group meditation, during which I spent a shameful amount of time wondering if all three of the Lentil Boys were in love with Yoga Girl. They'd have to be, surely? She was so nice. And, of course, there was the litheness. When my mind should have been stilling, I was inspecting the unkempt trio and wondering if she ever slept with any of them. Or indeed *all* of them? She was absolutely beautiful, but one thing I've learnt is never to underestimate the confidence of the most unremarkable of men.

As well as meditating, we did a few yoga classes, ate vegan food at regular intervals and swilled down as much sage tea as we could stomach. A large part of Saturday afternoon was spent eating a single raisin. About half an hour in, I realized it was maybe the twentieth time I'd done such a thing: *every* course on mindfulness and meditation wheeled it out to demonstrate how to slow down and live in the moment. I sighed quietly. Maybe it was time to throw in the towel for good on this meditation thing.

Late on Sunday afternoon, just as the end was in sight, one of the Lentil Boys announced a LovingKindness Meditation—an exercise in intimacy where you sat opposite another person, staring into their eyes, thinking kind and loving thoughts for ten long minutes.

It was *excruciating.*

Uneven numbers meant I ended up being partnered with the most whiskery of the Lentil Boys and from the way his pupils flared and dilated, he was clearly giving it socks with the LovingKindness thoughts. The only way to cope was to disappear deep inside myself.

Eventually, someone chimed something chime-y—probably a Tibetan prayer bowl, it usually was—and the longest ten minutes in eternity came to an end; this was our cue to break the gaze and start with someone new. I gave a pained smile and twisted away.

Yoga Girl called, 'Has everyone swapped partners?'

I looked at my new person. A man. His face was as expressive as a poker but there was something going on in his eyes. Almost a smirk. Something to do with the 'swapping partners' comment.

Juvenile.

And yet.

I stared at him. He stared at me. I thought, *I feel kindly towards you. I feel lovingly towards you.*

Holding his unblinking gaze, I decided that he was returning the kind and loving thoughts. Then I *actually* felt something. Some sort of relief.

No one was more surprised than me.

Even as I gave a wobbly smile, tears started to spill from my eyes. Heavy drops plopped into my cupped hands and there were none of the awkward pats or fumbling for tissues that usually accompany public crying. We simply sat still and held the gaze.

When the bowl chimed, the man tilted his head, asking a silent question: was I okay?

I nodded and smiled, dashed away the surprise tears, then turned to meet my next partner.

Maybe half an hour later, the weekend came to a close and our last instruction was to remain 'non-verbal' until we were off the property.

Upstairs, in the dormitory, as I threw my few possessions into my bag, my heart was lighter than it had been in a long time. The peace of meditation still eluded me—it probably always would—but, entirely unexpectedly, I felt absolved. It didn't make sense but that man, that stranger, had cleared away some of the wreckage of my past.

One of the Lentil Boys returned my electronics then I stepped out into the chilly evening—and saw the man standing there, pretending to fiddle with his phone.

This felt awkward. Something good had taken place in that room and that room was probably where it should stay.

After a quick nod, I made for my car, slightly startled by the long, low, cream-coloured Merc in the space beside mine. It looked as if it had come direct from a seventies' police show, very at home screeching through narrow streets and doing handbrake turns. It was hard to know if it was beautiful or just flashy.

'Hey,' I heard. I turned.

'I'm Quin.'

Well, *he* sounded sure of himself. *And* he'd broken the rules.

Then I decided that it didn't matter. 'I'm Rachel.'

He walked up to me. 'Could I . . . ?' he asked. 'Could we . . . ?'

'I don't know,' I said. 'I'm not looking for, you know, that sort of . . .'

'I don't think I am, either,' he said. (A lie, as it turned out.) 'But whatever happened in there, it touched me, and it helped you?'

Even though less than an hour earlier I'd stared into his eyes for ten unbroken minutes, this was the first time I paid attention to the bigger picture. His brown hair was shorn tight and he was taller than me (I was five foot nine, this wasn't always a given). On closer examination, his hiking boots, his technical-looking top, the way his skin was pulled tight over his cheekbones were characteristic of those men who did *lots* of gruelling physical challenges. Men who always had three protein bars on their person and whose physical make-up was 0 per cent body fat, 87 per cent sinew, 13 per cent rage.

He didn't look like he belonged here. 'Can I ask something?' I surprised myself by saying. 'Why did you do this weekend?'

'Because . . . I never feel like I'm done.'

I waited.

'I want something,' he said. 'Then I get it. Then I want a better version of it. Or I don't want it any more.'

Oh my God, one of those *men.*

'My happiness is always over there, just out of reach,' he said. 'Mr Upgrade, that's me.'

I actually laughed. 'Well, no one can say you didn't warn me.'

'So?' he asked. 'What brought *you* here?'

Okay, here we go. 'I'm in recovery. Meditation is recommended.'

If he responded with a blank stare, this burgeoning friendship would immediately hit the skids.

'I'm an addict,' I elaborated.

Baldly, he said, 'I know what "in recovery" means.'

That was a good start because most people haven't a clue. Then, when they get it, they usually run for the hills. I've often said there should be a Tinder for us Twelve Step types.

'Have you been clean for long?' And *that* was an excellent question, an informed one. He wanted to know if I was stable or if I was likely to slide and lapse.

'Years.'

'O-*kay!*' Suddenly he no longer looked tightly wound. 'So can I have your number?'

Why not? That was what I thought. What harm could it do?

He said he'd be in touch, then slid into his 1970s, flashy-stroke-beautiful car and roared away.

3

A client leaving before completing their six weeks was always disappointing. But this was the second time Simon had broken the rule forbidding sexual contact with other clients. And *still*, even as he was being bounced from rehab, he had that flirty gleam. He just couldn't help himself.

'You're thirty-seven,' I reminded him. 'Too old for this behaviour.'

'And you're . . . what?' He studied me with a dirty grin. 'Thirty-five? Thirty-six?'

I'd never see my thirties again and he knew it. 'Old enough to know I'm being played. Do your cheesy lines ever actually work?'

'All the time.'

'They ever work on women who *aren't* vulnerable?'

At that, a shadow scudded over him.

'If you don't get serious about recovery,' I said, 'your addiction will kill you.'

He shrugged. 'Live fast, die young.'

'That option is no longer available, Simon. You're too old.'

But he was impervious. He was going back out into the world and the first person he'd call would be his dealer.

Between fifty and sixty addicts a year passed through my hands and I cared a lot—maybe too much—about every one of them. If there was anything I could do to help Simon, I'd have done it. Letting him go was really painful.

I over-identified with my charges. Of course I did. I'd once been one of them.

Walking into the Abbot's Quarter (in reality, just a draughty ex-dining room) for this morning's group, the chatter was both anxious and giddy— rumours were hard currency in here. The possibility that Simon had been expelled would have unsettled them all. Intense bonds formed very quickly in rehab. That's not to say that everyone got on—often they absolutely hated each other. But indifference was rare.

Chalkie was the first to notice me. 'Sketch!' he hissed. 'She's here.'

I took my seat—the second worst one in the circle. That was the bad thing about being late to group, all the comfortable chairs were gone. I'd have to endure at least two hours in this low-backed upright thing with the wonky leg—and do it without demonstrating discomfort. Any display of vulnerability would erode my power.

My little flock of ducklings was quiet now, flicking looks at the last empty place—where Simon would have sat—waiting for me to speak. But their response to this upheaval was information for me, so I assumed my blandest face and prepared to wait it out.

Would today be the day that FedEx delivered my new sneakers, I found myself wondering. I'd only ordered them yesterday but sometimes they arrived the next day. Usually, though, it took two days. Occasionally, *three*. (*That* was hard. I'd be all geared up, my head generating pre-dopamine and then the cupboard would be bare . . .)

'Someone say something,' Dennis pleaded. 'I'm sweating like a pig from the silence!'

Right, back to work! Dennis, an alcoholic who had arrived yesterday, was still locked tight in the fiction that there was nothing wrong with him. Apparently, he was only here to 'shut up the wife'. Today—just like yesterday— he wore a wrinkled suit with soup stains on the trousers. His tie was askew, two buttons were missing from his shirt and his straining belly overhung his belt. A local councillor in the town he hailed from—one of those close-knit places in the middle of nowhere—I found him impossible to dislike.

'What's wrong with silence, Dennis?' My voice was cool but the rocky chair leg, tilting me forwards, then backwards, as I spoke, definitely undermined me.

''Tis too quiet.'

Couldn't argue with that.

'Can I ask a question?' Harlie's voice shook. 'Has Simon been kicked out?'

When he wasn't romancing Prissie behind the couch in the rec room, Simon had flirted outrageously with Harlie. She'd sparkled beneath his sketchy charms and they were shaping up to be a situation. Maybe it was as well he was gone.

'Simon has left,' I said.

Distraught, she crumpled into herself. Giles, another smoothie with an eye for the ladies, shifted uncomfortably, perhaps wondering if he was next to be ejected. Working-class hero Chalkie twitched, primed to sniff out a miscarriage of justice. Roxy, leaving in a week, frowned with concern. Dennis watched the others for hints on how to react. And Trassa exclaimed, 'You fancy him!'

'And what if I do!' Dennis was unable, as always, to resist making a joke.

'Not *you*,' Trassa said. 'Harlie.'

'I don't!'

She did, though. I'd keep an extra eye on her over the next few days.

'So Simon's *gone*, gone?' Chalkie asked. 'Just thrown out on his ear? No chance to say goodbye.'

'None,' I agreed. I had to plant my foot firmly on the floor to stop my off-putting swaying.

'Chalkie, why are you even bothered?' Roxy asked, doing my job for me. They get like that when they're nearing the end of their six weeks, thinking they know it all, it's sort of lovely. 'You couldn't stand him, said he was "a middle-class prick—"'

'"—corrupted by his own privilege". Same as yourself, nothing personal, like.' Chalkie's blue eyes burnt with fervour. 'But he's still entitled to a fair hearing.'

Chalkie was a self-educated firebrand from Dublin's inner city. I wasn't supposed to have favourites, but if I had, it would have been him. Articulate, angry and compassionate (unless you lived in a leafy suburb, in which case he wouldn't 'piss on you if you were on fire'), he was in danger of burning up in his own rage.

With his star quality, he was great at galvanizing his community behind a cause—for example, he took on and won breakfasts for hungry school kids. He did a lot of good. But every now and then—often at the most important part of one of his campaigns—he lapsed and began taking heroin again.

'Simon broke the rules,' I said. 'Twice.'

'Well, maybe those rules are bullshit.'

At this, Giles began to chafe. A well-heeled cocaine addict in his mid-fifties, he was no fan of Chalkie and his causes. A dazzlingly successful, thirty-year career in advertising had imbued him with the conviction that everyone made their own luck.

'"The most effective way to restrict democracy",' Chalkie said—he was quoting somebody, probably Noam Chomsky; it was usually Noam Chomsky, '"is to transfer decision-making from the public arena to unaccountable institutions."'

'*Christ.*' Giles recrossed his lanky legs and hissed through clenched teeth.

Chalkie fixed his gaze on Giles. 'Got a problem, man?' He paused. 'Ya tennis-playing prick.'

'Chalkie.' My voice was low but very firm. The patients were encouraged to go in hot and heavy when discussing each other's addictions but gratuitous insults were *not* okay. 'Apologize to Giles.'

'Sorry . . .'

Giles inclined his head, to demonstrate pained acceptance.

'. . . for saying you play tennis.'

Giles's head jerked up again, colour flooding his handsome, bony face.

'Prancing around in your white shorts, yelping, "Deuce!"' Chalkie scoffed. 'No wonder you got a taste for the snow. The shame, amirite?'

Laughter broke out. Nearly everyone loved Chalkie, that was part of his problem. He got away with far too much.

'Sorry, Rachel,' Chalkie said, with a grin. 'Sorry, Giles.'

Abruptly, Giles began to weep. Entering his fifth week, it was textbook behaviour. His denial was stripped away, his selfishness detailed by everyone in his life, he'd moved through rage and was currently mired in grief.

'All right, Giles?' I passed him a tissue.

'Fine,' he choked, his face in his hands.

Okay, time for Trassa. Married for fifty-one years, with five children and eleven grandchildren, she projected cosy respectability, underscored by cardigans, shapeless skirts and reading glasses on a chain. A compulsive gambler, she'd admitted herself here to convince Ronan, her middle son—the only one of her children still talking to her—to pay off her latest round of debts.

'Trassa,' I said. 'Your life story, please.'

It was the first written exercise the patients did and usually kick-started their thawing out.

'It's not finished yet.' Her smile was sweet. 'Might I remind you I'm sixty-eight, I don't have the energy these young ones do.'

'Have it ready tomorrow.' I was stern. 'In the meantime, why don't you tell us again exactly why you're in rehab.'

'Well . . .' A wide smile creased her soft, powdered features. There was something about her that always reminded me of a bap. 'Ronan, my young fella, overreacted.'

I let that hang in the air for several long moments—then pounced on Dennis. 'I've seen you having chats with Trassa. What has she told you?'

'Hey!' Chalkie jumped in. 'Don't make a snitch of him!'

'No, you're all right.' Dennis was confident. 'No one is snitching. Poor Trassa was unlucky, is all. Took cash out on a credit card for a dead certainty on the Grand National. Never saw the bills from the bank because they sent them online. The interest mounted up—the rates are criminal, as I needn't tell any of ye—and first thing Trassa knew was when debt collectors arrived at her front door, upsetting her husband, Seamus Senior. *Who's in a wheelchair.*'

Yes, this sounded familiar. Except in the version I'd been told, the race was the Kentucky Derby.

'By then the amount she owed had trebled. How could the poor woman pay it? She's on a pension! One of her sons said he'd cover it, but that she had to "go to rehab". Same as meself, we're both here to please another person.'

A rhythmic, high-pitched squeaking noise was now emanating from Giles. He didn't know how to cry properly because he'd had no practice. Before last weekend, he hadn't cried in forty-five years. Really, he should have been howling and banging on the floor, mourning his lost decades and the trail of abandoned women and children he'd left in his wake, but he was too repressed. Still, it was encouraging that he was crying at all.

'Trassa?' I asked. 'How much money did your son pay off for you?'

Sharply, she said, 'That's private.'

I gave her a look. 'You're in rehab. Nothing's private in here. How much?'

I knew that Trassa had, without mentioning sums, given the impression that it was about fifty euro.

'I took, I think it was . . . two thousand euro out from the cash machine.'

Shock bounced around the room. *Two thousand?* Even Roxy, who was far enough along to understand denial, hadn't expected that.

'*Two* thousand?' I asked.

'Oh, look, I don't know.' Trassa went the full-on, dithery granny. 'My old head.'

'It was four thousand.' She knew it. I knew it. And now everyone else knew it too. 'How did you get the credit card?'

'The bank offered it to me.'

'The bank *offered it* to you?'

Pink heat spread across her face.

'You mean you applied for it?' I said.

'Yes, yes.' She was desperate to shut me up.

'In your husband's name. Because your personal credit is shot to pieces.'

The mood in the room was dismayed—Trassa was regarded with great fondness—and this story didn't fit their picture of her. Dennis in particular looked desperately confused.

At lunchtime I stuck a hopeful head into the admin office, hoping to see a FedEx box in the corner, but Brianna said, 'Nothing. Sorry. What have you ordered this time?'

'Sneakers.'

'*More* sneakers? Anyone would think you were an addict.' We both did fake-wheezy laughs.

Like any sensible person with a job, I got my online purchases delivered to work. Brianna was as good as a personal concierge. Ted disapproved: our personal lives shouldn't overlap with our professional lives. If any of my ducklings stumbled across me gleefully tearing boxes open and shrieking with delight, it might be difficult to retain their respect in group.

But what was the alternative? Arriving home from work to find a little card bearing the dread words, 'Go to depot'? I don't *think* so.

Despite the disappointment, I got on with my day and around 5 p.m. I was in the office typing up the daily notes when my phone rang. As soon as I saw who was calling, my heart nearly stopped. What on earth . . . ? Joey. *Narky* Joey? Why was he . . . ? He would *never* be ringing for a friendly chat.

But mixed with the shock was curiosity and—madly—hope. My heart was pounding in my ears as I answered. 'Joey?'

'That you, Rachel? Listen, Luke's ma died yesterday. He's on his way home. Funeral's on Friday.'

'Luke? What . . . How . . . ?' I had so many questions. How had he been for the last six years? Had he got married again? Had kids? 'How . . .' I stammered. 'How is he?'

'His ma just died. That's how he is, Rachel.' Then Joey was gone.

At the best of times, Joey would never have won a Mr Conviviality contest. That hostility, though . . .

My hands were shaking so much that I needed to sit on them. Had that really happened? Did Joey just call me? Momentarily I worried that I'd imagined it.

'You all right?' Murdo gave me a sharp look.

'Mmmmm.' My lips felt numb. 'Fine. Just . . . stuff.'

'Sure?'

Silently, I nodded. Feelings flooded me: loss and longing and . . . yes, anger, and while it would probably be better if I didn't see Luke, I knew I still wanted to.

Why had Joey called? Because Luke had asked him?

But that wasn't very likely.

Unless . . . it *was*?

Should I go to the funeral? Or stay away? Back in the day I'd been very fond of Mrs Costello but we hadn't kept in touch.

I waited to see if the friendly voice in my head had anything useful to offer. But all there was, was silence.

Really? I asked. *Seriously?*

Still nothing. So I was on my own with this. Maybe I should pretend that there'd been no phone call? Just push it down and get on with my life until Monday, maybe Tuesday, whenever Luke had left the country again and gone home.

But what if I regretted it? Missed the chance of seeing him? Or felt guilty about not paying my respects to a decent woman who'd been good to me?

I hadn't felt this unravelled in—God, I literally couldn't remember when. The right thing was to ring Nola, my sponsor and the Wisest Woman I Knew, clean and serene for almost twenty-seven years.

'What's up, pet?'

'Luke.'

'What about him? No, don't tell me, come straight over. Drive safely!'

Half an hour later, I was pulling up outside Nola's beautiful red-brick house.

Unbelievably, it was twenty years since *I* had been a patient at the Cloisters and she'd come in to tell her story of recovery from addiction. With her beautiful highlights, zippy little sports car and impressive job, I thought she must be an actress in the pay of the treatment centre.

However, when I left rehab, I discovered she really *was* an addict. But she was drug-free, happy, hilarious and robust enough to weather all emotional storms. I wanted to be *exactly* like her so she took me under her wing and helped me to grow up.

My time in the Cloisters had revealed that I was an addict, but Nola had convinced me that, without taking anything mood-altering, I could live a normal life, a *better*-than-normal life. That I could cope with unpleasant emotions, that I could aspire to a healthy relationship with a man, that I could aim for whatever job I wanted—a life I was sure could never happen to a person as worthless as me.

I parked my car, hurried up Nola's black-and-white chessboard path and Harry, her delicious husband, opened their smartly painted front door and welcomed me inside.

In my early days in recovery I'd a *right* crush on Harry, he was just lovely—always keeping a respectful distance but never less than kind. I *yearned* for a man as good as him.

Nola used to tell me that if I stayed clean long enough, I too would get a life 'beyond my wildest dreams'. That was hard to believe.

Yet it had happened. All of it. Including a man as lovely as Harry.

Nola put a mug of tea in front of me. 'Go on, tell me.'

It didn't take long. 'So?' I asked. 'Should I go to the funeral?'

'Was Joey ringing off his own bat? Or on Luke's say-so?'

'I didn't think to ask, and I'm not ringing him back—I have *some* pride.'

'Grand.' She laughed. 'No one's making you. Okay, let's look at the facts. On the one hand you and Luke have unfinished business—'

'Do we, though, Nola? It was so long ago. Isn't it—what's the word when accounts have been inactive so long that they no longer exist?—moribund? Inert?'

'This might be the chance for you to tidy up some of that mess.'

'But what if I see him and end up devastated all over again?'

'What's your inner voice telling you?'

'Nothing. Radio silence.'

Nola lapsed into thought. 'In which case, you must Golden Key it.'

'No!' This was a device Nola was *far* too fond of: when a problem has myriad possible solutions but no clear answer, you put the whole snarly mess into an imaginary box and lock it with a Golden Key—also imaginary. Then, you *do nothing*. You don't even think about it: as soon as it pops up in your mind, you put it back in the box and wait until the universe unfolds the answer.

You don't drive your friends and sisters insane by discussing it until everyone is crying from tedium. No. You just keep your mouth shut and wait it out.

(The reasoning is that humans are weaklings who want the solution which gives the quickest gratification; we deliberately blind ourselves to any medium-term damage. I *knew* all of this; I just didn't want to hear it.)

'Ah, Nola! Can't you just tell me what to do.'

'It doesn't work like that and you know it.'

'Sorry. You're right. Absolutely. Yes. Thank you. Golden Keying it *right* now.'

Feck that. I was getting a second opinion. But I had to choose my person carefully, so they'd tell me what I wanted to hear. Even if I wasn't sure what that was.

My sister Margaret was very cut and dried, imbued with a bone-deep sense of right and wrong. I could hear her insisting, 'You have to go to that funeral! She was once your mother-in-law—have some decency.'

Mum would agree, but only because she *adored* funerals, beadily checking out the quality of the coffin, the mawkishness of the hymns and the enthusiasm of the crying. Though she enjoyed robust good health, she was constantly planning her own send-off—'The saddest hymns you can find'—and was adamant about one thing: 'There's to be none of this "life being celebrated" codswallop! I want people in *floods*.' An expensive, hardwood coffin had been earmarked. ('Do *not* get me a flimsy wicker thing. I heard of a man who slid out, *slid right out* and fell onto the church floor as he was being carried up the aisle. And he had no trousers on, nor underpants either, only his shirt and jacket. Do *not* let that happen to me.')

Helen would tell me there was no need to go. 'Fuck him!' she'd say, her voice dripping scorn. 'You owe Luke Costello nothing!'

Anna? She had a strong fondness for woo-woo codology. She'd probably agree with Nola.

Claire? Hard to know which side she'd come down on.

Dad? If he dared to express an opinion at all, no one ever paid any attention.

My best friend, Brigit? She'd be so here for this but she was *busy*. A mother of three boys, aged fifteen, fourteen and ten, and a girl of eight, she lived in the gorgeous wilds of north Connemara, at everyone's beck and call. Working from home (but oh my God, *what* a home), her job description was 'part-time' but the hours looked suspiciously closer to full-time.

A breezy text would be the way to go with Brigit. That way, if she liked the sound of things, she could get involved and if she had too much on, she could pass.

I hugged Nola and hurried back to my car, having decided to consult all of my sisters. At least that way I'd get to explore every possible option.

I reached for my phone then—spookily—*at that very moment* a WhatsApp arrived from Claire. Need to talk. Dilemma.

I replied, I've a dilemma too. Calling a summit for 8pm tonight. You round?

Yep, she said. My dilemma a private one, tho. Need a pre-summit with you.

Our family summits usually took place in Mum and Dad's house because

18

they lived equidistant from my sisters and me. But Claire and I arranged our sneaky *pre*-summit for seven forty-five.

Then I WhatsApped the Walsh family group: Mum and Dad's, tonight, 8pm. I need advice, Luke's mum has died, should I go to the funeral?

Immediately my phone blew up with messages, texts, voice-notes—like the internet when Beyoncé drops a surprise album. All of my sisters were on for meeting up, except for Anna, who rang to rage about the inconvenience of her living in New York. (And who advised me to 'Put it out to the universe.')

My next act was to call Mum, to check she'd be home. Even if she wasn't, we'd still meet there, eat her biscuits and frighten Dad. She greeted me with, 'Rachel? Good of you to ring. I could have been lying in a *crumpled heap* on the hall floor, dead for four days, without a person to notice I was missing.'

I called Mum daily and so did Margaret; Mum lived with another adult—Dad; she played bridge approximately twelve times a week; four hours each day were spent on the phone to her pals, complaining about things—she was healthier and more sociable than me.

'Are you in this evening?' I asked.

'Why?' She was instantly suspicious. 'What do you want? But hear me now! I'm not minding your dog, I'm not hemming your skirt and you can't borrow my car. I've a life too, you know.'

'Advice is what I'm looking for.'

'Buy the thing.'

'What thing? No, Mum, that's not—'

'Just buy the thing, whatever it is. Life is short. That's my advice.'

'I'll be there about eight.'

'We've already had our dinner. Gluten-free sausages.'

'Since when are you gluten-intolerant?'

'Hah! We're not! We're just being adventurous. I'll tell you something, you wouldn't know the difference. Next week, we might try vegan cheddar.'

I whizzed home to feed an ecstatic Crunchie—she always behaved as if I'd been gone and given up for dead for about three hundred years—then left again to meet Claire. Foolishly I arrived on time and parked five houses down from Mum and Dad's. Seven minutes later, Claire's car bounded over the speed bumps. Even before she came to an abrupt, ear-piercing halt, her electric window was whining open and her stylish, oyster-grey nails were beckoning me over.

She refused to ever get into my car. The heating didn't work and it made her depressed.

The night was misty. Scuttling along, hugging the wall, hoping to avoid any neighbours, I slid into her warm, fragrant, leather-lined Audi. 'Lovely smell,' I said.

'Diptyque,' she said. 'Tuberose. They do air fresheners for cars now.'

That was Claire all over. Right at the front of the fashion vanguard. Ever-questing, snuffling out new brands—skincare, handbags, lifestyle. *Devoted* to *Porter* magazine! Never afraid to spend money!

She gave me a quick hug. 'Am I late? God, I am. So, are you okay?'

Her hair, in a fashionable shade of mouse brown, was in a fabulous, falling-down French twist, her skin glowed and although I didn't know what age she was currently claiming to be, she looked good for it.

'Your face.' I took a second look. 'Where'd your pores go? It's amazing.'

'Had a thing done.'

She was always having things done. Her favourite phrase was, 'I'm not going down without a fight.' (That, or 'Make it a strong one.')

She deserved to look as great as she did. She had a personal trainer and—crucially—*showed up for her sessions*, instead of texting ten minutes before the start, pretending she had a sore throat (which was what I'd kept doing the few times I'd signed up). The only carb to cross her lips was vodka and she was very susceptible to Goop, obediently buying their powdered unicorn hoof or whatever their latest thing was. Her one blind spot was a fondness for fake tan but, on that matter, she couldn't be reasoned with. Everyone has their weakness.

She was so invested in her youthful look that she didn't like spending time in public with Margaret, *who was younger than her*, because Margaret had 'aged gracefully' (according to Margaret). Or 'gone to hell, entirely' (according to Claire).

Their battleground was Margaret's hair. Margaret had stopped colouring it a few years ago, but as far as I was concerned she was the real winner because it was now this amazing cool silver colour. I reckon she actually looked better than she had in her twenties.

Sometimes I thought about doing the same thing myself—the freedom was alluring. Think of all that time and money I'd save. Even more importantly, consider all the *emotional* energy saved—the last ten days before my roots got done were *hard* going.

'Did it hurt?' I asked Claire. 'The thing you had done?'

'Oh Christ, yeah! Even after six co-codamol.'

'Six? Claire!'

And there you had at least two of the differences between Claire and me: I too would like the poreless skin, but I wasn't prepared to suffer for it. Instead, I spent a fortune on serums, doing constant ongoing research. It was one of my many micro-obsessions.

The tragedy in all of this was that our second youngest sister Anna, had The Best Job in The World, an executive at McArthur on the Park, a PR company which repped some of the most exciting skincare on the planet.

In practical terms, it meant that we had glorious, giddy-making access to free products. And even so, I *still* couldn't stop buying things. Free stuff is always lovely. But nothing is as alluring as New and Exciting. Or *More*.

The second difference was that Claire mood-altered with happy abandon and never developed a dependency: she was an enthusiastic drinker and had a whole suite of pills at her fingertips.

Me, though? I'd been to rehab twenty years ago for being too fond of cocaine and other drugs. It was the best thing that had ever happened to me and these days I lived a normal, happy life—so long as I steered clear of *any* 'mood-alterers'. Which meant no codeine, no occasional Xanax for anxiety, nothing at all—not even alcohol.

Which baffled my 'loved ones' (my sisters and parents). Alcohol hadn't been a big problem for me back in the day, it had been all the other stuff. But I was a person who could get addicted to rice cakes. To tap water. To tofu, magnolia paint, nude lip gloss, boiled cauliflower—*anything*. No matter how bland, how unremarkable, I could get addicted to it. So, no alcohol for Rachel.

'How're you bearing up?' Claire asked.

'We'll save it until we're inside. Tell me what's going on with you.'

She pressed her lips together. 'You know Adam?'

The man she'd been with for twenty-three years? 'Er . . .'

'And you know our friends, Piet and Beatriz?'

'Mmmm.' They were fairly new but Claire and Adam seemed to see a lot of them. They were a bit flashy. Very Claire. No offence meant.

'So, turns out that they're swingers.'

Oh, *here* we go. The real surprise was that Claire hadn't taken up swinging much sooner.

Valiantly, I said, 'No judgement.' My personal brand was 'In Recovery but Still Great Fun'; it was important to seem breezy about all lifestyle choices in case I stopped being invited to things. People were already uncomfortable around me when they wanted to get hammered and I was sitting there, nursing a Diet Coke. I worked hard to *never* seem disapproving.

But the truth was that I had *a good deal* of judgement here. Based entirely on the fact that I wouldn't like to swing with Piet—he was too big, he shaved his head and he wore chunky gold rings.

'They want to, you know, *swing* with us. Beatriz fancies Adam and Piet fancies me.'

Well, they were all adults.

'Piet wants to date me. And Beatriz would, yeah, date Adam.'

Dating? I'd visualized swinging as a more generalized sort of thing, that they'd all be flubbing round together, like kids in a ball pit. But *dating?* That sounded a lot more . . . intimate.

Unless 'dating' just meant 'riding'?

'Piet suggested it to Adam. Adam told him to sling it. But I'd, you know . . . I think I want to.'

'You can't *make* Adam swing if he doesn't want to.'

'. . . yeeeahh. Maybe I should just have a thing with Piet? He's always giving me hot stares and saying things like "If I didn't know that Adam would throttle me . . ." It's sexy.'

'Having a thing with Piet is different from swinging.' Then, 'Claire, are you sure you want to be a swinger? It sounds to me that you just fancy Piet.'

She exhaled. 'I really fancy Piet. On the *mercifully rare* occasions I have to have sex with Adam, I pretend it's Piet.'

To each their own. In my opinion, Adam was a showstopper. Big and tall but not in that meaty, Piet way. And he *suited* Claire. They were both immensely social, great fun and said yes to everything—at least everything that involved alcohol and other people. It would be hard to find a more perfect couple.

'It would upset Adam if I had an affair on the sly—'

'—ya *think?*'

'—but if we were swingers, it would all be out in the open.'

'Listen to me, Claire. Swinging is grand if everyone is on the same page. You and Adam need to talk about this. And remember, you and Adam have a good thing going. It's rare and wonderful. Seriously, you don't know how lucky you are.'

'Ah, stop! No need to be all serious. Just tell me what to do. You're wise.' Jokily, she elbowed me. 'Yes or no? G'wan, say yes!'

'Okay.' I sighed. 'I'll tell you exactly what to do.'

Her face lit up. Eagerly she said, 'Yes?'

'Golden Key it.'

'NOOOOOOOO!' Then, 'Christ, here's Margaret, in her anorak of doom. Say nothing.'

Claire and I clambered from the car, while Margaret gave us a wounded look from inside her navy nylon hood. 'You'd think that, by now, I'd have got used to being left out of things,' she said as the three of us hurried through the strangely wet mist to Mum's front door, Claire holding her Bottega pouch over her wonderful hair. 'But it still hurts.'

Luckily that was the moment when Claire's high leather boots skidded on the damp pavement, sending her flying into Mrs Kilfeather's hedge. By the time the diversion was over, Mum was hooshing us into the hall.

'In, in, get in,' she said, rotating her arm. 'Before we're all drowned.'

'The soles of new boots should be sandpapered,' Margaret said. 'If you don't want to slip.'

'You're right. They should. I'd do it, only they're Louboutins.' That was Claire's version of an apology.

'Take off those coats and shoes,' Mum said. 'Don't be bringing the rain into my Good Front Room.'

Margaret obediently slung her anorak on the knob at the bottom of the stairs, I threw my coat over it but Claire refused to remove hers. 'It's not a coat, it's a shirt-dress.'

Again, that was totally Claire. You'd see a photoshoot in a magazine, say of a woman wearing a floor-length, organza shirt-dress, over flared trousers and a clingy fine-knit sweater, and you'd think, That's beautiful, but no normal person would ever wear it. Claire would, though.

'Shirt-dress, coat-dress, call it whatever you like,' Mum said. 'It's still wet. Take it off.'

'For the love of God!' Claire said, but she complied.

The three of us stuck our heads into the television room to say hello to Dad. Anxiously he looked up, like a badger peering out from a burrow. 'What's going on?' He clutched his beloved remote control against his chest.

'Summit meeting.'

'Feck.' Longingly, he eyed the telly. Golf, from what I could see. 'Am I needed?'

It would be cruel to interrupt his viewing. 'Just tell me. Should I go to Luke's mother's funeral?'

'She's dead? That's a terrible pity, she was a lovely woman. Who told you about it?'

'Joey. He rang me. Out of the blue.'

'Narky Joey rang you? I see.' He paused. 'Lookit, my opinion counts for nothing around here.' This was uttered without a hint of bitterness. Poor Dad had accepted his place at the bottom of the pecking order a long time ago. 'But it sounds to me that you should go. If you can face it, like.'

'Seriously? Okay. Thanks, Dad. Look. In that case, you're absolved from attending the actual summit.'

'God, that's great.' He looked pitifully grateful. Then, 'Did you hear about our gluten-free sausages?'

'I did. I hear you couldn't have told the difference. And—'

'Vegan cheddar next week!'

'Here's Helen!' Mum yelped, opening the front door to a small, drenched creature, dressed entirely in black. Her silhouette was that of a twelve-year-old girl.

'I need a towel!' She unzipped her long waterproof coat with a whizz and flung back the hood with such force that droplets flew everywhere. 'Old Woman, you!' She clicked her fingers. 'Bring me one.'

As Mum happily disappeared up the stairs to do her bidding, Helen yelled after her. 'Nothing flowery or pink!' Helen had a loooooong list of things she hated so much she wanted to hit them in the face with a shovel. (Perhaps unsurprisingly, it was called her Shovel List.) Flowery patterns and the colour pink were among the countless items which featured on it.

'I'll get the gin.' Margaret ducked into the kitchen and returned with a litre of Aldi gin, a bottle of tonic and a selection of mismatched glasses. Nothing for me, but I'm used to it. Even after all these years they still act as if my being clean and sober is a temporary self-indulgence.

When the drinks were poured and we were in the sitting room, Helen wearing a giant turban of a towel (yellow), I told my story. The responses were as predicted.

'Of course you're going.' (Mum.)

'You have to go.' (Margaret.)

'Are you mad?! She doesn't have to go!' (Helen.)

Claire was the only one who asked, 'What do you *want* to do?'

'I know it'll hurt but I want to go. I think.'

'What's the big deal?' Margaret asked. 'You've met someone else. You and Quin are solid.' Then she had a think. 'But why won't you move in with him?'

'Because . . . if I moved in and things went bad I'd have to move out again.'

'Why would it go bad? You're punishing Quin for what Luke did.' Sometimes Margaret could cut to the heart of a messy situation with sharp insight. 'You're stuck.'

At times, that was something Nola also said.

'Have you anything for a headache?' Helen asked.

'A good, hard whack in the skull with my stick,' Mum replied, and they both creased with laughter. Then, 'Margaret, go out to the fruit bowl and get your sister some tablets.'

A question had been playing on my mind. 'Do you think Joey told me about the funeral out of the goodness of his heart?'

This caused a spirited and united response. 'Narky Joey? Joey *Armstrong*? He isn't a goodness-of-his-heart person! He's one of the most terrible men I've ever met!' (Said by Helen. With admiration.)

'Maybe Luke asked him to tell you?' Claire said.

In which case . . . 'I might go. Don't judge me but it might be good to be back in touch. The way it ended was horrible—'

'That's all on him,' Helen interjected.

'But we *were* happy for such a long time . . . Shouldn't we at least be civil?'

Margaret had returned, carrying the fruit bowl, which bristled with boxes of tablets, pipette-bottles of drops, tubes of ointment, three blackened bananas and a wizened mandarin orange. 'You've *everything*. Can I have this tube of Fucibet? There are three here.'

'Work away.'

'Headache,' Helen reminded her.

'Tablet, caplet or soluble? Aspirin-based or ibuprofen? Codeine—'

'Surprise me.'

'If Rachel's going to the funeral,' Claire announced, 'we need a plan.' She was a great strategist, a big high-up in a charity—which often confused people into thinking she was kind-hearted. Giant mistake. Claire could fire people without having to go to bed for a week with guilt and she got really pissed off if the Crimson Ribbon Day collection was disappointing. ('Lazy bastard volunteers! All they had to do was stand in the rain, shaking a bucket in people's faces, it's hardly rocket science.')

After subjecting me to a dispassionate appraisal, Claire was thoughtful. 'You look good. That weight you lost, I thought you might put it back on now that you're happy again, but fair play, you haven't.'

Only Claire could turn the greatest trauma of my life into a positive.

'Could she get Botox?' Mum asked.

'I *have* Botox!' While I'm nowhere near as bad as Claire, I too have my pride.

'Where?' Mum lunged at my face. 'But you can move your eyebrows!'

'Botox has improved. Frozen foreheads are a thing of the past.'

'But then how are people to know you've got it?!'

'Hey!' Claire exclaimed. 'Nice earrings!'

It had taken her a while. Granted my hair was long and loose enough to act as camouflage but Claire had an instinct for fancy things. At first glance they were just triangles of orange Perspex. What made them special was that each sported a not insignificant diamond.

'Give me a look.' Claire was tucking my hair behind my ears and coming in for a close-up. 'Christ,' she breathed. 'Quin?'

Of *course*, Quin.

Helen and Margaret were also on top of me, trying to see.

I twisted my face from side to side so they all got a look, then I was told to take the earrings off, so they could be examined at closer quarters.

'Are the diamonds . . . real?' Helen's tone was sceptical.

'But why would you put a diamond in a cheap piece of orange plastic?' Margaret sounded confused enough to cry. 'I don't get Quin's taste *at all*.'

There were times I agreed with her. Quin amused me. He didn't really care that gifts were supposed to be what the person on the receiving end liked. If something appealed to *him*—and his taste was nuanced and niche, not for everyone—that was usually enough for him to reach for his credit card.

'They're horrible,' Mum said.

'They're so not.' Claire was adamant. 'Quin is really cool. What's the name of the jeweller? Text me when you know, so I can find out the price.'

'Oh, do!' the other three exclaimed.

Sometimes Quin got it *so* right—a fifties bracelet in chunky, blue Lucite was one of my favourite things. These orange Perspex earrings, though? Diamonds or no diamonds, I'd never have picked them. But because I cared about him, I wore them.

'So this is what you do,' Claire said. 'Go with Quin. Waltz into the church with him.'

'It's a funeral,' Mum snapped. 'No one's waltzing anywhere. *Don't* go with Quin.'

'Don't,' Margaret agreed. 'It would be inappropriate.'

'Luke left her!' Helen exclaimed. 'She can do what she likes!'

'Anyway, Quin's in New Mexico,' I said. 'He's not back till Sunday.'

'Do you want me to go with you?' Mum asked.

The answer was no. But how did I tell her?

'Girls,' she said with sudden anxiety, 'go easy on the rouge while I'm reposing in my coffin.'

'I'm sorry but I can't come,' Margaret said. 'I've no more holiday leave left, not until July.'

'Nor can I,' Claire said. 'Big meeting. Sorry.'

We all turned to Helen who looked uncomfortable and said, 'I've a thing.'

'*What* thing? You work for yourself!'

'Not a work thing.' Helen gave Mum a cool stare. 'And not something I can reschedule.'

This was like dropping a lit match into a gas can. Instantly everyone was agog. We were far too enmeshed in each other's lives, my sisters, Mum and me.

'You're up in court?' Mum asked. 'For assault? For stalking? For trespassing?'

'Nope. Nope. Nope. And nope. You can keep on asking, but you're wasting your breath.'

'You're getting married?' Mum asked hopefully. 'Artie's finally making an honest woman out of you?'

I was *so* interested in her answer to this. You know the way you sometimes can't figure relationships out? Well, that was Helen and Artie. To me, they seemed bafflingly ill matched. Helen courted trouble: she spoke her mind, changed it frequently and was prone to sudden, passionate grudges. Artie—an intensely clever man who worked in financial policing—was cool, calm and impossible to ruffle. He barely spoke, which Helen said suited her because she wasn't with him for his conversational skills but for his expertise between the sheets.

You could see her point: Artie was phenomenally handsome—huge and broad-shouldered, with the flaxen, blue-eyed, unkempt appeal of a Viking.

From one or two things Helen had let slip, I gathered that Artie took no nonsense from her. Well, not much. You couldn't say he'd tamed her because he hadn't, but he was probably the first of her boyfriends who hadn't been destroyed by her tendency to break nice things.

Helen smirked. 'I'm not getting married. Like, *ever*.'

'Whatever it is,' Margaret said, her tone kind, 'you'll tell us when you're ready.'

'Yeah. I will.' And Helen actually blushed.

In wonder, we watched the flush creep its way up her pretty, cat-like face.

'Something to do with Your Best Friend, Bella Devlin?' Claire pounced.

Bella Devlin was Artie's youngest daughter and had been Helen's best friend since Bella was nine and Helen thirty-three. (Bella was now fifteen.) Such unorthodox behaviour was typical of Helen but it was a relief that she had a friend at all.

'Leave Bella Devlin, My Best Friend, out of this,' Helen said.

'Tell us!' Claire commanded.

'Nope.'

'Flowers.' Mum had lost interest. 'I want lots of flowers. I want a wreath that says "GRANNY" from my grandchildren. Shiny pink nail varnish and I want my good rosary beads, the mother-of-pearl ones that Father Fergus brought me back from Fátima, threaded through my fingers—'

Claire was clicking on her phone. 'Rachel. Kate's not rostered to work in Blossom Hall on Friday, she could go with you.'

Unless . . . I looked at Helen. 'Is she working for *you* on Friday?'

'Let's seeeeee.' Helen had a think. 'Go on then, yeah, she can have the morning off.'

'You better not be giving her all the dodgy jobs,' Claire told Helen.

Helen had another think. 'Ah, she's grand. Nothing too . . . dangerous.'

'Actually, I really should go to this funeral,' Mum said. 'To show respect. She was my opposite number in the Walsh–Costello marriage.'

But almost from the word go, Mum had taken against poor Marjorie Costello.

She'd never have admitted it, but back in the day Mum had decided that because Luke's dad, Brian, was a mere electrician—contrasting with Daddy Walsh, the accountant—the Walshes were somehow better than the Costellos.

It made no difference that both Mum and Daddy Walsh had come from humble backgrounds and that Daddy Walsh had gained his qualifications via a correspondence course instead of spending four free-and-easy, duffle-coated years swaggering about Trinity College like an entitled young buck.

For once in her anxious, status-obsessed life Mum had relished her position as top dog.

Until the Costellos had extended an invitation to tea. Poor Mum had swanked along, prepared to be generous about their mean little abode—and then Dad had parked the car outside.

'This?' she'd asked, staring in green-tinged shock at the well-kempt, handsome house. Yes, it was a suburban semi-d, but it boasted double glazing, up-to-the-minute gutter work and a fibre-glass front door.

Once inside, the square-footage appalled her. A large extension into the spacious back garden had resulted in an attractive conservatory and an enormous, light-filled kitchen. The converted attic yielded up two extra bedrooms, both boasting built-in wardrobes and en-suites.

Worse still, the workmanship everywhere was excellent: doors hung straight, they shut easily and silently, the light switches didn't deliver mild electric shocks and you could run your hand along the banisters without your skin being torn to bits by stray splinters.

Mum kept swallowing and swallowing. When Mrs Costello produced an array of pretty cakes and mini-tarts she stuttered something about how they must have spent the day baking.

Mrs Costello had a good laugh at that. 'Life's too short for making quiche. The Laden Table did all this.'

The Laden Table! Mum was borderline obsessed with the place. How she yearned to be like her friends, who could casually pick up the phone and place an impromptu order for beef stroganoff for ten. But Mum was held back by shame—certain that buying from the Laden Table was the same as paying for a series of Facebook ads, confessing to being an appalling cook.

It had been a tough eighty minutes. In fairness, it often is when two random sets of parents are brought together because their respective children have fallen in love. Luke and I churned out most of the chat and even Dad made a stab at it, but because he spoke so rarely it was hard for him to gear up.

Mum managed the occasional strangled sentence. 'That rug . . . it looks like a Gooch luxury hand-tufted Berber. Oh, it is? Eighty per cent off, well . . . lovely.'

On the way home, Mum remained silent for most of the journey. As we crossed the Liffey, back into the southside, she murmured, in the tiniest of voices, 'It was like a small hotel.' Then, 'How did they get eighty per cent off the rug? I never see anything but rubbish in the sales.'

Back in the present, I said, 'Mum, no need for you to come to the funeral. You'd lost contact with her.'

And I needed to be free to leave at a moment's notice, without being told I was being disrespectful.

'Now that's settled, I need some advice.' Claire got to her feet and began removing her fashion-forward flares.

'What's going on!' Mum cried. She was terrified of naked skin.

'Francesca says my kneecaps look like the faces of two old Russian women wearing headscarves. Do they?'

Francesca was Claire's seventeen-year-old and shaping up to be a handful. But she could be very funny *and* on the money. Interested, I focused on Claire's kneecaps. They were bumpy, certainly, but I wasn't seeing actual old women.

'I don't know,' Mum said. 'If you stare at anything long enough, it starts looking funny.'

'Like the man who saw Michael Bublé in a slice of toast,' Margaret said.

'I *do* see old women in headscarves, yeah,' Helen said. 'But I don't know if they're Russian.'

'D'you know what's a funny thing to do?' Mum exclaimed, obviously bored of Claire's knees. 'If you stare at your own face in the mirror for long enough, you start to look like the devil.'

'Ah, never mind.' Claire was also bored. 'It's not going to stop me wearing short dresses.'

'Put your trousers on again, good girl,' Mum said.

4

Crunchie launched herself at me in ecstatic welcome and Kate declared, 'Rachel, hey, you're home!'

'Hello. Hel-*lo*, who's a good dog?' As Crunchie danced around, I rubbed her ears. '*Who's* a good dog? You are!'

In the living room, Kate pointed at her paused screen. 'Korean series. *Completely* insane. But I love it. Maybe you should give it a go. So would you like some tea? Camomile and rose.' She'd clambered off the couch and was already in the kitchen, getting me a cup. 'Helps with sleep.'

'What about you, my clean-living little niece! How'd your surveillance go today?'

'Good! Your man turned up; I got lots of photos.'

'Can I ask a question? Theoretical at this stage? Would you mind missing work on Friday morning?' Quickly, I added, 'Helen says you can have the time off. But not if you need the money.'

'What's going on?'

'You know Luke? My ex-husband? His mum died, funeral's on Friday—'

'—Quin's away and you need a wingman? On it.'

'You sure? You don't mind missing work? Maybe Helen will pay you anyway.'

That was our cue for hollow laughter, which turned into the real thing.

'When did you last see him?' Kate asked.

'Twenty twelve,' I said. 'Six years ago. The day he left.' Even remembering it—me crying and begging him to stay—made me feel nauseous.

'Wow! That's . . .' Twenty-somethings usually think people like me, a woman in my forties, have evolved past all painful feelings, but Kate was better than most. 'So how was the legal stuff done? Your divorce?'

'Lawyers, mostly. Sometimes his mate Joey was the go-between. But Luke and I haven't exchanged a single word.'

Thousands of times I'd ached to talk to him but he had blocked my number, email, everything.

'And you never bumped into him?'

'He sold his business and moved to Denver, Colorado. Got a new job, had friends living there. That's all I know.'

'. . . Social media, though?'

'No.' I had to laugh at her shock. 'He was on Facebook for a while, back in the day, but *barely*, you know?'

He'd even blocked me on that. But, according to Anna, he hadn't posted anything in literal years. And I'd never found him on anything else. For two or three years after he'd left, I'd done regular, obsessive checks on Instagram and Twitter but always came back empty-handed.

'This could be hard for you.' Kate considered. 'After breaking up with Isaac, I was good until Chloe's kid's naming ceremony. Soon as I knew I'd see him there, I was in bits.'

'Yeah. I'm still not sure I'll go.' For a long time I'd felt I'd never forgive Luke. The whole business had been horrendous and I was very grateful it was in the past. Maybe the past was where it should stay.

I wondered about calling Quin. Dublin to Taos, New Mexico, would have involved at least three flights if he'd been going under his own steam. But as the client had flown both him and the architect on a private jet, he might have arrived already.

'Rach?'

'Quin.' I felt a rush of warmth at the sound of his voice. 'How are you? You got there okay?'

'God, yeah.' He groaned. 'Private jets are just so great. But also so terrible. Whenever I travel on one, it takes me months to readjust to normal class.'

Quin designed bespoke audio-visual systems for the homes of very rich people. He was regarded as having a magic touch, which periodically bumped him up against great wealth.

'It's amazing here,' he said. 'We're outside of town, in the desert. I've put some shots on Insta, if you want to take a look.'

I clicked on his grid and found images of a high desert plain. In the distance, a sudden eruption of jagged granite exploded from the flat nothingness, looking like a cathedral made of raw stone.

'Oh, Quin, it's *beautiful*. So, listen, can you talk for a minute?'

'Sure.' His voice was instantly alert. 'Let me just go into another . . .' There came the rustles of movement and the sound of a door closing. Then, 'Okay, I'm here. What's up?'

'I got a call today. From a friend of my ex-husband's.'

Quin's sharp inhale was audible.

'His . . . Luke, I mean, his mother has died. The funeral's on Friday morning. I don't know whether to go or not.'

'Right.' A pause. 'Rach . . .' Another pause.

Quin knew everything about me and Luke.

Well, *nearly* everything.

One of the great things about having met on a weekend where our very presence was an admission that we were struggling with life, was that, right from the start, Quin and I were admirably straight with each other. In our early days I'd felt okay to say to him, 'I could never love another man the way I loved Luke.'

'Ow!' Quin had been visibly pained. 'Radical honesty can go and fuck itself.'

But we'd been able to laugh about it.

For a moment the connection to New Mexico went loud and crackly. When I could hear Quin again, he was asking, 'What's your "inner voice" telling you?'

'Nothing at the moment. But, like, would you mind if I went?'

'If I did, that's my stuff. Right?'

'Haha.'

'Sleep on it. See how you feel tomorrow. But', he growled, 'you'd better not fall for him again.'

'I won't.'

5

I turned out the light and hoped for sleep. But behind my eyelids, my eyes were wide open. I was cast back in time, to over twenty years ago, when Brigit and I were living in Manhattan.

There had been a gang of Irish lads we used to see around. All of them about six feet tall, with mad-long hair, tight, *tight* jeans and an abundance of neck and wrist accoutrements, they'd looked like they belonged in a hard-living rock band from the early seventies.

They drank Jack Daniel's, which they called JD, were no strangers to leather waistcoats or a denim jacket worn over a bare chest and were always accessorized by skinny blonde girls in groupie chic.

Dying of embarrassment that they were Irish, *terrified* we'd be lumped in with them by the cool New York types whose approval we craved, Brigit and I had, oozing irony, named them the Real Men.

But when, inevitably, we got talking to them, they were actually lovely. It was a relief to talk to men who were funny and halfway normal.

Those were the days when Brigit and I were scouring New York City for boyfriends. I was hoping for someone chiselled, hot, well paid and worthy of respect. In fact, *so* great at generating respect that simply by being his girlfriend, I would also engender some.

What it came down to was, I was waiting for a saviour. But my saviour had been unaccountably delayed. So while I was killing time, I'd ended up having a passionate but messy sort of a thing with one of the Real Men—Luke Costello.

The mess was entirely my fault. With his long hair, as glossy as a blackbird's wing, and his hard, fit body, Luke was an utter *ride*. I was happy to spend time—lots of it—in his bed but not to be seen with him in public (seriously, I was awful). He finally ran out of patience with me at the same time as I crashed, burned and ended up in rehab in Ireland.

Almost a year and a half later, when a new, clean-and-sober me returned to New York to make amends to Luke, it quickly became clear that the connection we'd once had was still there.

And we were so happy, *all* about Doing Things Right This Time. Even though we had full-time jobs we both started evening classes—neither of us had been to third-level but now we were keen to 'better ourselves'.

Then shit got *really* real when I instigated the 'kids conversation'.

'Luke, do you want to have babies? Children?'

He paused. 'Not right now.'

'How strongly do you feel about it?'

Another pause. 'I see my brothers and, like, they're wrecked the whole time. And they live in Ireland, close to family, who help out. We're here and we don't have anyone to pick up the slack. What do you think?'

'Same. I think I want them but it's safer to get a career sorted, steady income, maybe even a mortgage and all that, first.'

'Cool!'

So we were agreed that there was to be no rushing, no crazy impromptu decisions, nothing like the way I used to live. I had become one of those women with a five-year plan. Worse, I was proud of it.

The only worry was that my GP had said that we—and she mostly meant me—might be already on the decline, fertility-wise.

'So,' I remember saying to Luke, 'in case we need a contingency plan, we're getting checked out next Tuesday.'

'Oh yeah? How does that go down?'

'I have a scan to count my eggs and your sperm would get tested, to see if it's . . . healthy?' Was that the word? 'Enough of it? Good at swimming?'

'But how would it be tested?' He seemed a little anxious. 'Where would they get it?'

'At the clinic. You'd, aaaah, do it there.'

'You mean, I'd have to . . .' He went pale. 'Oh God, *Rach*el. I'd have to . . . do it, right *there*?'

'In a cubicle, I guess. Not, like, in the waiting area.'

I wasn't wild about the idea either. Luke in a small, bare room with a load of pre-used porn made me feel squeamish, jealous and oddly turned on.

He put his face in his hands and groaned. 'Rachel . . .' Then, 'This is important to you?'

'If everything is okay, we can park that issue while we get the rest of our lives in place.' I added, 'It will give us peace of mind.'

'You sound like a dodgy insurance salesperson.' He exhaled, long and loud. 'Okay. On one condition. That you never use the word "sperm" again.'

'Done. Do you think I *like* being this person?'

The afternoon of our appointment, as we arrived at the building in midtown, I was surprisingly nervous. All medical stuff was anxious-making, even if it was just a precautionary check. What if I was infertile? Or Luke was?

But we'd cope. It would be a shock, but we'd weather it. My faith in us was strong.

As we waited for the elevator to the doctor's suite, Luke cut his eyes to me. 'Peace of mind, you say?'

'Peace of mind,' I intoned. 'For you and your family.'

After ringing the clinic's bell, the door buzzed and we pushed it open—and the receptionist half rose behind her desk. Her glance flickered from Luke, to me, then back to Luke, his long hair, his leather jacket, his woven wristbands, the silver chain around his neck. For a moment I think she was considering calling security.

Who could blame her—the waiting room bristled with neatly pregnant women in bland Michael Kors dresses and Ferragamo flats, their accompanying menfolk in thousand-dollar suits.

Luke saw the receptionist's concern. 'It's okay.' His voice was gentle. 'We have an appointment. And,' he added, 'insurance.'

I watched him smile at her; she stared, gave an abrupt half-giggle, then slowly flushed a deep red.

Clipboards and pens appeared for us to input our information. After a lengthy wait, we were ushered into the presence of Dr Solomon, a tiny woman with lots of curly hair.

'You don't plan to get pregnant just yet?' She speed-read our forms.

'Not right now.' I sat up straight. 'But if there were any issues, that might change things.'

She flicked back to my form. 'You're, hmmm . . . almost thirty-one? And Luke . . . ?'

'Same,' he said.

'We're late starters.' Defensively I wanted to blurt out our convoluted story and to reassure her that Luke and I were *very* together. *We just moved in with each other. In twenty months he'll be a Certified Public Accountant—I know, you wouldn't think it to look at him, but a steady heart beats inside that sexy exterior. I'm doing a degree in Addiction Counselling, plus both of us are working full time. Once we're qualified, our student loans must be repaid, then we want to buy a place to live. All of that needs to be tidied away before we can even think about having a baby.*

'It's okay,' Dr Solomon said. 'Thirty-one is not old, not these days. If everything is in order, you've got plenty of time. So!' She clapped her hands and a nurse entered the room. 'Rachel, while you have your scan, Tomaka will take Luke for his semen extraction.'

Luke shot me an anguished WTF look.

'You'll be alone,' Dr Solomon added. But there was a wry turn to her tone that made me wonder if she'd alarmed poor Luke on purpose.

As he stood, Dr Solomon gave him a good, long look. 'I'm not saying you'll have motility issues. However, in that eventuality, you should know that tight jeans are frequently a contra-indication.'

And on that note, Tomaka took him away.

Fifteen or twenty minutes later, we were reunited in reception. Luke—clearly mortified—kept his eyes downcast. In the elevator that returned us to ground level, he remained silent. Only once we were out of the building and onto the teeming streets of midtown did it feel okay to speak.

'Luke? Was it . . . bad?' I asked. 'Magazines with the pages stuck together?'

'What?' He seemed startled. 'No, babe.' He slung his arm around my neck and pulled me closer, out of the path of the crowds. 'No.' Our foreheads touching, his dark eyes held mine. 'There was no need for any of that. I just thought about you.'

6

As soon as I woke up, I heard in my head, *You need to go to the funeral.*

Well! I thought. You took your time!

Yeah. Lol.

So there we were. Whether I liked it or not, I was going to the funeral. Then I went to work.

'Giles had a bad night,' Hector said at the morning meeting. 'Overwhelmed with guilt. Crying non-stop.'

Ted looked at me. 'You want a session with him? Murdo, you're available to cover group?'

Murdo nodded.

'And sorry for the short notice,' I said. 'But, Murdo, can you cover tomorrow morning too? I've a funeral to go to. Ex-mother-in-law.'

'*The* ex?' Murdo exclaimed.

'You sure this is a good idea?' Ted said. 'Will the ex be there?'

I almost laughed. 'Ted. It's his *mother*. Anyway, I'll be back in time for afternoon group.'

'Grand. And your new client arrives tomorrow morning,' he said. 'Priya will email the file.'

I went to find Giles and, in the corridor, passed Dennis who was huddled with Roxy, *deep* in chat. God only knew what Dennis wanted with her, but certainly not advice on recovery, from the wheeler-dealery energy he was giving off. More like he was trying to sell her a septic tank ('one careful owner') or doing his best to buy a roller disco at a knockdown price . . .

He spotted me and an expression of theatrical fear crossed his face. 'Jez, there's Rachel,' he declared. 'I'm quaking in me boots!'

(Said boots were cut-off wellingtons, which the bottoms of his exhausted trousers were tucked into. Dennis, though a townie, was the kind of can-do operator who'd happily jump in to help with some emergency lambing, if he thought it would drum up a couple of votes in the local elections.)

'Morning, Dennis, Roxy.' I tried to sound lofty.

Being mean didn't come naturally, but it was important that they were terrified of me.

'Quaking,' Dennis repeated, in a fake undertone.

You should be, I thought, almost sadly. *I'm accumulating so much information on you and your shenanigans and soon I'm going to rain terror down on your head.*

In the dining room Giles, flanked by Chalkie, was buttering toast and crying.

'Wudja stop, ya big thick,' Chalkie was saying, not unkindly. 'Making a show of yourself.'

'Let him cry.' Trassa was all sympathy. 'After the terrible, *terrible* things he's done, the lives he's ruined, who wouldn't cry?' As Giles scanned the length of the table, she asked, 'What are you looking for, pet?'

'Marmalade,' Giles squeaked.

'Harlie!' Trassa yelled. 'Pass the marmalade along to poor Giles.'

'Giles,' I said. He looked up, his face drenched. 'I'll see you in Consulting Room Three at ten o'clock.'

Mutely, he nodded.

'You not doing group this morning?' Chalkie was aggrieved. 'Who's covering?'

'Murdo.'

'Okay.' Several expressions moved across his face, eventually landing on disappointment. Murdo, my heavily inked, much-pierced young deputy, was *tough* and that didn't suit Chalkie because he was still trying to avoid who he really was.

Six minutes later, Giles, leaking tears, slid into the armchair opposite me. (The seats were much more comfortable in these small one-to-one rooms.)

A successful, entitled man, he'd spent his life accumulating and discarding wives and children. Everything had come easy to him. In recent years, though, his rarefied life of tennis and sailing had slid off the rails as his fondness for good times crossed the line into raging addiction.

But his second and third wives had been in competition to enable him for as long as possible. As soon as one tentatively voiced the opinion that starting each day with four lines of coke wasn't perhaps ideal, he'd upped and left for the other. This ex-wife ping-pong had carried on for over a year, Giles bouncing back and forth.

His colleagues also protected him because he was 'high functioning'— which translates as 'still able to charm potential clients'. (For as long as anyone keeps making money, everyone seems happy to pretend they're fine.)

Only after having a paranoia attack on a press trip was he finally cut loose by his board—which was the catalyst that propelled him in here. I'd never yet seen an addict seek help if they weren't in danger of losing—or had already lost—someone or something important to them.

Over the past four weeks, I'd unleashed a bombardment of truth on Giles. His friends, wives, ex-wives and adult children had all showed up to reveal the truth about him.

It had broken him wide open and now he sat weeping, a box of tissues on his lap.

'Why are you crying?' I asked softly.

'All of it,' he said thickly. 'Leaving Danielle.' His first wife. 'She was devastated . . . and I didn't care, because I thought I loved Ingrid.' His third wife. (Yes, he'd somehow managed to slot in an extra wife between his first wife and the woman he'd left her for. Giles was full of plot twists.) 'And my children. They were just babies and I neglected them . . .'

This was a tricky time for anyone in rehab and Giles needed to be guided gently. If he became too overwhelmed with grief or regret, there was a chance he'd leave, to run back to his old painkiller.

The Cloisters regime was tough. Yes, the patients were pushed way out of their comfort zones, but always with exquisite care. They were monitored with a gimlet eye so that we knew when to hold back, when to press hard, when to abruptly change strategy and show them some love.

'You've come a long, long way in the last twenty-nine days,' I said. 'You're becoming a whole new person. It's painful, all this clarity, but it'll be worth it. Over time, you can try to make things right with the people you hurt.'

'They'll never forgive me.'

Who knew if they would or they wouldn't and if they didn't, that was their right. But . . . 'No matter what,' I said, 'you can live through this and anything else life throws at you, without relapsing.'

I walked him back to group and, on a whim, crooked a finger to extract Harlie, just to check she was okay after Simon's departure.

She swished into the consulting room, everything on point—brows, lashes, skin and hair. In the outside world, she managed a CosMedical clinic (called Rich Girl Face—I *loved* the name), where she had access to all kinds of tweakments.

'So,' I said. 'Simon?'

'What about him?' She was cagey.

'You and he were . . . close?'

'You mean I fancied him?' Her glare was combative. Then, 'Maybe I did. For thirty seconds. Big mistake.'

'Don't beat yourself up about it,' I said. 'Happens all the time in here. When your drug of choice is taken away, you'll look for other ways to make yourself feel good.'

'Yeah, but,' she said, 'I heard about him and Prissie. They're all trash, aren't they? Liars and cheaters, the whole shower of them.'

'Who *exactly* are you talking about?'

Immediately her mouth bunched up, as if it had been pulled tight with a string. She didn't want to let the name escape. In our first session, two and a half weeks ago, she'd growled, 'That fucker is dead to me.'

'Who?' I repeated.

'Nnnnnn,' she hummed, from behind her sealed lips, her eyes bright and popping. I swear to God, despite her fury, she was hilarious.

Eventually she exhaled and let herself speak. 'Caleb.'

Her ex-husband. He'd left her about a year ago. I'd texted, emailed and called, trying to persuade him to come in to confront her, but all I'd got was a deafening silence. He was probably trying to move on with his life—who could blame him?

However, two of her friends had shown up and their colourful, exhaustive accounts of her drunken capers had horrified her into seeing she wasn't just a party girl but an actual alcoholic.

'Other than Simon, how are you?' I asked.

'Peachy, Rachel. Yourself?'

I waited.

'I only came in here to learn how to drink normally.' Her voice wobbled; I wasn't sure if it was with grief or fury. 'But according to you, I can never drink again. My life is over and I'm only twenty-nine.'

'What about Tegan?' I asked. 'What if she'd had the chance to stop drinking?'

'Stop trying to guilt me!'

Gently, I reminded her, 'Tegan died. From alcohol poisoning.' Tegan had been one of her closest friends. After her death, Harlie's parents and friends had done an intervention, so that Harlie wouldn't be the next casualty.

'If Tegan had been given the choice between dying or getting sober, which do you think she'd have taken?'

'I don't know.'

She did know. But right now, it was too painful for her to accept.

After she'd left, I opened the file on the newbie who was arriving tomorrow. Ella Black, aged twenty-eight, her particular poison apparently prescription sleeping tablets. She'd been persuaded she needed rehab after she'd taken her boyfriend's car for a drive at 3 a.m. and crashed it into the front window of a house. Despite breaking her collarbone, she'd climbed out, walked home, gone back to bed and woken up with no memory of what had taken place.

There had also been a few late-night Facebook incidents. She worked as a social media content provider for an airline—a high-status, well-paid job, according to her boyfriend Jonah, the owner of the crashed car.

Twice in the past seven weeks, Ella had posted odd stuff on the company account—a mad-sounding conspiracy theory about the US government and a wildly libellous claim about the 'real' father of Prince Louis. If it hadn't been for Ella's boss—someone called Boyd—taking them down before they'd gained any traction, she'd definitely have been fired.

It was always a rush when a new person came into my care; the chance to help them change their lives was exciting. The potential, the possibility of it—of *them*. Sometimes, of course, it didn't work out. They didn't think they really were addicts, or they weren't ready just yet to give up their best friend.

Frequently, they reappeared in the Cloisters a year or two later, a lot more battered, much more humble.

I started sending emails and making calls to the significant people in Ella's life, trying to establish as much detail as possible. As well as Jonah, there was her best friend Naaz, plus her parents and two brothers. In here, clients gave only the most sanitized, tragic version of themselves. To get the full picture, you had to talk to everyone who knew them. It was a little like investigating a crime.

Speaking of which—Dennis! Although I had several *written* testimonies on his shenanigans, it was proving difficult to get actual human beings in here, to confront him.

His wife Juliet had blackmailed him into rehab by threatening to leave him. But the few times we'd spoken since, it was clear she'd burnt up all of her energy getting her husband as far as us. What she wanted now was some magical transformation and for Dennis to be delivered back, all fixed. But it wouldn't take place without her input, so I rang her again.

'I don't know, Rachel,' she said. 'This coming week is bad . . .'

'What about your daughters?'

'They don't want to. It was hard enough for them to write those testimonials.'

I'd already been spurned by Dennis's GP *and* his best friend *and* two men he worked with on the local council. They were scared, all of them, and this was far from unusual. Outing a loved one as an addict or alcoholic was usually a painful, protracted process. Because you loved them, you wanted them to get help, but you also wanted to avoid confrontation.

Sometimes a friend or family member arrived here, blazing with righteous fury, all set to tear the addict a new one. But just as often, people were tangled up with guilt and confusion.

'Juliet, you need to come. Otherwise, you're wasting your money.'

'Maybe the week after next. What about . . . ?' Her voice lightened. 'You could try his brother, Patch. I'll text him your number, tell him to call you.'

'But—' She was gone.

My sneakers had arrived!

'Three pairs?' Brianna asked.

'Different sizes.'

She slid me a knowing glance. 'That right?'

HemHEM, it's not healthy to lie, even about the small stuff . . .

'No,' I admitted. 'They were all beautiful and I couldn't decide and, as I was paying for one delivery, I might as well take a look at the others . . .'

'Other stuff came.' She pointed a pen at a neat stack of parcels. 'If I was a betting woman'—she passed me a small square parcel—'I'd guess it was a Pomegranate Noir candle.'

It actually was. Then I read the card. 'How nice! From—remember Fiona Headley?'

'Sex addiction? About fourteen months ago? She's obviously still okay, if she's sending thank-you candles.'

'Yep.'

'I help them too!' Brianna said. 'I do all their paperwork perfectly. But *I* never get sent fancy candles.'

'Have it.' I thrust it at her. 'Seriously, you more than deserve it. I *insist*!'

'Okay, thank you, I *accept*!'

'Pass me that other package. What is it?' I read the sender's details and exclaimed, 'It's my planting trowel!'

'Open it!'

Like me, Brianna 'dabbled' in gardening.

Pulling the stainless-steel implement from its packaging, I bounced it in my hands. 'Feel how light it is!'

She took it from me. 'Even though the handle is cherrywood.' We marvelled at such ergo-dynamic efficiency.

'You can never have too many trowels,' I said.

'Or watering cans.'

'Or hoes.'

'Or shears.'

And it was the truth. Once you started down the path of buying gardening tools, there was always going to be something fancier, stronger, lighter, in a better metal, or in a nicer colour.

Like I said, I could get addicted to anything.

7

In the staff room, Carey-Jane was microwaving her revolting minestrone soup. The smell would stay on my clothes for the next seventy years. Hell is other people's food. Trying to numb myself to the different stenches doing battle—Priya's tuna bap, Yasmine's beetroot salad—I ate my own (civic-minded, stench-free) hummus and crackers and zoned out for a while, thinking about Luke.

I'd see him tomorrow. Which was almost unimaginable. A wash of gratitude for Quin hit me.

Granted, my feelings for him weren't what I'd felt for Luke. But how could they be? Quin wasn't Luke. And I wasn't the starry-eyed hopeful who'd fallen in love with Luke, but someone older and wiser.

Sometimes, when I considered that things with Quin might not have happened, I went cold.

The relief I'd felt during the LovingKindness exercise at the meditation weekend had been real—but in the twenty-four hours afterwards, I'd wondered if, actually, it had had anything to do with Quin? Perhaps it had just finally been time for me to forgive myself and Quin had appeared as a catalyst? 'When the pupil is ready, the master will appear.' (That's the kind of thing we say in 'personal-growth' circles. Nola says it, Anna says it, even Brianna says it occasionally and she believes in *nothing* unless it can be signed for or filed.)

Less than two days after we'd met, Quin texted, then rang. 'So. We should meet. Properly.'

His self-assurance was impressive. Entertaining, almost. But to say I was out of the habit with men was a giant understatement. In the previous year I'd gone on a couple of dates, once with a cousin of Brianna's and another time with a colleague of Claire's—but only because Brianna and Claire *made me*. It was no surprise that nothing further had ensued.

'Let's do an escape room,' Quin said. 'If things go south and we've nothing to say to each other, at least we'll have fun trying to unlock the puzzle.'

'Hold on there, mister, what if we can't? Unlock it, I mean? Are we stuck there forever?'

'Haha, no, they let us out after an hour. You've never done one? Okay, wear comfortable clothes, like, no high heels or tight dresses.'

Tight dresses? I thought. *You'd be lucky!*

'Is it maths and stuff?' I asked. 'Because I'm terrible at that. I don't want to be responsible for us losing.'

'Not maths. Basic cop on, mostly. And I'm really competitive; we'll definitely win.'

Well? I asked the voice in my head. Should I go?

But that day, she remained frustratingly silent.

So I ran the whole thing by my sisters.

'What age is he?' Claire asked.

'Same as me? Maybe a bit younger?'

'Kids? Ex-wife? Job?' Margaret asked.

'I don't know. But by the law of averages, he's likely to tick *some* of the boxes.'

'And you're okay if there are kids and an ex-wife?' Claire asked. 'Like, you'd better be. At your age, everyone has baggage.'

'Is he a Feathery Stroker?' Helen asked. '*Has* to be if he was trying meditation.'

The term 'Feathery Stroker' originated years ago in New York after Anna's friend Jacqui slept with a kind, respectful man who'd spent most of the night stroking her body with featherlight pressure. Un*bear*able, she'd said. Being flung across a bed and ravaged was much more her thing.

To be fair, many people would adore a session of feathery stroking but the phrase caught on and spread to condemn all straight men who were a bit, I suppose, *earnest*. Perhaps slightly humourless and pompously right-on: men who pontificated about their homemade tamarind marinade with its secret ingredient (which was always tabasco); who defended public breast-feeding even when there had been no objections; who sought your opinion about putting their cat on Valium or who pronounced 'artisanal' in a non-existent French-meets-Dutch accent ('oar-tijj-in-owwl').

I, personally, wouldn't have been keen on *actual feathery stroking* but more and more blameless men came to be written off as the circles of definition expanded: those who habitually used the word 'groceries'; had opinions on fabric softener; spent more than thirty seconds going down on you; or had no reservations about eating a mango in the street.

If any of those misfortunates fancied one of my sisters or their friends, they were laughed out of it. And if you liked a man, the very *last* thing you wanted was for him to be categorized as a Feathery Stroker.

As Quin had done a meditation weekend, he was about to be written off and—surprising myself—I said, 'He's not a Feathery Stroker. He looks like he does triathlons and might bore on about clothes that wick away sweat.' Hastily I added, 'But he might not, either.' (Boring on about clothes that wick away sweat was also suspect.)

Helen groaned. 'Christ, one of *them*. Betcha he has a spork.'

And I was in the clear! 'Might own a spork' was a different kind of insult.

A quick survey revealed that I was the only one of my sisters who'd never done an escape room.

'Honestly, it's such fun!' Margaret declared. 'Garv and I did one with the kids. The clock is ticking down and you're trying to decipher the clues and when you beat the clock—we escaped with like ten seconds to spare—you feel a million dollars!'

'They're the most stupid fucking things ever invented,' Helen said. I took this to mean that she had *not* beaten the clock.

'Angelo and I *adore* them.' Anna, starry-eyed, was on one of her many visits home to Ireland. She dropped in every six weeks or so, for a weekend. 'It's like being a kid again. If you go to a high-spec one, it can blow your mind. We went to a zombie hunt in a deserted mall; it was amazing!'

'This is Dublin,' Helen reminded her. 'We don't do high spec. Or low spec. Or any spec at all. We're shit.'

'Not always,' Margaret said. 'Our one was in a science lab. A virus had escaped and we were—'

'Oh yeah,' Claire said vaguely. 'I was at that one. Team-building exercise for the volunteers.'

'*You?*' Margaret said. 'And did you do all the stuff?'

'*Me?* In Simone Rocha? On my knees slithering through a crawl space? Not bloody likely.'

'Who's on their knees?' Mum had come into the sitting room for the first time in this conversation.

'Rachel's going on a date,' Helen volunteered. 'He's taking her to an escape room.'

Mum's face filled with outraged colour. 'A *Shades of Grey* thing?'

'WHAT?'

'He ties her up and whacks her with a riding crop? She has a ping-pong ball in her mouth and tries to escape? I heard about it on *Liveline*.'

'Hashtag for fuck's sake.' Helen sighed.

Quin's escape room was in an industrial park of anonymous grey warehouses beyond the M50.

He had offered to pick me up, but I'd declined. 'What if things—as you said—go south? Then you had to drive me home? Sitting side by side in your car for forty-five minutes would take ten years off my life.'

'Mine too. See you there.'

I got to the place on time and there was no sign of Quin. I stared at my phone and watched the numbers click into two minutes late, then three . . . When he was six minutes late, a car roared into the parking lot and, with a screech of brakes, pulled up beside me. It was Quin, this time in a jeep.

Late? Two flashy cars? I was having serious doubts.

He jumped out. 'Sorry I'm late. My son couldn't find his inhaler.'

A son? Okay, so he has at least one child. 'Maybe you could have texted?'

'I did.' There was an edge to his voice.

A quick look at my phone showed that he had. 'Why didn't I see it?'

'Spotty coverage out here.' He softened. 'But, yeah, sorry.'

I needed to know about his kids. 'Have you just the one child?'

'Two. A boy of eleven, a girl of thirteen. They're great. I'm forty-two, been divorced for five years. My ex-wife and I get on.' Seeming slightly entertained, he said, 'Anything else you'd like to know before we start?'

I shook my head.

'Over this way.' All business, he walked us into one of the giant ware-houses. 'I know it doesn't look promising,' he said, 'but trust me, these guys are great at this.'

Giving me a once-over, he said, 'You look good.' At first I thought it was a compliment; then he said, 'Sensible clothes.'

His gear was the stuff from my memory—dark, sleek athleisure wear.

Setting off down a long, empty corridor, we passed an endless sequence of shuttered rooms, until Quin stopped at a door. 'Here.'

In a small but fancy reception area, a neatly combed man, wearing black tie and tails, was holding a little round tray that served no obvious purpose. He looked like a butler. Flanking him was a woman wearing the black dress and white apron of a *Downton Abbey*-style domestic.

'Mr Quinlivan? Ms Walsh?' Butler-man asked. 'Thank goodness you're here! I am Smythe, purser of the *Queen Anne* ocean liner. A pair of diamond earrings has disappeared from the stateroom of Lady Glenrother. Suspicion has fallen on young Mabel here, Lady Glenrother's personal maid.'

At this point Mabel curtsied.

Unsure of the etiquette, I half curtsied back.

'I know Mabel to be an honest soul,' Smythe said. 'She is entirely innocent. But if you do not locate the missing jewels, Mabel will be sent for trial and found guilty.'

'You're my only hope,' Mabel said. 'Do you accept your mission?'

'I accept,' Quin said.

Then they were all looking at me.

Oh God. I didn't do well with that sort of pressure. 'Okay, I accept too.' *Jesus, could we not just have gone for ice-cream? Ice-cream dates had become an actual thing and I was so there.*

Smythe relieved us of our coats and phones, then declared, 'You have one hour to find the jewels and save Mabel. The clock starts ticking . . . *now*!' Next thing, we'd been ushered through a doorway and the lock had clicked behind us.

We were in a small, dim room, perhaps an old-timey office. A jacket and official-looking cap hung from a dusty coat-rack. A still-smoking tortoiseshell pipe lay abandoned on a heavy wooden desk, over which a bare yellow bulb was suspended.

In a corner, a heap of vintage leather suitcases and trunks were piled high. On one wall, a noticeboard showed the times of the tides and a sepia photograph of a military man with a luxuriant moustache glared down at us. Another wall was almost entirely covered with leather-bound ledgers.

It was surprisingly un-shit.

'So we're looking for keys, switches, weird stuff in paintings, anything.' Quin was already pulling at the locked drawers in the desk.

'Like this?' I held up a heavy brass key.

'Where d'you get *that*?'

'I put my hand into the jacket pocket.' I indicated the coat-rack.

'Wow.' His grey eyes glittered.

Sweeping my gaze around the small room, I homed in on a tray in a corner, bearing a teapot and two china containers. I just *knew* something was hidden in there. The first container was full of tea leaves, I gave it a good shake, rearranging the leaves and sure enough, a small laminated card saying '67' appeared.

I held it up to Quin.

'Jesus, you're a natural!'

I could actually see his respect for me expanding.

'Hold onto it,' he said. 'But first we should try opening this desk with your key.'

The desk had nine drawers, all of them locked. On my fourth attempt, one of them opened—to reveal a trove of six more keys. 'Jesus! I guess now we try all of them in every lock?'

We split the task, three keys each. Our bodies close, we fumbled our way through but nothing worked until—of course—the last key opened the last drawer, which slid open to reveal a leather-bound ledger. We flicked through it at speed, trying to discern a clue, but all the pages were empty.

'It must mean something,' I said.

'Not always, there are lots of red herrings.'

Focusing hard, I scanned the wall of ledgers.

Quin started, 'What about that card—'

But, way ahead of him, I'd spotted a teeny gap between two ledgers. There was no need to check that the numbers on either side of the space were 66 and 68; I was *certain* they were. In slid the ledger—then came a loud click, followed by a whirring noise. 'Quin! What's going on?'

Astonishingly, the wall of ledgers was splitting open from floor to ceiling. 'There's another room.'

Quin sounded pleased. 'Behind this one.'

Feeling as if I were dreaming, I slipped into the new space: a huge, high-ceilinged art deco bedroom, a marvel of Lalique glass, smoked mirrors and pale parquet flooring. Along one wall were large portholes, through which you could see an actual ocean. I could hear it too, the wash and slap of the waves and the screeching of seabirds.

Some sort of audio-visual miracle, it was thrillingly convincing.

'Mind. *Blown*,' I said. 'Oh my God, Quin, I absolutely *love* this.'

'You do, do you?' He slanted some approval my way. 'But think of poor Mabel. Start looking.'

'Yeah, but.' I pointed at the headboard on the bed, a dramatic fan of overlapping slices of mirror. 'Like, it's *class*. And the light fixture!' A giant supernova in chrome and opaque white glass stretched in a frozen explosion above our heads.

'Rachel, we've thirty-four minutes left.'

'Oh! Okay.' My gaze flickered around the room. 'That painting?' I pointed.

'Take it down, I bet something is stuck to the back.' I touched the silver-grey walls. 'Quin, this is fabric! Maybe silk!'

'Thirty-three minutes.' Then, 'Rachel. You're scaring me now.' He'd lifted the painting from the wall and was unfolding something he'd found stuck to the back of it. 'A riddle. How are you so *good* at this?'

'Beginner's luck?'

Hurrying through, I found an opulent bathroom of black marble and diffused white lighting. Then a decadently mirrored dressing room, containing a set of matching luggage so beautiful it almost brought me to my knees: five pieces in the palest blue leather—a large trunk, a smaller suitcase, a hatbox, a vanity case and one that could have been a doctor's bag.

'Hey!' Quin had followed me in.

'I *know*.'

'No.' He was pulling at the combination lock on the biggest trunk. 'I bet that's what we're looking for, the numbers for this. Head in the game, Rachel.'

Finally, I focused.

The riddle from the painting led us to four different numbers, hidden around the room. The chrome legs of the nightstand, which were in the shape of a giant X, gave us 1 and 0. A recurring geometric pattern in the weave of a rug revealed itself to be an 8. And on the wall of the bathroom, a hidden number 9 appeared in the beam of an ultraviolet light.

But we still had to find the correct combination of the four numbers and only three minutes remained.

I was so invested in the outcome that I could barely breathe. First Quin input the numbers and I remembered them, then he said, 'My hands are too fumbly. You take over.'

Input. Nothing. Input. Nothing. Input. Nothing. Input. Then—a click.

'Oh God, Quin, I think this is it! If the earrings aren't in here . . .' I was trembling with anticipation and anxiety. '. . . I will legitimately *die*.'

The lock slipped free, then both of us were pulling the case open and the rush of adrenaline when I saw the two twinkling clusters within almost sent me into orbit.

'Oh my God, yes, there they are!'

Fuelled by the rush of victory, I high-fived Quin at the same time as he went in for a hug and I accidentally smacked him in the face.

'So?' he asked, later. 'You're certain you didn't sneak in there last night and do a trial run?'

'I'm certain.'

'But you're a natural at finding all the hidden stuff.'

I shrugged. 'I'm not. They just seemed obvious hiding places. The whole thing was risky, though. If we hadn't found the earrings and poor Mabel was a goner, we'd have blamed each other.'

'I knew we'd find them.'

'Is it a man thing? That confidence?'

He shrugged, 'It's a me thing.' Then, 'I like you.'

'You don't know me.'

'There's something here. You know there is.'

'I'm not looking for anything.'

'I hear you. I'm a commitment-phobe. I'm lonely and I crave intimacy, but I still fuck it up. What's your story?'

'My husband—' It was still too difficult to say the words, *My husband left me*. I began again. 'My marriage broke up. We'd really loved each other . . . I'm not sure I'll ever get over it.'

He seemed entertained by this. 'Of course you will. You were just waiting to meet me.'

'Why did you and your wife split up?'

'Yeah. Look . . . I slept with someone else.'

Even though it was the oldest story in the world, I was still upset.

'This is the thing.' Quin sighed. 'I thought if I was honest with you? But if I don't say upfront what I did, people get angry when I *do* tell them—'

'By "people" you mean women?'

'Yeah. So I get judged either straight out of the gates or further down the line.'

'Maybe you shouldn't have cheated.'

'No maybe about it. I'm flawed, like, *very*. But I'm trying to do better. I've been seeing a therapist. Eleven weeks now, I haven't missed a session. And I'm voluntarily . . .' He hesitated over the word. '. . . celibate.'

'Oh?' I was astonished. Celibate friends was really *not* the vibe I'd been getting.

Quickly he said, 'It was never meant to be forever. I just needed to stop the meaningless stuff.'

'Has there been a lot of "meaningless stuff"?'

Warily, he eyed me. With the tiniest little shrug, he said, 'Some, I guess.'

I could believe it. 'And how long has this "voluntary celibacy" been going on?'

'Let's seeee . . . I want to say five months?'

'So, since October?'

He thought about it. 'Maybe not *five* months. When are we now? March? There's been no one this entire calendar year.'

'That's not even three months.'

'. . . I thought it was longer. It's certainly felt it.'

Rachel! This is red flag central.

I was in full agreement with my internal voice, something that didn't always happen. It wasn't that I worried Quin would hurt me—I'd never love another man the way I'd loved Luke, which made me invulnerable. But the last thing I wanted was drama.

There had been a moment in the escape room when, as our bodies had been working diligently side by side, trying to unlock drawers, something had sparked in me. Quin had smelt . . . the only way I can describe it was *attractively not-safe*. For the first time in years, my body had reacted like the animal it was and felt full of longing.

So now, in light of the red flags, I was *disappointed*.

I picked up my keys and phone. 'Thank you, Quin, I had a good time today but I'm leaving now.'

8

Jesus, it was nearly two o'clock! The best seats were already gone in the Abbot's Quarter but I got a mid-ranking one. Last to arrive was Trassa—who looked pointedly at the sole remaining chair: a two-hour stint on it was hard going even for those without elderly joints. Immediately Chalkie stood up and directed Trassa to sit on the upholstered armchair he'd been colonizing.

Okay, it was time for Trassa's life story.

There were times when listening to a client's version of their life was actually a pleasure, almost like being at a good one-man play. Chalkie's, for example, had been insightful, almost unbearably moving and, at times, hilarious. Roxy, who worked in the music industry, had presented a tale of travel and glamour.

Trassa, though. Christ alive. Snooze city.

And no surprise. Trassa was far too skilled at protecting her addiction to let any truths slip out.

'I was born in . . .' We got a ream of blah about a happy childhood in rural Carlow: school, brothers, soda bread, fudge . . . We were treated to a couple of would-be funny stories, one about her and her brothers trying to catch a runaway ram. Naturally, somebody slipped in the mud and 'needless to say' (although it was said anyway) the ram was recaptured.

Meeting and marrying her husband was one cliché after another, as was the birth of her five boys. The phrase, 'the happiest woman in Ireland' was used several times.

But would someone *really* be 'the happiest woman in Ireland' by the time they gave birth to their fifth son in eleven years? Without any pain relief? Knowing she'd be bringing him home to an overcrowded, three-bedroomed house? Where she would spend four weeks on maternity leave before returning to her job on the production line in the local concrete factory?

Pages of tedium on the school years of her sons followed, plus far too much about Seamus Senior's health woes. It struck me suddenly as a very lonely life. No mention of female friends, just her three brothers, her five sons, her invalid husband, useless men everywhere, overrunning her days without bringing any real joy.

Her gambling addiction was dispensed with in two lines—she loved the sociability of the bingo and a scratch card on a Saturday evening was 'a bit of fun'. The reason she'd borrowed four thousand euro on a credit card was because she had a dead cert in the Kentucky Derby. (And it was the Kentucky Derby this time, not the Grand National; addicts tell so many lies that they often can't keep up.) It wasn't *her* fault the horse had fallen.

'The end,' she said, with a soft smile.

As always, the group were invited to comment, but today they were curiously reluctant. Only Roxy went for it. 'You told us nothing about your addiction.'

Helplessly, Trassa said, 'Roxy, love, I'm sixty-eight years of age, I've eleven grandchildren, I'm waiting on a new hip. I've *no* addiction.'

'You're trying to manipulate us,' Roxy scolded. 'Like, we can't call you an addict because you're an elderly lady.'

'If I had any notion what you were talking about . . .' Trassa's face was a picture of benign perplexity.

I turned to my left. 'Chalkie.'

'Yes, missus!' He sat up straight and saluted me.

'Why did you give Trassa your chair? At the start of the session?'

'Because this one'—he rocked himself so hard he almost fell over—'belongs in Guantánamo Bay.'

'Would you have given up your chair to Giles?'

'Um, *no*. Because I can't stand the head.'

'Or Harlie?'

'Harlie? That one is young and hardy . . .' Suddenly his voice trailed off.

'And Trassa isn't young and hardy? You gave your seat to Trassa out of respect for her age?'

'. . . no. Yeah. I don't know. Maybe.'

'None of you are helping Trassa by shielding her from the truth.' I was stern. 'This is what you should have said: "Trassa, doing a Saturday-night scratch card is nothing like borrowing four grand on a credit card you'd dishonestly got in your husband's name, putting it on a horse and being unable to repay it."' I focused on Chalkie. 'Say something helpful to Trassa.'

'Ah, here, *Rachel* . . .' He squirmed. 'Snitches—'

'—get stitches, Chalkie, no need to tell me. Trassa needs your help. Go on!'

'Trassa.' He cleared his throat. 'I thought that bet was, like, a hundred euro. Four thousand is very different. That's big money.'

Trassa's expression sharpened into scorn. 'You're a heroin addict, the lowest of the low.'

The group were shocked. Addicts tended to go on the attack when their lies were called out, but this was the first time they'd seen Trassa do it. Suddenly, everyone was staring at their feet, terrified I'd pick them.

'Giles,' I prompted.

Oh shit zipped across his face. Nervously he said to Trassa, 'Why did you take the credit card out in Seamus Senior's name? Is that not . . . fraud?'

Mimicking Giles's accent with impressive spite, Trassa replied, 'Having a threesome with your first wife and your second wife, while you're married to your third wife. Is that not . . . *fraud*?'

Shame silenced Giles. Eventually he managed, 'To be accurate, it's adultery. Morally wrong. What you did, though, that was an actual crime.'

After a brief, stunned silence, Trassa began a stuttering defence. 'Well! It's fine and dandy for Mr Cokehead Giles! You've plenty of money. But for the likes of me, *decent* people, who earn their money *honestly*, we do what we can to get by. What's mine is my husband's and what's my husband's is mine.' Witheringly, she said, 'You and your exhibition openings and sailing around the Greek islands listening to opera, you'll never understand what it's like for a woman like me, so keep your posh mouth shut!'

Giles promptly did. *Everyone* had their mouths zipped. Trassa's control of the group was extraordinary.

'Trassa,' I said. 'You're not getting it. What you did is illegal.'

'But not wrong.' Trassa was loud.

Harlie, who until now had been twirling her hair and staring into the middle distance, sat up so abruptly that the whole room looked at her. 'I'm sick of your shit,' she declared. 'You lied by acting like you'd only borrowed about fifty euro.'

My heart leapt. For almost a week Harlie had been angry but worryingly aloof; this outburst indicated progress.

'Lied!' Trassa exploded. 'When did I ever lie?'

'It's called "lying by omission",' Giles supplied, suddenly brave.

Harlie flicked him a scornful glance. 'Thanks, Giles, I had, like, literally no idea.' She shifted back to Trassa. 'You're a liar.'

'No, but . . .' Trassa ran out of words. She seemed confused.

We were finally getting someplace. Trassa was no longer entirely convinced by her own lies and I needed to park this for a while, to let her truth begin its sacred rearrangement.

9

It was Thursday night before Brigit called me back.

She and I could go for weeks without speaking but our connection was as strong as when we'd shared an apartment in New York, more than twenty years ago.

Around the time I got into recovery she fell for a man from County Galway, with soft-voiced banter and devilment in his eyes. Like everyone, he 'worked in IT'. They suffered a tough few early years, crammed into a small apartment in Queens with their two young boys, then returned to Ireland, built their dream house (which was also my dream house) on Colm's family's remote, rocky farm, and had two more children.

As life transformations go, it was dazzling stuff. 'The bigger the city the better I liked it,' she'd said. 'I tried so hard to make New York work for me. Who knew I'd be so much happier living on a remote peninsula, with four feral children, twelve minutes of rough road from the nearest off-licence?'

More than once, she'd said, 'I'd have had four more kids, no bother. I was happiest when I was pregnant. But Colm and I were too tired. We'd have died.'

All of the big-city stuff had fallen away from her—blow-dries, fashionable clothes, exhausting ambition—but lit by joy and an intense curiosity about everyone, she was gorgeous. 'How lucky am I?' she often remarked. 'To land up in a place where conversation is a legitimate hobby?'

Because, by Christ, they talked in Maumtully (the site of the off-licence. Also an ATM, a hardware store, a 'gentlemen's drapery', a pharmacy/vet's suppliers, several art galleries, approximately a hundred Aran sweater shops and one small hotel). Chats broke out in lineups, in the middle aisle in Lidl, around a can of paint which had been mysteriously abandoned on the path in Main Street.

More than anyone, Brigit had witnessed the worst of my addiction. She'd done a lot to protect me and, at the vital moment, she was the person who realized I'd taken too many pills and rang the ambulance. That I was alive today was probably thanks to Brigit.

'Sorry it took so long to get back to you,' Brigit said.

'Tell me what happened.' Her stories were the *best*.

Perhaps the motor on the boat taking the botany students out to the island had broken down, so Brigit had had to drive to Galway for a new one, then row it out to the boat, along with eight tinfoil blankets because the students had suspected hypothermia? Or the hotel had had a flood on the day of Geraldine Skerrett's wedding to the Welsh TikTok star, meaning nineteen visitors urgently needed accommodation, so Brigit and Lenehan (her eldest son) had to clean and heat their Airbnb barn at lightning speed?

'Nothing dramatic this time,' she said. 'Just a series of small disasters. So, right. Luke's mum—'

'I've decided to go,' I said.

'Good.' She sounded pleased. 'It feels . . . *right*.'

I pounced. 'Why's that?' I credited Brigit with modest psychic abilities. Which, might I say, she did nothing to disavow.

'It just feels . . .' She paused. '. . . the *decent* thing to do.'

'That's disappointingly prosaic.'

'Poor Luke. And if you see Joey Armstrong, give him a wink from me. For old times' sake . . . So when are you coming to visit?'

I groaned with longing for that Atlantic peninsula, a place of spectacular, twisted beauty, where lichen-patterned rocks sprouted from the land alongside crippled trees.

And Brigit's house! Three walls were constructed from the local blue-grey stone but the rear was almost entirely glass. Befitting a busy family, the common areas were all airy, Scandi-style flow but the bedrooms, with their high wooden beds and simple quilts, were solid, cosy affairs. Whenever I visited, I slept like the dead.

The drive, though, was the issue.

'It's barely four hours,' she said now.

But it felt a lot longer.

'It's the shite roads,' she admitted.

'They're grand as far as Galway.' That's what we always said.

But after Galway they got narrower and rougher, until they became bumpy single-tracks, where if you had the misfortune to meet another vehicle, you had to reverse for about five miles, trying very hard to prevent your back wheels from swerving into the ditch.

(And—although I was mortified to admit to this—driving down there in the twilight scared me; I was afraid of meeting the pooka. Even though there was no such thing.)

'Would you come for Queenie's birthday? March the twenty-ninth? Come for the weekend with Quin.'

'Hold on till I check . . . Sorry, Bridge! I'll be in Barcelona. My anniversary with Quin.'

'Ooooh. Barcelona for your anniversary! That sounds . . . serious.'

'Hahaha, stop!'

'But it does, Rachel.'

'I love you, goodbye, talk soon!'

Friday morning, the day was dry, the sky blue. At the church, the giant parking lot was nearly full and Kate and I had to park right at the far end. It was almost ten o'clock by the time we got to the front entrance. The undertaker and a few other official-seeming people loitered on the forecourt, but there was no sign of any of the Costellos.

'God, it's *freezing*.' I shivered in my black coat. But what else had I expected for early March?

'It's not, though.' Kate looked concerned. 'Rachel, are you okay?'

'Yeah. I—Is it really not freezing?'

'It's really not.'

'It must be just me then.' I was trying for a laugh but it didn't work.

'Come on, let's go in.' She took my hand.

Suddenly, there came a shift, a murmur, among the waiting officials. *Here they are.*

Stuck to the spot, I watched the hearse draw up, followed by two other black cars. Everything lapsed into slow motion as a cluster of Costellos, all dressed in black, got out. There were Luke's two brothers, their wives and kids, his sister, her husband, their children—there had been a time when I'd belonged in that family.

One of the nephews looked so like a young Luke that, briefly, time collapsed and I was twenty-seven all over again.

'Rachel . . .' Kate whispered—and I realized I was digging my nails into the palm of her hand.

'Sorry!' I let her go.

Luke was nowhere to be seen . . . Then, oh my good God, there he was, lifting an old man—his poor dad, he'd got so frail!—into a wheelchair. Tenderly, he settled his father's limbs and tidied his jacket.

It was shocking how little Luke's appearance had changed. No tight jeans and leather jacket, of course; because of the occasion, he wore a dark suit and an even darker expression. His hair was as thick and shiny as ever but shorter than it used to be. Back in the day, I used to cut it for him; I wondered who was doing it now.

'Rachel.' Kate stroked my arm. 'Stop staring.'

Too late, I noticed the woman who'd slipped her hand into Luke's. Just a brief impression of a slim, black coat, bright lipstick and elegant shoes. Despite feeling cold, I was suddenly drenched in sweat.

Is this real? Is this actually happening?

From the back of the hearse, the coffin slid out and the able-bodied men of the family surged forward to shoulder it—Luke, his two brothers, his brother-in-law, the Luke-a-like nephew and another dark-haired lad.

'We should go in,' Kate whispered, guiding me forward.

Claire had said that the most important thing was to write my name in the Book of Condolences, which would be just inside the door. 'So if anyone checks,' she'd said, 'they'll know you showed up. You don't even have to stay, you can just sign it and leg it.'

But with the coffin hot on our heels, there wasn't enough time.

Claire had also advised sitting near a side door in case escape became necessary, but the place was packed and seating was at a premium. Kate and I hurried up the aisle, the heels of my boots like hammers on anvils as we desperately sought a couple of empty spots. Christ, if we didn't find something soon, we'd be up at the front, alongside the family! The very thought . . . the ex-wife, crashing the funeral, like some heartbroken madzer.

'In there,' Kate hissed, jolting me into a spot about six rows from the front.

We shouldered our way through. 'Excuse me, excuse me, sorry.' There was really only room for one person, but any port in a storm.

Feeling as though this was all a dream, I noticed the group of men on the right side, a couple of rows up. Older but undiminished, the Real Men were out in force. My immediate impulse was to try to disappear down into my black coat. (Claire—who appeared to know everything there was to know about funerals—had told me that people didn't really wear black these days but it had felt like the mannerly thing to do.)

From inside my collar, I took a stealthy look, wondering how the boys had fared in the last six years. Once upon a time, they had been my friends; when I'd lost Luke, I'd lost them too.

There was Narky Joey, the breakout star. (Back in the day, Brigit and I initially agreed that if you *had* to sleep with one of the Real Men—say, in a last-man-on-earth-style situation—the obvious one would have been Joey, who was sexy in an angular, sneery way. As it turned out, Brigit *did* sleep with him.)

These days Joey was looking moneyed and hot, in a beautifully cut elegant suit beneath a beautifully cut elegant head of hair. Not so Gaz, who was still rocking alarmingly tight black jeans, a black leather jacket and what looked like half a can of hairspray holding the back-combed knots in his straggly 'do. Fair play to him. Stayed true to his principles. Johnno, barely recognizable, had gone the full, baldy, someone's-dad decline. And there was Shake, looking good, still sporting the excellent head of hair which had given him his nickname.

The strains of the organ started and a shoal of Costellos shot up the aisle to their seats at the front. I tried to get a better look at the woman who'd been holding Luke's hand, but her head was bowed, so there was just an impression of shoulder-length blonde hair and a delicately boned face.

Here came Mr Costello, his wheelchair being pushed by Luke's sister, Vanessa. As he came level with our pew, our gaze met. His dark, button eyes flared with surprise and—maybe?—warmth.

Now came the coffin. Luke was on 'my' side and as he passed by, his face rigid, my heart pounded so loudly that I thought he'd hear. He delivered the coffin to the stand near the altar then stepped into a pew near the front, 'excuse-me'-ing his way along, till he was next to his girl. From behind, I watched as she took his hand in hers and they sat down together, their bodies close.

With throat-clearing and shuffling, the mass began and reality began to settle. Luke was over there, on the other side of the aisle. With another woman.

In the months, even years, before today, I'd been fine. The way we'd ended would probably always hurt, but I'd been okay about it. At peace, really.

But now, in this church, the time-jump was making me light-headed—one minute Luke and I were each other's most important person in the world, the next it was more than half a decade later and we'd been long since consigned to each other's pasts. It was *insane*.

It was then that I noticed something terrible going on below my knees—a throbbing sensation, as if my lower legs were going to burst their way out of my leather knee boots, like the Incredible Hulk splitting his T-shirt.

The problem was my calves. Overall, I was an average size, but my lower legs seemed to be abnormally girthy. It was almost impossible to find boots which zipped up to my knees. This pair had made the cut because if I lay on the floor and got Kate to use a metal coat-hanger, they almost closed to the top. But I shouldn't have wasted my money. And I *certainly* shouldn't have worn them today. Foolishly, I'd hoped that their black leather sleekness in conjunction with my black coat would impress people.

Well, let's see how impressed they'd be if my legs exploded.

Next thing, bumping me from my worries about detonating shins, the priest announced that Luke would do a reading.

In his dark suit, he climbed the steps to the altar and settled himself at the pulpit, his face as blazingly pale as his white shirt, his demeanour so austere it was impossible to believe that there had been a time when his chat-up line had been a twinkly 'I suppose a ride is out of the question?'

Fixing his gaze downwards, he swallowed, then started, his voice low and husky, '"Remember me when I am gone away . . ."'

Oh God, not *this* poem. Instantly, tears filled my eyes and began to pour down my face.

Luke paused. It was a second or two before he continued: '"Gone far away into the silent land."'

Another break. 'When you can no more hold me by the hand—"'

His voice cracked on the last two words but he pushed on. '"Nor I half turn to go . . . yet turning stay."' This time the pause went on too long. His brother Mattie was already on the way up to rescue him.

As Luke stepped down, white-faced and bowed, he suddenly looked up, sweeping his gaze over the congregation. In the sea of appalled faces, he saw me. Our eyes locked and his blazed with sudden recognition.

I tried to read something—anything—from his expression, but his eyes went blank and then, dismissively, he looked away, leaving me trembling in every part of my body.

I was utterly mortified. Only then could I admit that I'd been carrying a nugget of hope, an absurd fantasy of Luke falling to his knees, declaring that he'd never stopped loving me.

I felt humiliated. Stupid. Absolutely devastated.

The rest of the service passed in a haze, ending with the coffin being wheeled down the aisle, the family trooping mournfully after it. As Luke passed our pew, his head remained bowed.

The family would be waiting at the front of the church, where people could personally pay their respects, so I said to Kate, 'We'll go out the side door.'

'You don't want to meet him?'

Jesus Christ, *no*. I needed to get as far away as possible. There was no hope of us being friendly. His flat-eyed glance had left me in no doubt.

The reality was that a long time had passed, he'd met someone else and so had I. The situation was as fixed as it was ever going to be.

'We'd better sign the book,' Kate said.

There was no need, he'd seen me, he knew I'd been there.

Quietly, we slipped outside but to get to the parking lot, we had to cross the forecourt of the church, where the crowds were congregating. Ducking our heads, Kate and I scurried at speed, my shins in agony yet—inexplicably— also numb.

'Rachel?' someone called.

'Oh no,' I whispered. Kate and I scurried even faster.

'Rachel!' The voice was a lot nearer.

There was no escape, so I stopped and turned to see Luke's brother, Justin and a younger man, the one who looked like the twenty-something Luke.

'I thought it was you!' Justin declared.

Hugging him felt natural. 'I'm so sorry about your mum. She was lovely.'

'Margie was a character.' He managed a half-laugh. 'It's a sad day.' He turned to Kate and stuck out his hand. 'Justin Costello.'

'We've met,' she said shyly. 'A long time ago. At their—Rachel and Luke's— wedding. I'm Kate, Rachel's niece.'

'Jesus.' He looked mildly shocked. 'You don't feel the years passing.' He shunted forward the young man. 'This is my eldest, Devin.'

'Devin?' I couldn't hide my surprise. 'The last time I saw you, you were about twelve!'

Up close, he wasn't really that similar to the young Luke. He had the same black hair and a similar body type, but his eyes were nothing like Luke's pools of darkness.

Politely, he shook hands with both of us.

'Will you come back to the house?' Justin asked. 'My place in Rathmichael. Everyone's invited, we'd love to have you.'

Go to the house.

There wasn't a hope. I needed to get away from the Costellos, all of them.

'I don't think it would be the best idea . . .' Especially not with Luke and his new lady there. 'But . . .' My tears started again. 'Just tell me, is he well? Is he okay?' Half laughing, I added, 'Apart from the fact that his mother has just died, I mean.'

Justin looked sad and embarrassed. 'He's good, he's good. Don't worry about him.'

'Could you . . . pass on my condolences?'

'You can tell him yourself if you come for the lunch. Come on, Rachel, we'd love to see you. Dad really wants you there.'

Automatically, I looked past Justin to the collection of Costellos who were gathered near the hearse. From his wheelchair, Mr Costello was watching us. He met my eyes, then lifted his hand in a friendly way. What the *hell*? *Go to the lunch.*

I clenched my jaw. 'Okay. We'll come.'

'Great. We'll see you there.'

Clutching Kate's arm, we scuttled back to the car. When we were far away enough that it was safe to speak, Kate asked, 'Are we *really* going?'

'No. I can't go just to please Luke's dad.'

'You lied?'

'Just being Irish. Justin would have kept at me until I agreed. It was easier to pretend.'

I I

Ted took one look at me. 'Go home.'

'No. I'm fine.' Well, I *would* be—diving into work always helped.

'You don't look fine,' Murdo offered. 'And where are your shoes?'

'Boots, actually. I had to take them off before my legs erupted. Just need to change my clothes now, then I'm set.'

'Rachel,' Ted said. 'Murdo can cover for—'

'Ted.' I fixed him with my most earnest gaze. 'I'm fine. Thank you. And thank you, Murdo. Is my new arrival here? Yes? Okay, I need to find Priya.'

I ended the argument by walking away.

I'll be okay, I told myself. I'll be better than okay, I'll actually be fine . . . won't I?

Hard to say. Maaaaybe you should have gone to Justin's house?

Sometimes the voice in my head could be irritatingly smug.

Twenty years ago, Nola became my sponsor on the condition that I 'found a higher power'. I *very much* didn't want to—giving up drugs was hard enough without having to be spiritual into the bargain.

Eventually though, a vague, gentle thing developed, where I had chats inside my head with something that wasn't me. At the time, that was as specific as I could manage. But over the years the voice in my head had evolved and grown, developing an entire personality of its own. At times it could be borderline unbearable.

'Rachel!' And there was Priya.

In the front office, she brought me up to speed on Ella Black. Ella had kicked up about surrendering her phone for the duration of her stay—nothing unusual there. They all did—I'd have done it myself if I'd had a mobile back then.

Nor was it a surprise to hear that Ella had asked about yoga classes—nearly all the women admitted here were *obsessed* with exercise, thinking that the real benefit of rehab would be the chance to drop a dress size. Like, never *mind* learning the tools to overcome an addiction, what really got them excited was six uninterrupted weeks to get strong-not-skinny. (That had been me.)

Discovering that we had no gym, no pool, nothing, was usually quite a moment—high-pitched, angry objections where phrases like 'natural high', 'keeps me sane' and 'human rights' were flung about. (Also me.)

Funnily enough, though, when they discovered they'd be getting plenty of exercise scrubbing bathrooms, hoovering hallways and generally keeping the entire house clean and sparkling, they were even more furious. (Me again.)

Ella's bags had been searched and the inevitable contraband seized. (Once again me. When I'd arrived at the Cloisters, I'd tried to smuggle in a jar of Valium.)

'But her bloods came back clean,' Priya said. Which meant she was in.

In the dining hall was a young woman with her arm in a sling—this had to be Ella. In yoga pants, running shoes and a raggedy-edged sweater that I owned in a different colour, there was a real bloom about her: shiny dark hair and freckles, she was pretty and wholesome-looking.

'Ella? I'm Rachel, your therapist. Come with me, we'll have a chat.'

In a consulting room, we sat opposite each other. 'How are you doing?' I asked.

'Oh, you know.' Her eyes filled with tears. 'This was hardly part of my life plan.'

'Getting addicted to sleeping tablets?'

'No, I meant . . . I mean, ending up in rehab.'

'What about getting addicted to sleeping tablets? Was that part of your life plan?'

'Well, no, because I'm not.' She was clear-eyed, earnest. 'I haven't.'

'So . . . ?' I feigned confusion. 'Why are you here?'

'My boyfriend and my best friend, they kind of had a freak-out. There was a thing with Jonah's car—they overreacted.'

'And Boyd, your boss?'

She seemed startled that I knew who he was. 'He overreacted too.'

'That's a lot of people who've overreacted.'

'I know how it looks.' She was so keen to explain. 'On paper, the facts are bad. But I know myself fairly well—I'd *know* if I had a problem. And believe me, if I had one, I'd want to deal with it.'

'So why are you here?'

'I thought if I came in for a few weeks, they'd stop freaking out.'

'Riiiight. So you've come here to prove you're not an addict?' I could play good cop now and again.

She met my eyes. 'And I know how that sounds too. But they were on my case so much it just seemed easier to give in.'

They never stopped amazing me, my clients. They could convince themselves that day was night, in order to keep on using. Now and again reality might break through but in most cases, they truly believed they could justify drinking or taking tablets or placing bets or making that booty call. Reasonable people, intelligent people, educated people—it made no difference. Addiction was the wave that washed away facts, common sense, kindness, everything good.

'Okay. So I'd like you to start writing your life story,' I passed her a printout. 'This is a template. As you can see, we'd like particular emphasis on your relationship with drugs.'

'But I'm not a—'

'But do it anyway.'

'Sure!' She was so perky and positive. 'Why not?'

'You can head back to the dining hall and I'll see you in group in fifteen minutes.'

No sooner had I secured the best seat in the Abbot's Quarter than Ella tumbled in, commandeered by Giles. No surprise there, he womanized as automatically as breathing.

Singling out my wonky-legged chair from Wednesday morning, he instructed Ella, 'Avoid that seat at all costs. And that one too. This is fine, though.'

Almost as soon as she was seated, Dennis barrelled through the doorway. Here less than a week, he already had 'his' chair; he stopped short at the sight of Ella sitting in it. Ella—keenly attuned to the moods of others—sprang up. 'Sorry! Is this your spot?'

Dennis, with his bone-deep need to be loved, declared, 'Not at all, not at all,' somehow managing to convey that yes, it most certainly *was* his chair, but he was such an extraordinarily decent skin that he'd let her have it and welcome.

'Sit down, sit down, sit down.' He waved and, with a shy, 'Thanks,' she did.

Next to arrive was Chalkie, then Harlie—and the energy in the room changed. She and Ella assessed each other and some vibe flashed between them. It was obvious that Harlie thought Ella, with her freckles and wayward, natural hair, was pathetic. And Ella thought Harlie, with her hair extensions and elaborate make-up, was ridiculous.

It was instant mutual hate.

'Ella,' I opened with, 'can you introduce yourself?'

'Mmm, yeah, I'm . . . My name is Ella, from Waterford originally, live in Dublin now and I'm mummy to the best cat in the world.'

'Any dogs?' Dennis asked. 'I've a lot of respect for cats, but . . . do you ever think your fella is judging you? A dog wouldn't care what you did but a cat—'

'Not at all. Mooch is *awesome*, he—'

'*Jeeeeezus*,' Harlie hissed.

'Excuse me?' Ella's tone was sharp—which made Chalkie smile. Which, in turn, made Ella focus on him and his blue-eyed charisma, then flush slightly.

'Ella,' Roxy interrupted. 'Why are you here?'

'Sorry.' She giggled and went a darker pink. She was lovely, very charming. 'I could talk cats all day. So, it's crazy, I had a weird reaction to medication. *Prescribed* medication. By a doctor.'

'But . . . ?' Dennis asked.

'My boyfriend was freaking out,' Ella said. 'So was my best friend—about the way I reacted to the tablets. They were all, *You're gonna end up dead*.' She said it in a funny voice and got a laugh from Dennis and Trassa. The rest, however, remained unimpressed. 'I know I'm okay, but so they could stop fretting, it seemed easier to check in here.'

'Would you like to tell your group the events that triggered everything?' I said.

'. . . Ah . . . Okay! So, yeah. Last February, like February a year ago, I was coming home from work. Late. So it was dark. I was walking from the Luas stop to my house and two people—men—just *appeared* and . . . and . . .' Her head dropped to her chest and she whispered, 'Sorry . . .'

'Take your time, Ella.'

'They grabbed me and . . . pulled off my backpack. Everything was in it, my phone, my purse, my laptop, all my work and stuff—'

'Did they rape you?' Dennis asked. Ever sensitive.

She lifted her head and stared at him. 'No . . . But they hurt me and they scared the shit out of me.' She looked in my direction. 'Sorry for swearing.'

That was hilarious, her mannerly apology. In a matter of days, if she was like everyone else, her effing and blinding would be out of control.

In silence, I waited. I had a feeling Harlie would get this for me.

Sure enough, she swished her thick curtain of hair and asked, 'Then what happened?'

'How do you mean?'

'You're not in rehab because you got mugged.' Oh, the *scorn*. 'What did you get addicted to?'

'Nothing.'

'Tablets,' Harlie reminded her. 'You said you were taking tablets. And your friends said, *You're gonna end up dead*. So, what did you *do*?'

'I stopped being able to sleep. Every time I closed my eyes, I, like, felt their hands on me and I was so scared. My doctor said I had PTSD . . . My GP gave me a prescription for sleeping tablets.'

'And?' Harlie demanded. 'No one is in rehab because their doctor gave them a prescription.'

'. . . Okay . . .' Ella looked to me for guidance. I remained poker-faced. It was something I'd found very hard in the beginning—the whole impassive thing. My impulse was always to jump in and help them out. Left to my own devices, I'm a dyed-in-the-wool people-pleaser too.

'So, yeah, a weird thing happened. I took my boyfriend's car out for a drive one night last week. I'd taken my sleeping pill, I was in bed asleep, and it's insane but I don't remember doing it—'

'You don't remember *driving the car*?' Harlie pounced.

'That sometimes happens with these tablets.' Ella was all earnest explanation. 'In the US, there are court cases now. It's the fault of the pills.'

'Did you get home safely that night?' I asked.

'Um, no. So I drove the car into a wall—'

'—the front window of a house,' I corrected.

'Hold up, there!' Roxy exclaimed. 'Is that how you broke your collarbone? Was *that* "the accident"?'

'Yes!' Ella was smiling but red-faced, caught out.

'I thought you'd slipped on the ice or something,' Roxy said.

Of *course* Ella had been vague about how she'd come by her injury, trying hard to muddy any link between broken bones and sleeping tablets.

She'd try to stick to a simplified, sanitized version of what she'd done but the real story would be revealed over the next days and weeks. Unless, of course, she started having sex with one of the other patients behind the sofa in the rec room. And from the longing glances she kept giving Chalkie, anything was possible.

I 2

In the staff room, I gathered up my stuff.

'You sure you're okay?' Murdo asked. 'Quin will be back . . . ?'

'Sunday morning.' I wished he was back already.

'What are you up to now?'

'Meeting Claire in Dundrum for a burger.' And a debrief.

'Dundrum.' He winced. 'All those shops and shit. The fake waterfall . . . So, enjoy it. If that's actually possible. See you Monday.'

'Well?' Claire asked as she briskly deconstructed her burger, discarding the bun and offering me her chips. 'Did you get to talk to him?'

I shook my head. I was already regretting not having gone to Justin's house. I'd had a chance to corner Luke, maybe quiz him about the reasons he'd left me, but I'd turned it down.

'He saw me, though. He knows I was there.'

'Good stuff, good stuff.' A meaningful pause. 'How did he look?'

'Upset.'

'Well, yeah, *obvs*.' For about half a second her expression was fake-sorrowful, then she lost interest. 'But is he still . . . hot?'

Hey, there was no getting around this. 'Yeah, Claire.' I sighed. 'Still hot.'

'Full head of dark hair? Eyes intense and brooding? Body still sexy af?'

My stomach felt sick. 'Yes.' Then, 'Yes. And yes.'

'Yeah.' She lapsed into thoughtful silence, then hit me with her full beams. 'You know, I was going to say, "That's a shame." That maybe it would have been better for you if the wheels had come off. But a man as hot as Luke Costello, it would be, like, a terrible loss to the world.'

'This isn't making me feel any better. Just in case that was your intention.'

'Sorry, babes. Eat your . . . whatever it is, vegetarian thing. So listen, you're going to feel weird for a few days. Your sleep will be affected, you'll eat lots of ice-cream and the sneaker-makers of the world should brace themselves for a spike in sales. But this too shall pass.'

She was right. That was the great thing about being not-young: knowing through practical experience that feelings, even the worst of them, calm down and eventually ease. They're probably not gone forever—that was another thing I'd learnt: the notion of 'closure' is unrealistic. If I'd felt an emotion once, it stayed on file *for-ev-er* and could be reactivated if the conditions were right—or, more accurately, *wrong.*

'What was he wearing?' she asked.

'A suit.'

'Pics?'

'Claire . . .'

'Tight trousers?'

'Not obscenely so.'

'Now that *is* a shame.' Then, 'Yeah. Sorry, Rachel, sorry. Anyway! Why would you care about Luke when you're getting it from Nick Quinlivan on the regular! Sexy man, is Quin, is all I'm saying.'

Even before Claire had met Quin, she'd liked the sound of him. She'd scolded me for writing him off after our first date.

'He was honest with you,' she'd said. 'He made a mistake by cheating on his wife, and now he's trying to do better. And do you honestly think you're going to meet someone who hasn't fucked up at some stage? It's human nature, we all do it. Give him a chance, would you?'

And, surprising myself, I'd decided I might. There had been a shift in how I felt about myself since the meditation weekend. There was definitely some forgiveness, some healing. That alone made me feel positively towards Quin.

And—unexpectedly—I'd fancied him.

This, I'd discovered when Claire had asked, 'How would you feel about him pounding away on top, hoofing it into you?'

'*Hoofing it into me?*' I'd winced.

'Sorry,' she said. 'It's the testosterone gel. Since I've started, I think about sex twelve times a second. I guess this is what it's like to be a man.'

It was a mystery why Claire's doctor had put her on, of all things, testosterone supplements. It wasn't as if she'd ever been lacking in confidence. Menopause seemed like a strange country with some very odd practices and I did my best to pretend I'd never be old enough for it.

As it happened, I could *well* have been perimenopausal, but it was hard to be sure, seeing as I already had several of the symptoms. Insomnia? Step right up! Tiredness? Well, that's just modern life.

'So?' Claire had insisted. 'The hoofing?'

I'd thought about it and . . . *oooh. Definitely* something there.

'My God,' she'd declared, vivid with delight. 'You like the sound of it! You'd better reply the next time he messages you!'

Back in the now, I took a forkful of chips from Claire's plate.

'Take them all,' she said. 'Save me from the carbs. So, Rachel, if you ever get tired of Quin . . .'

Oh Jesus, we were, once again, skirting dangerously close to swinger talk. I was so hoping she'd forgotten about it.

In a high voice, I blurted, 'Have you found a dress yet for Mum's party?'

Mum was turning eighty in four weeks' time and we'd been ordered to throw her a surprise party. Between Claire's dynamism and Margaret's meticulous nature, arrangements were well advanced: eighty of Mum's family and frenemies had been invited to a champagne reception and sit-down dinner in the SugarLoaf Inn; an elaborate frock was being constructed by a 'couturier' that Margaret had managed to unearth and, in New York, Anna was in negotiations with her employers to secure huge amounts of free make-up and skincare for the party bags.

'Jesus, the dresses,' Claire declared. 'If it was only me I had to worry about . . . But I'm also ordering them for Kate, Francesca *and* Molly.'

Molly was her stepdaughter, Adam's daughter from another relationship. Around the same age as Kate, Molly was willowy, gorgeous, charming and had a high-status job as a scientist for a clean-energy company. All of us were in love with her but Mum was the worst—absolutely *fascinated* by Molly's impeccable social skills. She was also prone to frequent bouts of anger triggered by how far short all of her own children and grandchildren fell by comparison.

'Then there's Luka to worry about. I ordered him a studded hoodie from Balenciaga and he's refusing to even try it on. "The planet," he says. What other fifteen-year-old boy gets the chance to wear Balenciaga!'

Luka was an incredibly tall, incredibly thin, incredibly earnest young man. Not much fun, to be honest. And not his fault. Like teenagers everywhere, he rejected the value systems of his parents—and his parents were all *about* fun.

'Seriously, Rachel, the *stress* of it.'

'You're not stressed,' I said. 'You love it!'

'Ah, yeah, I do.' She gestured for the bill. 'Gotta go.'

'What you up to?'

She nodded in the direction of the fourth floor, where the medi-spa lived. 'An oul' spot of radio-frequency body contouring.'

'What does that do?'

'Tightening.' She pursed her lips with evident satisfaction. 'Tight. En. Ing. See you tomorrow.'

This was news to me.

'Committee meeting for Mum's party.'

Another one? There were so *many*. 'Listen, any idea what's up with Helen?'

'Not one clue. But we'll have to get it out of her. Right. Bye!'

After Claire had gone, I had a moment of freefall, of not knowing what to do next. The shops were there . . . I could always stagger around them, killing time. But no.

FaceTime Quin? Again no. I was so raw that I'd probably say something to accidentally hurt him. Call Nola? Jesus Christ, no! My worst idea so far—no *way* had I the energy for the deep-dive she'd make me do on my emotions and motivations.

Go to a meeting.

If I drove fast, there was an eight thirty NA meeting that I could probably make. It was oh-so-tempting to skip it and just go home and collapse on the couch . . .

Go to the meeting.

All right! I'm going!

People who haven't been to a Twelve Step meeting think it's all about addicts bemoaning their miserable drink- or drug-free existence. But it's nothing like that. In meetings we talk about whatever's going on in our lives, good or bad, managing our responses to rogue emotions, celebrating all that's good and identifying old destructive habits, so that we don't lapse.

Once I got there, I was happy. It was good to sit on a hard chair in a circle with others of my kind and check in with myself—yes, my name was Rachel; yes, I was an addict; yes, my feelings today were painful but yes, I could cope with them.

What more did I need?

13

There was no sign of Kate at home. After taking Crunchie for a speedie turn around the block, I tumbled straight into bed, and FaceTimed Quin. A quick in and out was what I was hoping for—just your basic bedtime courtesy call. This wasn't the right time for a deep and meaningful.

'How was the funeral?' he asked. 'Did you meet your ex?'

'No. But it was okay. We can talk about it on Sunday. Like, if we need to. But really, it's all good.'

We said our goodbyes—then I was hit with a wave of gratitude that, two years ago, I'd listened to Claire's urgings and given him a second chance.

'Ask me *anything*,' he'd said. 'And I'll answer you honestly.'

'Why did you cheat on your wife? Because you're Mr Upgrade?'

'Nah, I wasn't like that with Shiv. But she was messing around, you know, *flirting* with a man she worked with. I was . . . hurt. Hurt, scared, humiliated . . . so I decided to get back at her. Which is pathetic, you don't have to tell me. I hoped she'd see what she was missing but thing was, she'd had enough of me and I was too stupid to realize.'

'That's a lot of drama, Quin.'

'Shiv is a . . . she's a strong personality. She and I, we're quite similar. But all of that drama was temporary. And five years ago. These days we care about each other. But not the way we used to.' He paused. 'You, though, I *really* like.'

'Why?'

'Why does anyone like anyone?'

'I get the feeling the only reason you want me is because you think you can't have me.'

'*Can't* I have you?' he shot back. 'Then why did you text me?' This was the first time I'd ever seen him smile. 'Rachel, maybe you're right, maybe the only reason I want you is because I think I can't have you. But we won't know until we know. You're just going to have to take that chance.'

He held my gaze and I was frozen by his being Not-Luke. I'd honestly thought I'd never again consider another man, and even though that seemed to have changed, Quin's unfamiliarity confused me.

That beautiful fantasy of 'After ten minutes I felt I'd known him all my life' didn't occur so much in reality. Nobody likes to hear this, but intimacy isn't a gift granted by the Gods of Love at First Sight, but is something that has to be worked at—like learning to stay upright on a unicycle.

This relative stranger wanted things from me—my time, my thoughts, access to my body. And for the first time in forever, the idea wasn't horrifying. Which I put down to whatever strange business had gone on between us at the meditation weekend.

It wouldn't be easy. I was out of practice. But if I wanted a life with love, I'd have to spend time with this person I didn't know, I'd have to sit in silences that were sometimes far from comfortable, I'd have to accept all the ways he wasn't Luke.

Suddenly I was okay with that.

It'll never last. That's what I'd thought at the start. I laughed at Quin's impatience and couldn't be arsed to be intimidated by his fast-changing moods. And that, without me knowing it, was the perfect attitude.

He was interesting. Intriguing. Frequently entertaining.

And sexy. Oh God, yes. There was an edge to him that sparked something in the flat battery that was my heart.

But there was plenty that was wrong with him. Even though there were one or two heartbroken women in his recent past, it was safe to say he wasn't a charmer—not immediately anyway. His smiles were rare and he could be blunt to the point of offensive. His moods had a tendency to spike and then plunge, his energy was inquisitive, almost acquisitive, and he was too hungry for quick fixes.

This was the sort of thing that happened a lot: one Saturday, skimming the paper, he came across a rave review of a book. 'Rach, listen to this!' He read out a few sentences, then declared, 'I'm buying it!' Immediately he downloaded it to his Kindle and dived in, but about half an hour later, abandoned it, complaining that the reviewer 'hadn't a clue'.

'You didn't give it a chance,' I'd said.

'I did!'

'Everything disappoints you.'

'Not you.'

'But I will. Just give me time.'

So I was going on dates with him, and enjoying myself, but I held off on anything physical. It was always going to be a massive deal to be intimate with a man who wasn't Luke—and Quin more than most. He was acting smitten but he was really *quite* judgy about appearances. There was a good chance he'd conclude that my forty-something body was too slack or too cellulite-y. Too *something*, anyway.

'Have I been friend-zoned?' he demanded around the five-week mark. 'Is there any point being patient?'

'So you don't want to hang out if there's no chance of . . . ?'

'Nope.' He was quite clear about it.

'I'm . . .' I tried to find the right word. *Terrified*, that was it.

It was nearly twenty years since I'd slept with anyone other than Luke. I had fancied Luke so very much, I only needed to smell him for my body to light up. But our sex life had been straightforward stuff. It had worked for both of us—but it left me at a disadvantage now.

Claire had asked me, 'What *precisely* are you afraid of with Quin?'

'That he'll be too "technical". That he'll be barking instructions, like, "C'mon, Rachel, do the three-legged dog!" Or, "Side-straddle me!" As if we're acrobats putting on a show. I've been out of the game too long and, from what I hear, it's changed. I need tenderness, I need emotional connection as well as the physical side. And I want to take it slow.'

'Well, *tell* him.'

What other choice did I have? 'Okay.'

So I laid out my specific concerns, which he received so calmly that I told Claire, 'It really would be no hardship to sleep with him.'

'"It really would be no hardship"?' she repeated. Then, molto-sarcastically, 'I'm off to buy a hat for the big day! You've idealized Luke; you're like an old woman with a *shrine*. It's time you moved on. You'd swear you and Luke were perfect.'

'We were.'

'If you were, you'd still be together. Off you go—*enjoy* sleeping with Quin.'

And I actually did! Facts were facts—without the disinhibiting effects of half a bottle of wine, I was shy. However, our first time, it was . . . 'Actually . . . sort of . . . fabulous,' I told Claire. 'He's *interested* in what I like, but not in a feathery-strokery way. And he kept checking I was okay.'

'This sounds *wonderful*. Any acrobatics?'

'. . . Aaaaahhhh, nothing too complicated. But he *did* know the right . . .

buttons to press. He, ah . . .' I cleared my throat. 'Knew his stuff. But not enough to *worry* me.'

'Any Costello flashbacks?'

'. . . No.' It was nothing like being with Luke when, long before the end, we'd fallen into tried and tested routines. With Quin, I felt we were embarking on an adventure with countless thrilling possibilities.

'I think it's going to be . . .' It took me a long time to locate the exact word. '. . . *fun*. He's focused on what he wants. And he wants . . . me?' We both fell around laughing. 'I thought I'd never fancy a man again.'

'And you fancy Quin?'

'Oh my God, yes! I am *weak* for him.'

Claire clapped her hands together with happiness. 'Life in the old dog yet. And I'm talking about you, not him!'

'Now that I know how . . .' I felt myself colour. '. . . *lovely* it is, it's all I want to do.'

'That rock-climbing he does? Has he . . . abs? And stuff?'

'Yes. Abs! Arms! Some manscaping! But not too much. Definitely not enough to make me feel inadequate.'

'He sounds perfect.'

14

'Great news, Mum!' Claire read from her iPad. 'All five of your sisters have RSVP'd.'

'They have?' Mum looked pitifully happy. 'Even Imelda?'

'*All* of them. That's what "all" means—*all*, you cretin! And their husbands. *Everyone's* coming.'

Mum's eyes were suspiciously shiny. 'That's just . . .' Her mouth trembled. '. . . great news. So when I arrive at the hotel, I'm thinking that Margaret and Dad will lead me in. Should I wear a blindfold?'

'No.' Claire was brusque. 'Health and safety. In other words, you're bound to trip and fall. Not a chance worth taking.'

Mum's iPad started bing-bonging. 'Here's Anna,' she said. 'Sweet Jesus, what do I press?' She made some panicky jabs and, more by luck than judgement, Anna's face appeared on the screen. 'Hey, Mum, hey, Claire. Rachel! How was the funeral? Did you see Luke?'

'Saw him, he saw me, but we didn't speak.'

'So, how did he . . . seem?'

'Still hot,' Claire called.

'I didn't mean . . . I was wondering if he was . . .' She was fooling no one.

'No leather trousers,' Claire elaborated. 'Just a suit.'

'That's too bad . . . Are you okay, Rachel? Call me if you need to talk. So how are the party plans going?'

Mum said, 'Do you swear to me, Anna Walsh, on your bended knees, that you have eighty Lucerne Bio serums for the party bags?'

'I swear to you. And loads of other stuff too. Your sisters will be so impressed, they'll be sick.'

A disturbance at the door heralded the arrival of Helen, in a dark form-fitting tracksuit, her hair up in a high pony.

'You look like an assassin!' Mum was all admiration.

'Fecken wish I was.' Helen scanned the room and focused on me. 'You, girl! Report on Luke Costello. How was his crotch?'

'It was his mother's funeral,' Mum said, her tone sharp. 'Have some respect.'

'He was in a suit,' Anna called from New York.

'Suits can be tight,' Helen said. 'Remember their wedding? Sweet. *Jesus.* Remember the debate we had, wondering if he had the trousers specially tailored or if it was just down to . . . him?' At my stricken face, she muttered, 'Anyway, he's an asshole.'

'Stop talking about him,' I said. 'Like, *please.*'

If they didn't knock it on the head, I'd have to leave. Since yesterday, I'd been awash with humiliation—both old and new. Every time my memory reran the little home-movie of the dismissive flick of his eyes in the church, fresh shame flooded in.

Underneath the shame was an appalling sadness.

But I'd be okay. So long as I didn't take anything to sidestep the pain—and I wouldn't—this awful discomfort would eventually disperse.

'If I could have your attention,' Mum called. 'Claire, Helen, before I arrive at the hotel, you're to have the guests all fired up. Make them practise yelling, "SURPRISE!" Do it a few times. My sisters, but especially Imelda and Philomena, won't want to, and some of the cousins are right bitches too, but tell them there'll be no goody bag for them if they don't. Ah, here's Margaret. What's that you're wearing?'

'A shirt-dress. It's new!'

A blue-and-black checked flannel button-down, the sleeves rolled back over a slubby grey T-shirt, it was very Margaret. With flat black leather knee boots and her choppy bob, she looked comfortable and stylish. It was a great look and it really suited her.

'You're . . . well turned out.' Mum sounded surprised.

'You look like a social worker,' Helen said.

'. . . who's having an affair.' That was Claire trying to be nice and it made Margaret laugh. Not that there was any chance of Margaret having an affair. Of all of us, her relationship was the most convincing. She and Garv were *lovely* to each other.

'How are you, Rachel?' she asked. 'How was Luke?'

'We didn't speak.'

'Oh. Well. How did he . . . look?'

'Do *any* of you care about my surprise party?' Mum exploded. 'Or do you just want to talk about Luke Costello's tight trousers?'

'I'll take Luke Costello's tight trousers for five hundred dollars,' Claire said.

'Ah now! Bitta respect for Dr Spork!' Helen said.

'Who? Oh, *Quin*.' Mum snorted. She didn't like him. 'Cocksure of himself,' was her sour assessment.

Confidence was usually seen as a positive. But Mum was from that generation of Irishwomen who prided themselves on raising children with rock-bottom self-esteem. Nothing galled them as much as an offspring with confidence. Quin might have got away with it if he'd put the effort into charming her—because he could be *very* charming when it suited him—but, contrary fecker that he was, he decided not to. ('Why should I?' He'd declared. 'I shouldn't have to apologize for who I am.')

'Is Spork coming to my party?' Mum asked.

I laughed. 'Mum! We've been together for nearly two years.' As she well knew.

'Two years? How's he going to mark your anniversary? By flying you to . . .' She cast about, trying to find a location adequately exotic. '. . . *Bora Bora* for the weekend?'

She had a point. Quin liked to visit countries that other people couldn't pronounce, like Laos, or that the Department of Foreign Affairs advised you to avoid, such as Iraq. (It wouldn't surprise me if Quin said, 'Yeah, no, there's a province in the north of Iraq, absolutely beautiful, looks like Switzerland. I *know*. Totally peaceful, the entire population are red-haired Rastafarians— some genetic throwback. We should go.')

Last summer we'd gone on a walking holiday in Transylvania and I suspected his main reason for wanting to go was because of the name.

'Not Bora Bora,' I said. 'But Barcelona.'

'Oh!' Margaret was enchanted. 'Barcelona!'

'Well!' Mum sounded horribly smug. 'I hate to piss in your punchbowl—'

'Mum!' A clamour of voices rose. 'That's disgusting!'

'*That's* disgusting? You all say far worse! Anyway, Rachel, I hate to piss in your punchbowl—'

'You don't,' I said. 'You love it.'

'But you'll be mugged on the Las Ramblas street. Everyone gets mugged there. Now can we please stop talking about Rachel's men. The thing is'—her voice wobbled—'I've never had anything nice, *ever*. I have five sisters and I was always overshadowed. I've spent my *life* wanting a surprise party. This is my one chance to be special, so commit to it!' She turned to Margaret. 'What's the thing you say?'

'Lean in.'

'Yeah. Lean. Fucking. In!'

'I'd lean in a lot better if I had some chocolate,' Helen said, zipping towards the kitchen.

She looked . . . actually . . . a bit pale. I went cold. She wasn't sick, was she? Like, seriously sick?

When we'd all been younger, Helen had seemed invulnerable—brave, judgemental, deliberately contrary. People—men in particular—were dazzled and maddened by her.

However, in the last eight years, she'd endured three spells of suicidal depression, each culminating in a stay in a psychiatric hospital. She'd been well now for a couple of years but since the first bout, I'd never not been worried about her.

Sometimes my fear was so small it barely registered, but it was always there, like a faint background whirring sound.

Today it wasn't her mental health I was afraid for—but it had been such a shock when she'd first got sick that I'd got used to jumping to worst-case scenarios.

She'd drive you up the wall—only a fool would deny it—but at some point over the years I'd understood that she wasn't doing it on purpose. She couldn't help how she was. With her unmanageable impatience and robust opinions, life was often difficult for her. For every person she enchanted, there were about ten more who became instant enemies.

And the thing was, Helen would speak unpalatable truths when everyone else was too scared to open their mouths. The world needed more Helens.

I followed her as she opened the treat cupboard and a mini-avalanche of chocolate and biscuits tumbled out. '*Mint* Aero?' she asked. 'What is *wrong* with her?'

'Are you okay?' I asked.

'*Me?*' She paused in her rummaging. 'Grand. Apart from the appalling selection of candy in this house.'

'Have you got cancer? Is that your big secret?'

'What? No! Jesus. No. Nothing like that. Ah, for the love of Christ . . .' She waved a packet of biscuits at me. '*Mint* Jaffa Cakes? She needs *help*.'

My phone rang.

'Who is it?' Helen asked.

'Unknown number.'

'G'wan!' she teased. 'Live a little!'

'Okay. Hello?'

'Is that Rachel?' a male voice bellowed. 'It's Patch here. Patch Dooley.'

Who? Oh *right*, Dennis's younger brother.

'You were looking for me, I believe?' he yelled against a background of chugging noises. 'Juliet says you want me to come in about Dennis?'

'Thanks for calling back,' I said. 'You're aware that your brother Dennis is in a treatment centre for alcoholism?'

'I'm "aware", right enough.' He sounded amused. 'How does Wednesday morning suit you? I'll be in your area, visiting a man in Baltinglass about some bagels.'

'Bagels?'

'Bagels. Dogs! For hunting rabbits.'

Oh, *beagles*. 'Great. But we need to talk things through beforehand. Patch, how close are you and your brother?'

'Best buddies. But I've to go now.' Farm machinery—by the sounds of things—was revving away. 'I'm fond of me leg, I don't want to lose it.'

'I'll call you on Monday to talk—'

'Do that! G'luck!' He hung up.

Back in the sitting room, Mum was quizzing Margaret about what she planned to wear to the party.

'I'll see what I have in the wardrobe.'

Mum, an inveterate spender, was appalled. 'But you have to buy something new!'

'I don't.'

Mum threw her a wounded look, then turned her attention to me. 'If you show up in jeans, you can go straight home again!'

Claire and I exchanged a smirk. For weeks, Mum had been pestering me to 'make an effort' to wear 'something *glam*'. And it was all coming together.

Two weeks ago, a dress from the Vampire's Wife had arrived. Quin had been very pleased—it was everything he liked—expensive and beautiful, with cult appeal.

But with its high neck, long sleeves and muted ivy colour, it would probably be the wrong sort of glam for Mum, who appreciated bright sheaths of polyester satin, festooned with blingy appliqués.

The only thing she might approve of was that it was short. I'd also bought a teetering pair of black platform sandals. When I'd done a dress rehearsal for Claire, she'd tried to persuade me to go bare-legged—I swear her hand literally *twitched* for her beloved fake tan—but I wasn't having it. 'I need the safety of tights.'

'But sexy ones,' she'd pleaded. 'None of your sixty denier shizz, gimme a sheeny fifteen.'

'What if they get a run in them? Claire, I *can't*, that night will be stressful enough. I'll maybe go to twenty.'

'Any chance you'd do hold-ups instead of tights?'

'No. Me and sexy underwear are *done*.'

It wasn't entirely true. But the last time I'd tried, at a restaurant with Quin, my knickers became so savagely uncomfortable that, after the starter, I'd had to go to the ladies, take them off and hide them in my handbag. I still wasn't sure what had gone wrong—they'd felt okay when I'd left the house but perhaps I'd been sitting on them incorrectly? Or eaten too much bread?

'Get your father,' Mum ordered me.

'Why?' I asked.

'Just get him, for the love of God!'

'I'm here.' Dad, who had clearly been primed to expect the summons, was at the door. He came in and sat down and we all stared at him. What was this about?

'Right.' Mum flicked a look at Dad. 'At the party. We've. Decided. There's to be.'

Both of them took a deep breath and delivered the fatal line, 'An open bar.'

'*All* night?' Margaret was scandalized. 'With your relations? You might as well file for bankruptcy right now.'

'And we're having champagne on arrival. *Not* prosecco.'

'That's right,' Dad echoed. 'Champagne on arrival. *Not* prosecco.'

'But—'

'Nnnh!' Mum held up a hand to silence Margaret—who promptly turned to Dad and said, 'The cost will—'

'Nnnh!' Mum declared. 'Dad says we can afford it.'

'We can afford it,' Dad said.

'Yes, but—'

'And we've finalized the menu.' Mum spoke over Margaret. 'Asparagus to start, beef for the main course—'

Helen groaned long and loud. 'Just *how* tragic can one woman be. Asparagus is the fanciest thing you can imagine?'

Hotly, Mum said, 'Asparagus is a seasonal delicacy and if we don't serve beef, they'll say we're poor or mean.'

'We *must* serve beef,' Dad echoed.

'There are nicer things that cost more, if that's your yardstick,' I said. 'Is there a vegetarian option?'

'None of my relations are vegetarians.'

'I'm a vegetarian and I'm your daughter.'

'You're not a vegetarian, you're just a notice-box. Eat the potatoes and vegetables. Or bring a KitKat in your handbag.'

'We should have a vegetarian option,' Dad said. 'I'll ring them tomorrow.'

'On your head be it. Now, girls, the dessert! We're having a chocolate mousse with *real gold leaf* on it. I had it once in that restaurant in New York—remember? Where Dad got food poisoning—'

'Which time?' I asked. Dad got sick whenever he left Ireland—something *always* went wrong. We were such a neurotic family.

'It was a lovely place,' Dad said. 'It wasn't their fault.'

'Well, if it was food poisoning, it kind of *was*,' Helen said.

'Maybe it wasn't actual food poisoning—'

'It'll be hilarious,' Mum mused. 'Those bitches won't know whether to eat it or bring it home!'

'How about we have a special cocktail made for the night,' Claire said. 'We could name it after you.'

'That's a great idea!' Dad said.

Mum considered it, then shook her head. 'They'd say I was showing off.'

'I suppose they would.' Dad seemed disappointed.

God almighty, the world Mum inhabited had complex, illogical rules. I'd *never* understand them.

15

'Off you all go now,' Mum said. 'Dad and I need to watch our show.'

'Rachel, come to ours for dinner?' Margaret offered. 'Garv is making enchiladas.'

It was an attractive offer. Margaret, Garv and their two children, JJ aged fifteen and Holly aged thirteen, were a lovely family—very *harmonious*. A calm household where there was always homemade cake in a tin, armloads of wildflowers bursting from vases, and stacks of elderly Agatha Christie novels waiting to be read.

Of all of our homes, Margaret's would be the best in which to recover from a nervous breakdown.

In the bleak days after I'd sold the apartment Luke and I had owned and left New York, I'd lived there for five months. In the most gentle way, that little household had kept me going. If ever I was flat on my back, staring at the ceiling, wondering about the point of anything, a light rap would sound on my bedroom door and somebody would ask for my help to make a casserole or walk the two elderly dogs or rake a flower bed.

It was where my love of gardening ignited. Margaret's husband Garv had me out there every weekend, weeding, composting and planting. Obediently I was going along with it, half-heartedly enjoying myself, until one Sunday morning, he said, 'Something to show you.' Drawing my attention to an expanse of wildflowers pushing their way up through the soil, he said, 'The seeds you put down seven weeks ago? This is what happens.'

To say I was impressed was an understatement. This, my first time to witness the cycle of life in such a fashion, was a revelation which affected me deeply, because we Walshes had grown up to shun the Outside, mostly because the lead on the telly didn't stretch that far. The small back garden beyond our kitchen window was a frightening, unpredictable place, which we all agreed was best avoided.

But on that Sunday morning with Garv, I'd exclaimed, 'Let's plant more! What grows the quickest?'

He'd laughed and said he'd find out. Then I'd told him not to, that I really needed to work on my desire for instant gratification.

It was hard to believe there had been a time when I'd despised Garv, when all of us had—with the exception of Margaret, of course. But things change and these days Garv might even have been my favourite brother-in-law—it was between him and Adam. He was such a *good* man.

'Enchiladas?' Margaret repeated.

'Thanks, but . . .' I checked my phone. Still nothing from Kate. 'I've to go home. Crunchie needs to be walked.'

Kate was great at providing back-up but at the end of the day, Crunchie was my dog.

Still, I lingered, then heard myself say, 'You know, I can't stop wondering if Luke actually *asked* Joey to tell me?'

'Maybe you should have gone to Justin's lunch.' Out loud, Claire uttered the thought that had been plaguing me.

Maybe I should have. It had been my one chance to get answers. But perhaps if I'd gone, I'd be even more conflicted than I already was.

'Is it too late?' Margaret, ever practical, asked. 'To see him now, I mean. He's probably staying with his dad; you could go to his house.'

'No!' Helen exclaimed.

But it was tempting. The full weight of six years of silence upended themselves and fired me with adrenaline. The fizzy possibility of *knowing* was so alluring!

But what if Joey *had* called me off his own bat? What if Luke had been horrified to see me in the church—because God knows, he'd looked it? What if I turned up on his doorstep and he treated me with the same callous indifference he'd displayed when he'd left me?

No. No way. There was zero chance I'd risk *that* scenario. Which made me glad. It meant I'd changed, that I was no longer a desperate mess but a solid woman who knew her own worth.

'Don't go anywhere near that asshole.' Helen was fierce. 'Come home with me and have a three-way with Artie.'

'Now there's an offer!' Mum said, warmly.

'Or we could get pizzas and watch stuff?' Helen said. 'Whatever you want. Just don't start driving around Dublin looking for Luke Costello.'

'Thanks,' I said. 'Everything's been all stirred up by going to that funeral, but it'll settle down again soon.'

At home, Crunchie tried to jump out of her fur with delight when she saw me.

Out we went, for a quick turn in the woods near our house, and even though it was nearly seven, it wasn't fully dark yet. The clocks would be going forward in two weeks' time; spring was definitely on the way.

Back at the house, I got my iPad, flung myself on the couch and clicked straight onto Luxury Exchange to gaze at the pre-loved Chanel shoulder bag I was currently consumed by. My life had no room for something so ladylike—or so shockingly expensive—but I kept zooming in on the beautiful blue calfskin, so soft and squishy that I wanted to actually *bite* it.

From there I went to the RealReal and found two similar bags, then to Vestiaire, where there were *dozens* of little leather beauties, all of them way out of my price range. Clicking and scrolling, I was suspended in the happiest state of loved-up longing.

I was never not prone to obsessions but thanks to the discomfort churned up by Luke, I was extra keen for the dopamine hits generated by those beautiful bags.

At least I know what I'm doing, I told myself robustly. Then, *All the same, I'd better stop. Before I actually buy one of them.*

Because it wouldn't make the longing go away. Paradoxically, it would make it worse.

I suffered from the Disease of More—if one of something was good, then ten was excellent. If a recipe said half a level teaspoon of cumin, I put in a heaped tablespoon; if I bought one unbearably wantable bag, I'd want twenty more immediately.

So I forced myself away from the calfskin and popped over to Vulture, looking for new Netflix recommendations, and from there to Mr Fothergill's Flower Seeds, where I bought ten packets of hollyhocks when two would have done, then onto the Atlantic, mixing culture and commerce in a way that was profoundly enjoyable.

Yes, I knew I was actually *enslaved* to my device, yes, I had lost literal *weeks* of my life to it, when I could have learnt conversational Tagalog or trained as a humanist minister, but I always had such a lovely time that it was hard to mind.

Before bed, I lit a candle and set the timer on my phone—I was giving meditation yet another go. Surprisingly, considering all that was going on, my mind actually stilled. I was delighted. Then, ruining it, a memory popped up, vivid and complete, of a July afternoon, in Connemara, over a decade ago.

Ah, for God's sake!

Not long after Brigit and Colm had moved into their spectacular glassy home, Luke and I had visited.

Back then, the astonishing house was still partially under construction. As Luke asked, the moment we arrived, 'How was it possible to build anything here at all?'

Beyond the giant windows of Brigit's kitchen, it looked as if a perfect landscape had been torn apart and reassembled in any old fashion. Nothing was level out there, *nothing*.

'Oh my God, stop!' Brigit said. 'I cried every day for seven months. Every. Single. Day. Living with my in-laws, going round the bend. A miracle Colm and I survived.'

Five sheep, coolly chewing grass in a field that was almost vertical, watched us without curiosity. Small, gnarled trees, their ancient branches spotted with moss, sprouted from the land at head-meltingly unlikely angles.

'Your bedroom is actually finished,' Brigit said. 'But, as you can see, the rest of the place . . .' She gestured around at the raw concrete walls. '. . . which is where you come in.' Solemnly, she gave me a paint roller.

'Anything for me?' Luke asked.

'Oh yeah! How does laying floorboards sound? We've hired an electric saw.'

Luke's eyes lit up. He loved electric tools.

It was a magical week, toiling alongside Brigit and Colm, their two little boys trying to get in on the act. The work was hard, but gloriously rewarding, every day punctuated by a ten-minute walk to the stony beach for a reviving dip in the Atlantic.

Evenings were passed hanging out in the 'garden', talking, laughing, watching swifts circle overhead, black against the otherworldly Connemara summer light, where it never got fully dark.

'So what'll you do when the house is finished?' I asked one night after dinner. 'What's your next project?'

'Another baby,' Brigit said.

'And I suppose we'd better get married,' Colm said.

'Is that . . . a *proposal*?' Brigit asked.

'Well . . . why not.' Colm shrugged. 'Be easier for the kids when they go to school.'

'Now *that's* a story for the grandkids.' Luke was highly entertained.

'What about you two?' Brigit nodded at Luke and me. 'Any plans to . . . ?'

'We're fine.' I was brief.

A couple of times, Luke had asked me to marry him and I'd talked him out of it. My excuse was feminism, but really it was good, old-fashioned superstition. My life was as good as it could possibly get—what Luke and I had was too precious to risk by looking for more.

On our last day of that perfect week, Colm, Brigit and the kids had to go to the bright lights of Galway city on some official business. Luke and I decided to walk the boundaries of the property.

At the far edge of Brigit and Colm's eight acres was an expanse of lime-stone, shaped like a shallow bowl, perhaps ten metres by twenty. With the strangled trees and the total absence of signs of human life, it was almost too much for me. 'It's like being on another planet.'

A sound interrupted us. A splash. Startled, we looked down. Water was gushing up from the cracks between the rocks, as if from a burst pipe.

'What the—' Frightened, I moved away, as water spouted from a wider expanse of the land, then from all around us. We seemed to be in the centre of whatever this was. 'Luke! What's going on? We'd better . . .' What? Ring the authorities? But this wasn't anything as civilized as a burst pipe. Was it natural or . . . *super*natural? I couldn't be sure.

'It's okay.' Luke seemed excited as he moved us to higher ground. 'I think I know what this is.'

Bamboozled, frightened, I watched as a pool began to form.

'It's a disappearing lake.' Luke sounded full of wonder. 'Colm told me about it. Beneath us is a source of water.'

'*Right* underneath us?' Quickly, I stepped back.

'The rock is porous. Sometimes enough water bubbles up to fill the hollow. It creates a temporary lake.'

'What if it doesn't stop? And we all drown?'

He just smiled.

'We should get Colm,' I said.

'He's in Galway. Babe, there's nothing to be afraid of. This is . . . miraculous.'

Astonishingly quickly, the hollow became a pool. Before long, it was deep enough, if you'd wanted, to swim a few strokes in. Reflecting the sky, the water was an intense turquoise, with a strange opaque quality.

'Why does it look milky?'

'Sediment,' Luke said. 'Minerals. Calcium.'

It was too logical an explanation—all of it—for this very strange event.

'It's years since this last happened,' Luke said.

'Why is it happening now?'

Again, he just smiled—beguiled by it all. Slowly my fear turned into awe.

'It's weird,' I admitted. 'But . . . it's good weird?'

He laughed in delight. 'It's amazing. You were right earlier. We *could* be on another planet. I could be the last man on earth.'

'In that case, lucky me.'

And I thought, *If you asked me now, I'd say yes.*

I turned, about to tell him—but he saw whatever was written on my face and laughed softly. 'Really?'

'Ask me. Say the words.'

'Rachel Walsh, will you marry me?'

'Yes, Luke Costello, I will marry you.'

16

'Hi,' I said to the perfectly groomed young woman, 'I'm here to pick up Nick Quinlivan.'

'Of course! I just need to see your ID. Perfect! I believe his plane landed a few moments ago. Valeria will take you through.'

Valeria was even more alluring than her colleague: radiant skin, shiny hair swept up into a heavy bun and *such* a dazzling smile—almost too much beauty for this early on a Sunday morning. Although I was guessing that in the rich-person, private-plane universe, it was always 2.45 a.m. in a nightclub.

'This is your space.' It was a small, tasteful sitting room, the kind they have in boutique hotels. 'What may I get you? Champagne? Mimosa?'

'Erm . . . no thanks, I'm fine.'

'Or something to eat? Seriously, our chef can make you *anything*. She's just itching for the chance.'

When I shook my head, she laughed. God, she was a doll.

'*Loving* your willpower,' she told me. 'Mr Quinlivan should be with you shortly.'

I sat on a beautiful low armchair. Lovely. Then I swapped to the couch. Even lovelier. A bowl of fresh fruit—perfectly ripe bananas, lustrous grapes and giant, shiny apples—sat on the coffee table. It would be okay to eat whatever I wanted but I'd feel bad about disrupting the perfect proportions.

Even more tempting were the boxes of handmade chocolates stacked on a shelf. But if I started on that lark, who knew where it would end? With me trying to break into the Cadbury factory in Coolock, probably. (I could do *nothing* in moderation. *Nothing*.)

I eyed the fridge, wondering what was inside. Milk, maybe. And butter. Boring basics. All the same, it continued to exert a draw. I *love* other people's fridges—they're often exciting places, much more so than, say, store cupboards (chickpeas and their dull ilk).

The thing was, I was very nervous. Sometime yesterday, I'd gone hot-cold at the realization that there was a chance of bumping into Luke today. A *small* chance, admittedly, because only rich people or their lucky employees used this private terminal.

Also, I'd no idea when he was flying home. But they got so little time off work in the US, even for bereavements, that I couldn't imagine him sticking around for much longer than today. Tomorrow at the very latest.

Which meant that by tomorrow night, I could exhale—even though I knew I'd also feel disappointment and a devastating sense of anticlimax. That's feelings for you. Irritatingly contradictory.

To calm myself, I listed out the good parts of my life, things that I knew to be *facts*. I was drug-free and well, had a job I loved, good friends, a peculiar but loving family and I was in a healthy relationship with a good man.

Quin and I were quite different people but we had *such* fun. Even when we disagreed, it was always good-humoured.

He was interested in me—my opinions, my thoughts, everything. He was in my corner, in a major way.

And I fancied him. Unlike Brigit, Claire and Brianna at work, the suggestion of sex didn't make me exclaim, 'Jesus Christ, isn't my life shitty enough! I col*lapse* into bed after an absolute *arse* of a day and then *he* shows up, jabbing his lad at me! He's nearly fifty! Can somebody please tell me, *when* does it stop?'

Mind you, I was far from smug about this. My libido still flickered with regular life because Quin and I didn't live together. But if I moved in with him, I knew that the very second I'd lined up the last of my sneakers on the floor of the wardrobe, I'd start yelling, 'Birthdays, Christmas and our anniversary! Any other night of the year? Don't even think about it!'

I was fairly sure that I loved Quin but I hadn't—yet—told him, because those words shouldn't be thrown around until I was absolutely certain I meant them.

The thing was, the way I felt about Quin was very different to how I'd felt about Luke. After Quin and I had been seeing each other for maybe four or five months, he'd pinned me down about it.

'What's the difference between me and your ex?' he'd asked. 'Be honest, Rach. I want to know what I'm dealing with here.'

'Luke was like . . .' Carefully, I picked my way through the words, trying to be accurate. '. . . a French sauce that's been reduced and reduced.'

Quin flinched. 'Christ. And what am I?'

'You're like . . .' In a panic, I was trying to find something that would wipe away his hurt. 'Like Jo Burger's cheesy fries. Absolutely *delicious*. And moreish. Just different.'

He wasn't happy but he didn't labour the point. Except for now and again, maybe after he'd made me laugh like a drain or we'd had a lively couple of hours in bed, he'd mutter darkly, 'Jo Burger's cheesy fries . . .'

Quin hinted heavily that he loved me, but, being Quin, he was too competitive to run the risk of saying it, then being left hanging by my silence.

Sometimes I wondered how long we could go without saying, 'I love you.' If we could last an entire relationship? An entire lifetime?

But having seen Luke, I was asking myself if I'd been wrong to have held out on Quin. It was as if a spotlight was suddenly illuminating different types of romantic love. The version of me who had fallen for Luke was much more innocent than the woman who had met Quin. I was so much wiser now, shaped and changed by all that life had given me, good and bad.

And Quin was a very different man to Luke. So of course the love I felt for Quin—and I was starting to accept that it *was* love—would be different to how I'd felt about Luke.

Alerted by a noise at the door, I stood up and there he was: Mr Quinlivan. Abandoning his wheelie case, he crossed the floor, swept me into his arms and kissed me. His macho presence was a huge comfort—he was real, my life now was *real*—but as the kiss went on I couldn't help thinking, *Just say Luke happened to be getting a private plane back to Denver and he saw us? That would show the fucker!*

I put my face in Quin's neck. 'You smell fancy!'

'I had a shower.'

'On the *plane*?'

'Yeah. I know!' His eyes sparkled. 'I'll tell you everything. So? We right?' He scanned the room. 'You get yourself any free things?'

'There are some chocolates . . .' I indicated the stack.

'Go for it.' He picked up two extra boxes. 'Give these to your mum,' he urged with a sly smile. 'After she's eaten them, tell her they're from me.'

I laughed. 'Stop it, come on now.'

Another benefit of the private terminal was being able to park literally right outside the door, instead of the usual four-kilometre, concrete-coated trudge. Quin slung his bag onto the back seat and we hit the road; we had a plan, one that Quin had lobbied hard for: going swimming in the perishing March sea in search of the famous Cold Water High.

Two years ago, at the meditation weekend, my initial impression of Quin had been correct: he was an adrenaline junkie, his particular poison being rock-climbing. Two or three times a year he, with a group of friends he'd had since junior school, went off to a granite-y part of the world to place metal things into cliff-faces, hang off ropes and generally put his life in danger.

But he was also an endorphin stalker, convinced that constant happiness was achievable if he could just assemble the correct life ingredients together in the right way. He was always suggesting *stuff* and trying to involve me: 'People swear by ayahuasca' or 'Should we join a choir?'

Sometimes I obliged him. Let's be clear here—Quin wasn't for everyone. But my interests frequently overlapped with his because when you don't drink or take drugs, you have to generate your own dopamine—and shopping, while wonderful, can only do so much.

Despite it being 7.50 a.m. on a bitter March morning, business was brisk in the narrow roads around the Forty Foot. Salt water hung in the frigid air, people with rolled-up towels were disappearing through a gap in the stone wall and others were coming out, looking wet but elated. Several were wearing strange coats—huge, padded, poncho-like things in waterproof fabric.

There wasn't a parking space to be had but then Quin spotted a woman wrapped in a towel approach a car.

'Hey,' he called from the open window. 'Can we have your spot?'

'Sure.'

'She looks happy, doesn't she?' he asked me. 'We're doing the right thing, Rach.'

'I *am* happy,' she called. 'This is better than Effexor.'

He leant out of the window. 'Do you mind me asking, what dose were you on?'

'Quin!'

Like almost every well-paid person in South County Dublin, Quin was on antidepressants. In my opinion, there was nothing wrong with him, he was simply annoyed that money couldn't buy full-time happiness. Instead, he bought antidepressants which didn't fix him but numbed the edge of the disappointment.

Quin retrieved his togs from his case, I threw him a towel and in we went, both of us—but especially Quin—trying to look like regulars.

'That must be the changing place,' he muttered, steering me towards something which resembled a concrete bus shelter. Sugar Beach, St Lucia, it wasn't.

Undressing, we nervously scanned our surrounds, trying to get the lie of the land. There were maybe twenty people here—all shapes and sizes, which was a relief. I was nothing like as neurotic about the size of my thighs as when I was younger, but I suspected it would never really leave me, that body shame.

The sea, though . . . It looked deep, cold and profoundly uninviting. I had to wonder about Quin. There were times I was glad I'd done whatever fool scheme he'd cooked up, but there were other times, like now, when I worried that he was slightly off his rocker? That we both were?

Still, though, if Luke were to see me now, he'd think I was an impressive and interesting person. Wild swimming in wintertime was only done by brave, questing types.

Our options were to dive into the water or inch down some steps—neither appealed. The done thing then was to swim out a bit and chat with other swimmers. Clusters of three or four heads bobbed in the water, their happy voices floating towards us on the chilly air.

My teeth were chattering and my feet in my flip-flops were already numb—I'd have jumped at a chance to back out. But Quin took my hand and approached the steps with a breezy nonchalance. Displays of weakness were not his thing.

The air temperature was just above zero—I could actually *smell* the cold. 'Talk about showing a girl a good time,' I exclaimed.

'At least you're never bored with me.' He squeezed my hand. 'Three, two, one!' And we jumped.

It was so shocking, I thought I might have a heart attack. Gasping for breath and wheezing, 'Jesus Christ, oh Jesus Christ,' I turned in a circle, looking for Quin. 'Oh my God,' I yelled at him, exhilarated. 'We did it!'

He caught my wrists in his hands and his eyes were shiny with delight. His body came nearer, and it became clear he was moving in for a snog.

'Quin, no PDAs!' Urgently, I nodded at the solid citizens in their robust swimwear. 'We're not in the Maldives.'

He laughed, a bit too much, as if he were stoned. 'Sixty seconds,' he said, droplets of salt water falling from his spiky eyelashes. 'That's all we have to stay in, to get the benefit. Should we count down?'

'Already doing it!' I could hardly speak, so numb were my lips.

The moment the sixty seconds were up, we were out of that water, our skin tingling, our mood sky-high. Wrapped in our towels, with our coats thrown over them, we stopped off for take-out coffees, then drove to Quin's house, an extensively renovated, end-of-terrace Victorian four-bed with a huge modern kitchen extending into the large back garden.

Look at me now, Luke.

Quin dumped our stuff on the kitchen island. 'Which first? Coffee or shower?'

'Shower.' I was already halfway up the stairs. 'I need to warm up.'

'I'll warm you up!' he called meaningfully.

'You've no chance when you say things like that!'

Under the deluge of scalding water, I shuddered with pleasure. Quin appeared in the bathroom, putting his towel in the laundry basket. I stuck my head out and said, 'Come here.'

'You sure?' The relief in his eyes shot tenderness through me.

Poor Quin—unsettled by Luke's sudden reappearance and trying to not make it about him. I pulled him in, laying the palms of my hands on his chest, smoothing my way along the width of his shoulders, pressing the length of my body up against his. He was solid and real and I needed that.

The past was terribly sad, but it was the past. This was my life now and it was a good one.

Look at me now, Luke.

'Y'okay?' Quin pulled back to look at me.

'Yeah. Just . . . I'm glad you're back.'

'Me too.'

In the gaps between our words, a lot was being communicated.

I love you.

I love you too.

I could just say it. It would be so simple.

But to tell him, for the first time, two short days after I'd seen my ex-husband would somehow sully it, I felt.

Quin switched off the shower and wrapped me in towels. In the bedroom, while I gulped my coffee, he combed my damp hair and dried it with the ridiculously expensive, multi-function hairdryer he'd purchased back when I'd finally conceded we were in an actual relationship.

'So, tell me,' Quin said.

Choosing my words carefully, I said, 'I'm okay. Mostly okay. Seeing him has stirred up things which I'd thought . . . I never thought they were gone *forever*, but they'd settled to the bottom, I'd forgotten about them. I wasn't ready to feel them again.'

'And you feel . . . ?'

'Sad. Very sad . . . It's like wanting to visit a country that doesn't exist any longer,' I said. 'But soon everything will settle down again and I'll be fine.'

'Did you . . . do you still, like, *love* him?' It cost him a lot to ask this and my heart squeezed painfully.

I rolled nearer. 'No, hon. But I remembered how it felt to love him back then. It was once a big deal. I'm a bit shook, but all of this belongs in the past.'

He compressed his lips, nodded—then decided we'd talked about this enough. 'So! More coffee?'

I checked the time—ten past ten—too late for caffeine if I was hoping to sleep tonight. 'Decaf.'

When he returned from the kitchen, he was reading from his iPad. 'Dry robes,' he announced. 'Those weird coats everyone was wearing at the Forty Foot? They're a sort of changing room/coat mashup. We need them.'

'You want to make it a regular thing?'

'To get the benefit, I'd have to do it every day. And I don't want to do it without you, so you'd need to be here every day too.' He enlarged something on his screen. 'Would you like a black one with blue lining? Or red lining?'

'What? One of those giant coats?'

'*Dry robe*. Not a coat.'

I was *so* grateful I lived in a time when oversized was fashionable. A giant top made the rest of me look less giant and, God knows, you'd think I'd have outgrown that sort of thinking, but I hadn't and from the looks of things I never would.

But those coats were insane. *And* once had been enough to know that the freezing water wasn't for me.

'Stop, Quin, you loon. Don't get me one.'

'The colours are a bit basic,' he was muttering. Then, 'You don't want to make the swimming a regular thing?'

'. . . Ah, I don't think so. I'm not as dissatisfied with life as you are.'

That made him laugh. 'But what if you lived here *all* the time, Rach?'

It kept coming back to this.

'Our lives are busy,' Quin said. 'Both of us, we're out a lot in the evenings. It would be so good to come home to each other. And Crunchie loves it here.'

She did. But . . . 'Crunchie loves it anywhere.'

There were a lot of considerations about moving in with Quin, the most important being his two children. I got on fine with Liberty and Finley but it would be different if I moved in full-time.

And what about my house, which I *loved*? And my garden, which I actually might have loved even more? When I'd first moved in, five years ago, I was still in shock that Luke and I were over and had no interest in making a home. Functional was all that had mattered—a bed to collapse into, a couch to slump on, a microwave to make popcorn when I remembered to eat.

The furniture that Luke and I had owned in New York had gone to Goodwill. I'd arrived back in Ireland with very little money, so only the barest essentials were purchased.

But time really *is* a healer—because one day I'd found myself shelling out an unholy sum of money for a sixties-style dressing table. From Ebay! I hadn't even seen it in real life, but some certainty was humming in me that it would work—and it did.

It must have been around then that Claire and I took to haunting a second-hand furniture market, because Claire's best frenemy had come by a fabulous low-slung Mad Men-esque coffee table there. But Claire found the scratched wood and torn upholstery of the market repellent. 'Life's too short to see potential in something. Give me the completed article, don't waste my time.'

But I was all *about* the potential. The day I found two battered but deliciously angular mid-century armchairs at a stall, I immediately asked the price. Claire said, genuinely confused, 'What d'you want *them* for? Mulch for your'—she threw a snigger into the word—'"shrubs"?' (Her garden was gorgeous because she paid a lot of money to a landscaper and his team of skilled Slovakians. She had never picked up so much as a trowel and my little hobby baffled her.)

Feeling thrillingly directional, I'd had the chairs reupholstered and now they occupied pride of place in my 'study'.

'You'd better not become one of those smug fuckers,' Claire had warned. 'With their one-off "pieces".'

It was an identity I'd have been delighted to embrace but, to date, the chairs remained my biggest success.

'I love my house,' I said.

'It's great—if it was just the two of us. But the kids need their space.'

'I know.'

'We can dig up your cherry blossom and replant it here.'

But there was another reason I was resistant: the terrible way Luke and I had ended. 'Quin, if things went sideways for us . . .' I tried to find the words. 'And I had to leave . . .'

'Things won't go sideways.'

I could have laughed. It didn't take him long to snap back to his cocky, confident self.

'Even if they did,' he said, 'you'd be okay. You've survived a lot, you're *able*.'

He was right, I saw, slightly surprised.

The years in between Luke and Quin had been very painful, especially at the start, but I didn't go under. By the time I'd started seeing Quin, I'd changed:

I'd got used to never feeling 'safe'—or maybe I'd got better at providing my own version of safety, a skill I wouldn't have learnt if Luke hadn't left me. Which meant that when I met Quin, there wasn't as much of me to surrender as there once had been. It's not that I was tougher, I was just better at self-care. And that had to be good.

The facts were: Luke had moved on—I'd seen it with my own eyes—and so had I. All that needed to stop now was the running commentary in my head, where I kept presenting my nice life to Luke to demonstrate how fine I was.

'Is it this house?' Quin asked. 'Because we can change things. Or move somewhere new? Fresh start?'

He'd lived here since the end of his marriage, seven years earlier.

'Maybe we could start in this room,' I said. 'Give it a bit of a makeover.'

'You don't like it? But . . . I bought us a new bed.'

It had been purchased at the same time as the hairdryer, along with new bed linen, towels and tons of scatter cushions. ('Women love cushions, right?')

I waved at the exposed brick walls and the sleek dark furniture. 'This room is very . . . *male.*'

'You should have said!'

But redoing Quin's décor, making even small changes, would have implied a commitment I hadn't been ready for.

'So, Rach, let's do it up! Whatever you want, we'll do it.'

'Even a "Live, Laugh, Love" light?'

'You would never get a "Live, Laugh, Love" light. Which is the main reason you're my favourite person.' Then, 'Hey! They're all sold out! Those dry-robe things. This is *bullshit.*'

17

'Those ones,' Quin said. 'Definitely that pair.'

I'd been modelling the three pairs of sneakers which had arrived on Thursday.

'Mmmm . . .' I was still undecided. 'And not these ones?'

'Get both.'

I laughed. 'No! Honest to God, Quin, you're worse than me.'

If it were down to my most basic instincts, I'd keep all three of them, but I *had* to do things in moderation.

I picked up my phone and checked the screen. Still nothing. 'Quin.' I made an apologetic face. 'I need to go home to walk Crunchie.'

'No word from Kate?'

'No.' I'd texted a couple of times, but she hadn't got back to me all day—which wasn't like her.

'I'll come with you,' Quin said.

The idea appealed—everything was nicer if I did it with him. 'No. You're shattered. I'll go now, be back in an hour.'

'Okay. I'll sort out dinner.'

I was tipping food into Crunchie's bowl when Kate's key rattled in the door.

'In the kitchen,' I called.

'Hi!' Her eyes were bright. Too bright.

'Hi . . . are you okay?'

'Rachel, can we talk? I need to tell you something.'

Instantly I was alarmed.

'That funeral on Friday? Devin's granny's?'

Hold on a minute here—'Devin's granny's'? Surely she meant *Luke's mum's*?

'Devin and I . . .'

Ah no, you're *joking*. You are fucking JOKING me! 'Devin and you, what?'

'We . . . ah, yeah, we've been talking—'

'"Talking"?' Even I knew that that was a euphemism for an entirely different kind of communication. 'How did he contact you? No, it wasn't a real question. And?'

'I like him. I think he likes me.' More euphemisms. 'I like him' meant they'd probably spent the entire weekend in bed. 'I think, maybe, we might be a thing.'

'. . . You've known him *two days*?'

Colour flushed her cheekbones. 'Nothing has actually, like, *happened*, he lives in his mum and dad's and I didn't want to bring him here until you and I had spoken . . . Look, it's probably nothing, just a . . . nothing. But it didn't feel right that you didn't know.'

Guilt got me. Not only was she the sweetest person I knew, she was also an adult: she owed me no explanations.

'Wait,' I said. 'Thank you for telling me. Sorry for being weird.'

But already my head was racing ahead, going the Full Catastrophe: Kate and Devin having noisy sex in the bedroom next to mine; Kate and Devin sprawled on the couch watching Netflix, me brooding on an armchair, third-wheeling with jealous tension.

Much as I loved Kate, we could no longer share a house, not if there was a chance of bumping into Luke's nephew on the regular, seeing him emerging bare-chested from the bathroom, a towel wrapped low around those narrow Costello hips.

It might be uncomfortable. But it's an opportunity.

An opportunity for what?

Personal growth.

Internally, I sighed. Wretched personal growth. Always so unpleasant.

'So, ah, tell me about Devin,' I said, making the effort. 'What age is he?'

Kate's face lit up. 'Same as me! Twenty-three. Our birthdays are only seventeen days apart, we're practically twins!'

Oh God.

Shyly, she admitted, 'It's the first time since Isaac that I've really liked someone. And he's in a band so he gets who I am. Except'—she pre-empted my question—'they haven't made it yet. So he's got no money. Another thing we have in common.' Her laugh was nervous and I felt shitty.

'I'm delighted you've met someone.' I was able to at least half mean it. 'It makes no difference whose nephew he is.'

'Oh, really?' Her face flashed with relief. 'I'm so happy you're not raging with me. It's just, you know that thing when you meet a person and you feel like you've known them forever?' Dreamily, she added, 'Not just that, though. He is *SO* hot.'

No disagreeing with that.

I got Crunchie's lead and, delirious with delight, she came running. Usually we just did a lap of the village, which took twenty minutes at most. But tonight we went up into the woods.

My house was one of sixteen, hidden on the edge of a sleepy Wicklow townland. With granite cladding and plenty of the original foliage, an effort had been made to blend them with the landscape. But the locals weren't keen on us blow-ins. Apparently, after we'd lived here for seventy years, they might talk to us in the shops. In the meantime, every transaction was a bit of an ordeal.

Still, it was lovely to live walking distance from Actual Nature.

Crunchie was off the lead and snuffling around in a state of frenzied bliss but she kept coming back to check on me. I'd had a rough few days—ever since that call from Joey—and she'd noticed.

With this Kate–Devin business, I wondered if the universe was telling me to move in with Quin?

For too long I'd held Luke and me as the Gold Standard. But, with a few adjustments, I could live very happily with Quin. And there was no need for us to start fresh in a new home that we'd bought together, no need to uproot his kids.

Would Quin and I last long term? I hadn't a clue and what did it matter? I'd thought Luke and I would be together forever and I couldn't have been more wrong. All there was, was now. And now was good.

18

On Monday morning it wasn't even seven thirty when I let myself into the Cloisters. After waking at 6 a.m. I couldn't get back to sleep so decided I might as well be doing something useful.

Down in the kitchen, someone was giving a very loud, high-pitched version of a schmaltzy song. The name 'Demis Roussos' flashed in my head. 'La la, la la la, la lala la lala, you'll BEEEEEEEEEEEE THE WAN!!!'

I followed the noise and found Dennis serenading Ella while they prepared breakfast for the house. The newbies always got the worst jobs.

'You'll BEEEEEE THE WAN!!'

'Stop,' Ella was pleading, doubled over with hilarity. 'I'm officially deceased.'

'Did I ever tell you about the time I entered *The Voice of Ireland*?' Dennis was saying. 'No word of a lie.'

'I almost believe yo—Jesus Christ!' Ella had spotted me. She looked as if she'd seen an apparition. 'Where did you come from? Have you been here all night?'

I gave my enigmatic smile.

'Bacon sangwidge?' Dennis offered.

Another of my enigmatic smiles. 'Is that a yes or a no?' he beseeched.

'It's a no.'

And here came Ted, hungry for details. 'How *are* you, Rachel?'

'Fine, Ted. Everything is fine.'

It wasn't entirely true but in time it would be.

'Your ex has left the country?'

'Probably.' I made myself smile again. 'Either way, it's grand.'

My gut was telling me Luke was gone and, now that it was too late, I still felt the panicky regret that I hadn't gone to Justin's lunch. A freefalling sense of loss whispered that I'd missed an opportunity to . . . *what* exactly?

Magic away the last six years?

Because that could never happen. The truth was that some things just couldn't be fixed. My challenge was to live with that—and I could. The yearning that had been stirred up inside me would slowly eddy back down to the bottom, to where it had been living, and in time life would return to business as usual.

I was the first to arrive at the Abbot's Quarter. A couple of minutes later, Dennis and Ella piled in.

'There she is again!' Dennis was in great form. 'You missed a top-notch *bricfásta!*'

Frowning, I focused—Mother of God, the utter *state* of him! Just how many more days did he need before he noticed that his clothes were absolutely filthy? Obviously, at home, his wife did everything for him.

Not that Ella seemed to mind Dennis's manky threads. With her good arm she gave him a playful shove, both trying to claim the second-best chair. Ella and her ilk survived by being lovely to everyone, even those who hadn't changed their underpants in six days. She could have been literally choking from the stench from Dennis and she'd never admit it.

'Wow.' Ella had noticed my new sneakers. 'Your kicks slap!'

They *did* slap! Mostly white but with leopard-print stars and a trim at the front. I opened my mouth to enthuse with Ella—and caught myself just in time. Jesus, I was off my game.

With a small, silent incline of my head, I smiled with just one side of my mouth. Over the years, the feedback had been that this odd smile was quite terrifying. When you consider the hours of practice I put into it, it was gratifying to hear.

Poor Ella, though. Compliments and praise were how she bonded. When people wouldn't play that game, it left her with nowhere to go.

Here came Giles, lanky and debonair. He was displeased when he saw Ella with Dennis. Dear God, you can take the coke out of the womanizer . . .

'. . . and next thing,' Dennis read out, 'Your man sits up in the coffin and says, "Whose lipstick am I wearing?"!'

The Abbot's Quarter erupted with hilarity. We were being treated to Dennis's life story and it was a rip-roaring romp—story after hilarious story. Alcohol got an occasional mention but only ever as a necessary ingredient of 'a great night out'.

I'd seen this a lot—an alcoholic taking ownership of their drinking by hiding it in plain sight, with dramatic, entertaining accounts of wild sprees. It *sounded* as if he was admitting he had a problem, but in reality it was just one big deflection. Any shame that Dennis felt—and there was bound to be plenty—was buried beneath an almost impervious shell of distracting anecdotes.

He seemed to own half the town he hailed from—proprietor of a pub, a fish and chip shop, a taxi company and a small funeral home. The taxi company (which was just himself and his brother, Patch, sharing the one car) operated from the same premises as the funeral home, which led to some 'hilarious' mix-ups.

'Jez, I've just thought of another one!' Dennis abandoned his written script. 'My Near Death Experience! Picture the scene . . . The afters of a funeral. Now, I'm a man who loves a funeral, there's nothing as nice as a funeral ham sandwich . . .'

I could certainly visualize it: Dennis pressing the flesh amongst the mourners while mentally totting up how much was being spent at the open bar in *his* pub. Like Chalkie, Dennis was burdened with great likeability. It meant that people enabled his drinking, made excuses for him, covered up his gaffes and couldn't bear to confront him.

Dennis was actually on his feet now, acting out various people from his anecdote. I'd let him finish this one and then he wasn't getting any more airtime until his brother Patch came in on Wednesday morning and blew the lid off things.

'. . . I was clinically dead! For four minutes, can you credit it? I knew I was on the hospital table but I saw the corridor of white light. So I sez, "Have ye an open bar in heaven?"'

Ella snorted with laughter.

'I was deadly in earnest.' Dennis's curls bobbed. 'If there was an open bar, I'd keep going towards the light. But a voice sez, "No bar. Heaven is dry." So I sez, "Good luck! I'll see ye again. And back I came!"'

When the laughing quietened, Ella declared, 'You could get a job as a stand-up!'

'If he doesn't die from alcoholism first,' Giles said quietly.

A blanket of silence dropped on the room and six heads whipped around to stare at Giles. In fairness, I was surprised myself. But Roxy was leaving in three days and, clearly, Giles had begun his transition to the Elder Statesman of the group. The poacher had become a junior gamekeeper.

'But . . .' Ella was appalled to hear her buddy Dennis being accused like this. His story—that his wife had bullied him in here—she'd bought wholesale. It copper-fastened her conviction that she too was here just to please others.

'What the hell's got into *you*?' Chalkie asked Giles.

Giles shrugged. 'Dennis almost died from alcohol poisoning. It's not funny.'

'Ah, stop!' Dennis protested. 'We're only having a bit of a laugh.'

With a sharp nod of agreement, Ella glared at Giles.

At the end of the session, when they rose to stream out, I said, 'Dennis, stay behind for a moment?'

'Oh, lads, I'm in the soup!'

After shutting the door, I said, 'Dennis, your clothes.'

He plucked at his suit jacket. 'Made by the fair hands of Makee's of Mullingar. No doubt you've some husband or boyfriend that needs "bespoke tailoring", a fine-looking woman like yourself? Mention my name to Mossie Makee and he'll look after you and the lucky man in question.' His exaggerated wink indicated that a hefty discount would be mine.

'Dennis, your clothes are filthy.' I indicated the stains on his tie, the unidentifiable blobs on his shirt. 'You need to do your laundry. Also you've been here almost a week and you haven't had a shower.'

'I have a bath every Easter Sunday,' he declared. 'Whether I need it or not! Harhar.'

'Dennis, you need to shower every day. And get someone to show you how the washing machine works.'

'Shur, the wife will be in with clean togs for me next weekend.'

'Wash your clothes.' I could be quite frightening when I really made an effort. 'Tonight, Dennis.'

As I left the room, he yelled after me, in sudden, real rage, 'What's any of that got to do with drinking too much?'

Plenty. Addicts hated themselves and many couldn't treat themselves with the barest of civility. He'd learn.

When I switched my phone on, there was a message from Helen. Meet me? Need to talk to you.

This sort of thing—Helen proposing a one-on-one casual hang—was a bit weird. She must want to talk about whatever she'd been doing the Friday morning of Mrs Costello's funeral. Impossible to guess what—she could be splitting up with Artie, embarking on a solo expedition to the North Pole—knowing Helen it could be anything. But I hoped she was okay.

When? Today? Red Kite Farmhouse 5.45?

Immediately she replied, Not Red Kite Farmhouse. Hate that place. Full of Scummy Mummies.

Of course. Everyone else adored Red Kite Farmhouse—their twee aesthetic, their artfully mismatched trestle tables, their giant over-priced cherry scones. Helen *had* to be different.

Then another message arrived. Okay, Red Kite Farmhouse it is. Just don't bore on about the fucking scones. I get it, they're BIG.

I was mildly offended. I'd never in my *life* bored on about the size of the Red Kite Farmhouse scones. They were big, too much for one person, but I was happy enough to let them be.

Because it was late in the day, it was easy to get parking—the marauding clusters of Lululemon-clad yummy mummies usually emptied out around three thirty, piling into their Range Rovers to pick up the kids from private school.

Helen was already at a table, studying her phone and looking faintly murderous.

She spotted me and chirped, 'Oh, Rachel, haai!'

Helen *never* chirped. Chirping was on her Shovel List.

A rictus smile appeared on her perfect little face and I was picking up a very bad feeling here.

'Sit down.' She pointed at the chair opposite her. 'Got you a mint tea, that's the right one, is it? And a brownie. Couldn't chance it with the scones.'

'So what's up?'

Her gaze dropped to the table. 'So look. Artie and I, we've been thinking . . .'

Suddenly I knew what she was going to say.

She met my eyes. 'We want to have a baby.'

That was what I'd been braced for.

'I'm sorry, Rachel. I know it'll upset you and I'm genuinely sorry.'

We were still locked in an endless eye-meet. My face felt hot and the right words wouldn't come.

'You're going to say you're a big girl and your stuff is your responsibility and all that, but . . .'

'It's true, though,' I managed.

'You don't have to be brave. Not to protect me.'

'I—' There were too many emotions lurching around in me, just one big mess.

'Tell me you hate me,' she urged.

'But I don't. Like, of *course* I don't. My ship sailed a long time ago. You have to do your thing—I couldn't bear it if you didn't because of me.'

'Should you eat your brownie? Would the sugar help?'

'I thought you didn't want kids.'

'I didn't. Then suddenly I did. I thought there was something wrong with me so I went to the doctor. I thought she could give me tablets to make it stop. But she said I was "broody". Broody!' she exclaimed. 'Me! I was impressed by her nerve. Listen, should I have got you a giant scone?' She scraped back her chair. 'I'll get you one now.'

'Sit down, you eejit. So . . . ah . . . where are you at, in the process?'

'Riding for Ireland.'

'Lovely . . . or is it?' My experience was that having sex according to a time-table took a lot of the enjoyment from it.

'We've only just started, so it's okay right now. On Friday morning I had an exploratory thing done, you know, a *procedure*, that's why I couldn't go to the funeral. The doc said that even though I'm nearly forty, I've a good few eggs left. So it might work. If it doesn't we'll have to "explore other options". IVF maybe.'

'The best of luck, Helen, and I really mean it. I hope it works.'

'Really? So we're good? You and me?'

'Totally.'

'Thanks.' Then, 'Hey! What's this about Kate and Luke's nephew? I met them this morning—'

'*Both* of them?'

'She was on surveillance and he was "just hangin'".' I'm no judge but they seemed . . .' She paused and considered the word. '. . . keen. Yeah. *Very* keen on each other. What if they, like, get married and you have to see Costello at the wedding?'

'Ah, Helen. Let's not jump any guns here.'

'Okay. Anyway, why would you care? You like Dr Spork, he's a good boyfriend.'

'He's a great boyfriend.'

'Even if he does own a spork. And you're sure you're okay with my baby thing?'

'Absolutely. Don't give it another thought.'

'Right. Just one thing. The word "trying"?'

'Shovel List?'

'Very high on it. Never say it. I'll head off, so.'

19

I watched Helen drive away, then my face was free to show how I really felt. Which was sad, very, very sad.

But you'll be okay. You'll absolutely be okay.

God, though, everything was happening at once—crossing paths with Luke again, Kate falling for Devin and now this. If you believed in planets and patterns you'd be sure something big was going on—juxtapositions and whatnot.

Even already, though, my spirits had lifted a little: if Helen and Artie wanted a baby, I'd love it. Two contradictory feelings could exist at once— hope for Helen and sadness for me.

A sudden yearning for Quin kicked in but tonight he was on a conference call, in the thick of his New Mexico project.

It was almost a surprise how strongly I felt because until recently our relationship had been like an incomplete patchwork blanket—lots of different positives which, taken all together, didn't quite create a whole. Still, it had worked. But something extra had been flung into the mix, and all the separate parts that hadn't quite added up to the genuine article suddenly did.

This change could be traced back a couple of months to one of those unexpectedly meaningful conversations that people accidentally wander into.

Quin had once again referenced the Jo Burger's cheesy fries thing and instead of me laughing it off, I said, 'I wish I'd never said that.'

'You said it because you meant it.'

'But I was in a different place then. When we met, it was hard to trust you. You were quite open about, you know, your tendency to be a player. If I'd met you, say, ten years ago, I'd have steered *so* clear.' Suddenly I understood something. 'Even now, I know you care about me but . . .'

'What?'

I had to tell him. 'Say, on one of your work trips, if you met someone and liked her, I don't think you'd agonize too much about me before sleeping

with her. And I think you'd 'fess up—not to hurt me, but because . . .'
I swallowed hard because it was a horrible thought. '"We're all adults here."'

'You're wrong.' To my surprise, Quin sounded angry. 'How do you know I *haven't* met people—and walked away from a situation?'

'Have you?'

'Yeah. Couple of times.' His eyes bright, he glared. 'Rachel, you've hurt me.'

'I'm sorry.' This—his upset—was unexpected.

'I make it my business to not hurt you. But this . . . *thing* of me being a shagger, it's handy. You can commit some of yourself to me, but it means you don't have to go the whole way. You're saying you're with me because we don't have the potential to be serious. That's pretty damning, Rachel.'

'I'm sorry.' I meant it. 'I had it wrong. You're different now. I just need . . . to let my feelings catch up with the facts.'

Since then, my attachment to Quin had become steadier and deeper.

However, he wasn't available tonight, so I went to a meeting, my regular Monday night anchor group, and it helped. When I got home, though, I was *shattered* and I fell in the door, rummaging in the kitchen for something easy for my dinner.

Not for the first time, I wished my address existed on a Deliveroo map.

Kate was out, I'd no idea where. She and I didn't keep tabs on each other— I wasn't her parent and didn't want to act like one—but the news about Devin had changed that. Was she with him now? What if—as Helen had suggested— this became serious and they decided to get married? I'd have to see Luke at the wedding. If only I hadn't brought her to the funeral . . .

A box of Raisin Bran turned up in the cupboard—but there was no milk in the fridge. No problem! I curled on the couch, eating handfuls of it straight out of the box and opened up my iPad, clicking here and there, looking for lovely feels.

I dropped in on Luxury Exchange to say hello to 'my' Chanel shoulder bag. After gazing at it lovingly, it hit me that, sooner or later, someone would buy it—someone with more money than me, or even less restraint. One day, I'd click and click and there would be no sign of it. No details on who had bought it, whether they deserved it, if they'd get as much happiness from it as I would have. Just . . . *gone.*

Crunchie gave a warning bark and the doorbell rang—local kids looking to be sponsored for something or other, no doubt. Not a week went by without them shaking me down for cash. I grabbed my purse, keen to hand over the money quickfast, then swung the door open—and standing outside was Luke.

Shock wiped me blank.

In my head he'd already gone back to wherever he lived these days. So to find him outside my house, the drizzle beading his silky hair and the shoulders of his dark overcoat, was simply too strange.

'Can I come in?'

In an obedient daze, I stood aside, making room for him to step into the hall. Crunchie skittered around, her claws clicking, sniffing at him.

Why was he here? Maybe he'd come to apologize . . . ?

I pointed towards the living room.

'My shoes okay in the house?' he asked.

I looked down at his boots. 'Yes, no, fine. Go on.' Christ, who *cared*?

I followed him in and indicated the couch. 'Sit down. Can I take your coat?'

He shoved his hands into the pockets of his coat and remained standing. 'This won't take long.'

He didn't seem terribly friendly. Two grim lines ran from the corners of his nose to the edges of his mouth. They hadn't been so visible in the church.

Well, he'd got older, so had I.

'What can I . . . Why are you here?'

'Devin and Kate?' Suddenly he was animated. 'What the *hell*? Did you put her up to it?'

Anger. That was the emotion he was giving off, I recognized it now.

'Put her up to what?'

'Getting into something with a man who *just happens* to be my nephew.'

Wounded, I stuttered, 'I only found out last night, I wasn't happy either.'

Angry and silent, he stared at me, breathing hard.

'Why would I, quote, "put her up to it"?'

'To get back at me.'

His hostility was shocking.

'I wouldn't do that.' My voice was small and confused. 'But what's it to you? They're both adults, they can do whatever they like.'

'Can you imagine how I felt when I walked into Justin's house and there, sitting at the kitchen table, was *your niece*. What if she fucks him over?'

'She wouldn't, she's an absolute sweetheart! What if *he* fucks *her* over? That's far more likely, if he's anything like you.' His pupils flared with shock— oh yes, I'd *gone* there. 'Either way.' I heaved in a breath and tried to calm down. 'Either way, it's none of our business. They might not last five minutes. And you don't even live here.'

'I'll probably be here for a few more weeks.'

'What? Why?'

'Dad's not well. Mum was his carer but she's . . . So I'm here until we find someone else . . . He's narky, hard to please . . . Well, we'll see how it goes.'

Despite everything, I felt for him. 'I'm sorry. About your dad. And your mum.'

'Yeah, well.' He sighed heavily. 'It never rains but it fucking well pours.'

For an uncomfortable moment, his dark eyes searched mine; then, with a swirl of his coat, he turned and left the room. The front door opened and shut. Moments later an engine started up outside and roared away.

Trembling, I had to sit. *You'll be okay. Not just yet, but you'll be grand. Time just needs to pass, that's all.*

It would be good if I spoke to someone, but who? Nola? Quin? Brigit? Claire?

Not Quin, he was busy. Claire? No, she was too bossy. Brigit? She'd be in bed by now. Nola, then. I reached for my phone, then realized I'd put it on airplane during my NA meeting and forgotten to switch it back. As soon as it reconnected, two, three . . . no, *four* missed calls popped up from Kate, trying to warn me that Luke was on his way.

Feeling light-headed and speedy, there was a real chance I might vomit. I was probably in shock. It was never going to be easy, meeting him after so much time. But experience had taught me to wait it out.

A sharp bark from Crunchie made me jump, then Kate hurtled into the room, looking horrified. 'Rachel? You okay? Did Luke come here?'

'. . . What happened?'

'Devin and I were at his mum and dad's. Luke came in, met me . . .' Helplessly she spread her hands. 'Went ballistic.' She was on the edge of tears. 'Asking why I was there. Devin explained but Luke didn't believe him. Made me tell him our—your—address, then grabbed the keys to Justin's bike and, like, just *left*, leaving Kallie behind with us.'

'Kallie?'

'Luke's girlfriend, partner.'

'She's still here?'

'Yeah. I tried to call,' Kate said. 'But your phone was off. So I said I was leaving, hoping I'd be fast enough to get here before Luke, but Devin's dad said it would be good if you guys talked? Was it?' she asked, delicately. 'Good to talk?'

My thoughts lurched and heaved alarmingly. Nothing was solid. 'What's she like?' I blurted.

'Kallie?' Kate looked dismayed. 'I barely met her. She's, ah . . . Rachel, are you sure you want to do this? Okay. Well, she seems cool. It was so awkward when he left and she tried to joke about it. "So you meet a guy and he says he doesn't do complicated." They live in Denver. She's . . . fortyish, I guess? But cool. Like you,' she added brightly.

There was so much more I wanted to ask, but I said, 'I'm fine, Kate, don't worry. C'm'ere.' I pulled her into a tight hug, then she went off about her business.

I rang Nola and brought her up to date. 'There are too many feelings in me,' I said. 'Every one of them horrible.'

'The only question is,' she said. 'Are you going to take something?'

'I haven't got anything to take! Sorry. No. Of course it's a no.'

'Then you'll be fine. All part of the process, just some more emotional and spiritual growth for you!'

She made it sound like a good thing, like I'd won a small prize. 'And when I've emerged from the growing I'll be . . . what? Stronger? More resilient?'

'Time will tell.'

'But it hurts. Will the Luke stuff never not hurt?'

'Shur, how would I know, girl? Golden Key it.'

Aargh! It's what she always reverted to when we talked about Luke. I'd been Golden Keying him for years and the universe still hadn't sorted it out.

'Off to sleep with you now, pet. Ring me if you need me. Harry never minds.'

Again, I thought about ringing Quin, maybe going over to his and climbing under his duvet, where he'd hold me tight. But it would be a mistake to let him see the state of me. He'd be hurt. Mistrustful even. And that would linger long after my feelings about Luke had returned to normal.

More in hope than expectation I went to bed. *Please make me sleep.* But that wasn't how my higher power rolled. There was no point *ever* in me asking for something specific—Chanel bags, global cooling, green traffic lights all the way home—the only thing I had consistently been given was an eventual acceptance of my situation, whatever that was.

Sure enough, an overload of adrenaline powered through me—I'd be awake all night at this rate. I had to get back out of bed and huff and puff my way through allegedly calming 'breath-work' for all the good it did.

As the clock ticked past 1 a.m., anger began to build. I'd always been a person of delayed reactions, absolutely *useless* at defending myself in the moment, instead having fabulously articulate middle-of-the-night back-and-forths in my own head, several hours or days or even weeks after the appropriate time.

How dare Luke Costello barge into my home and hit me up with a load of nonsense allegations? All the times I'd tried to get him to talk to me and it took this?

And the absolute nerve of him acting like the wronged party! *He* had left *me*.

At about 2 a.m., admitting defeat, I got dressed, summoned Crunchie, found the flashlight and went outside. (The flashlight was one of my touch-stones, a sure sign that I was an adult. It was the first thing I'd spent money on that I didn't need immediately, but 'in case of a power cut'. It wasn't even a nice colour.)

We headed for the trees, Crunchie casting me uneasy glances: was this middle-of-the-night wood-walking going to become a thing?

'Who knows?' I said to her.

I was never more grateful for her because once you've a dog, you can go *anywhere*. A long-haired woman in her forties walking alone in the forest in the dead of night is a candidate for being burnt as a witch. But throw in a dog and suddenly everything is grand. ('Stand down the pyre, lads, she has a dog!')

As I tramped along in the dimly lit darkness, details that had registered only subconsciously at the time were coming into focus. The big boots Luke had been wearing had given him an extra inch or so over me, making him even more daunting. Had it been deliberate, I wondered. Who knew? Anything was possible because he was not the man I'd once known.

He'd even smelt different—we'd been so near to each other in my living room that the angry heat of his body had reached me. But everything which contributes to the unique smell of a person—detergent, soap, food, environment—had changed.

Also, his overcoat wasn't very him. Maybe he'd borrowed it from one of his brothers? Or maybe that was his look now—because his jeans were different too. Definitely not as tight as they used to be. My sisters would be devastated.

Beside me, Crunchie was panting. Part corgi, part golden retriever, her short little legs weren't able for this. 'Okay, we'll go home.'

Sometime around 3.30 a.m. I dropped off. Only to be woken at seven twenty-five by my phone ringing—Luke.

Jesus Christ.

'Luke?' My mouth tasted of rage. 'What have I done now?'

'I'm sorry,' he said heavily. 'Last night. Losing the head. Calling to your home. I shouldn't have done it. Any of it. I'm sorry.'

I hadn't a clue *what* to say.

'. . . You still there?' he asked.

I took refuge in therapy talk. 'Your mum has died,' I said. 'You're in shock.'

'I don't know what got into me.'

'It's okay. Let it go.'

'You sure?'

'Yes. Take care of yourself.'

'Uh. Okay. You too.'

'Okay.' Then, 'Bye.'

'Bye.'

His breathing was still audible when I hung up.

20

Luke *had* to be put out of my head; big work stuff was going down today. I printed out all the information I needed and went to the morning meeting. But sitting at the table, a wave of exhaustion hit. I could have fallen asleep there and then.

Luckily, Murdo stuck his head into the room and crooked a finger: Trassa's son Ronan had arrived. The adrenaline from this would keep me going.

'He's in the drawing room,' he said. 'I'll see you in group.'

I found a nervous-looking man in his early forties, staring at an untouched cup of tea. An equally untouched plate of 'visitors'' biscuits were on the table before him.

'Ronan?' I shook his hand. 'I'm Rachel. Thank you for coming.'

He half stood and, in a voice filled with anguish, asked, 'What do I have to do?'

My heart hurt for him. The people who care about addicts have it very hard. So much of their time they're plagued by suspicion, fear, thwarted hope, frustration, anger, and then, when they've finally convinced their loved one to get help, they usually feel terrible guilt.

'Just be honest,' I said. 'I'll guide you.'

'Do you think she'll . . . lose the head at me?' God love him, he was terrified.

'She might. She needs to protect her addiction and one way of doing that is to blame other people.' We'd already been through this on the phone. 'She might cry. She'll probably try to make you feel guilty. Or like you're overreacting.'

'This is very hard.'

'You managed to get her in here, you've already done the toughest part. Just try to be brave a bit longer.'

He nodded, white with dread.

As soon as I was certain that everyone was safely in group, I took Ronan into the corridor, opened the door of the Abbot's Quarter, ushered him in and guided him to the 'visitors'' chair Waldemar had parked there earlier, draped with a piece of A4 paper saying 'Don't Sit Here'.

Murdo was already in the room—he always provided backup when we had 'visitors'.

You could have heard a pin drop. Ella didn't understand what was going on, her head was flipping from person to person, seeking answers. The rest of them, though, couldn't help but be a little buzzed. These confrontations were often edge-of-your-seat stuff so long as you weren't the person in the spotlight.

'Trassa,' I said. 'Would you like to say hello to your son?'

Her mouth worked but no words emerged. Eventually she managed, 'Who's minding down home while you're up here?'

'Keith.'

'He knows nothing about cattle.'

'It's one day, Mammy.'

'Tell that to the poor cows who won't get milked.'

Already I was losing Ronan. He was wilting before my eyes.

'Have you *any* idea of the suffering of a full udder?' Trassa asked him.

'Have *you*, Trassa?' I said.

'I'm not a cow!'

'And neither is Ronan. Take a look at these.' I passed her a sheaf of credit-card bills.

After a bit of a production with her reading glasses, she scanned them . . . As the penny dropped, the blood visibly left her face.

'Telling my business to all and sundry!' she slung at Ronan.

'Would you like to tell the other members of your group what you have in your hand?' My tone was reasonable. 'Or should I?'

'I . . .' Her rage at Ronan was colossal. 'I'm your *mother.*'

'Trassa, I have more copies of those pages.' I rustled them. 'Should I distribute them?'

'No,' she muttered. 'I'll tell them. They're . . . credit-card bills.'

'Whose?' Dennis was always bursting with curiosity.

'. . . Mine.'

'How many credit cards?' I asked.

'Eleven . . .'

'Totalling how much?' I asked.

'. . . I don't know.'

'You do. So do I. Should I tell everyone?'

Tearful and defiant, Trassa sat up and looked around at her group members. 'It's a lot. But I was unlucky. It's the fault of the banks and the government for the high interest rates—'

'Trassa?'

'It's . . . about fifty-nine thousand euro.'

The shock in the room was immense. The session the previous Thursday afternoon had done a lot to reveal the true Trassa and everyone had thought that that was as bad as it would get. This latest revelation was too much to take in immediately.

Ella paled so dramatically that her freckles popped. *Oh my God*, she was thinking, *I am nothing like this Trassa. There's no way I should be here.*

Dennis was even more shaken. He'd believed Trassa, he'd identified with her, but if she was an addict, where did that leave him? The sacred time when the denial of an addict begins to crumble, and the truth of their situation starts to land, always made me visualize a river meeting the sea: fresh water churning into salt water, two powerful, separate streams having no choice but to merge, to become one new blended body.

'Ronan,' I said. 'Can you tell your mother how this has impacted your life?'

Haltingly, reluctantly, he said, 'I've had to take out a second mortgage on my house to get the money to pay this off and—'

'You'll get your money back!' Trassa exploded. 'You'll get the house when Seamus Senior and I are gone.'

'It's not just about the money,' he blurted.

'Course it's about the money.' A glint of steel had appeared in her. 'All I heard from you was fifty-nine thousand euro this, fifty-nine thousand euro that. But you won't be out of pocket.'

'But . . . Mam. Listen, can you?' His body was clenched tight. 'The sheriff came to your house to seize goods—'

'How do you know?!'

'Dad told me. He's not well,' Ronan whispered. 'It was an awful ordeal for him. Then *I* had a visit. From Collie Byrne.'

Trassa was stopped in her tracks. This was something she hadn't expected. 'What . . . what did he want?'

'His twenty thousand euro.'

'*Twenty* thousand?' Trassa exclaimed. 'It was only twelve thousand the last I heard.'

'Trassa. Tell the group who Collie Byrne is.'

Looking stunned, she managed, 'He's a . . . a local moneylender.'

'He works in the bank?' I knew he didn't.

'No. He's . . . freelance.'

'He's a loan shark.' For the first time Ronan was angry. 'He came to my house—'

'*Why?*'

'He knows I'm the only one still talking to you. I couldn't tell Keith where I was going today because he'll do nothing to help you ever again.'

'What did Collie do . . . say?' Trassa looked genuinely shamed.

'He said it was nothing personal but if he wasn't paid back by the end of this week that things would get messy.'

'Messy?'

'Yes, Ma, messy. Which means rough. He gave me a choice between it happening to Dad or me.'

'And what did you say?' Trassa's eyes gleamed with terrible interest.

'Me, Ma, I said me.'

A sharp nod of approval. 'Good boy.'

Ronan couldn't cope with much more so I finished the session early and ensconced him in the drawing room where, white as a sheet, he jigged his leg compulsively.

'Did it do any good?' he stuttered.

'Hopefully. Probably.' I couldn't make promises. This might have broken open Trassa's denial, but addiction is a powerful thing. 'You were very brave. Thank you for coming. Will you be . . . okay? With this Collie Byrne character?' This wasn't part of my job. I couldn't take on the problems of the family and friends of my clients but I felt very tenderly towards poor Ronan.

'It'll take some juggling. Moving money around. Some of the credit cards will have to wait. Collie's money is a priority.'

'Good. Good. Are you okay to drive home?'

'Ah, yeah. Better get back before Keith's killed the entire herd.' He attempted a lacklustre smile and trailed out to his car, looking small and young.

21

When Ronan's car had disappeared from view, I switched on my phone, to discover three missed calls from Luke, then a text asking me to ring.

What was with all the calls? Apart from Mum, no one I knew made them. *Everything* was done through text or voice-notes.

For privacy, I went out to my car. My hands, as I pressed the buttons, were shaking. 'Hi. It's Rachel.'

'Thanks for calling back.' He sounded exhausted. 'Sorry about this, but I get it now, why I was freaking out. Can I explain?'

'Um . . . sure.'

'She looks like you. Kate, I mean. When I saw her sitting at that table, for a split second, I thought . . .' He sighed heavily. 'Everything's mixed up in me. The past and the present, you know?'

'. . . Well.' I strove for humour. 'I don't need to remind you that your mum's just died.'

'Yeah.' Another world-weary sigh. 'I thought it would be just about missing her, but everything is fucked up. Justin and I are scrapping the way we did when we were kids—so much for any mad fantasies about moving back to Ireland. Forget it. We can't address a civil word to each other. Which isn't ideal when we're living in his house.'

'Aren't you staying with your dad?'

'Maybe you don't know? They sold their house a few years back, now they—I mean *Dad*, Christ, I keep forgetting—is in a one-bedroomed flat. I could sleep on the couch but it's not fair to do that to . . .' He hesitated. 'To Kallie, my partner.'

WhoIsSheWhereDidYouMeetHerDoYouLoveHerMoreThanYouLovedMe . . .

I cleared my throat. 'How's your dad doing?'

'A good day today. He has lung disease, COPD, in case you didn't know.' How *would* I know? I didn't even know what it was.

'Used to be called emphysema. It's a hard thing to see. To be honest, after a day there, I'm glad to escape back to Justin's.' After a short pause, he blurted, 'And yeah, I feel super-guilty about that.'

'Try not to feel guilty.' More therapy-speak but it was the only way I felt safe talking to him. 'Carers always feel guilty, they never think they do enough. But they need to take care of themselves too.'

'Ah, I'm grand,' he said. 'I don't need to take care of myself.'

Yeah. Whatever. 'So I'd better get back to work.' He couldn't miss the sudden snippiness of my tone.

Quickly, he said, 'You got a dog?'

'Um, yes, Crunchie.' Just thinking about her warmed my heart. 'Rescue dog.'

'Part golden retriever? Part . . . ?'

'Corgi. She has cute corgi legs. She makes me really happy.'

'Yep, dogs are great.'

'True that. Do *you* have . . . ?'

'Ah, no. I wasn't sure if . . . No. No dog. Not yet, anyway. Sorry for disturbing you at work.'

'It's okay, it's my lunch break.'

'Joey says you're still an addiction counsellor. At the *Cloisters*, of all places?'

'Head counsellor, actually. I train up the newbies.'

'Seriously? Wow. And how does that work? They do regular tests to check you're clean?'

'. . . What? *No*. They trust me. And *I* trust me.'

'Is Nola still in your life? Tell her I said hey.'

My lips tightened. He could fuck off, acting like we were friends again.

'So. Thanks for being so cool about me showing up at your home. That sort of shit—it's not who I am.'

Well, technically you =are, *because you* did *it*. But I just said, 'Okay.'

I hung up and sat in my car, breathing hard, waiting to calm down. Him offloading his stuff onto me—after all he'd done—it was confusing.

On a whim, I FaceTimed Anna. It was 8.20 a.m. in New York so maybe I'd catch her before she started her day.

And there she was! My heart lifted.

'Great timing,' Anna said. 'I'm just getting dressed.'

Anna was a rarity among successful New York women; she had no fear of sugar and stayed in bed when everyone else got up in the dim dawn to go to Barry's Bootcamp. 'If I turn into a blimp, so what?' she always said. 'We get one life, I want to enjoy mine.'

She didn't turn into a blimp, though. Unlike Claire, Margaret and me, who were Model A Walshes—tall Never-Slenders who took after Mum—she and Helen were Model Bs: short and slight, with a whippet-y ability to burn calories.

I brought her up to date with the latest on Luke.

'Yeah.' She sighed. 'You and Luke were *such* a love story. This was always going to be painful. But you ignore the universe at your peril.'

'Excuse me?'

She was shimmying her way into very skinny jeans. With a hoick of the waistband and a whizz of the zip, she was neatly contained. It was a pleasure to watch.

'You and him, it was a . . .' She threw a silky T-shirt over her head and spoke through it. '*Brutal* finish.' Her delicate face reappeared. 'But now he's in Ireland.' She slung several fragile gold chains around her neck. 'It's like the universe has put him there so you and he can make peace.'

'So the universe has given Luke's Dad COPD just so Luke and I can learn to be civil?'

'Oh, Rachel.' She clucked sympathetically, shucking on an oversized blazer, flicking a hand back to free her swingy ponytail from the collar. 'You're not that sneery cynic.'

'Oh, Anna,' I replied. '*You're* not that space cadet who thinks the universe gets personally involved on my behalf.'

'I am. It does.' She extended her arm, which sported a big, brass bangle. 'Too much?'

'No. Show me your shoes.'

The camera wobbled downwards to show a pair of beige and black Valentino Rockstuds.

'You're walking to the subway in *them*?'

Apologetically, she said, 'They send a car for me now.'

I was so proud of Anna. She managed to thrive in the bruising US corporate world but she was still her own sweet self. It was a matter of great personal pride that she'd never sacked anyone. If an underling wasn't flourishing in their role, she either reassigned them to something more suitable or sat them down for a genuine chat which usually ended with the employee unilaterally deciding to change careers and thanking her for her insight.

'How's Angelo?' I wanted to keep her talking.

With his long, lank hair, gaunt face, dark clothing and multiplicity of tats, Anna's partner wasn't exactly Mum's idea of the perfect son-in-law. ('You wouldn't want to meet that fella down an alley on a dark night.') But he was *great*: compassionate, interested, sure of himself without being obnoxious.

And no matter what Mum might mutter to herself, hot in an intriguingly ugly-beautiful way.

At first glance you might think, *No. No way*. But after two seconds of talking to him, you'd go, *Waaaait a minute*. Then you'd be full-on, *Right! I get it! He's far from typical and I love it!*

Spacey but grounded was the best way to describe his unusual outlook on life. His energy (and he spoke a *lot* about 'energy') was wise and calming, which meant he was skilled at talking people down from ledges.

Now, *he* meditated—and, unlike me, he actually did. Twice a day, every day, for at least a decade and it seemed obvious that he didn't spend each twenty-minute session worrying because he'd forgotten to take the curry out of the freezer for that evening's dinner.

Considering he was the most non-pushy person you could imagine, it was a surprise that he worked as an art agent. New York art sellers tended to be total sharks. But instead of harrying people into buying things they couldn't afford by inventing other fictional purchasers who were right outside, flinging handfuls of money at the door, Angelo was full-on 'if it's meant to be'. If a client was dithering over a painting, he'd say, 'Why don't you guys take it home, see if it works in your space? Nah, no need for a surety, you've good energy—*honest* energy.'

When Mum heard, she declared that Angelo was a complete fool who deserved to have dozens of paintings stolen.

'Never happened,' Angelo said. 'Not once.'

'Not *yet*,' riposted Mum, who launched an immediate enquiry into his income, interrogating him until he admitted he earned 'a fortune'. (Her words.) (He'd never be so crass.)

As Anna was an ex-spacer who had infiltrated mainstream society but still had floaty tendencies, she and Angelo made perfect sense.

'He's great,' Anna said. 'He's always great.'

22

'Roxy,' I said. 'As you're leaving on Thursday—'

'AWWW!' Dennis bellowed.

I gave him a stare that abruptly shut him up.

He was looking better today, a lot cleaner and neater—because last night he'd persuaded several women to launder his clothes, to sew missing buttons back onto his shirts and to dab away the worst stains on his suit. He'd out-sourced all the labour and it was a metaphor for his life—there would always be someone to save him.

'Roxy,' I said again. 'In light of your upcoming departure, would you like to say something to each person here? Perhaps some advice or . . . ?'

'Sure!' A music executive in her late thirties, cross-addicted to alcohol and marijuana, Roxy had undergone a huge transformation in the last six weeks. My hopes for her were high.

'Trassa.' Roxy studied her and nodded slowly. 'You're getting there.'

'Getting where?' Trassa asked, tremulously.

'To where you need to be.' As the most senior member of the group, Roxy was heady with wisdom. In the kingdom of the blind, the one-eyed woman is queen.

Chalkie was next. 'Everyone loves Chalkie.' Her smile was warm. 'You're talking the talk, my friend, but are you walking the walk?'

She was spot-on. Chalkie was so generous with the sordid details of his drugging that it could fool you into thinking he'd embraced recovery. But his war stories were deflections to keep me from probing too deeply. Buried in Chalkie was either a bottomless sorrow or a burning rage—I didn't know which—that accounted for his relapses. His partner, Skye, had already been into group but her tearful testimony hadn't brought about the breakthrough I'd hoped for.

Roxy turned to Giles. 'My man Giles, you *sure* coke is your drug of choice? And not sex? Just saying.'

'As for you.' Roxy addressed Dennis. 'Too much ha-ha-ha hee-hee-hee.' She held up her hand. 'Don't. I am so over you.'

Dennis's belly laugh was no surprise, but a sliver of pain was audible.

'Harlie. You're breaking my heart. Yes, you're an alcoholic, yes, it sucks. But deal with it. Stop. Being. So *angry*.'

Harlie flat-eyed her.

'Oh, honey, it's okay,' Roxy said. 'My soul *hurt* when I got that I could never make the drink and drugs work for me again. But what I remember now is how shit I felt *all the time*—waking up in a stranger's apartment, not knowing if it was morning or evening. Living that way was such hard work.'

'Won't you miss drinking?' Harlie blurted out.

Roxy shrugged. 'Been there, done that, got the DUI. It's *over*, baby. My choices are I stay clean and sober or . . . I say goodbye to any kind of good life.'

'If I can't drink again, my life is over. I'll never enjoy myself again.'

'How much *were* you enjoying yourself, though?'

'Oh my God, *stop*! You're worse than Rachel!'

Roxy gave her a sympathetic smile, then turned to Ella. 'Soooooo.' Roxy made a steepling gesture with her hands. I really approved of what she was doing with the small amount of power she had. 'I look at you and I think—a person who stands for everything stands for nothing.'

'Whatnow?' Ella's voice shook.

'You're so, "Oh please like me, please love me. I'm your friend, hey, I'm *your* friend too."'

What Ella did next would be very interesting. If she played along with Roxy, it was a bad sign.

Happily, though, she reacted. 'Excuse me, Roxy? You're what? An alcoholic? And addicted to weed? No judgement, but who are you to think you know me? I shouldn't even be here.'

Roxy laughed and several of the others gave knowing smirks.

'I *shouldn't*,' Ella insisted. 'No offence, you all seem cool—'

There was another exchange of glances.

'Yeah.' Ella was snippy. 'Whatever.'

'Ella,' I said. 'Can you tell us about the three cards of sleeping tablets which Priya found sewn under the lining of your handbag the morning you arrived?'

The blood drained from her face. Even her lips were white. She cleared her throat. 'But why didn't you—'

I hadn't mentioned it until now, so she'd decided I didn't know. But we all knew *everything*.

'If you're not an addict, Ella, why would you need to smuggle in sleep-ing pills?'

'. . . I was . . . afraid I wouldn't sleep in here. That's all.' She stumbled through her explanation. 'It's hard at the best of times since I was attacked. I thought it would be even tougher in a strange bed.'

'How have you managed these past four nights?' I asked.

'Oh. Okay, I suppose.'

'According to Moze and Hector, you've been sleeping fine.'

'Were they *spying* on me?'

'Yes.'

'Seriously?'

'*Yes.* You're in rehab. That's how it works.'

Momentarily, she looked confused, lost even, then she turned away.

A text had arrived from Claire. Call me. URGENTLY.

What *now*?

With shaky hands, I hit her number and she answered immediately.

'Kate?' she gasped. 'Luke's nephew?'

'Yes . . .'

'What's he like? Nice? Kind? As sexy as Luke?'

Jesus *Christ.*

'Is it too soon to invite him for dinner?'

'Yes, Claire, *yes.*'

'I'll get some dates from them. Would you like to come?'

'. . . No. Thank you.'

'You don't? Okay, grand. Does he eat shellfish?'

'Bye, Claire.'

23

'Hi.' Quin, wearing an apron and a tea towel slung over his shoulder, gave me a distracted kiss. 'You haven't seen the tahini?'

I hadn't seen the tahini and I planned to keep it that way. I enjoyed cooking but Quin was making one of his needlessly complicated dinners and only a fool would get involved.

I had to tell him about Luke's visit and phone calls, but now wasn't the time, not when Quin was charring aubergines and generally stressing about making a dinner elaborate enough to impress his ex-wife.

Even though they'd split up seven years ago, he and Shiv still had this weird competitive thing. She was an interesting one: quick and clever, always analysing situations to find the money-making angle. Her dark hair was cut in a chic elfin cap—daring, right? Other than that, she was fairly ordinary-looking, but no one noticed because blasts of confidence puffed from her at regular intervals, as if she were a battery-operated air freshener.

For a long time she'd worked for a mid-market fashion chain. When retail began to die, she pivoted to online, setting up a site selling cool children's clothes. This was hugely successful, so much so that she was now consulting for the Irish fashion board. Next she'd started a business importing mobile saunas and that too was a winner.

According to Quin, she'd put the fear of God in his previous girlfriends. But while I thought she was really kind of mean, she didn't scare me.

I sat at the table, scrolling emails, stress-eating edamame beans and stealing glances at Quin. Coming face to face with Luke had sent my past crashing into my present and my head was melted. I'd one foot in my old life and another in the now and, as a result, my set-up with Quin seemed slightly . . . unfamiliar.

'Quin?' I asked. 'Can we talk? For a moment?'

'Okay.' With grim energy, he was whisking something in a saucepan.

'Luke came to my house last night.'

'What?' The whisking stopped abruptly. 'Is he still . . . I thought he'd gone back?'

'Still here. He came to complain about Kate and Devin.'

'Seriously? What's it to him?' Then, 'Are you okay?'

'Yes.' Well, I would be.

'. . . Why didn't you tell me sooner?'

'Last night, I was . . . shocked, I suppose is the word. Then today, work, you know? Quin, it was nothing, though. He rang to apologize this morning.'

'Oh. Okay . . .'

Finley wandered in. 'Any food?' He opened and closed cupboards until he found a bag of Doritos and began horsing into them.

'You'd better eat your dinner.' Quin's threat sounded half-hearted.

'Course I'll eat my dinner.' Finley grinned through a mouthful of half-crunched crisps and swung from the room.

He was a cheerful kid. Other than eating non-stop and needing new shoes on an almost weekly basis there was very little drama.

Liberty was a trickier proposition. In the time I'd known her, she'd gone from age thirteen to fifteen, two of the toughest years in any woman's life.

In the beginning, I was introduced as Quin's 'friend'. I stayed over only when they were at Shiv's. But Liberty had cornered me. 'I'm not stupid. You're Dad's *girl*friend. And you're not my mum.'

Trying to sound calm, I had agreed. 'You already have a mum. You don't need another one.'

I was *pathetic*, trying to be all Cool Adult. In my happiest imaginings Liberty and I would have a Movie of the Week relationship where I whispered ways to conceal the crop of angry-looking spots along her jawline or told her not to worry that her torso had had a growth spurt so that her legs looked disproportionately short because it would all come good in the end.

But it hadn't exactly worked out that way. Although I steered well clear of any disciplinary matters, every couple of weeks there was a meltdown where she flung things, yelling that she hated Quin, she hated me, she hated Shiv, she hated Garrett and that she'd never asked to be born.

I didn't take it personally. My earlier life had been Tantrum Central: Liberty was a rank amateur compared to Claire and Helen. Being honest, I'd gone the full poltergeist once or twice myself.

'So what did he expect you to do about Kate and the nephew?' Quin asked.

'I don't really know. Nothing, maybe.'

The doorbell rang and Quin looked harried. 'That'll be Shiv. Can we talk about this later?'

'There's really nothing to talk about, but sure.'

Shiv and her partner Garrett had arrived with two bottles of alcohol-free wine. Of all the things I loved about Quin, Shiv and her boyfriend, Garrett, were bottom of the list. Brash and flashy, they got excited by rich people and they thought cocaine was glamorous.

Garrett, curly-haired, big and loud, was 'in property'. He wasn't my favourite person, and I wasn't his, but we all kissed hello, because we were middle-class.

Quin took a break from his steamy clattering to assess the alcohol-free wine. 'And we're doing this . . . why?'

'To cut down on mid-week drinking,' Shiv said. 'We still get the experience of wine, without the actual alcohol.'

'Cool.' Because this was fashionable, Quin wanted to try it.

'Rachel would know about that,' Garrett said. 'No alcohol mid-week.'

'Or ever,' Shiv added.

'That's me!' I smiled gamely. 'No fun!'

(Once, when he was very drunk, Garrett had confided how worried he and Shiv had got when they realized I was sticking around. 'We love going to France. For the wine? We used to go with Quin and Elin.' (Elin had been the girlfriend before me.) 'Not going to happen now, is it? Q-Dog's mad about you.')

'I'm wondering', Shiv admitted, 'if this, the alcohol-free wine, might become a thing . . .'

That was Shiv very much on-brand—what people earned and how they could be persuaded to spend it seemed to occupy about nine-tenths of her brain.

The third time we'd met, she'd quizzed me on my finances: 'Do you get a bonus? No? Wow.' 'Could you make more in private practice?' 'You could? So why don't you do that?' Questions that became ever more personal until I found the courage to say, 'That's enough about me. How much do you earn, Shiv?'

She'd given me a long stare, followed by a short laugh and a nod. 'You'll do.'

Shiv looked around Quin's kitchen and asked, 'Where's Liberty?'

'In her room, crying.' Finley supplied. 'She's on her period, she says.'

Garrett muttered, 'Jesus *Christ* . . .'

If Claire had been there, she'd have squared up to him and said, through gritted teeth, 'Fifty per cent of the population experience it every month for thirty years, it's as natural as breathing, get over yourself.' Sadly, I wasn't Claire.

'I'd better go up to her.' Shiv left the room.

Quin resumed his clattering at the stove and Garrett and I eyed each other.

'How's work, Rachel? The junkies behaving themselves? Cool, cool.'

He and Shiv were baffled by my job—they thought I was a do-gooder.

'Why don't you open the fake wine?' I suggested. Gratefully he dived onto the job.

Shiv had returned, trailing Liberty, who looked pale and very young. Also, as her lower half still hadn't caught up with the growth spurt her torso had enjoyed, she looked as if she'd been sawn in half and reassembled with the wrong legs. My heart went out to her.

'Dinner's ready,' Quin said, and there was a rush to the table.

'What is it?' Shiv examined the artfully presented platter.

'Pasta with burnt aubergine, pomegranate and tahini cream. Ottolenghi.'

'Ottolenghi!' Shiv was impressed, then irritated that she'd shown it. 'Here, have some fake wine. Rachel? Fake wine?'

'No thanks.'

'Why not?' Quin asked. 'It's got no alcohol.'

Trying to hide my embarrassment, I said, 'Not recommended for me to replicate the drinking experience.'

And he knew it. Usually he was cool about me not drinking or taking drugs; the few times he'd given me the baleful Captain Buzzkill eyes tended to coincide with the presence of Shiv and Garrett.

Or maybe tonight it was because I'd hurt him by taking too long to tell him about Luke's visit?

'Oh?' He shrugged. 'Okay.'

Garrett swirled the pale yellow liquid and sipped it thoughtfully. 'You know, it's not *bad*.'

'Tastes like the real thing,' Quin agreed. 'So, cheers!'

They clinked glasses.

I'd give it forty minutes.

Finley began to shovel food into his mouth, then mumbled, sounding surprised, 'This is really good.'

Finley would eat anything, but it was genuinely great.

'Bit ambitious for a weeknight, though.' Shiv pointed her fork at Quin.

'That so?' Quin looked amused.

'You really did *all* of this prep just before we arrived?' Her stare was bold, as she watched him.

He smiled some more, skimmed his glance away, then slid it back to her. 'Did some of it last night.'

'Hah!' Shiv was delighted. 'Knew it!'

Everyone kept ploughing into the food until literally everything was eaten. As soon as the kids left the table Quin set down his glass with an air of surrender. 'The pretend wine isn't doing it for me.'

Garrett exhaled. 'Thank God someone said it.'

'Usually, two glasses in,' Quin said. 'I feel good, but right now life still feels . . .'

'. . . too real. Totally.' Shiv turned appraising eyes on me. 'Must be how it is for Rachel all of the time.'

Once again I summoned my game smile. Sometimes I wondered about the energy I expended making drinkers feel okay about the fact that I didn't drink. With all of that effort, I could have sailed around Ireland in a crate.

Quin was on his feet and opening a bottle of real wine. Gratefully the three drinkers gulped it down.

'That's more like it,' Garrett gasped. He'd drained his glass. 'Making up for lost time.'

'We'll try again with the other stuff,' Shiv said. 'But not tonight. And seriously, the dinner was great. Especially with it being vegetarian.'

'Vegan,' Quin said.

'*All* of it?'

'Yeah. Plant-based living. That's me.' Then, 'Except for the times I'd prefer a rare steak—'

'Me too.'

'—but got to get with the programme, right?'

'Right!'

They grinned at each other and, glad to see Quin in better form, I asked, with affection, 'Why did you two ever split up?'

'Because he was sleeping with my best friend's sister.'

I knew that. It hadn't been a real question.

'You started it,' Quin replied. 'Sneaking off for long, flirty lunchtimes with your boss's boss!'

They both laughed loudly and for a small, very scary, moment I wondered what I was doing with these people.

*

'Are you going to meet him again?' Quin asked. 'Do you want to?'

I didn't know. For the first time in a long time, I knew where to find Luke. I could corner him and all the conversations I'd had with him in my head I could have for real.

'No ... but ... it might be a good idea if we talked out some of the bitterness. Look at you and Shiv, you get on great.'

'Yeah, we're friends, because there's nothing left, no love.'

'There's no love between Luke and me either.'

The wound still hurt, but it was a shadow of what it once had been. 'Maybe this is a chance to tidy up a painful part of my past? But I'm not going after him to try to make it happen.'

'Okay.' Suddenly he looked very tired. 'Just keep me posted. And now I really need some sleep.' He turned on his side and I hooked my arm around him, pulling myself tight against his back. In no time, he was snoring softly but even though I was absolutely exhausted, my head kept racing.

I couldn't let Luke undermine the life I'd rebuilt. That moment earlier when I'd wondered what I was doing with Quin and the others? There couldn't be a repeat of that.

Yes, Quin had flaws—so did I, so did everyone. No one on earth was perfect. Maybe even the Dalai Lama left the light on all night in the bathroom, keeping the fan running, even though he'd been repeatedly asked to turn it off when he'd finished cleaning his teeth.

It was absolutely okay to have moments when you thought, *This person is a bit of an arse*. It was normal. Quin wasn't a perfect person—but Luke hadn't been either. It had taken a long time to realize that, because I'd idealized everything about him. Which was why his behaviour at the end had seemed so unexpected and terrible.

When I finally got to sleep, it was probably no surprise that I dreamt about Luke and Yara. She was in his arms. His eyes were closed, his lips were pressed against her forehead and he was holding her with unbearable tenderness.

He was the first to notice me. His eyes opened and, silenced by shock, he stared straight into my soul.

Then, still in his arms, she turned to me and smiled.

24

Ah, for God's sake! Patch Dooley had promised he'd be here at 9.15 a.m., it was now ten twenty-five, there was still no sign and no one was answering his phone.

Murdo was holding the fort for me in group, but I hadn't expected to be so late. Just then, an old-looking, low-to-the-ground, brown Merc turned into the drive and bumped towards the house. Something about its energy told me it had no tax, no insurance, no suspension and had failed its last five NCTs. Dennis's brother, I'd stake my life on it.

The car swung itself in, straddling two parking spots, then the driver's door opened, releasing a cacophony of high-pitched barks, which ceased abruptly when the door slammed shut again.

I went to reception and moments later Patch burst in. He was a second Dennis—the same ill-kempt saunter, the same hail-fellow-well-met likeability, the same bang of low-level lawlessness.

Bright eyes met mine. 'Rachel?' His greying curls bounced. 'I'm late and you're hopping with me! Blame the bagel fella. Drove a hard bargain. But to make it up to you, didn't I get you one!'

'Got me what?'

'A pup. A bitch. Fine size. On the back seat—will we take a look?'

What? 'Ah, no . . .' His chaotic energy was affecting me. 'But will the pups be okay in the car?'

He grinned. 'Be grand! There's a window open! They'll probably scutter all over the place but nothing worse than goes on in that car on a Saturday night!'

Christ.

'It's the Dooley Cab.' He jerked a thumb over his shoulder. 'You know Dennis and meself run a taxi firm? Well, you're looking at it!'

'Do you need anything? Tea? Bathroom? To go over things again?'

'Divil a bit. I'm grand.'

'Remember, Dennis will probably try to make you feel guilty—'

'Lookit, don't worry. Let's go.'

I ushered Patch in and watched Dennis closely. Gratifyingly, his mouth fell open and his face was stamped with shock. But the shock quickly shifted to wonder and he leapt up, hurling himself at his brother. 'Did they ketch you as well?' he bellowed, the very picture of happiness. 'Are you an "alcoholic" too?'

'What do you take me for!' Laughing, Patch thrust his hand into Dennis's. 'They'll never ketch me!' He tapped the side of his head. 'Up here for thinking.'

Together they pointed at their feet, 'Down there for dancing!'

Oh no. No, no, *no*.

Murdo was staring at me and I turned away, shamed by his shock.

'Are you here to get me out?' Dennis demanded of Patch. 'In time for St Patrick's Day on Saturday!'

'The great escape!' Patch agreed. 'Thelma and Louise! We'll cut the roof off the Merc!'

'Dennis.' I was desperately trying to restore calm. 'Return to your seat. Patch, please sit here. Dennis! Dennis.' I cleared my throat. 'Dennis. Can you tell us who this visitor is?'

'He's my brother!'

'We didn't need to be told.' Ella was charmed and starry-eyed.

'Patch. Patch, hello.' Reluctantly, everyone settled, then I carried on. 'You know that your brother is here because he's an alcoholic. Dennis says he's not an alcoholic. So can you give us some examples when you've been worried about his drinking.' We'd been through all of this on the phone on Monday. 'His daughter Abigail says there's been a lot of drunk-driving.'

'Well . . .' Patch looked thoughtful. 'I wouldn't exactly call it "drunk".'

'And I wouldn't exactly call it "driving"!' Dennis finished.

The room erupted with hilarity.

I'd got this *so* wrong.

I persevered a while longer but Patch was way too wily for me. All his visit had done was strengthen Dennis's conviction that he shouldn't be here. After twenty minutes, I ended things.

As I walked Patch out, he asked, 'Was I any help?'

'No,' I said.

'Do you want that bitch?'

'No.'

'Well, g'luck, so.'

'Bye.' I didn't tell him to drive safely.

I hoped he didn't. I hoped he drove into the canal and lost his licence.

As tears of rage and shame gathered behind my eyes, I stomped back inside to ring Juliet Dooley. She needed to get herself and her daughters in here sharpish and this time I wouldn't let myself be fobbed off.

Under normal circumstances, I was good at my job. Like, *skilled* at reading people, knowing when to go easy and knowing when to go in for the kill. But in the week since all the Luke stuff had kicked off, things had been—what was the phrase?—sub-optimal. My sleep had been more broken than usual and I was just . . . disrupted.

I mean, seriously—what kind of half-decent counsellor would have taken a chance on Patch Dooley? The moment he'd swanned up here with his carload of bagels, I should have shown him the door.

There was only one person responsible for this debacle and it was me. But I didn't like that feeling, so instead I decided to blame Luke.

It was *his* fault that my decision-making abilities were off. If Dennis Dooley didn't get sober, if he drank his way into an early grave, leaving behind a devastated widow and two fatherless daughters, Luke Costello was to blame.

Would this lunchtime *ever* end?

For once, I was entirely caught up on my work. My caseload was always heavy and my obsessive tendencies probably didn't help—I usually researched my patients so thoroughly that I could have gone undercover and lived as them. But I'd emailed and called every relevant friend, colleague or family member of my charges. In addition, I was up to date on all the new drops on the many, *many* online stores I liked. I'd ordered new secateurs with cheery pink handles. I'd visited 'my' Chanel bag and wondered what exactly I'd have to sell in order to afford it. Then I'd looked up articles on living with a single kidney and come to the conclusion that selling one of mine might be a mistake. In short, I'd run out of ways to distract myself so it was probably no surprise that I flashed back six years to that terrible Thursday afternoon when I'd realized Luke was going to leave me.

I'd been asleep but I woke with a jump, terribly afraid, without knowing why.

A strange air of industry drew me to the living room. His back to me, Luke was removing books from a shelf, his damp T-shirt sticking to him.

The floor was strewn with CDs and books. I couldn't make sense of the scene.

'What's going on?'

Luke gave me a quick look. His hair was in his eyes, in damp points. 'Packing my stuff.'

'. . . Why?'

'You know why.'

What does he mean? 'Have I . . . missed something?'

He shrugged, eyes as cool as slate.

'Wait. What. Talk to me, please!'

With fluid actions, he moved to a stack of corrugated brown cardboard— flattened packing boxes, I realized, *baffled*. Where had they come from?

I tried to intercept him but with cold efficiency he sidestepped me. 'Busy here, Rachel.'

With one punch, a flat slab of brown cardboard 3-D'd out and became a large box, into which he began loading things.

Stunned, I stared. 'Are you really going?' My voice was faint.

He didn't answer. So I asked, 'When . . . are you planning . . . ?'

'Tomorrow morning.'

I didn't believe him. We'd had a terrible time and we'd stopped being kind to each other. But it was temporary. Things would change—things always changed—and we'd be fine again.

But he just kept on putting his possessions into that cardboard box, the muscles in his back and shoulders working efficiently under the tight, white cotton.

'Where . . . ? Will you stay with Joey?'

'I'm moving to Denver.'

Denver? Honestly, I thought he'd gone insane. 'But . . . what about your business?'

'Selling it to Gustavo.'

That he had an answer was devastating. This might actually be . . . *real*?

'Why Denver?'

'I've a job there. I'll stay with Johnno and Elaine until I get my own place.'

Even all these years later, that memory still had the power to make me shake.

Hoping that a little light espionage would distract me, I went along to the dining hall. About ten of them were in a rowdy knot at a table, everyone talking at once. The chocolate run. Had to be. Nothing else got them as agitated.

Every day, two patients were permitted to leave the grounds and, jingling with change, go to the nearby village, tasked with sourcing a long list of confectionery and cigarettes from the garage.

People who'd never eaten sweets in their lives became devotees while they were here. I remembered it well myself—when the days were so challenging, the small comforts became very important.

Only those who'd been here for more than two weeks were trusted to go out: today's chosen pair were Rudy from Carey-Jane's group and Chalkie.

I settled myself in a chair by the wall, close to Harlie, who had hived herself off from the main throng. A short, angry glare came my way, then she returned to painting her nails. (In Little Miss Sparkle—it gave me a small thrill that I knew.)

Chalkie had a pen poised over a sheet of paper and Rudy was accepting banknotes and doling out change. It looked as if they were running an impromptu betting shop.

'Read my lips.' Dennis seemed to be remonstrating with Chalkie. 'No to: Mars Bar, Mint Crisps, Chomps, Boosts, Curly Wurlies, Twirls and Daims—I don't even know what Daims *are*—'

'They're Swedish.' Stanley, a new client, a beardy, bear-like man, one of Yasmine's charges, called out.

'So's ABBA, but I don't want to ate them ayther!' Then he muttered, 'Except maybe the blondie wan . . .'

'*Nomnomnom,*' Ella said. 'Daims are gorgeous.'

'Hard on the dentures, though.' Trassa threw in a note of caution.

'My teeth are my own!' Dennis insisted.

'Yeah, you bought them in Dealz for a tenner.'

'A tenner? He was robbed.'

'Hahaha. Ah no, it cost extra for that lovely yellow colour!'

'Lookit,' Dennis said. 'I'm just asking for something that—what's the thing they say? "Sparks joy".'

'Joy!' Chalkie scoffed. 'A middle-class thing if ever I heard one. In Maslow's hierarchy of needs—'

'Dennis, hear me out,' Trassa said. 'How about Wispa Caramel!'

'*Nomnomnom.*'

'There's no such thing,' Giles said loftily. 'It's called Wispa Gold.'

'How the fuck would *you* know, Mr Green-and-Black?' Chalkie asked.

They called on Stanley to adjudicate—but Stanley took offence. 'Hey!' he said. 'You've got me all wrong.' He gestured at his chunky physique. 'I'm here for steroids, not food, okay?'

'Jez,' Dennis murmured, 'for a lad who doesn't have a *grá* for the chocolate, he knows an awful lot about it.'

'Anyway, yeah.' Stanley was suddenly more peaceable. 'Wispa Gold is a Wispa with caramel running through it. Giles is right, Wispa Caramel isn't a thing.'

A grumbling mutiny broke out around Trassa.

'Hey, hey, *hey*,' Stanley said. 'Everyone be cool, it's an easy mistake to make.'

God, I wouldn't have minded a Wispa Gold myself. But I couldn't *possibly* ask. For the briefest moment I wished I was a client here, then several things shifted in me, like planks collapsing, and the thought got banished.

'Look,' Dennis said. 'I like a Bounty—'

A hue and cry rose. 'Bounties are rotten!'

'Like eating air freshener!'

'Coconut-flavoured mould!'

'*Nomnomnom.*'

'Not gonna lie.' Harlie didn't even look up from her diligent nail-painting. 'I'd take a bullet for a Bounty ice-cream.'

'Okay,' Giles said. 'Work with me here—what about a *red* Bounty?'

'*Nomnomnom.*'

'What's the difference?'

'Red is dark chocolate.'

'Christ!' Chalkie declared. 'Bounties are bad enough but *dark* chocolate?'

'*Nomnomnom.*'

Startling me, Harlie leapt to her feet and exploded at Ella, 'Would you stop saying "NomnomfuckingNOM"!'

'*Nomnomnom.*'

Thanks to Patch Fecking Dooley, I was mortified going back into group for the afternoon session, afraid that none of them would have any respect for me, ever again. But fake it to make it, so I put on my impervious face. As they all filed in, Dennis paused to wink—*wink!*—in my direction.

I managed a small smile, while thinking, *I'll fucking get you, you charming, loveable bastard.* Then my focus switched to Trassa.

In the wake of yesterday's revelations from Ronan, it was time for the mop-up operation. Most people in rehab are broken open by a public airing of their wrongdoings, but the first reaction tends to be defensive rage.

'Trassa,' I asked, 'how did you feel when Ronan was talking?'

She gave a twisted smile. 'He was always disloyal. A coward. But I'll still be signing the house over to him.'

'Hey! He's no coward,' Chalkie said. 'The poor lad was in bits.'

It was interesting—heartening, actually—how most of the people here could challenge each other in group, go in hot and heavy at times, then traipse back out into the dining hall, the best of friends.

'A coward,' Trassa said. 'And he'll get his money back.'

'It's not just about the money, Trassa.' Giles sounded shocked. 'Debt collectors visited your home.'

'And scared your husband,' Chalkie said. 'He's not a well man. Holy *fuck*. I'm agreeing with Giles. Get me out of here.'

'Seamus Senior will outlive us all.' Trassa gave us an I've-got-an-apple-tart-in-the-oven smile.

'But if he does, Ronan will never get the house,' Harlie said.

'I just meant . . .' Trassa blustered. 'You know what I meant.'

'Fuck's sake!' Harlie surprised us all. 'Am I the only one freaking out that a loan shark is going to hurt your son if he doesn't pay him twenty thousand euro by Friday?'

'He's not a loan shark!'

'He's definitely a loan shark,' Chalkie said.

'You're the man who stole the bail money your community raised!' Trassa flung at Chalkie. 'And used it to buy heroin for yourself! You've no right to criticize me! Because of you an innocent man spent seven months on remand waiting for a trial.'

'At least I won't be responsible for my son getting his fingers sawn off!'

'Who said anything about saws?' Trassa was scandalized. 'Or fingers. Collie Byrne's not that sort! A few slaps is as bad as it gets.'

'Chalkie's using his imagination,' Giles said. 'And he's on the money.'

'No pun intended.' Giles smiled at Chalkie—who returned the smile. Then both of them realized what they were doing and identical looks of horror appeared on their faces.

Right, that was enough of Trassa for the moment. She'd been set upon the right path; things were now just a matter of time.

25

'It's in the Dublin mountains,' Kate said. 'And it's *big*. Rooms for *everything*. Laundry room. Cinema room. They have a boiling-water tap.'

'Ooooh.' We laughed. We both lusted after those taps.

That evening, Kate and I were both home. She'd spent the previous night with Devin and, at the best of times, Other People's Houses exerted a huge draw on me but my obsession was worse than usual because of Luke.

Maybe I shouldn't have been nosy-poking around but maybe it was impossible not to? Luke was on my mind the whole time, humming away like background noise. Memories kept popping into my head—at work, in traffic, midway through a conversation with Mum.

But it was hardly a surprise. We'd broken up in a way that had left me hanging, with a million unanswered questions. Now, all of a sudden, Luke was answering my calls again. If I tried talking to him about what had gone wrong, I suspected he wouldn't make a run for it.

Not just yet though. Since the funeral, my skin had felt like it was on inside out. I needed to wait until I was less raw.

'Devin has his own space away from the main house where his band practises,' Kate said. 'It's set up with all the equipment.'

'How many bedrooms in the house?'

She thought about it. 'Devin's room, his mum and dad, his sister, his kid brother, the room Luke and Kallie are in . . . five, anyway. A *gazillion* bathrooms.'

'And his parents are cool with you, um . . . staying over?'

'Uh-uh,' she said. 'They're really nice. Well, Justin, you know him. And his mum—Sarina?—she's lovely too.'

Don'tAskDon'tAskDon'tAsk. '. . . Have you seen'—it was difficult to say her name—'Kallie again?'

'This morning.'

I waited.

'Rach, don't be mad, but I feel sorry for her. She knows nobody here except Luke and he's gone all day, over with his dad. Devin's house is off the bus route and she can't drive a stick shift—is that a car with gears?'

'It is.' God, this was hard. But I needed to nip something in the bud. 'Of course I'm not mad. The stuff with me and Luke has nothing to do with . . .' It was easier to say it a second time. 'Kallie.'

'Oh, okay, good.' She smiled.

I had to go to bed—this had turned into a very rough week and I wanted to check out for a while.

But instead, I ended up thinking about Luke.

Long, long ago, back in the days before I'd been to rehab, he and I had had lots of amazing sex. It was the part of us that always worked. The urgency with which he'd wanted me was the hottest thing ever and even when I was embarrassed by his clothes or his friends (seriously, I was *awful*) I found him head-spinningly sexy.

But the uncomfortable truth was that when we'd start tearing the clothes off each other, I'd often be slightly out of it—though never a lot. Any time it was obvious, Luke refused to touch me. It confused him—or it made him angry.

He couldn't understand why I overdid it, and the thing was, neither could I.

Huge amounts of my energy went into pretending to him, to Brigit and most of all myself that my drug use was as harmless as a couple of glasses of wine with dinner. And sometimes it *was* that innocuous. Say the words 'drug addict' and everyone immediately envisions a needle-strewn alley. But there were times when Brigit and I stayed in to watch a movie and shared a joint instead of a bottle of wine.

When Luke saw I had a problem he tried to help but instead of seeing a kind man who *really* cared, all I saw was a killjoy. Just before I went to rehab, he broke up with me.

Fast forward a year and a half, when I returned to New York and quickly realized I was in love with Luke—and he was in love with me.

However, I knew I needed to wait before sleeping with him again. Just for a while. My previous life had been all about instant gratification and it had done me no good. Things were different now. I was serious about Luke; it was important to try to do better.

Not that it was easy—Luke was so hot. Not to mention *keen*.

But when the night eventually came, and I was spread, naked, across

Luke Costello's bed, shyness paralysed me. I'd spent the previous weeks in my single bed in an all-women's hostel, fantasizing about his beautiful skin, the shock of dark hair at his groin, the heat of his mouth on me. But the reality of his body, the undeniable want in him, scared me sideways.

Which didn't make sense—we'd already done this countless times. Except we hadn't—the me that had had wild sex with Luke Costello had been a different person. Now I was stone-cold clean and sober and didn't know how to be present in my body. 'Can we . . . ?' I pulled him towards me. I wanted this to be over, to be on the far side of it, just to prove I could do it.

'Already?' He shot me a look, his dark eyes confused.

'Yes.'

My eyes squeezed tight, I felt his body slide over mine, then the fullness as he moved inside me. He paused, and groaned my name, tangling his hands in my hair, then began to move. *Okay, okay, I can do this.* I tried to let my body take over, to reduce it all to a collection of sensations.

'Rachel,' he panted on top of me, 'open your eyes. Look at me.'

But I couldn't. I just wanted him to come and for it to be done.

'Don't stop,' I begged, arching my hips upwards.

He slowed, then, to my horror, pulled out of me, and in the sudden shock of emptiness I began to cry. I'd failed him, I'd failed us both.

I sat up, searching for my clothes, but gently he pulled me back to lie next to him. Stroking my hair off my face, he kissed away my tears. 'It's okay.'

'It's not.'

'You're afraid of intimacy,' he said.

I cry-laughed. 'What would you know?'

'I read the books you gave me. They say that addicts fear intimacy. Because you don't feel good enough.'

'I'm *not* good enough.'

'You are *so* good enough. I love you. But you're scared.'

'C'mon, let's get dressed.' I was heartsick, certain I'd never have the confidence to try this again.

'Hey.' He rolled over onto me. 'We don't have to do anything you don't want. But would you trust me?'

'To do what?'

He sat up in bed. 'So if you come here to me . . .'

He helped me to clamber onto his lap. I clasped my arms tightly around his neck, pulling at his thin silver chain and braided leather cord, praying that whatever we were trying would work.

'It's all okay.' His voice was almost a whisper. 'Just keep looking at me. So can you . . .' Gently, he moved his hands to my thighs so that my legs slid around his hips, shifting us even closer. 'And forget about . . . that.' He dismissed his erection. 'Just look at me and breathe.'

'Breathe?'

'At the same time as each other.'

Ooookay. I inhaled, so did he and together, our rib cages expanded. I exhaled, he exhaled and our shoulders dropped. Focusing on my breathing dialled down the discomfort of that unbroken stare.

After a couple of false starts, a rhythm built until we were inhaling and exhaling in perfect synchronicity. The intimacy of matching our bodies in this way was unlike anything I'd ever experienced.

'Was this in one of the books you read?' I whispered.

He nodded, still holding my focus.

As our eye contact endured, he went from being Luke, to an unrecognizable stranger, then changed again to a man with whom I shared a deep connection.

It took a while to notice that, keeping time with our breaths, he'd been rocking us gently. A fire had built in me, unexpectedly hot.

This was different.

'Okay?' he murmured.

'Yes.' My voice was high with surprise. 'Maybe we could . . . ?'

'Don't do anything you don't want to do,' he repeated.

'I think I want to.'

'Maybe not today.'

'*Yes*, today.'

He laughed softly and as he slid into me and our bodies slotted together, his pupils flared. All that eye contact became suddenly too much and my gaze moved sidewards.

'Come back to me,' he whispered.

Several seconds passed before I was able to face him again—then there he was.

Over time the speed of our bodies increased and my breaths became shorter. Still I kept my eyes on his and it was *intense.*

As I began to lose myself, he said, 'Stay with me.'

But the wildness in my body made me feel vulnerable.

'Rachel, stay with me,' he repeated. 'I love you, it's all okay.'

I felt exposed and shy, but he held me tight, he held me *so* tight and all I had to do was take a breath, then the next breath, then the next. There were moments when the sensations in my body became almost too much to bear.

But I stayed.

26

'Like, I wasn't banging up every day,' Chalkie said. 'It was more in binges. I'd be clean for months—twice I nearly managed a whole year—but both times I started again just before I got my chip from NA. I think I thought I was cured. But guess what? I was still a junkie.' He shot a veiled smile at me. 'Sorry, Rachel, I mean *addict*.' Then, with more animation, 'Have you ever noticed middle-class kids are never "junkies"? Right? But poor fuckers, brought up in the flats—'

I cleared my throat. 'Chalkie, stay on track . . . So you decided to get clean? Why?'

'I dunno, really. There I was in some manky sitting room with three other heads, all of us on the nod, and I just knew I didn't want to do it. Not any more. A new path to the waterfall, amirite?'

'What was different about that day, Chalkie?'

He shrugged, his eyes burning blue. 'Hard to say, Rachel. Nothing I can think of. Just, I was *done*. Other times would have made more sense. After Maarit died . . .'

Maarit had been the mother of Chalkie's second child, a daughter, Vida. Maarit had struggled with addiction and about two years earlier had taken her own life.

'When I stole Rixer's bail money and stuck it in my arm . . . the shame of that will be with me till my dying day . . . But it wasn't enough to make me stop. And then I just . . . decided.'

Even though we knew the outcome of this story, we were barely breathing. 'Was it hope?' Ella breathed.

He fixed her with his blue stare as he considered. 'I dunno exactly if I'd call it hope. But I wondered if I tried a new way, if things would be different?'

'If nothing changes, nothing changes,' said Trassa—and received a number of startled looks.

'What's up with *you*?' Dennis squeaked.

Trassa looked confused, as if she didn't know she'd spoken.

'I knew what I was facing . . . withdrawal, like, it's no joke.' Chalkie's short laugh turned into a grimace. '"Let this cup pass from my lips." But I was *doing it.*'

'It's called "a moment of clarity",' Giles supplied. 'Priya talked about it in a lecture.'

Giles was right. Usually a crisis was what shocked an addict into recovery—a job loss, a relationship breakdown, a brush with the law. Sometimes even the threat was enough.

But there were times when, without any immediate drama, addicts just decided to stop, when a rare break in their clouds of denial illuminated how exhausting it was to maintain a habit, how gruelling it was to hurt themselves and others, over and over.

However, moments of clarity were usually preceded by months, maybe even years, of people begging them to stop.

Either way, it was to be seized upon—moments of clarity didn't usually last long before the window closed up and it was once again Denial City.

Unexpectedly, I was flung back in time, to a morning long ago, in New York. I'd woken early and alone—and I felt different. Inexplicably calm. Something had shifted and my soul was quiet.

I opened my bedroom curtains. Outside the window, the first hint of dawn hazed the horizon. As I watched, the sun peeped out and light began to spangle over the city. My window was wet—it must have been pelting down earlier. As the sun continued to rise, a ray caught on a raindrop on the glass and broke into the seven different colours of the rainbow, becoming smudged stripes of transparent colour on the wooden floor, right before me.

Seeing 'signs' had never been my thing but the same strange calm I'd woken up with was insisting that my personal rainbow was a very clear message: *Be brave. Say goodbye. You'll be fine.*

Chalkie was still talking and hastily I tuned back in.

'I was going to give NA another go,' Chalkie said. 'I'd done lots of stints there.'

But he'd never stayed long enough to do any healing—and there was so much for him to heal from. Born to a single mother, an addict, he wasn't even three years old when she overdosed and died in their home. For seventy-two hours, he sat by her side, trying to wake her up. He'd even attempted to feed her, putting a saucepan on the hob and trying to open cans of soup by tearing off the paper labels.

His father had never been in his life so he lived with his grandmother. Sadly, she died when he was fifteen.

'Then Skye tells me I'm on her health insurance.'

It was hard to know precisely what to call Skye's relationship with Chalkie. She was the mother of his eight-year-old son, Tito. After Maarit died, Chalkie had asked Skye to adopt Vida. Now Vida lived with Skye full-time, but Chalkie came and went.

Skye was a social worker and a community activist. Chalkie had said—with warm admiration—she was 'a working-class woman trapped in a middle-class body'.

'The health insurance meant I could come in here.' Chalkie gave me a bold smile. 'Be the beneficiary of Rachel's *considerable* wisdom, get three meals a day, a warm bed at night. But spare a thought for the poor scumbags nodding out on stairwells in the fla—' He saw my face. 'Soz. Yeah. You know, I think that it was just my time to stop. You don't see till you see, you don't hear till you hear. "The truth must dazzle gradually, Or every man be blind." Emily Dickinson.'

Ella took in a short, gaspy breath. Her chin trembled as she stared, love-struck, at Chalkie.

'Yeh.' Chalkie slanted a look at Giles. 'What would someone like me know about poetry?'

'Well, I—'

'Ah, you're all right, Gilesy man.' Chalkie grinned. 'I'm just fucking with you.'

Call me delusional, but I was sure there was affection in there somewhere.

Ella's tears were now in full spate and Harlie was watching, her contempt visible.

I was concerned about Harlie—she seemed to have got bogged down in anger.

Usually, when the truth dawned on addicts, anger was one of the reactions. But people tended to move through it and on to grief, back-and-forthing between the two, often throwing some bargaining into the mix while they were at it. Harlie, however, had landed on anger, liked it and decided to stay.

Since her arrival, I hadn't made her cry once, a failure that I felt keenly. What if I couldn't get any further with her? Sometimes—very rarely, mind, but it had happened—people withstood everything I flung at them during their six weeks and left, still in the tight grip of their addiction. It was the *worst*. Obviously, I felt for the addict and all the people who loved them but—and this was shallow and shameful—*I* felt like a failure.

I wondered about trying again to get her friend Tegan's parents to come in. Maybe if they talked to Harlie about their dead daughter, something would shift?

Meanwhile, Ella was still sobbing.

'What's up?' I asked.

'Nothing,' she gasped. 'Just happy that Chalkie is here. That he's going to be okay.'

'What about you? Are you happy you're here? Happy *you're* going to be okay?'

'But I *am* okay.'

As they filed out at the end of group, Trassa, looking haunted, hung back.

'Rachel. Would you know if . . . ?' She clutched my arm. 'I'm thinking about Ronan.'

I waited. Her grip on my arm tightened and she leant close to me.

'I'd be afraid'—her voice was hoarse—'that Collie Byrne might hurt him.'

Still I waited.

'He's not really a violent type, Collie Byrne. He'll probably just take some of Ronan's machinery for the debt. But I was lying awake and I couldn't stop thinking of . . .' Her jaw clenched and her skin was as white as paper. 'Ronan's not tough,' she said. 'He's a gentle sort of a lad, he wouldn't be able to defend himself and—can you help me, Rachel?'

'What would you like to do?'

'I could maybe talk to Collie Byrne? Make a plan to pay back the money?'

'As I understand it,' I said, carefully, 'you had already made promises to Collie Byrne. In the past.'

'But this time I mean it. I meant it the other time too,' she added quickly. 'But it's different now.'

'What way? You always knew that Collie operated outside the law.'

'I never really thought about it.' She looked lost and frightened. 'I just . . . knew I'd get the money from somewhere. But tomorrow is Friday, the day Collie Byrne said he'd . . . I don't want anything bad to happen to Ronan.'

At long last, she broke down. Fat tears sprang from her eyes and a storm of sobs shook her. 'He's my little boy,' she gasped. 'I don't want anyone to hurt him.'

27

'So! When I first got here I thought you were all insane!' Roxy was up on a dining chair, giving her farewell speech. 'And I wasn't wrong!' The room erupted into laughter.

The twenty other clients and four of the therapists had come along, as well as Brianna, Nurse Hector, Starling who taught art, Florian the grounds-man and Karlin the cook. Karlin had made a special farewell Gateau Diane, Roxy's favourite. Most people got fobbed off with a preservatives-riddled thing from the garage. No doubt about it, Roxy had been a big hit.

'I came in here to save my job.' Roxy beamed around the room. 'Then discovered I was an alcoholic and drug addict. Fuck my life!' Radiant with gratitude and optimism, she was a very different woman to the resistant, surly creature who had arrived here six weeks ago.

The one off-note here was poor Trassa. Planked on a chair, with Giles and Chalkie hovering protectively, she looked catatonic. One of her two per-mitted weekly phone calls had been used to speak to Ronan, to discover that heaven and earth were being moved to get Collie Byrne his twenty grand by tomorrow. That immediate worry had gone but there were much bigger rearrangements taking place in her.

'Six long weeks ago,' Roxy declared, 'I thought an addict was one of those people sleeping in shop doorways! Imagine my shock when I got it—even though I had a job and an apartment I was an alkie.' She grinned. 'Let me tell you, I was *not* happy! I was very, *very* not happy. Next, I decided I could keep drinking and using, I just needed to be careful.'

'Bargaining!' someone yelled.

'Yep, bargaining. Didn't last long though. Rachel, over there'—she pointed to me, leaning against the doorway—'said I'd never drink or drug normally again. Ouch! Gurl, you need to learn how to break bad news! Then I cried for eight days solid.'

'How are you feeling about going Back Out There?' Chalkie called up to her.

'Sad, you know? Which is weird. Six weeks ago, I hated this place, hated everyone here.' Ruefully, she shook her head. 'Especially Rachel, not gonna lie.' Then, 'Sorry.'

'No need.' *Sort* of true. It wasn't the real me she'd hated.

'Wow, though!' She widened her eyes. 'You knew my bullshit up and down! You are *really good* at your job. Times even *I* didn't know I was lying—but you did. That's some training you got!'

I allowed myself a little smile.

'Until I got here, I had no clue how exhausted I was. All. The. Time!' Roxy said. 'All the planning . . . where my next drink was coming from, where I'd get the money to score, having to keep track of all my lies. So let me hear your suggestions for staying clean and sober.'

'Meetings,' someone called. 'Lots of meetings! Get phone numbers from the other women there. Go to your aftercare, every week.'

'Never forget you're an addict! Never think you're cured!'

'Can't *believe* I'm saying this,' Roxy exclaimed, 'but I'm relieved everything caught up with me. I was so ashamed all the time. You know?' She laughed as she scanned the semi-circle of faces. 'Yeah, you *do*.'

'When are we getting the cake?' Ella muttered.

Confused and uncomfortable, Ella wasn't enjoying this. And Dennis even less so. Despite me getting it so wrong with Patch, Dennis was wobbling. Plucking him from his everyday life, bombarding him with lectures and AA meetings, removing any access to alcohol and surrounding him with other addicts who'd once been just as resistant, was starting to work. I could see it on his face—a terrible suspicion that he wasn't that different to Roxy.

'Some of you here don't want to stop.' Roxy said. 'And I get it, it's like saying goodbye to the love of your life.'

At her words, something squeezed in me, something I hadn't felt in a while—the agony, the grief of turning away from the thing I loved the most. It had been excruciating. I'd been clean for a long time but it was good to be reminded that I was still an addict, that I'd never be cured.

'But addiction is a killer disease, so if you want to stay alive, you've no choice. So do it! Now, take one last look at me because in ten minutes' time, when I walk out that door, no offence, guys, I am never coming back.'

Amid rowdy applause, she climbed down from the chair and embarked on a bout of enthusiastic hugging. I waited till everyone had dispersed, then collared her.

'I'm very fond of you, Roxy,' I said, 'but I do *not* want to see you in here again.'

'Got it. Thank you, Rachel. Thank you for everything.'

It didn't always feel right to hug a departing client but with Roxy there was no way I couldn't. I held her tight and hoped she'd be happy, and when we pulled away from each other, we both had tears in our eyes.

28

I needed a T-shirt from the airing cupboard so, in my sturdy pyjamas, I zipped from my bedroom onto the landing—at the *very moment* that the lock on the bathroom door clicked and Devin Costello, wearing only a towel wrapped low around his hips, emerged, in a cloud of steam.

We took one startled look at each other and speedily I retreated to my bedroom, where I raged at the terrible timing. I'd deliberately waited until I'd thought there was no chance of meeting him! The water was still running! What was he doing leaving the bathroom when the shower was still on?

Devin and Kate had shown up late last night. Giggling and sweet, they'd tumbled into the living room to say hello, then commandeered the kitchen, where they did stuff with halloumi. Even with the door shut, I could hear them exclaiming, 'Squeaky. It's so squeaky.' Then laughing like drains.

Young love.

Very young.

Devin seemed very child-like to me, much younger than Luke had been when he'd been only a few years older. Maybe because all kids were more cosseted these days? Or maybe because his parents weren't short of money?

. . . Or maybe I was just old . . . ?

They'd gone to bed shortly after I had. For a while the low murmur of their voices and occasional laughter was audible from Kate's room, then it all went very quiet and I drifted off. Until the sound of a stifled groan—a male one—reached me in my sleep.

Suddenly I was wide awake, assailed by catastrophic thinking. No *way* could I keep living in this house if I had to listen on the regular to a Costello man doing sex noises in the room next door. I'd have to move out. Or Kate would.

. . . But poor Kate, that brutal commute from Claire's. No, it would have to be me. I'd move in with Quin and find someone to help pay my mortgage by sharing with Kate. A young, easy-going type, who didn't mind a home with inadequate sound insulation.

But I couldn't take things with Quin to the next level just to escape Luke Costello's nephew.

Or could I?

It had taken me *hours* to get back to sleep, only to land right into a nightmare. It was New York, more than twenty years ago, and Luke was yelling, 'You're lying.'

'I'm not, I'm not, Luke, I'm not,' I stuttered with fear.

'But I've found your hiding places! See!' Dramatically, he ripped a strip of paper from the wall and hundreds of tablets tumbled out, bouncing to the floor and around the room. 'Why did you lie? You know that's *worse* than taking drugs.'

At the start of the dream, we were both in our twenties, then, as happens in dreams, we changed and looked like we do now, him with his shorter hair and unfamiliar coat, me with my smooth Botoxy forehead and new sneakers.

When I woke up, I was shaking. God, that had been *awful*. Since that phone call from Joey Armstrong, so many long-buried feelings had been flung to the surface.

It was 7 a.m., anyway, nearly time to get up. Then I heard, 'It's so squeaky!'

So, they were awake.

Moments later, one of them (Devin, it transpired) went into the bathroom and shut the door. Then opened it again and called, 'Which shower gel do I use?'

'The Origins one. Guess why?'

'Because it's *so squeaky*?'

'Yeah!'

He laughed, she laughed, they probably laughed next door in Benigno and Jasline's, Crunchie was doubtless in convulsions downstairs in the kitchen. *Good job I was already awake*, I wanted to yell.

Then it occurred to me that I'd have to wait until Devin finished because the heating system couldn't handle two hot showers simultaneously. Breathing angrily, I stomped about, organizing my clothes, only to remember that all of my T-shirts were in the airing cupboard.

The shower was still running. Good stuff, I thought, I was *safe*. So, out I went—and disaster struck.

During her time living here, other boyfriends of Kate's had stayed over—twice or three times the infamous Isaac (an arse), and there was some other one-off randomer she'd found somewhere. I couldn't have cared less what they'd thought about me, but there was a real fear that Devin might suddenly drop some disparaging remark at the dinner conversation, with Luke present. You know the way young men carry on about any woman over the age of sixteen? The utter scorn they pour on us? 'Ew, the state of Kate's auntie. I saw her in her literal pyjamas! Imma poke myself in the eyes with a rusty compass before I'd go through that again!'

Fuckers, the lot of them.

Seriously, though, what the hell had he been at?

Maybe he'd been keeping the water running so it was nice and hot for Kate? In which case, wasteful! Think of the planet! Or perhaps he'd planned to lure her into the shower for some early-morning shenanigans? In which case, bad manners!

This was very, *very* uncomfortable.

You'll get used to it.

'I fecken won't,' I muttered.

You'll see. You will.

'Parcel for you,' Brianna called as soon as I got to work. She held a wrapped box up to the light and squinted. 'Looks like chocolates. Lily O'Brien's.'

I groaned with longing but the mood I was in, if I ate one, I'd eat them all. 'Keep them.'

'Seriously?' Brianna was delighted.

'Seriously.' I opened the attached letter, which was from a man who'd been in for alcoholism about two years ago. I went straight to the end of the letter to see if he was still sober—he was—then folded it into my bag to read later. Right now, Trassa needed to be checked on.

'I'll share them,' Brianna said.

'Whatever you like, just don't give any to me.' Not today.

Trassa was at the breakfast table, holding a cup of tea and staring into space. Apparently, she'd eaten almost nothing of last night's dinner and had gone to bed at eight o'clock.

Twenty years earlier, I'd been the same when I could no longer outrun the fact that I was an addict—when it was suddenly clear that I wasn't simply a recreational user, that I couldn't stop.

The avalanche of truth had been overwhelming. Seeing the damage I'd done to others—and myself—had shocked and shamed me. Worse, suddenly knowing in my bones that my best friend, the thing I loved most in the world, the only substance that brought me genuine relief, could no longer be part of my life, well, it was like a death. The end of the greatest love story ever.

But it had to be gone through. I'd had to do it. Trassa had to do it. There could be no recovery without it.

My new arrival was due this morning. Ducking into one of the small interview rooms, which had a window overlooking the front grounds, I skimmed her file again. 'Bronte, forty-three, a heroin addict. Married to Eden Tollemarche, Viscount Kilsharvan.' It wouldn't be the first time a member of the aristocracy had landed in here: addiction was no respecter of titles.

Has been abusing heroin on and off since her twenties, but it got out of control six years ago. After a year of intravenous abuse, she went to rehab in the UK. Stayed clean until she broke her ankle last June and was prescribed opiate painkillers. She blames them for her relapse. For the past eight months she's been injecting heroin. At the assessment her husband seemed supportive.

My attention was caught by a muddy Land Rover coming through the gates, slightly too fast. It whizzed into a parking spot and almost immediately a tall, ruddy-faced man jumped out, strode to the trunk, extracted a bag and hoisted it onto his shoulder.

Bronte was slower to appear. Reluctantly, she extracted herself from the car. Dressed in jeans, a shrunken jacket and a giant felt scarf wrapped around her neck and shoulders, she looked about fourteen.

She paused to cast the house an apprehensive look. For most people, being checked into rehab is the worst moment of their life. They can't believe it's really happening—for a long time their lies and manipulations have kept them ahead of the posse but the game is finally up, and everything is about to change forever.

However, this was Bronte's second time—and second time round was worse. There was so much shame in a relapse. When an addict first got clean or sober, they had to work hard to win back the trust of the people they loved—but when they got it, it was beautiful. Relationships often became honest and pure, perhaps for the first time ever.

It was infinitely harder to pull it off twice. People were willing to forgive once, but a relapse soured everything.

Outside, Bronte and the husband exchanged a few words. He touched her face and she nodded, then they turned towards the steps which led to our door and disappeared from my view.

Even though I wasn't needed, I went to the admissions office, where it was all go. Brianna and Eden were processing the paperwork and Priya had Bronte's luggage up on a desk, rummaging through the contents, looking for contraband.

Passively, Bronte sat on a chair, her arm bent at the elbow as Nurse Moze took a blood sample. She was as pale as milk, except for a cluster of delicately broken veins in the middle of each cheek. Not a scrap of make-up—her eyebrows and eyelashes were so fair they were invisible and her wispy, faded hair was carelessly caught up in an elastic band. I itched to tell her that she should use a proper bobble, that it was no wonder her hair was broken and flyaway, the way she treated it. But sadly that wasn't part of my remit.

Her clothes were really quite something—her jeans looked as if they'd time travelled from 1973, where they'd last been seen on a ten-year-old boy haring around on a Chopper. Was this an aristo thing? Long, elegant fingers, no nail varnish, but there was no avoiding the ring on her wedding finger, a monstrously ornate Victorian-style gold and ruby affair.

'What are these?' Priya had found a card of tablets in Bronte's wash bag.

'Her birth control.' Eden's voice was too boomy for the small room.

'Are they, Bronte?' Priya asked.

'Oh? Um . . . yes.'

Priya examined the brand name, made a note in Bronte's file and moved the tablets to an in-tray.

'She needs to take them.' Eden's face darkened.

'We need to check what they are.'

'You think she would try to smuggle . . . ?'

Wouldn't be the first time, buster.

Pleasantly, Priya repeated, 'We need to check them.'

'Give her her birth control. She's my wife and I *insist*.'

Coolly, Bronte followed the exchange.

Frankly, I was *delighted* I'd gatecrashed! This sort of insight was priceless.

'Bronte is in our care now.' Priya was firm.

'Eden . . . ?' Bronte shook her head at him. 'Please . . .'

'Okay.' Visibly trying to calm down, he said, 'I should go.' He flicked an angry look at us. 'May I have privacy to kiss my wife?'

'No,' I said. 'She's in rehab now.' Christ, were they *all* in denial? You'd expect the clients to be, it was part of their condition. But when the very people who were checking them in were also at it, you'd seriously wonder.

Incredulous, he asked, 'You think I'm going to slip her something as I kiss her?'

'It's happened!' Moze, Priya, Brianna and I exclaimed, simultaneously.

In foul form, Eden Tollemarche departed.

It was time to start group and as Bronte was here, she might as well come with me.

'The bloods that Nurse Moze took?' I asked her. 'Are they going to come back clean?'

'I don't know . . . I mean, I was detoxed, I haven't taken anything since . . .'

'Okay. Let's go.'

In the Abbot's Quarter, as Bronte sat down, Harlie gave her a thorough scan—and I could read her mind. *A lash and brow tint, some red-cancelling primer followed by a decent coverage foundation. Maybe even a handful of hair extensions to give those poor, broken strands some body.*

Bronte removed her jacket to reveal a T-shirt that said 'I'm Sorry I'm Late, I Didn't Want To Come'.

'Morning, all,' I said. 'As you can see, a new member has joined us. Bronte, would you like to introduce yourself?'

'Um. Okay.' In a low voice, she said, 'My name's Bronte. I'm . . .' She cleared her throat. '. . . addicted to heroin. I was clean for over four years. Nine months ago I broke my ankle, got put on Vicodin and . . . relapsed.'

Chalkie was checking her out—the humongous ring, her slender, elegant limbs, all of it.

'Nice T-shirt,' he said.

'Oh?' Bronte barely glanced at it. 'It's my daughter's.'

'You've kids?'

'Three. A daughter, eighteen. Two sons, sixteen and thirteen.'

'What age are *you*, Bronte?' Dennis asked. 'Yourself, like.'

'Dennis!' Giles hissed. 'You crass oaf! You should know better than to ask.'

'It's okay.' Bronte shrugged. 'I'm forty-three.'

'How do you make ends meet, Bronte?' Chalkie asked. 'Feed your kids? Pay your rent?'

'So . . . my husband . . . It's his money.'

'What way does he . . . *earn a crust?*'

'He—well, we run a farm.'

'He's a farmer?' Troubled eyes roamed over her. 'You don't look like any farmer's wife I've ever seen.'

'How would you know?' Giles rounded on Chalkie. 'Have you ever left the, quote, "impoverished inner city"? You told us you wouldn't sully your man-of-the-people lungs with the "oxygen of privilege"!'

'Where's your farm?' Chalkie kept his eyes on Bronte.

'County Meath.'

Dennis interjected. 'How many acres?' This was one of his areas of interest.

'. . . Two thousand.'

'Fuck!' Chalkie almost levitated.

'*Is that a lot?*' Ella asked Dennis out of the side of her mouth.

"'Tis fecken huge.' Dennis leant towards Bronte. 'That's a fierce big amount of land ye have. Are ye dairy? Tillage? Mixed?'

'. . . Most of it is leased. We breed horses.'

'Horse-breeders?' Chalkie was delighted. Here was a chance for real outrage. 'Lady Bronte.'

'Actually, I'm a viscountess—'

'—you're joking!'

'Chalkie,' I asked. 'How relevant is any of this?'

'If I was living in privilege,' he spluttered, 'because I'd stolen land from other people, the guilt would have me racing off to buy heroin. No wonder Lady fucking Bronte here—'

'Lady fucking Kilsharvan,' Bronte interrupted.

Dumbfounded by her arrogance, Chalkie swivelled to stare at her.

'But there's no need to use my title.' Her tone was tart—but her smile was minxy.

29

'Ella, you're reading your life story,' I said.

'Sure!' Perky as can be.

She'd been here a week now and, other than with Harlie, she was popular. In fairness, she put enough effort into making everyone love her. She was funny, kind and, even though one of her arms was still in a sling, she did her chores without much complaint.

A week of lectures, NA meetings and immersion with twenty other people who were at various stages in their recovery process meant that the erosion of her denial was already well under way. But writing and reading out her life story should move her on further.

Off she went. The youngest of three, her early years had been fine. Ella was a much-longed-for girl, so after having had two boys, her mother had doted on her. She'd liked school but not sports; there had been enough money but not loads; her dad was firm but fair; her brothers teased her but not too badly.

As with everyone, I'd asked Ella to relate happy and unhappy memories from her childhood. There were lots of happy stories—when she'd been snuggled up in bed, recovering from the chicken pox, being fed flat Seven-Up by her mum; a Christmas Eve when it snowed; the whole family going to London for her tenth birthday.

Yes, yes, lovely. I was impatient to hear the less happy stuff. Always far more telling. Finally we got there—the unhappiest time had been in her last year in primary school. 'Over the summer, my periods had started and—' She flicked a look at the men in the room and hesitated. 'And my chest had got . . .' She stopped and began again. 'I'd started wearing a bra. My three friends wouldn't hang out with me any more. They said I was showing off—'

'That's hard,' I interrupted. 'How did you cope?'

'I, ah . . .' Tears started to spill down her face. Shocked, she wiped them away. 'God, I wasn't expecting this . . . I just got through it. But I had to do everything on my own, get the bus by myself, eat my lunch . . . I never had a . . . an ally, I guess is the word. I never got used to it. It was a long year.'

'You didn't make new friends?'

She shook her head. 'My ex-friends were bitching about me, saying they could smell period from me. Everyone kept away.'

'*Jez*. . .' Dennis looked faint.

'What about afterwards?' I asked.

'When we started secondary school, everything was different anyway. Maybe everyone had caught up? A friend of my mum's had a daughter in my class and we started hanging out. After a while things just got more normal.'

'Did your ex-friends ever apologize?'

'No.'

I'd picked up her hesitation. 'But?'

'One of them, we ended up being friends again, sort of. Like, there were five or six of us, hanging around together. She and I, we never talked about that year. I sort of . . . hated myself for not having it out with her. But at the time it was just easier to go along with things.'

'Are you in touch now?'

'Instagram. And only because I'm hoping something really, really shitty happens to her.' She giggled, then stopped abruptly and scanned the faces in the room, wondering if she was being judged.

'Did you learn anything from that year?' I asked Ella. 'Good or bad?'

She thought about it. '. . . Feeling safe isn't real. It can be taken away with no warning. It doesn't take much for a person to end up totally alone.'

She read on and it was all pretty tame: good results at school, a year spent travelling in Asia followed by three years in college. She moved to Dublin, got good jobs, met her boyfriend and her friend Naaz. Until the mugging which had set her on the path to addiction, her life had been close to perfect.

'Your doctor told you that sleeping tablets must not be taken for longer than two weeks?' I asked. (But I already knew. I rarely asked a question to which I didn't already know the answer.)

'But I was badly messed up after being . . .' She dropped her head and whispered, 'Attacked. I kept having flashbacks.'

'Did you go for counselling?'

'. . . Um . . . well, no. Counselling is expensive. And getting time off work to go, you know . . .'

'Well, if you're sacked—and you will be if you don't get a handle on your addiction—you'll have plenty of time.'

She looked devastated—then rallied. 'I've been off them for ten days now, I *can't* be addicted.'

Internally, I sighed. Every patient I'd ever met gave me some version of that. 'Easy to be clean while you're in here, Ella. Your every movement is monitored. It's very different in the outside world, where you've stresses and pressures—and choices.'

'But if I was addicted, wouldn't I be craving them?'

Another internal sigh. 'That word "craving" has a lot to answer for.' People think that addicts rail around, weeping and pleading for their drug of choice. 'Addiction isn't just a physical thing, it's emotional, it's mental, it's spiritual. Those are the aspects that drive almost every relapse, not a physical craving.'

She shrugged, not interested.

'Tell me why Jonah, Naaz and Boyd said you were addicted.'

'I think Jonah just wants to break up with me.'

'So he said you were addicted to tablets and made you go to rehab? That's a bit extreme.'

She shrugged. 'Guys.'

'And Naaz? What's her reason?'

She squirmed. 'There was a . . . moment, with her boyfriend. It was nothing. Just a . . . Seriously, it was nothing. But Naaz didn't see it that way. She's hella possessive of him.'

'And Boyd's reasons?'

Her discomfort worsened. 'Boyd . . . I think he had . . . Sorry if this sounds whatever, but I think he wanted to be with me. And when I . . . wouldn't, he decided to come after me.'

'So he sexually harassed you at work? Because that's a serious allegation.'

'No,' she gasped. 'I wouldn't say that. I just think he liked me—then he didn't.'

'Were you sleeping with Boyd?'

'No!'

'No?'

Better get him in here, get them *all* in.

While I'd been quizzing Ella, Trassa had started to cry. Giles's chair was the nearest to the tissues and fistfuls were being passed from hand to hand like buckets of water in a medieval-town-on-fire drama.

'Trassa, why are you crying?'

'Because . . . because . . . I'm a very bad person. I can't believe that I've saddled Ronan with a second mortgage and him with a young family.'

'Okaaay?'

'I did it to Keith too. And Michael, my eldest, he lent me fifteen grand to pay Collie Byrne another time and I never paid him back. It's so much money,' she gasped. 'How did I not see?'

Michael, my eldest. Something twanged in me—I'd have to come back to it.

'Did you not know how much Ronan had to borrow?' Ella asked.

'I did!' Trassa turned a tear-stained face to Ella. 'I did! But it didn't bother me. I don't know how it didn't.'

When people emerged from denial, it wasn't as if they suddenly remembered things they'd conveniently forgotten. The facts had always been there in plain sight, but the addict had managed to blur their importance. The details of Trassa's addiction were the same as they'd always been, but for the first time she was seeing them for what they actually were. She was in shock.

'I knew it was a lot of money,' she said. 'But my lads are educated, they have opportunities that I'd never had, they own their own houses. I knew they could afford it.'

'But they can't afford it,' I said. 'Ronan's had to take out a second mortgage. So has Keith.'

Her eyes pleaded with me. 'Maybe I just *decided* they could afford it?'

'Why would you do that?'

'I don't know. It must be because it suited me to? Because they were the only people who could get the money for me.'

'Why did you think they should help you?' I asked.

'Because I'm their mother! I gave birth to them and my life in that house was hard going. Never enough room and their GAA kit flung everywhere and they were always hungry, always looking for more dinners. Keith was forever sick, so I was up and down to the doctor with him and Seamus Junior was selling drugs for a while and I was afraid the guards would come to the front door and Seamus Senior was fucking useless and no one ever said thank you or offered to make me a cup of tea. There was never anything for me.'

'So, you thought that they owed you? How much of a factor did your bullying play?'

'Wh–at?' She was suddenly looking wary.

'They're frightened of you, your sons.' Well, I knew for a fact that Ronan, Joe and Seamus Junior were. Michael and Keith would have nothing to do with this. 'You knew if you told them you needed a lot of money they'd do everything they could to get it. Didn't you?'

Her tears had dried. 'They're *not* scared of me.'

'They are, but,' Chalkie murmured. 'That poor Ronan lad was bricking it.'

'And he felt fierce fecking guilty about you being in here.' Dennis was grim. In the last couple of days he'd put clear blue water between himself and Trassa, worried that addiction might be catching.

'He didn't feel guilty.' Trassa's voice was unconvinced.

'Trassa, if I may.' Giles radiated wisdom and compassion—and Chalkie rolled his eyes at him. 'There was a time when I felt exactly as you do now. I used a lethal combination of emotional blackmail and veiled threats to persuade my wives to support my addiction. I withheld money from Ingrid, said that without cocaine I couldn't do my job properly, and if I lost it, we were all penniless.'

'But you're a schemer, Mister Big Shot Moneybags and I'm just a poor old woman from Carlow. I'm nothing like you!'

30

On Saturday morning, Quin and I were dozing when my phone rang, startling us both.

'It's Kate.' The only time she rang me was during an emergency. 'Hi, honey, what's up?'

'Heyyy. Where are you?'

'Quin's.' My heart was pounding. 'What's going on? Are you okay?'

'Yeahhhh. I need your help. Well, not me.'

'Help how?' She sounded like she'd had a bang to the head.

'It's Kallie.'

'. . . *Kallie*?' Hurriedly I sat up in the bed. Beside me, Quin mouthed, *WTF?*

'She had an accident,' Kate said.

'Is she hurt?' In which case, what was I meant to do? I wasn't a doctor.

'Not that kind of accident. An accident with a . . . condom.'

It took me a moment. Oh, right. Sex. *With Luke.*

'She needs', Kate whispered the words, '*Plan B.*'

'The morning-after pill? Tell her to go to the pharmacy. Any pharmacy.' Agitated as I was, even I could see that this was elementary.

'She doesn't want them judging her.'

'They won't judge her.' Well, they might, it depended on the individual pharmacist, but it wouldn't kill her.

'She wants to see a GP.'

'No one's stopping her.' I paused. 'Or are they?'

'Luke isn't here, he's over with his dad, he's not answering his phone. She's uncomfortable asking Devin's mum, she doesn't want people knowing her business.'

'. . . But you know it. And I know it.'

'And I know it.' Quin had been listening avidly.

'She asked if I could get her an appointment with my—our—GP,' Kate said.

'But they've closed for St Patrick's Day. I guess I could ring Mum and ask her—'

This was absolute nonsense. 'Kate, she should just talk to Luke.'

'I told you, he's not picking up.'

Quin was clicking on his phone. 'How about my GP? There's a slot free at eleven forty-five. If she wants it?'

Silently, furiously, I shook my head at him.

But Kate had overheard. 'What's Quin saying?'

I didn't reply.

'Rachel . . . ?' Kate pressed.

Oh, for God's sake! 'He says he could get an appointment at his doctor's. At eleven forty-five.'

'Okay, great!' After a muffled consultation with another person—Kallie, I presumed?—Kate came back. 'Book it. Where should we go?'

'Tell them to come here,' Quin said. 'The appointment's for me, I'll have to go with her.'

As soon as I hung up, I turned to him. 'What the actual *fuck*?' This was the strangest thing. Did *Luke* know? He absolutely didn't, I decided. There were several hundred people he'd prefer his partner to ask for help before me.

'She wants to meet you.' Quin seemed entertained. 'Guess you're not going to yoga.'

'Why?'

'You know you want a proper look at her.'

Well, yes, I *did*. But also I *didn't*. Curiosity had me in a painful grip. The woman Luke loved was coming here. For me to—allegedly—help her. However this went down, there would be a price to pay.

I'd better start getting ready. 'I'm going to jump into the shower. Is my hair okay? Do I need to wash it?'

Quin studied me. 'Maybe. Yeah. Wait, I'll come with you, I'll do it.'

Having Quin in the shower with me usually led to a lot more than hair-washing. 'Hon, maybe not right now. I feel too . . .'

'Uh . . . Sure.' He was disappointed. But he'd live.

It was frustrating—*extremely*—not having access to my full range of clothes and make-up. Instead, I had to attempt a natural, hey-I-just-woke-up-like-this look with the random bits and pieces that had accumulated at Quin's.

'Ah fuck it!' I'd turned out my handbag and five lipsticks were lined up on the edge of the basin, every one of them wrong. 'My favourite neutral isn't here. Maybe I could ask Liberty? See if she has something . . . ?'

'Yeah, if you want to summon the Antichrist.'

True. If Liberty got woken early, she could burn down the world.

'Why does this matter?' Quin asked.

'Because!' I was exasperated. 'It *does*.'

I was applying a third coat of mascara when the clap of car doors shutting sounded down in the street. I hurried to the bedroom window to see that Kate, Kallie—and *Devin*—had arrived.

'Quin, they're here,' I hissed. 'How do I look?'

'Beautiful.' He grabbed me. 'You are beautiful. Remember that.'

Leaning side-on at the window, hoping to not be spotted, I spied on Kallie. She was slender and taller than I'd remembered. Her fair hair was shoulder-length and choppy with a heavy fringe. There was a vaguely Isabel Marant look to her clothes—clean-washed skinny jeans, slouchy pixie boots, a loose, gypsy-style top and an oversized jacket that seemed familiar. Then I realized it was Kate's. And before that, it had been mine.

Except it hadn't been oversized on me.

Down we went, Quin yanked the door wide open and there was a flurry of 'Hi! Heyyyy! Nice to meet you, so you found us, hahaha. Er . . .'

Kallie made directly for me. She slid her smooth hand into mine. 'So,' she twinkled, fine lines radiating from the edges of her blue eyes. 'This isn't awkward at all.'

Immediately my heart softened. She could, I understood, actually be for real. She might be in a genuine panic, trapped with her boyfriend's family in a foreign country, needing something as time critical as the morning-after pill.

'It doesn't have to be awkward,' I stammered, desperate to put her at ease. 'We can just decide that it isn't.'

'Okay!' Still holding my hand, she said, 'It's so good to meet you. Thank you for helping me.'

So this is who Luke loves now.

Quin was already discussing directions with Devin. 'Mens.' Kate rolled her eyes at them.

'How about we all jump in the one car,' Kallie said.

'Nah.' Quin was cool. 'Two is better.'

'Why?' I asked when we were in his car, leading the way.

'Because we don't want to be stuck with them after she sees the doctor.'

'That seems a little . . . harsh. So. What do you think of her?'

'Rock chick meets primary school teacher.'

'Not her look. I mean, she seems really . . . *likeable*?'

'Are you asking me? Because what I see is a lot of drama.'

'Maybe she's just really private?'

'Look at us.' He laughed. 'A two-car convoy of five people. That's not very private.'

'Ah, you're just being . . .' There was no point saying anything further to him. Anyway, I knew what I meant.

At the clinic, Quin, Kallie and I piled into the empty waiting room. Kate and Devin decided to wait outside and be *young*.

'So this is embarrassing,' Kallie murmured to me. 'Not the sort of thing that a thirty-eight-year-old woman should be dealing with.'

'No, no, no.' I rushed to reassure her. 'Accidents happen.' *So she's only thirty-eight? That's a little younger than I'd have preferred.*

'It tore,' she murmured, leaning in to me. 'The condom.'

'It happens!' I said gaily. 'Life is messy.' *Don't make me think about Luke and condoms.*

She turned her attention to Quin. 'So?' She was upbeat. 'What line of work are you in, mister?'

'I'd rather talk about you.' He sounded jovial. 'What line of work are *you* in?'

Quin was being a teeny-weeny bit of a dick, but no one except me would have known.

'Singer-songwriter,' she said.

What? Oh my God, that's so cool.

'Yeah?' Quin enquired. 'Would I have heard of you?'

'Kallie Lampart? No.' She laughed. 'Didn't think so.'

'What kind of stuff do you do?'

'Cheating men, heartbreak.' She elbowed me. '*You* know the kind of stuff. I've a real job too, that pays the bills. I'm a CPA. Like Luke.'

She'd said his name, she'd just thrown it out there. Although my breath caught at the back of my throat, the world didn't end.

'It's how we met,' she said. 'He hired me for a project.'

'And you still work together?' My voice sounded impressively normal.

She shook her head. 'I freelance around my music. Besides, not a good idea for your boyfriend to be your boss.'

'Kallie Lampart?' A man called. 'Hi, I'm Dr Benson.'

Off she went and she was back in no time, eyes lowered, a prescription in her hand. 'I'll just do the paperwork and then we can scoot.'

Scoot. Okay. I got back to my phone. But after too much time had passed, she was still at the desk. There seemed to be an *atmosphere*.

I got up. 'Everything okay?'

'Rachel, yeah.' She was flustered. 'They don't take my insurance here.'

'Because we're a different country.' The receptionist's tone was dry.

'And my credit card isn't good. So can I Venmo you guys?'

'Venmo?' Once again the receptionist was bone-dry. 'No.'

'I have no other way to pay. I guess I didn't think I'd have to.'

'I've got it.' Quin stepped in.

'Oh my gosh, you lifesaver!'

He wasn't really, he'd just got bored.

'So now I need to find a drugstore,' Kallie said.

'One just over there.' Quin nodded his head across the street.

'Then can I take you guys for coffee to thank you?'

Quin shot a look in my direction and whatever he saw made him say, 'That's sweet of you, Kallie, but we have plans.'

'Sure!' She flushed slightly. 'Of course! Thank you for your help.'

After a hesitation that I found charming, she launched herself at me in a hug. 'Rachel, it was so good to meet you.'

I wrapped my arms around her narrow back, smelling the eucalyptus-scent of her shampoo, and I felt a bittersweet type of happiness. The weight of what I'd lost and the warmth of healing were both present. In those first weeks and months after Luke had left me, I had thought I'd never get over him, but look at this, I marvelled. Look at me hugging the woman that he loved now.

As soon as we were in the car, Quin said, 'So. *That* was weird *af*.'

'Quin, trust me, no. I see it differently now. You're not a woman, you don't know what it's like to be judged.'

'But after all that she had to go to a pharmacist anyway. Rach, she was checking you out. And marking her territory. Letting you know she's having wild, condom-tearing sex with your ex-husband.'

'I . . . I'm not sure it's that. I think she was genuinely panicking.'

'Hoh-ho, *no*! You watch. Next she'll suggest double-dating.'

God, what a thought. Progress had been made but no way would I be able for that. All the same . . . 'Isn't it better to be on good terms? Why did you say no to coffee with her?'

'Because you've had a very tough week.'

As soon as he said it, a wave of weariness hit. 'I wanted to get my seedlings in the ground today but . . .'

'And you don't want them to become "root-bound",' he said, making me smile.

In our early days, I'd turned down a date with him for that very reason. 'We'll do them tomorrow,' he said. 'I'll help.'

But my little bits of gardening, I liked to do alone. My hands in the soil, gently transferring sprouted seedlings into my flower beds, helping living things to grow from almost nothing, did something good for me.

Quin had no real interest in my amateur efforts, so it was touching that he'd offered to help. But I'd see if I could leave work early on Monday and get it done while it was still light.

'You think you're able for BanDearg tonight?' Quin asked.

God, I'd completely forgotten. It had taken Quin *months* of logging into BanDearg's system at 7 a.m. every Friday morning to finally score a reservation. He was out of his mind with excitement. *And* we were going with Claire and Adam—there were too many people to let down here. 'It's hours away. I'll be fine by then.'

'Breathable Bread?' Adam read from the menu. 'What do you think that is?'

'I'd say we're about to find out.' Quin nodded at the waiter, who was making his way through the black-walled gloom of the restaurant bearing four tiny plates. Something about the manner in which he had materialized from the shadows reminded me of the reveal in *Stars in Their Eyes*.

'Indeed.' The young man smiled proudly at his plates, each topped with a mini glass dome containing white smoke. 'Instead of traditional dinner rolls, we have . . .' At this point my connection dropped out. I can only ever hear the first seven words in a lengthy food description. '. . . activated yeast, blah de blah of wheat and other codswallop. Enjoy!'

'Can't wait!' Claire said, then she placed an anxious hand on his arm. 'And, ah, the wine list . . . ?'

'Coming.'

It would be too, now that Claire had requested it. At the best of times she inspired respect and tonight she was looking particularly glossy, in a black flying suit with exaggerated space-age shoulders. Okay, the shoulders were ludicrous, but she pulled them off—and I'd have *loved* her hair. However, I simply couldn't master that chic, loose, falling-down thing no matter how often I tried.

'One, two, three . . . go!' Quin said. We lifted our domes and inhaled the tendrils of white smoke.

'Just like freshly baked bread,' Adam said. 'This place is awesome.'

'I know, right!' Quin was in great form. Getting a table here had been a personal crusade because he insisted he was the only person in Ireland who hadn't yet been.

When the smoke dispersed, nothing at all remained on the plates. Adam looked dismayed, then glommed onto me because he knew that Quin and Claire would mock him.

'Sorry to be a Basic,' he said. 'But there will be actual food at some stage tonight?'

That made me laugh. I was very fond of Adam. He was a bit Mr Expense Account and faaaar from his comfort zone here, but he was so game, always.

'You will definitely get fed.' I'd done my research. 'Although I'm not sure there's any pork belly here.'

'Is it tragic to like pork belly?'

'Pathetic,' Claire said at the same time as I said, 'No.'

The arrival of the wine list changed everything—suddenly the three of them had their heads together, the mood serious. I tuned out as the discussion raged about what wine would go best with Death by Parsley or Three-D Printed Quail.

'For you,' the drinks waiter said to me, 'we can do alcohol-free tinctures and infusions, specially created to complement each course. Start you off with a charcoal lemonade?'

'Sure!' I mean, why not? BanDearg was *totally* one of those places—mildly ridiculous but lots of fun. Granted I'd need four slices of toast when I got home but so what.

'Did you hear about today?' Quin asked Claire and Adam, then launched into the story about Kallie.

Gripped and wide-eyed, they listened *hard*.

'What do you think?' Quin finished. 'She just checking Rachel out?'

'Sounds like it,' Adam said. 'How many times did she mention the burst condom?'

'Once,' I said.

'Felt like lots more,' Quin said. 'Swear to God, I thought she was going to get it out of her bag and show us.'

'Quin!' I gave him a playful shove. 'You just decided you didn't like her. But she's lovely.'

'Seriously?' Claire asked.

'She's warm. *Really* warm. And lots of fun. You can tell.'

'And is she . . . ?' Claire looked at Quin. 'Hot?'

'Oh God, yeah. Not as hot as you, Claire, but yeah, hot.'

The pair of them smirked at each other. It was good that my boyfriend got on with my sister. But sometimes they annoyed me . . .

'Why is she still in Ireland?' Claire asked. 'Doesn't she have a job to go back to?'

'Her partner's mum has just died. She's being supportive.' But I'd wondered that too.

'Tell me her name.' Claire was already on Instagram, where earlier I'd done a deep dive. 'Oh my God, it's all a bit "Me and My Hot Man"!'

In fairness to Kallie, she had never actually posted the words 'Me and My Hot Man'. But in any photo with Luke, it was implied.

For example, a sidelong shot of Luke, busy at a cooker, frying pan in hand, a tea towel hanging from his jeans pocket, was captioned "Nothing tastes as good as . . . what I get from this guy". Followed by salivating emojis, winking emojis, then several hearts of different colours.

Kallie was fond of emojis.

But so was I.

Apparently, it was our age.

'She goes . . . horse-riding?' Claire was scanning Kallie's grid, the many shots of her, slender and gorgeous in jeans, a plaid shirt and a cowboy hat, flanked by a horse, standing around in glaring sunlight, their shadows short on the sunbaked ground. 'Yeah, I guess it's on brand.'

Then, Claire exclaimed, 'Oh, *HAI*!' She'd found the horsey shots that featured Luke. Contrasting with Kallie, Luke was often caught unawares or was deliberately avoiding the camera. There was one really beautiful photo where the brim of his hat cast a shadow over most of his face, except for his smile.

'You didn't say Kallie's a *singer*!' Claire was doing more clicking.

This fact I found quite humiliating. A singer-songwriter who did actual gigs to paying customers was a more high-status identity than an addiction counsellor. Luke had definitely traded *up*.

'Folksy pop. Acoustic guitar.' Quin was dismissive. 'She either does covers of Doobie Brothers' ballads or her own stuff, which is all a bit "2012 Taylor Swift called, she wants her identity back".'

Earlier, I'd immersed myself in Kallie's YouTube, trying to garner clues about her relationship with Luke. But as her songs veered from angsty ballads to tender love songs, it was hard to get a *fix* on things. Her voice, though, was light and attractively mournful.

'Jesus, look at this!' Claire had found a video of floaty-frocked Kallie on a high stool with a guitar. 'Let's have a listen.' But she cast a hunted look around the temple to gastronomy. '. . . And maybe not.'

'Ahem.' A polite cough from the waiter heralded the arrival of our I Dream of Blini course and both Quin and Claire morphed into photographers, taking dozens of photos of their food, then uploading them to Insta.

Briefly, I considered copying them before deciding that I couldn't be bothered. Instagram was a pain. The only stuff I was ever enthusiastic about posting was pictures of Crunchie.

Much later, we'd just finished our Seabuckthorn Seven Ways (dehydrated, jellied, frozen, charred, puréed, stewed and 'reversed') when my phone rang. The disapproval of the entire restaurant hit me—who was the woman who let her phone ring during an intense gourmet experience?

'LUKE' flashed on my screen.

My heart almost jumped from my chest.

'Another burst condom?' Quin asked.

I got up, moving towards the door. 'Sorry, lads, I better take this.' Then, 'Hello?'

'Rachel? It's Luke.' Hearing his voice was still very strange. 'Kallie told me about today. I'm sorry you were involved.'

Was he . . . ? He was blaming me, wasn't he? Somehow it was my fault that his girlfriend had asked for my help.

'Thank you for helping her out,' he said. 'It was decent of you.'

'Is this sarcasm?'

'No. It *was* decent of you.'

'Oh. Okay.' It took a few moments for my indignation to die down. 'It's fine.'

'She shouldn't have bothered you. There were other people who could have helped her.'

Was he telling me that she *had* been checking me out? Well, whatever. We'd met and nothing terrible had happened.

'So, aaah . . . how's your dad? Any luck with finding a carer?'

'Not yet. He's being an arse, probably on purpose—'

Suddenly Quin was at my side. 'Everything okay? They're about to serve the Fermented Hay.'

I nodded at him, then spoke into the phone. 'I've to go.'

'Enjoy your . . .' Luke paused. '. . . fermented hay. And thank you. Again, not sarcasm.'

The rest of the night passed without incident, until right at the end when Claire was in the ladies, Quin was sorting the coats and, briefly, I was alone with Adam.

'Rachel.' There was something urgent in his tone. 'Have you heard about Claire and me becoming swingers?'

'Yes.' I frowned. 'But—it's only theoretical?'

'You know your sister, though. Once she gets an idea in her head . . .' He sounded utterly miserable. 'But maybe I'll enjoy it.'

'I take it you don't want to . . . ?'

He took a breath. 'No, Rachel. I'm fine as I am. I like my life. I like my wife . . .'

31

Lying face down on my bed, I groaned with pleasure. 'Who needs sex when Nick Quinlivan is massaging your sore calves.'

Behind me, Quin laughed. We'd been out in the hills, a twelve-K hike through streams and bracken, with 'our hiking friends' Taryn and Timothy.

Although at first glance you'd never have taken them for rugged outdoor types: Taryn, skinny, nerdy and frowny, looked as if a small child could snap her in two. Her partner Timothy, with his spectacles and pale, scholarly air, looked like an aristocratic boy from Victorian times who had a weak chest and was fated to die young.

The four of us had met two summers ago, during a weekend in Brigit's. (They too 'worked in IT' with Brigit's husband Colm.) When they heard that Quin and I were planning to climb Errisbeg the following day, they invited themselves along.

Privately, Quin was scandalized. 'Who are these consumptive-looking randomers? No way will they keep up!'

But Brigit had a word with Quin: Taryn and Timothy were a lot fitter than they looked. And so it proved. Heading up the mountain, they had so much speed, stamina and enthusiasm that now and again Quin had to say, 'Slow it down there, lads. Don't forget about Rachel.'

They turned out to be delightful—they were open to life, to people, to experiences—and we had gelled in the loveliest way. 'You think you're too old to make new friends,' Quin said subsequently. 'Then you surprise yourself.'

Today had been fun. Now Quin and I were back at my house. 'Do the thing with your thumbs,' I begged. 'Press them—oh God, yesss!'

'You should have a bath,' he said. '*We* should have a bath. Loosen up those muscles.'

'Not enough time.' We'd been invited to his parents for 'supper' at five o'clock. Quin didn't care if we were late but I did. 'Quick shower,' I said. As his eyes lit up, I added, 'Nothing else!'

Ma and Da Quinlivan lived in a big, solid 1950s build, surrounded by what an estate agent would call 'a large, mature, south-facing' garden. There were full-grown trees, handsome shrubs and flower beds bursting with vivid daffodils.

As a family, the Quinlivans *fascinated* me—so accomplished, so confident, so certain of their place in the world.

The front door was ajar. 'Who goes there?' a woman's voice floated down the hall. Then, 'Nicholas! Rachel! Welcome!'

Quin's mum Genevieve—known as Vivi—breezed towards us, her Hermès scarf fluttering. Blonde, bony and capable, she'd been a high court judge until her retirement five years ago.

Kissing us briskly, she relieved us of our coats and directed us towards the kitchen for drinks. 'Daddy's down there, making some concoction.'

'First-born!' Quin's dad, Roly, set down the jug in his hand. He was delighted to see Quin—or Nicholas, as they called him. 'I'm making Dutch negronis! We drank them in Amsterdam, your mother liked them.'

Big and beardy, Roly was a nice enough man. Well-intentioned, if nothing else. The problem was that he'd been a constitutional lawyer, much renowned. His professional life had been spent advising the government of the day and generally being treated as an oracle. For the past few years, he'd been just a regular citizen but he still thought he knew everything.

It made for awkward games of Trivial Pursuit.

From the hall, Vivi called, 'Robert and Ava *sont arrivés.*'

Robert—a younger, quieter version of Quin—had a neat, pretty wife and three clean, obedient children. He worked as a commercial lawyer.

As did Quin's sister Michelle. The youngest of the siblings, Michelle looked like Roly rather than Vivi. Her scaffolding was robust and her face was large and square. But instead of raging that her mother's skeletal, high-cheekboned genes had passed her by, she was a buoyant, assured woman, living her best life. She'd made partner in a big, shiny law firm at the tender age of thirty-one, their youngest ever. Her husband, a red-haired charmer called Barry, was also a lawyer and their two kids were cute and hilarious. (Unlike Robert and Ava's, who were whispery and timid.)

Because Quin didn't work in the law *and* because his marriage had broken up, he was regarded as the family rebel—which they insisted they were proud of. 'Nicholas marches to the beat of his own drum. Struck out by himself and made his own path. That takes character.'

Graciously, they presented their own stellar careers and harmonious marriages as a little dull and predictable.

'Sit, Rachel, sit, please!' Vivi wafting past, in a discreet breath of Coty Chypre, directed me to the dining table. 'Wherever you please. No *placement* today as we're just family.'

'Jesus.' Quin shook his head. 'The Barbarians are at the gate.'

'Cheeky.' Vivi's eyes flicked from my glass to the smaller jug of juice on the worktop, checking that 'Daddy' had done things right. The Quinlivans would never be crass enough to make a drama of me being a non-drinker. Instead, they always had something special prepared—today it was fresh pineapple juice, laced with ginger—which they served without comment.

'Boys, come with me.' Vivi commandeered Robert's children and had them carry quiches and bowls of salad into the dining room. 'And genuine Dutch *stroopwafels* for dessert!' She smacked away Michelle's rambunctious children. '*No*, thank you, girls. We can quite do without your help. Everyone! *À table*!'

'So?' Michelle took a sip of her Dutch negroni and asked, 'How was Amsterdam, Mum?'

The senior Quinlivans observed (what seemed to me) a punishing schedule of cultural events. They were forever off to the Wexford Opera Festival or Oberammergau or a Mozart recital in a deconsecrated church. They followed rugby, they were tennis fans, chess was a particular passion and they were freshly returned from Amsterdam, where they'd spent four days immersed in the Old Masters.

'It was honestly bliss,' Vivi said, backed up by Roly. 'Although my favourite Bloemaert was away for restoration. But on our last day we visited the Moco.'

'Oh-oh!' Michelle made a disappointed face. 'Emperor's new art.'

Vivi nodded sadly. 'What a shame.'

My eyes stayed fixed on my plate. I'd loved the Moco when I had gone a few years back, but best to keep that to myself around here.

'What is it, Rachel?' Sharp-eyed Vivi had noticed. 'You disagree?'

I looked up and grinned. 'I'm saying nothing.'

'But do!' Michelle urged.

Not a chance. I'd have loved to say, 'I like it, you don't, let's leave it at that.' But a dissenting opinion at the Quinlivan dinner table led directly to a debate—they adored that lark, me 'defending' my position while being *savaged* by a hail of philosophical questions: 'But what is it *saying*?' 'Will it have merit in two hundred years' time?'

For them, it was a simple intellectual exercise but one they really did like to win. To me, though, 'debating' felt too similar to confrontation. I just wanted to get in, eat my *stroopwafel* and get out again. Alive, preferably.

Quin's family were really nice people, not a bitchy bone between them. Their confidence was the problem. They were so sure of who they were that they expected the world to reshape itself around them. Whereas I—being like everyone else—was in a constant process of recalibration, trying to negotiate emotional harmony with every new person I met.

Meeting Quin's family had explained so much to me: until Shiv had fallen out of love with him, life had always delivered exactly what he wanted—a great job, healthy kids and a tight circle of friends, many from his days in junior school. Shiv's departure had humbled him. Slightly. Like, you could never call him meek or self-effacing. But I was certain that if I'd met him in the Before Times, I'd have found him *far* too obnoxious.

32

'. . . So there's this hotel in the desert, it used to be a French Foreign Legion fort and—' While we were waiting for *Line of Duty* to come on at 9 p.m., Quin was at one of his favourite pastimes: researching amazing holidays. This time, Morocco was in the spotlight.

While any sensible person yearned for a gorgeous riad, replete with fountains and lush gardens, in the centre of Marrakech, Quin had to be awkward.

I'd often told him that his perfect holiday location would be an enclave nestled between seven competing warlords, boasting Michelin-starred street food and a Zegna store operating from a crashed Boeing 747.

'French Foreign Legion?' I asked. 'Don't tell me. One of the "Local Attractions" would be the chance to undergo some light torture?'

'Haha.' He liked that. 'It doesn't mention it, but who knows. So Danny, this guy I met in Taos, said they mix it up a little. Take you out into the desert and leave you there.'

'I'm not . . . *loving* this, Quin.'

'We'd be in a luxury tent, obvs, but they mess with your sense of safety. No phones, no roads, no other people. Danny says we'll experience real fear that we've been abandoned. The guys from the hotel are back at base camp, getting stoned out of their heads and won't fetch us until they're able.'

'Quiiiiiiiin . . .'

'So, on our third day, just when we're freaking out about having no water left, that's when I'll ask you to marry me.'

I laughed. Quin's grandiose proposal fantasies—touching lightly on the truth that we were both wary—was a running joke.

'And the moment I accept, the Toyota flatbed truck from the hotel will appear over the top of the sand dune, where it's been hiding all along. Great!'

My phone lit up—Luke, again! What the hell? These days he was ringing me more often than when we were married.

I snatched it up and answered with a snippy, 'Yes?'

'Rachel? Look, just say no, but I said I'd ask.'

'What?'

'Kallie says maybe we should get together, the four of us, you and your partner, me and her. Go for a pizza or something.'

No fucking *way*. Quin had predicted this—and I hadn't believed him.

'I . . . Look . . . I don't know.'

Anxiously, I looked at Quin who was mouthing *What?*

Say yes.

My head was racing through all the permutations. But I didn't have to do anything I didn't want to do—and I didn't want to do this. 'I don't think so.'

'That's fine. Cool. I said I'd ask. So I've . . . asked.'

'You totally did.' My tone was sarcastic-cheery. 'Consider me *asked*. Okay, *see* ya!'

I was suddenly in a terrible mood but it took a while to narrow it down to *offended*. Yes, I was *offended* by the presumption implicit in his suggestion that I had forgiven him. Did he really think it would be that easy? Like, without any apology or explanation? Because—why? Because six years had passed and there was a statute of limitations on Shitty Things Done by Ex-Husbands?

It didn't work like that.

'What's going on?' Quin asked.

'It was Luke. He wants us to go on a double date, just like you predicted.'

'Damn, I'm good! So what do you—'

'I need to talk to Nola. Sorry.'

As I left the room, Nola's phone already ringing, Quin called after me, 'There were three of us in that marriage!'

'Nola?' I said. 'Let me tell you what's just . . .'

When she was all caught up, I said, 'The last time I saw Luke I was crying in the street and begging him to stay. Like, *begging*, Nola. And he thinks I'm just going to forget everything and go for a friendly thin-crust with him and his new lady love.'

'Hot coal,' she said.

'No!'

'Holding onto your anger is like holding a hot coal in your hand.'

'I am not meeting up with Luke and his lady love.'

'Why are you calling her that? You like her!'

'I . . . don't know. Look. Even if I got through the dinner without crying, I'd be in pieces afterwards. Anyway, I've got as much healing as I'm ever going to get. I can live with the rest.'

'For the past few years I've been telling you to Golden Key the Luke question. The universe would untangle things when the time was right—*if* it was meant to be. He's here, he's willing to see you, this is an opportunity you'd be a fool to turn down.'

Nola was very wise and well intentioned. But I knew myself better than anyone—my limits, my weak spots. 'It took me a long time but I've found a way to live happily again. That's precious.'

'But you're stuck.' She sounded serious, almost angry. 'You need to sort this shit out.' Nola was always misleadingly blithe, full of sing-song suggestions rather than stern orders. This was the most forceful I'd heard her in a long time.

'Quin's never going to go for it.'

'Try him.'

'How solid are we?' Quin asked.

'Hundred per cent.'

'Okay. Then I wouldn't mind meeting him.'

'Seriously?' I was dismayed. 'But you don't like Kallie.'

'I don't *trust* her, that's different. And I'm . . .' He spread his hands. 'I want to know what he's like. Just need to check that I'm more built and better-looking than him.'

'You are.' Objectively speaking, Luke was good-looking but Quin's cast-iron confidence was very sexy. And, unlike Luke, Quin was lovely to me.

'Ah yeah, I know that.' Quin grinned. 'Look, I'm curious about him. What's the harm in meeting up?'

I heaved out a sigh. 'Your competitiveness has a lot to answer for.'

'How do you feel about it?'

'I can't think of anything more awful. *And* I want to go. Which doesn't make sense, but that's how it is.'

'So we'll do it. Call him back.'

When Luke answered, I blurted, 'Tell Kallie we'll have dinner with you.'

'Oh. Sure. When?'

'Tuesday evening.' Then I said, 'It's going to be exhausting.'

After a silence, he said, 'Likely. But probably still worth doing.'

'Have you been talking to Nola? No, never mind, nothing. Okay, where should we go?'

'How was the fermented hay place?'

That was typical Luke—no clue about how hard it would be to get in there.

'Forget I said that,' he added. 'I don't want to eat fermented hay.'

'It was delicious.' Actually, it hadn't been bad. 'You can see pictures of it on Quin's Insta.'

'Doesn't matter.'

That was one of the things I'd forgotten—Luke wasn't very adventurous.

'I'll book a place and text you,' I said. 'Any dietary requirements?'

'None.'

'You're not a vegetarian?'

'Not any more.' Was there a smirk in his tone?

'Fine.' I hung up and yelled, '*Well, fuck you!*'

Quin was good at restaurants. 'Not too cheap but not too showy,' I told him. 'No tasting-menu bullshit and plenty of bland food.'

'"Bland food"? No way, Rach.'

'Just do it!'

'Okay, don't take my head off. Can I just ask . . . ? How about Peruvian?'

'No.'

'Schezwan?'

'No. Quin, seriously. No! Okay, what about Jake's Place? They bring extra potatoes and vegetables with the main course, that's the sort of thing he likes.'

Quin blinked. 'Wow. That's—'

'—I know. But that's who he is. Or was . . .'

'The tables are very close together in Jake's Place—you sure about this?'

'Definitely. They're always quick there, wanting to get you out to ship another crowd in. Quick works for me.'

When the table was booked, Quin began vacillating between angst about Luke's good looks and strutting around, making muttery threats about 'putting some hurting' on him.

'Should I feed you across the table?' he asked.

'Do.'

At least we were able to have a laugh about it.

33

Dennis's wife Juliet was a surprise—high heels, expensive handbag, alluring perfume, excellent blazer. Her look was modern, very cool. I was wondering who she reminded me of and I realized it was—of all people!—*Claire*.

Okay, she wasn't as fashion forward as my eldest sister but she wasn't the downtrodden woman with red-raw hands I'd expected. The mistake was on me—Dennis was such a charmer it should be no surprise that his wife was a prestige version.

As for their seventeen-year-old daughter Joya, she was *fabulous*. Long lavender hair with two tight angel horns. Fabulously baggy jeans, a graffitied hoody, a neon-pink neck-purse and car-tyre sandals, worn with stripey socks.

Abigail, the elder daughter, hadn't come. But getting Juliet and Joya counted as a win. And because there was no way I was chancing a rerun of Patch's visit, I'd coached them until we were all blue in the face.

When Juliet and Joya followed me into the Abbot's Quarter, everyone looked startled at the onslaught of glamour. The high heels, the lipstick and the hair—these weren't things they saw much of these days.

Dennis stumbled to his feet. 'Joya—' he stuttered, moving towards her.

'Dad, no.' She gave him the hand. 'Don't touch me.'

You could almost taste the shock in the room—*this* fabulous creature was Dennis's daughter? *This* stylish, yoga-toned woman was his wife?

Juliet and Joya weren't even settled in their chairs when Dennis started, 'Before anyone says anything, can I—'

'No, Dennis, you can't.'

'What about my side of the story?'

'You've been here two weeks. We already know your side.'

'But how will—'

'Please stop talking. Start listening.'

I began with Joya, who was twisting her body into a pretzel of reluctance. 'I don't want to be here,' she murmured.

'Shur, g'wan away home!' Dennis exclaimed. 'No harm, no foul. Good girl, off you go.' He half stood, wrenching a fat roll of soiled-looking fifties from his hip pocket. 'Let me just give you some—'

'Stop,' I said. 'Joya is staying. Sit back down and put that money away.'

When everyone had settled, I asked, 'Joya, what kind of father is Dennis?'

'It depends.' Her voice was hesitant. 'On which version of him you get.'

'What does that mean?' Dennis sounded wounded.

'Like, he can be in great form. On those days you can ask him for *anything* and he'll say yes. On the bad days he yells a lot. Yells at Mum.'

'About what?'

'Stuff like, one of his constituents, her washing machine broke, so he said Mum would do it. But he didn't *ask* Mum, just came home with two bags of other people's laundry. Mum told him to do it himself but he said that it wasn't his job.'

'So who did it?'

She shrugged. 'Dunno. But not him, I bet. But that wasn't out of the ordinary, he's always making promises. Then breaking them. Like, a while ago, he gave Abigail and me each a credit card, with a limit of four hundred euro. He said we could buy whatever we wanted and he'd pay it off every month. But that never happened, not even once.'

'Money, money, money, that's all ye ever want!' Dennis exploded.

'We never asked for those cards,' Joya exclaimed. 'You gave them to us and of *course* we were psyched, don't be cross with us for that. Then we found out it was bullshit. *More* bullshit.'

'Can you tell Dennis what you've noticed about his drinking.'

Nervously, she said, 'Sometimes we don't see you for days, Dad. Then I get up to go to school and you're lying on your face outside the house, passed out drunk. Always, the first thing I think is that he's dead. It really scares me.'

Dennis looked stricken.

'You're never not drunk.' Joya's chin wobbled. 'But the worst was I was out in town with my friends and we saw your car. A lady was driving, you were in the passenger seat and you looked *lit*. My friends . . . they were laughing. It was so embarrassing. I said you were giving the lady a driving lesson, that was why you weren't driving. They didn't believe me, but they said nothing because they felt so bad for me.' She looked him in the eye. 'I was ashamed of you, Dad. I wished I had a different dad. I'm sorry, Dad,' she squeaked, and began to sob.

I asked her if she'd like to leave and she shook her head, so I turned to Juliet.

'You've been married twenty-two years? When did you realize he was an alcoholic?'

'He was always a drinker,' she admitted. 'But in the early days he was great fun. In later years, even when he'd get very drunk and make a show of us all, he could talk his way out of it—he could sell sawdust to lumber mills. But maybe about five years ago, it changed.'

'How?'

'He'd always been Dr Jekyll and Mr Hyde. The outside world got the chat and the jokes, but at home he had a terrible temper on him.'

'I never laid a finger on you!' Dennis declared.

'You didn't have to,' Juliet said.

'Dennis has told us . . .' I referred to my notes. '"My wife is never satisfied. She's always asking for things."'

'I have a job,' Juliet said. 'I earn my own money. I never ask him for anything. Not any more.'

'But', Dennis blustered, 'you're always whinging about wanting things done in the house.'

'Like what?' Juliet asked. 'Like? What?'

'Well, why wouldn't you do Mrs Fallon's laundry? You told *me* to do it.'

'In the end, who *did* do Mrs Fallon's laundry?' Juliet's eyes were narrowed and Dennis squirmed. Addressing me, Juliet said, 'He's a terrible husband and a terrible father—there are no boundaries or discipline, except for when he loses his temper. And he doesn't come home at least three nights out of every seven.'

'What is your wish for Dennis?' I asked.

'I don't want him drinking himself to death on my watch.'

'That won't happen!'

'Tell your daughters,' Juliet said. 'They're the ones who love you. I don't care any more. I'm ready to divorce you.'

'Wait now!' Dennis was the colour of parchment.

'You don't want Juliet to divorce you?' I asked him.

'I do not! She's my wife!'

'You love her?'

'With my life!'

To Juliet, I said, 'Do you know where he is on those nights he doesn't come home?'

Juliet nodded.

'I'm on Patch's couch,' Dennis said loudly.

'Where does he stay?' I prompted Juliet.

'With the woman he was "giving driving lessons" to. Her name is Maudie Letter.'

'That woman is an absolute lunatic! I helped her to fill out the forms for her mother's home help and she turned into a bunny-boiler lunatic. She had me pestered.'

'A bunny-boiler lunatic?' I repeated back to him and waited for him to nod. Then I got to my feet and opened the door. Standing outside were Murdo and a blonde-haired woman, whom I invited into the room.

Maudie belied her homely name; she had a very cute Reese Witherspoon look about her.

Dennis was dumbfounded. When he could speak, he looked at me and yelled, 'Rachel! Why did you bring them in on the same day?'

'You think this is a coincidence?' Juliet said. 'The three of us came in the car together, we're going to Harvey Nichols in Dundrum after this. By the way.' She took Maudie's left hand and demonstrated it to the room. 'Congratulations are in order. Dennis is engaged!'

As soon as they were gone, Dennis began to wail, 'She's making it up. They're all making it up.'

'Ah, you're grand,' Chalkie patted him. 'Come for a cup of tea.'

'Tea,' Giles said. 'And biscuits.'

'But she's ruined my good name!'

'I know, I know . . .'

As soon as they got Dennis back into group, they'd hit him with the truth, but for the moment they were his friends, his comrades, they understood his shame and fear and all they wanted to do was mind him.

. . . with the exception of Ella, who, right now, was watching him with contempt.

34

After lunch, when I led Chalkie's partner Skye into group, Ella had to suppress a squeak of distress—because Skye was gorgeous: a mixed-race beauty oozing charm and intelligence.

Bronte, by contrast, barely blinked, just let her eyes glance over Skye in a careless, uninterested way. Very impressive. Because no matter how cool she played it, no matter how much Chalkie appeared to disapprove of her, there was a spark there, potent enough to power Dublin for a week.

This was Skye's second visit to group because I was fast running out of ideas to break Chalkie. Rixer, the young man whose bail money Chalkie had stolen, had sat in this room and detailed the ways Chalkie's theft had derailed his life. It should have been devastating, but Rixer was too fond of Chalkie to really put the boot in.

The route to breaking an addict's denial was usually via the testimony of a person they loved. Chalkie cared about dozens of people—most of them members of disadvantaged communities—but from what I could see, there were only three people he actually loved: Skye and his two children.

'Chalkie,' Skye was saying. 'If you relapse, you'll die. I don't think you're getting that.'

My fear was that Chalkie *was* getting it and didn't care.

'Up to now, you've been lucky,' she said. 'Every time you've relapsed, you've survived. But one day you won't come back.'

'Ah, Skye . . . Baby, don't cry. I'm not worth it.'

'This is what I mean!' she declared. 'You put no value on yourself! But so many people love you.'

'Chalkie,' I said. 'Is there anything you're consciously aware of that's holding you back?'

He sighed. 'The God thing. I can't do it.'

'You don't have to.'

'Ah, don't gimme that! I've been to NA meetings, they're always going on about God. You know my feelings on religion.'

Well, I sensed I was about to find out . . .

'"Religion was invented when the first conman met the first fool." So said Mark Twain. Listen, I want to stay away from heroin, but don't insult my intelligence and ask me to believe in God.'

I knew how he felt. For a long time, I thought only stupid people believed in all of that.

Twenty years earlier, Nola had told me, 'It doesn't have to be the hairy oul' know-all in the sky, but you need *something*. If a normal person has a disaster, they can cope with their feelings. But the likes of you and me? We're not able. So we need to involve something else, bigger and better than us. Even if it's imaginary.'

To Chalkie, I said, 'The god they talk about in meetings has nothing to do with organized religion. Is it the word "god" that's too much? Could you use "higher power" instead?'

'It's the concept, missus! Why does there have to be anything at all?'

'Because addicts are egomaniacs. They tend to become their own gods. But your higher power can be anything, Chalkie. Anything other than you. Pretend, Chalkie. Fake it till you make it.'

'*Why?*'

'Because recovery is easier when you accept that you don't control everything. In fact, *life* is easier if you live it that way.'

Despite my own initial resistance, a cloudy, amorphous almost-belief had eventually settled, when I noticed that, no matter what was going on for me, I always felt better after an NA meeting. Even when I hadn't wanted to go. Even when several of the people there annoyed me. Somehow, by the time the last person had finished sharing, I could appreciate how our collective spirit created something greater and better than the sum of our individual energies.

If ever I tried to analyse the magic, it fell apart immediately. But eventually I could connect with that feeling even when I wasn't at a meeting.

Who knew, maybe in time Chalkie would find something?

'Think about it,' I said.

'No.' He was suddenly adamant. 'Only one person I can depend on and that's me.'

'But can you? Depend on yourself? Your own best judgement has had you using heroin for seventeen years.'

'I've stopped. I'm here.'

'Stopping is easy. Staying stopped is the hard part.'

'I'll stay stopped.'

My heart sank. *Some*thing needed to change with Chalkie, because the feelings that drove his every relapse were still stashed in some secret part of him. It wasn't his fault. Whatever, wherever they were, they were just too painful to be felt.

But without connecting with them, he'd go back out into the world, where his relapse was inevitable. And right then, I couldn't bear that thought.

As soon as group ended, I had a strong urge to call Gemma Kaye, the mother of Harlie's friend, Tegan—the young woman who'd died from alcohol poisoning. I didn't understand the urgency burning in me but suddenly it seemed imperative to persuade Gemma Kaye to visit. We'd spoken last week. She'd been reluctant but I'd sensed that if I kept pressing, she'd agree. I'd no clue what this had to do with Chalkie, but I did it anyway.

35

On my knees by the flower bed, I gently, gently, *gently* loosened the aster seedling from its pot, taking extra care with the roots, then placed it into the hole I'd dug with my beautiful new trowel. After the intensive mollycoddling the seedling had got in the warm utility room, it looked vulnerable and tiny as it set sail on the high seas of the great outdoors.

Don't worry, I instructed this little lad as I crumbled handfuls of compost around it. *Your soil is the right pH, you're in a lovely sheltered spot and you're surrounded by your pals.*

I didn't actually talk out loud to my plants but I couldn't deny that, in my head, a lively dialogue took place.

You're too big now to be eaten by the birds, I promised. *And if a late frost comes, I'll be straight out with the bubble wrap, to keep you warm. And don't worry about Crunchie, she's afraid of flowers.* Ever since she ate a bedful of daffodils and vomited for three days, but no need to go into the details.

When I'd bought my house, it had a lot in its favour—the perfect size, near to work and, handily, the right price (a low one). But it stood in a biggish patch of ground. There was *a lot* of grass, which I'd have to cut and I knew nothing about lawnmowers, about any gardening really. But thanks to what Garv had shown me, I was very interested.

So Nola took me to a garden centre and made me buy a load of 'beginners'' bulbs: snowdrops, daffodils, crocuses. Under her watchful eye, I planted them. Then, for several months, absolutely nothing happened except that the weather got very cold.

Just as I had started to wonder if this would be the year it stayed winter forever, strange white things began to push up from the frozen soil. My snowdrops!

'But how?' I asked Nola. 'They're such tiny delicate things.'

'Delicate?' she asked. 'Them? They've petals like *blades*. It's how they shove their way out of the dark into the light. Oh, they might look fragile, but they're well able to survive.'

I'd frowned. 'Are you metaphoring me?'

'So what if I am?'

Not long afterwards, the crocuses appeared, pretty and startlingly vivid, then the daffodils, in their exuberant bursts of yellows. Everywhere were fresh shoots of green, shocking against the January pallor—and I was 'in'. A gardener. On-board for wherever it took me.

My hands in the soil, helping living things to grow from almost nothing, did something good for me. Working in silence and solitude, caught up in concentration and care, was the closest thing to meditation I'd found. I could lose hours to it.

When, inevitably, flowers died off, I felt it deeply, but after the first couple of years, acceptance crept in. Everything had its moment, its time to be alive, and then it stepped aside to make room for fresh life.

'Hey!' Claire, followed by Kate, had come into the garden. 'Rachel. C'mon!'

'C'mon, what?'

'Dresses,' Kate said. 'For Granny's party. Mum's ordered lots for me to try on.'

Immediately I abandoned my tools. Following the pair of them up the stairs to Kate's bedroom, I said, 'I can't hang around too long, I'm going to a meeting.'

'Good woman . . .' Claire was never interested in that part of my life.

I stopped dead at the sight of several cardboard boxes on Kate's floor. 'Claire . . . Did you order *all* of Net-a-Porter?'

'Nearly. Okay, let's go!' Gleefully, Claire produced a high-necked, sequined mini-dress and swung it at Kate. 'Try that. With these . . .' She rummaged through one of the bigger parcels, emerging with a shoebox. '. . . flatforms!'

Kate complied, then stood before the mirror. I was biased and I knew it but with her long legs, shiny hair and clear, fresh skin, she was gorgeous.

'I don't think so,' she decided.

'You're wrong!' I exclaimed.

'It's too . . .' She shrugged. 'Shiny? I'm not a sequins person.'

'Try it with these sneakers.' Claire produced another shoebox.

'Better,' Kate concluded, once she'd put them on. 'But still not me.'

'No worries.' Claire was undaunted. 'Try this.'

'This' was a corset dress in pale pink. 'Burberry,' Claire said.

But once she was zipped into it, Kate shook her head, 'It looks . . . medicinal.'

'Then take it off.'

I had to hand it to Claire. There were no attempts to persuade Kate to change her mind. She just moved on to the next option—which was a black organza cape dress.

'God almighty,' I gasped. 'That's so *beautiful.*'

And it suited Kate. Unlike the previous two dresses, this was quietly *thrilling.*

'How much is this one?' Kate asked. 'Is it a million euro?'

'Who cares!'

'Ah, Mum!'

'Listen, I've to go,' I said.

'Rachel, stay!'

But I couldn't. Tonight was a special night: Nola's anniversary. She was twenty-seven years clean.

I drove like the clappers and got there just in time.

At the end of the meeting, an elaborately decorated cake, bearing twenty-seven candles, was placed before her. After we sang Happy Birthday, she blew the candles out. It took a while.

'Lord save us!' Laughing, she put a hand on her chest. 'You need strong lungs for twenty-seven of them.'

'Twenty-seven years.' The boy beside me stared at Nola. 'That's literally unbelievable. I'm sixty-four days.'

'Sixty-four days is amazing.' I was so eager to encourage him. 'We all have to start somewhere. And for any addict to get through twenty-four hours without using is miraculous.'

His eyes lit with interest. 'Seriously?'

'Of course. When you think of how hard it was—well, if you were anything like me—to just do a single evening without taking anything, sixty-four days is a triumph.'

'How long are you . . .'

Nola had appeared at my side. She slid her hand into mine.

'Months?' The boy asked. 'Years?' Mischievously, he said, 'You're not going to tell me you're twenty-seven years as well.'

Oh. I took a breath. 'It's a long time but I don't count it that way. All that matters is today. And I'm clean today.'

'Does that mean you don't get an anniversary cake?' He seemed disappointed for me.

'Haha, no cake.'

'I want a cake.' He said it with conviction.

'Do you, pet?' Nola seemed delighted by him. Although she was that way about most people. 'You'd better keep coming and keep staying clean, so. And when you're one year, we'll get you a fabulous cake.'

36

I'd blocked off Tuesday afternoon's group to focus on Trassa. 'How are you?'
I asked her.

'I'm—' Then she clutched her stomach and sobbed for what felt like
several minutes. The hand-to-hand medieval-fire-putting-out with the tissues
started up.

'I've been remembering things,' she eventually managed. 'I pawned my
engagement ring. It had belonged to Seamus Senior's grandmother and it was
worth something. Michael found out, he was raging, he gave me the money to
buy it back but I . . . you know, spent it. That's why he won't talk to me.'

Another storm of tears began. 'It's gone now. Long gone. And I feel . . .'
She choked. 'Like my heart is broken.'

'Why?'

'Because it was beautiful. It was the only good thing I'd ever owned. And
it meant something, when Seamus put it on my finger, I was glad of it. And
I gave it . . . awaaaay.'

'Did you enjoy what you did with the money?'

Suspiciously, she watched me through watery eyes. 'What do you mean?'

'The bet you placed, you enjoyed it?' Gently, I said, 'It's not a trick question, Trassa.'

'I did.' Almost apologetically, she said, 'There's nothing in the whole
earthly world like it. When the longing comes on me, I get filled up with . . .
it feels like sparkles, shiny things. Life feels like a Christmas tree.' Even
remembering the emotion was making her smile. 'You know on a Saturday
night, when your daddy and the lads are gone drinking and it's just you and
your mam at home. She's got sweets for the two of you and you watch a film
together on the telly? That's the feeling. It makes me *happy.*'

She broke down in fresh sobs. 'I miss my mother. I miss her so much.'

Half the room had lumps in their throats or tears in their eyes, myself
included.

'Since she went,' Trassa gasped, 'since she left us, I haven't ever felt safe. She was the only person I ever felt all right with. Now I'm always on my guard.'

'What age were you when she died?'

'Thirteen.'

'And when you got married?'

'Seventeen. I went from one lot of men to another.'

'Your first child—Michael—was born when, exactly? How soon after you got married?'

After a short hesitation she said, 'Four months.'

'Trassa?' I tried to sound light. 'Is there any reason you didn't name your first son Seamus Junior?'

Every one of my cells was on high alert, desperate to read Trassa's cues. This was her gig. If she wanted, we would shut this down immediately. Or we could save it for a one-to-one. But we couldn't magic it away.

'Seamus Junior is your second son?' I asked. 'Named for your husband, Seamus Senior?'

She nodded.

Our eyes were locked in an intense exchange of trust and responsibility.

'Trassa.' My voice was almost a whisper. 'Who is Michael?'

After a long, long silence, in which the world held its breath, she said, 'My father.'

Immediately I stood and ended the session. Subdued and silent, the other six trooped out, while Trassa and I went to a private room.

'I was showing at two and a half months. I made sure everyone could see. I was walking around the town, this great . . . big . . .' Trassa stuttered out the words. '. . . cry for notice. I'm sure everyone knew—there were no secrets, there still aren't, but nothing was said.'

'While she was alive your mother protected you?'

'He terrorized her too but she did what she could. After she died, it was a free-for-all.'

'Does your husband know?'

'He never said a word. But if I gave the child my father's name, I hoped he might . . . Because he knows I hated the man. But, no. And nobody ever asked me. Not one. Until you.'

'Were there no women in your life? A teacher? Aunts? Friends?'

'My teachers were nuns. I tried telling the girls at school, but . . . it's hard to describe. It was no good because nothing could be done. Going to the guards? I'd have got the blame.

'I was a girl of seventeen, no boyfriend. I was around the town, not hiding that I was expecting, hoping that *some*one would . . . All that happened was my father and Seamus's father cooked up a scheme—Seamus Higgins, with the asthma and the weak heart, married the stupid slut in the family way. But it could have been worse,' she said. 'Seamus is decent. But sick, always sick.'

I nodded, afraid to say anything, in case I got it wrong.

'Rachel, though!' Trassa's tone had lifted. 'Now that we know what my "root cause" is, can I go back to the scratch cards?'

My heart sank. 'Oh Trassa. I'm so sorry for what you went through. And we'll do everything to find the specialized help you need and deserve. But you're still an addict, nothing can change that. After what you went through, it's understandable that you'd seek escape. But I'm sorry, Trassa.'

'You mean, after all I've told you, I still have to stop?'

'You know you have to.'

She stared at me, stared and stared. And then she *bawled*.

37

This probably wasn't the best night to be meeting Luke. Even though I'd been given the tools to protect myself from my poor patients' pain, how could you not be affected by Trassa's ordeal?

But I'd done all I could for now—the evening nursing staff were on high alert and a consultant therapist, who specialized in sexual abuse, was with her.

When I arrived at Quin's, he was banging around in his bathroom, his back to me. From a shelf he grabbed a bottle of Lutens 5 O'Clock and slapped on a generous handful.

'I love that smell,' I said.

'Oh?' In the mirror, his eyes met mine. 'Should I—' He reached for the bottle once more and I yelped, 'That's enough!'

Obviously I wanted Luke to be impressed with my good-looking, fragrant boyfriend but at no point could it appear that he'd made an effort.

Quin turned, then he exclaimed, 'You look great!'

My lunch hour had been spent getting my hair blow-dried into shiny, beachy waves in the tiny hairdresser's in the village. (It was always the luck of the draw whether you got the young, savvy gay man or the older woman in thrall to her heated rollers. Fortune had favoured me today.) Then in a speedy post-work in-and-out I'd gone home to change into a deceptively casual shirt-dress and low-cut ankle boots.

Quin inspected my knees. 'I'm guessing your ex-husband is a leg man?'

I winced. 'This isn't the 1970s. But yes,' because I'd promised I'd never lie to Quin about Luke, 'he used to like my legs. I'm not trying to . . .' I waved my hands. '. . . win him back or any of that bullshit. But I wouldn't be human if I didn't want to look good.'

'I'm a leg man too, you know.'

'You can look at my legs any time you like.'

'Can I, though . . . ? When did I last see you in a dress?'

I pulled him close and hissed, 'Shut. Up.'

Then we both dissolved into laughter that was slightly manic.

At the noisy, crowded restaurant, Luke and Kallie hadn't arrived yet. Quin and I had just taken our seats when I felt him flinch. 'For *fuck's* sake,' he muttered. 'What a terrible day to have eyes.'

I followed his gaze: Luke was at the top of the steps. He'd just removed his jacket, revealing a white T-shirt and black leather jeans, which were carelessly tucked into motorbike boots.

Quin had also gone big on tonight's look. Wearing black twill track pants from Z (Zegna's 'affordable' diffusion) and what had been described in *GQ* as a 'power hoodie', he was sleek, understated cool.

But Luke Costello in leather was unbeatable. A power move, if ever I saw one.

Luke and Kallie were handing over helmets to the coat-man. They must have come on a bike, so Luke's leathers had a practical function. All the same, I felt slightly sick, wondering why I'd agreed to this terrible, *terrible* idea.

Luke spotted me and indicated us to Kallie. With his hand on her hip, he steered her down the stairs, the muscles at the front of his thighs flexing with each step he descended.

Quin stood up, stepped forward, then—I wasn't imagining it—stretched himself a little taller, made his chest a little wider—and shook Luke's hand. 'I'm Quin. Good to meet you, man. Sorry to hear about your mum. It's a hard loss.'

'Thanks,' Luke muttered. He nodded at me. 'Rachel.'

Kallie, in a handkerchief-hemmed floaty dress, was looking deliciously Stevie Nicks. 'Hi, hi, hi!' Her blue eyes were a-sparkle as she launched herself at me, then Quin, for a hug.

'You smell *gooood*,' she declared at Quin, all flirty approval. Then, 'Cool place, guys. Good pick. Should we sit? We should sit!'

She pulled me into the chair opposite her.

'Great dress,' I said.

'Zara! Today. I know!' Then, 'Whoops!' She swooped on the wine glasses in my place setting and plucked them out. 'Excuse me.' She'd grabbed a passing waiter. 'Can you take these away?' Her voice was stern. 'My friend cannot have any alcohol.'

'That's okay,' I said.

'Don't they trigger you?'

I laughed. 'No.'

'Oh, I just thought—No, okay, all good.'

Quin unzipped his power hoodie, then pulled it off to reveal a close-fitting T-shirt, which hugged his defined arms and pecs. Fair play, I thought. Nice countermove from the Quinster: *I see your leather-clad thighs and I raise you quietly impressive biceps.*

I slid him a sideways glance and signalled, *Nice one.*

With the tiniest smirk, he replied, *Got your back, babes.*

'Drinks?' The waiter who had removed the glasses was back.

'Fizzy water for me,' I said.

'That's right,' he deadpanned, 'I believe you cannot have *any alcohol.*'

He expected me to smile but I'd have felt bad—Kallie meant well.

'Water for me too,' Kallie said and Luke gave her a startled look. 'No wine, Kal?'

'No.' She flashed some urgent message with her eyes, then I understood.

'Kallie, don't let me stop you. I don't even notice. And Quin will be drinking, so go for it.'

'You're sure? I don't want to be inappropriate.'

'You're not.'

'But don't you worry?' She was asking Quin. 'That Rachel will relapse?'

'Rachel is the strongest person I know.' His voice had a slight edge. 'Besides, I don't own her.'

'So you guys aren't serious?'

'We're serious,' I jumped in, then rattled off, 'Together almost two years. Moving in with each other soon.' And I shouldn't have said that. 'How about you two?'

'Sixteen months.' She twinkled at me. 'Separate living spaces at this time. Luke is so independent. But hey, you know that.'

Well, I knew now. I just wished I'd known before we got married.

'It's our actual anniversary in a week,' Quin said. 'The following weekend I'm taking Rachel to Barcelona—'

'That's Spain, right?' Kallie asked.

'Nah, Barcelona, Texas.' There was Quin being a teeny bit of a dick again. Not that I minded. Not entirely. 'Sorry, joking—yes, it's Spain. I've hired out the entire Sagrada Família—you know, Gaudí's church? I'm gonna propose to Rachel there—'

'Whu-ut? Congratulat—'

'No. No. It's a joke!' Quin was flustered. Embarrassed. 'Rachel and I—' Desperately he signalled to me across the table. 'We joke about—'

'— marriage proposals in "obvious" places,' I explained.

At Kallie's blank face, Quin said, 'Top of the Eiffel Tower? Flying over the Grand Canyon in a helicopter . . .'

A pall of mortification lay on us all, then in a plummy, newscaster voice, Quin announced, 'And that is why private jokes should remain private. Sorry, Kallie.'

'Hey, that's okay.' Her smile was genuine.

For a short while, the discussion of the menu generated the pretence of a free-flowing conversation. But as soon as we'd ordered—and we were all keen to skip the starter, clearly no one wanted this night to be prolonged—it hit a wall. Kallie and Quin had to do most of the heavy lifting.

Luke, sitting diagonally opposite me, let nothing slip—but his mother *had* died less than two weeks ago, I could hardly expect him to be chatting away happily. Meanwhile, I was dizzy from successive waves of disbelief. Me, Luke and our new partners, out for a civilized dinner—*how* had this happened?

His hands were fiddling with the salt cellar. Three of his fingers sported silverware but there was no wedding ring. I remembered exactly when he'd taken it off.

Jesus.

It was taking all of my energy to avoid looking at him. Kallie, directly across the table, was the person I tried to focus on. But another of those woozy whooshes of memory lunged and my eyes cut to Luke—to discover that he was watching me. Our stare collided with such intensity that heat flushed my body.

Quickly my gaze dropped to the table-top but within moments I had to look again, to check that Luke Costello really *was* a mere arm's length away.

He was still scrutinizing me. There was a slight furrow in his forehead and a lot going on in his eyes—and I flashed back six years, to the morning he'd actually left.

We'd been in the hall of our apartment and a jingling sound had made my nerves flare—his wedding ring. He'd taken it off and discarded it on the hall table. Then, with the crunch of plastic and metal, he dropped his house keys.

A part of me still thought this was some sort of stunt—but the conviction that it was real was quickly taking hold. It was suddenly difficult to breathe.

I'd tried to physically stop him. But, cold and unknowable, he'd peeled my hands off him. Holding me by the shoulders, he kept me at bay.

'Luke, please, I'm begging you.' My face was drenched with tears. 'I love you so much. We can fix this, we'll go for counselling, whatever you want.'

Looking for a tiny piece of connection, a link to the man I knew, a way back in, I'd have promised *anything*.

From his wintery stare, it was clear he wasn't interested. I whispered, 'Have you no compassion?'

He met my eyes, assessing my naked desperation—and his response was indifference.

Shaken, I tried to reconnect with the present. I am *here* in 2018. I am *safe*. I *survived*.

Quin was asking Kallie, 'How did you get so much time off work? To be in Dublin with Luke?'

'Are you kidding?' Kallie exclaimed. 'I'm working remotely. I can work anywhere, all I need is Wi-Fi and coffee. I have a gig in, like, two weeks so I'll scoot back for that.'

'What about you, man?' Quin asked Luke.

'Same. Working remotely. Fitting it in around my dad.'

'He has his own company.' Kallie sounded proud.

Luke shook his head. 'Only small.'

'Eight members of staff, honey. Nearly double figures.'

For someone who never noticed other people drinking, I nonetheless noticed that the first bottle of wine had disappeared in no time.

'Should we . . . ?' Quin consulted Kallie, then Luke. 'Get another?'

'Sure!' Kallie was all for it. 'If it's still okay with Rachel?'

Quickly, I said, 'It's still okay with Rachel.' In *no* universe would I let myself be painted as Mrs Judgy! Not tonight.

'How did you guys meet?' Kallie directed her question to Quin.

Quin cleared his throat. 'On a meditation weekend.' He straightened himself in his chair.

'Cute! The couple who pray together, stay—'

'Haha, no one said anything about praying.' Quin shut that down fast. 'So, on our first date, we went to an escape room. That's when I knew she was the woman for me.'

'We've never done an escape room, have we, hon?' Kallie asked Luke. 'I'd love to!'

'When you do, you need Rach on your team.' Quin smiled around the table. He was working *hard* here. 'She found clues stashed *every*where.'

Call me pathetic but I enjoyed Quin's praise.

'She was an absolute natural,' he said.

'Really?' Luke spoke—and there was something weird in his tone.

'Yeah,' Quin said. 'She found things hidden in the most unlikely places. Unbel*ie*vable stuff.'

My gaze snagged off Luke's and bumped up against an emotion I couldn't identify. Some sort of distress? Or was it anger . . . ? Definitely something strong. Then, breaking the strange mood, a flurry of plates was being slung before us by a crack squad of fast-moving waiters, armed with insulated tea towels and promises of 'more potatoes'.

'Wow!' Kallie stared at her mountain of food. 'This looks . . .'

'Edible?' Quin asked, to awkward laughter. 'Let's hope.'

Light had appeared at the end of the tunnel. Quin had been instructed to say no to dessert and coffee, so the torment would end soon.

I picked up my knife and fork, but something was stopping me from launching straight into the food. I was waiting for Quin to photograph the meal, the way he often did in restaurants, that's what it was. Then, just as quickly, I knew there was *no way* he'd be bragging about tonight's dinner.

'Rachel, can I ask a question?' Kallie asked.

'Course.' It was only then I realized that she was already drunk.

'Do you ever miss . . . getting buzzed? Going a little crazy? It's so fun to get waved with your man. Do you miss that?'

'No.' I smiled through a jaw that was beginning—just slightly—to clench.

'Sometimes Luke and I smoke weed out on his deck and put on loud music and dance and . . . no? You don't miss that?'

'Kal,' Luke said. 'Maybe you could stop with this—'

'It's okay.' I was tight-lipped, I didn't need him to fight my corner.

'But, Quin, don't you sometimes wish you had a girlfriend who could drink. Get a little high? Hey, if I'm being offensive, please tell me. I just . . . want to understand.'

I tensed. There were times that Quin *did* mind but if he even hinted at it now, I would never speak to him again.

'Are you kidding?' Quin said. 'Rachel is amazing in a million different ways *and* I have a designated driver always. But hey.' With a conversational swerve that almost gave us whiplash, he said, 'Why don't you tell us what it's like living in Denver?'

'Our life is pretty outdoorsy.' Kallie looked at Luke. 'Right? Pretty outdoorsy?'

'Sure.' He gave a tiny shrug. 'When we're not getting stoned and dancing on the deck.'

Kallie's face fell. She looked from Luke to me. 'Oh no. I'm sorry, Rachel. I was an idiot?' She nodded. 'I was an idiot.'

Kallie tightened the clasp on her helmet, scooped up the handkerchief hem of her dress, revealing a slender length of lightly tanned thigh, then hopped onto the bike behind Luke, grasping him around his waist.

'Bye, guys!' she called. 'Missing you already!'

Quin and I waved them off.

'She'll freeze,' Quin said as we went back to my car.

'Good.' I felt queasy and diminished.

'I can't believe I let him pay the bill,' Quin muttered.

Yeah, that was bad. When it had arrived, both Luke and Quin had pounced on it but Luke had won. 'Tonight was our idea,' he said, with a hint of steel. 'You can get us next time,' Kallie said.

But there would be no next time. Quin had to content himself with leaving a far-too-generous cash tip.

'Can we please not talk about them,' I asked. 'I literally can't take them being in my head for a second longer. Tomorrow or some other time we can debrief, but right now, I need to watch two episodes of *Ozark*, maybe three, and think about nothing. Is there ice-cream at yours?'

'Unless Fin's eaten it all. But I'll go out and get you more if he has.'

There were healthier ways of dealing with the unpleasant emotions tonight had stirred up, but my endurance had run out. So I had my ice-cream and my two episodes. I couldn't stop thinking about Kallie. She *fascinated* me. What was it that had drawn him to her? Her light-heartedness? Was it even real?

When Quin got into bed, I asked, 'How hot is Kallie?'

'Hot.' No hesitation there.

'Who's hotter? Me or her? And Quin, the answer is *me*, okay?' Because sometimes Quin was just too honest.

'You, of course.' His expression was concerned and sincere. 'But there's something about her . . . Sheeeee's . . . interesting,' he mused, his arms behind his head. 'Mixed messages with old Kallie there. Sweet on the outside, all great fun. On the inside, she's . . . harder. Tough. I still don't know if I trust her.'

'Why not?'

'Maybe because she's a survivor. She'll always be okay.' Then, 'The neck of her implying we were holy. She has the bang of a Christian, doesn't she? Slightly?'

'Mmm. Maybe. She's very positive . . .' That made me laugh. 'There's nothing wrong with it, if she is. Look at us, pair of bitters, lying here, taking apart their characters.'

'They're probably doing the exact same about us.'

Oh no, that hurt.

'Do you think Luke is one too?' Quin asked. 'A church-goer?'

'We don't know for a fact that Kallie is. But Luke . . . When I knew him, he sort of had *tendencies*. He's quite . . .' I couldn't find the right word. 'Moral, I suppose. Not holy, as such. But traditional is probably the best word. Like the way he was about the bill tonight—from his point of view, he *had* to pay, because it was his gig. Or say he found fifty euro that some poor person had dropped in the back of a taxi? He'd never go, Wahey! Free money! And stick it straight in his pocket. He'd give it to the driver, even though the driver would keep it for himself. There would be no doubt in Luke's mind, not for a single second.'

'Wow.' Quin fake-blinked. 'That's just . . . wow.'

'Haha, I know. So tell me, am I a survivor, like Kallie?'

Quin's stare was appraising. 'You're more complicated. On paper, because you're an addict, you're vulnerable. But if you stay clean, you're a world-beater.'

'Who would you rather sleep with? Me or Kallie?'

Long and loud, he groaned. 'Now I'm thinking about a three-way with both of you.'

'Well, fucking *don't*!' He drove me mad but he made me laugh.

He strummed an invisible guitar and sang, 'My boyfriend's ex-wife is super-super-hot! I faked a burst condom to see just what she's got.' Then, 'You, of course, Rach, always you. I want you more than anyone—that's not going to change.'

We'd turned out the light and were settling into sleep when, into the darkness Quin suddenly said, in a squeaky voice, 'Our life is pretty out-doorsy!' Then in his own voice, 'Pair of fools.'

38

I woke early, my head full of last night. Playing on my mind was the tender way Luke had called her 'Kal'. Even more painful was the glimpse Kallie had given into their shared life—thinking about them getting stoned and dancing on the deck cut shards of envy into my gut.

It sounded so sexy. I could actually *feel* it, Luke sliding his arms around Kallie's waist, pulling her to him, against his hips. Kallie twirling away as he watched admiringly, then spinning back, landing hard against his body, discovering how much he wanted her.

Lucky.

Fucking.

Kallie.

This morning, my clean life of recovery seemed brain-numbingly boring— a very dangerous train of thought. I wanted to be the girl I'd been in my twenties, before my addiction had caught up with me, when there had been nights of wildness and adventure and no thought of tomorrow.

I'd have to ring Brigit. She'd detail how tragic and desperate I'd actually been.

It was only 7.30 a.m. but as I was awake, it seemed like a good idea to go to work. I was worried about Trassa. After yesterday's revelation, she was bound to be extremely vulnerable.

Often, during a person's time in the Cloisters, a trauma that had been stashed for perhaps decades broke the surface. Ultimately, casting the cold light of day on it was a good thing, but in the short term, Trassa would need a lot of minding.

All the counsellors were trained in crisis care and the nursing staff would have kept a watchful eye on her during the night, but she was ultimately my responsibility.

I was in two minds about waking Quin but he surfaced just as I was leaving.

'Come back to bed.' He pulled me against the warmth of his chest.

'No, honey. See you tomorrow night.'

'Not tonight?'

'Laundry,' I said.

'Bring it here,' he insisted. 'I'll do it.'

Hah! That was a laugh. His cleaner Irini would end up with the job.

'I also need to go to Aldi,' I said. *And hopefully talk to Brigit*, but I kept that to myself.

'Life hack,' he mumbled. 'Do your big shop Monday nights at twenty to nine in Dundrum. Best time of the week. Nobody else there to annoy you.'

But today was Wednesday and there was nothing in my house. 'Tomorrow night, you, Taryn and Timothy are coming to me for Transylvanian food. Remember?' I kissed him, then ran down the stairs and slipped out into the day.

As I was getting into my car, my phone vibrated—a WhatsApp from Kallie. Ohmigod, Rachel, I'm sorry, I'm sorry, I'm sorry!

In a mad rush of sympathy, I decided to ring her—she was clearly awake.

'Rachel?' She said, 'You hate me, right?'

'No.' Then I added, 'You big eejit. I mean that affectionately. An Irish thing, Luke can explain it.'

'I was anxious,' she said. 'I drank too much wine too quickly. Those questions I asked you and Quin, about your drugging, I am truly embarrassed. I am so sorry.'

'It's really okay.'

'My reasons . . . ? So Luke loves me, I know that. But in some ways—okay, *lots* of ways—he's unavailable. You know that, right? So when I found out he'd once been married, I . . . Wow, it was a *big* shock. She must have been one amazing lady.'

'Oh-kay.'

'I want to figure him out. I thought you were one of the clues.'

Should I tell her that she'd probably never figure him out? Let's face it, once upon a time he'd been absolutely *mad* about me and look at how that had turned out.

Somebody had bought 'my' Chanel bag! At first I couldn't believe it. I clicked and scrolled, up and down, up and down, changing the search parameters and starting all over again. When the truth dawned, I was almost as unsettled as if my *actual* handbag had been stolen. For a few uncomfortable seconds, I felt genuinely bereft. *Now* what would I obsess about?

However, going by past behaviour, finding something new to fixate on shouldn't prove difficult. As I cycled swiftly through emotions, I landed on anticipation, wondering what kind of surprising lunacy would snap me up. I hoped it would be another unattainable bag—they provided so much distraction in exchange for very little trouble. Not like, say, wheelbarrows, which were just-about-affordable *and* very unwieldy. (I'd bought one last summer after thirteen blurry days of head-racing obsessing. It was delivered to work, proved too big to fit in my car and Murdo had to borrow a friend's van to get it to my house. And after all that drama it had only been used three times.)

'I hate having to do this.' Jonah, a slight sprite of a boy, stared sightlessly at his cooling cup of tea.

'It's hard,' I said. 'I know. But you're helping her.'

'She will lose the fucking *head*.' Naaz bit her lip and reached for another biscuit. 'Seriously, Rachel—is it okay to call you Rachel?—it's going to be the apocalypse.'

'It might not. Will we go?'

Murdo was already in the Abbots Quarter. When I walked in, followed by Jonah and Naaz, Ella looked stupefied with shock. Her mouth half opened, then froze. Only her eyes moved, flicking anxiously as Jonah and Naaz took their seats.

I flashed back twenty years to when Luke and Brigit surprised me by appearing one morning in this very same room and promptly blew the gig wide open. Jesus, I'd nearly died from shock and shame.

'Morning, all.' I smiled. 'As you can see, we've been joined by two people.' I asked them to introduce themselves.

Jonah cleared his throat. 'I'm Ella's boyfriend, have been for about three years. We live together.'

'And I'm her friend Naaz. I share the house with her and Jonah.'

'And you've come this morning because . . . ?' I looked to Jonah to kick things off.

'Ella has been taking sleeping tablets—'

'Because I was *attacked*,' Ella interjected hotly.

Cool and calm, I said, 'Jonah has taken the morning off work to help you. Have the manners to hear him out.'

'But this is bullshi—'

'Stop. It,' Murdo ordered.

Startled, Ella did.

'You know about her crashing the car?' Jonah asked. 'But even before then, things were weird. She'd been taking a lot of time off work "sick". She was "sick" a lot.'

'What sort of sick?'

'Period pains. The flu.' He looked at Naaz for help.

'Food poisoning,' she supplied. 'Glandular fever. But she diagnosed herself with the glandular fever.'

'And the food poisoning didn't make sense,' Jonah said, 'because we'd all eaten the same thing. And she wasn't throwing up, just saying she had a pain in her stomach. Then about two months ago I was at work, she was home "sick" and she sent this *insane* text, that there was an intruder on the roof. I called, she didn't pick up, I was freaking *out*, so I came home. She was wandering around the kitchen, saying she was making pancakes. I asked her about the intruder and she had no clue. *Totally* out of it. Not drunk or slurry but completely blank. There was nothing in her eyes.'

'What did you think?'

'I thought something like, I dunno, a stroke? But I'd already been wondering about the sleeping tablets. We've all heard the stories. It's just that you don't think it'll ever be you.'

'What stories?'

'That after people have taken the tablet, they do things, they seem awake, but they're not. And the next day they don't remember.'

'That happened to Ella?'

'Well, yeah. Sometimes we'd have sex and the next day she wouldn't remember. Or she'd call people and make plans . . . One night she told her mum she'd drive down to see her after work the next day. Which was mad because it's a three-hour drive. Next morning, heading off to work, she asked me to do dinner that evening. I reminded her she was going to Waterford, but she hadn't a clue.'

'Another night,' Naaz said, 'she got into bed with me and my boyfriend, Oliver. Wearing nothing. Acting threesome-y.'

'You wish!' Ella exploded.

'Ella, no. You know that.'

'Did you call her out?' I asked Naaz.

'Yeah, but . . . she said Oliver fancied her and I was jealous.'

'I never said that!'

'You did,' Jonah said. 'I was there. But you were out of it so you don't remember.'

'Jonah, did you try challenging her?'

He shrugged helplessly. '. . . She'd been mugged. It affected her badly. Any time I tried to talk about the tablets, she reminded me. I was trying to be supportive, so I felt I should shut up. But we—Naaz and I—copped on that she must be taking more than the prescribed amount. So we went looking and found prescriptions from two doctors in Dublin and another from a doctor in Waterford. She'd also ordered some online. She didn't need a prescription for that but they cost hundreds.'

Doctor shopping. I saw this a *lot*.

'As well as the sleepers, she had prescriptions for Valium and Xanax. The tablets were hidden *every*where in the flat.'

'Like?'

Jonah and Naaz exchanged a shrug. 'In jacket pockets, zipped inside cushions, sellotaped to the underside of the couch.'

Deep inside me, a bell clanged. This type of subterfuge featured a lot in testimonials—what was different about this time?

For a second I puzzled over it but had to move on.

'She had cut the cards of tablets up into tiny amounts,' Naaz said. 'Twos, mostly, sometimes four. We found two tablets inside a bag of oven chips in the freezer. That was an accident,' she added. 'Finding those.'

'We laid them all out on the coffee table,' Jonah said, 'with the prescriptions, and called her in.'

'You're making it sound like there were thousands,' Ella yelled. 'There were literally, like, twenty.'

'There were thirty-one sleepers, eighteen Xanax and twenty-nine Valium,' he said. 'And it wasn't the number, it was that they were hidden.'

'But—'

Again, Murdo shushed Ella.

'We hoped it would shock her into stopping,' Jonah continued. 'But she went crazy. Crying. Saying we didn't know how traumatized she was. I felt really guilty . . . but angry too because how could I get her to stop if I couldn't say anything to her?'

'Same,' Naaz agreed.

'Before the mugging, did you ever notice a pattern of impulsive behaviour from Ella?' Leaving nothing to chance, we'd already been through this on the phone.

'Hey!' Ella's face was dark with umbrage. 'What's *that* got to do with sleeping tablets—'

With a look I managed to silence her but poor Jonah was agonized. I nodded at him to continue. 'Yeah. Like, she and I binge-watch stuff, same as everyone, but when Ella loves something, she literally stays up all night. That's a regular thing. Which is bad because of work. And bad because it's something we're meant to share. I always fall asleep but in the morning she's still sitting there, watching the last episode.'

Ella squeaked with outrage and Jonah whispered, 'Sorry.'

'There was a time we were watching a K-drama—' He looked at me. 'A TV series from Korea.'

I know what a K-drama is! Exsqueeze me, son, I'm down with the kids!

'We were saying how cool it looked and we'd love to go, but you know, it was just . . . talk. So I went to sleep and woke up to discover she'd booked us flights and an Airbnb. In Seoul.'

'Had she consulted you about getting time off work?' I knew she hadn't.

'No. And when I tried, I couldn't. *And* we couldn't afford it. We were able to cancel the Airbnb but not the flight. We had to take the hit.'

Ella stood up. 'Fuck you,' she yelled at Jonah. Then to Naaz, 'And you.' And to the rest of us, 'And all of you! I'm not staying in this fucking shithole another second!'

'Ella.' I bit out the words. 'Sit. Down.'

If Ella was really set on leaving, I couldn't stop her, so I had to channel Scary Rachel *hard*. 'Everyone who cares about you wants you to be here,' I said. 'Not just Jonah and Naaz, but your mum and dad and brothers. And the rest of us here in the group? Right?'

'Yeah,' Chalkie said. 'Yep.' Trassa, Bronte, Giles, even Harlie made agreeing noises. Poor Dennis, still in bits after his going-over on Monday, was the only one who couldn't muster enthusiasm.

Ella hovered, torn with indecision. I knew where she was at: utterly adamant that this was an outrageous travesty, but afraid that something strange and terrible was taking place which everyone other than her was in on.

'At least stay for your lunch?' Chalkie cajoled. ''Mon, Ella, who else will do the crossword with me?'

'Do, good girl,' Trassa threw in.

'Okay,' Ella mumbled. 'But I'm leaving this afternoon.'

That seemed like a good place to end things. The group rose and surrounded Ella, ferrying her off for tea and chocolate biscuits. She would rant and rave over the next couple of hours, but from my past experience, I was fairly sure she would stay.

39

And she did. At two o'clock, she slunk back into the room, looking wiped out. A confrontation like the one she'd had this morning was a total head wreck. Not to mention that all her private fears and suspicions about her tablet habit had cracked open, demanding attention. The next few days would be rough for her.

My plan for the afternoon had been to focus on Dennis but something made me decide to take a punt on Bronte. 'Bronte, tell us about your relapse.'

'My um, relapse . . .' She hadn't been expecting this. 'I'm writing my life story, don't you want to wait? No? Oh. Well. It was . . . I didn't plan it. It was an accident.' She waited a moment. 'I'd been doing so well. I never missed drugs, my life was *good*, then my horse threw me. Broke my ankle. First time to break a bone, the pain was much ·worse than I'd ever expected. I asked for painkillers.' She paused.

'And then? Did you tell your doctor that you were a heroin addict?'

'Yes. He gave me ordinary painkillers, but they didn't work. They were literally aspirin. I couldn't bear it, I needed something a lot stronger.'

Giles leant forward in his chair. 'I have to ask—did you exaggerate how bad the pain was? For the doctor.'

Something small and strange zipped through me.

'Oh . . . ah . . . *No!*'

'But did you, Bronte?' I asked. 'Did you think—Here's a chance to take opiates again and for it to be legitimate?'

'I promise you, the pain really was awful.'

'Both can be present—the pain and the temptation. In the four years of your recovery, you'd been going to meetings?' I asked. 'Had a sponsor? Did the steps? Accepted you were an addict? Accepted you'd never be cured?'

She nodded.

'Accepted that relapse was always possible?'

After a pause, she said, 'Maybe not. Four years was a long time. I think I'd forgotten about relapsing.'

'So you were in pain and your doctor had offered you opiates—did you call any of your recovery friends to tell them about your dilemma? Or your counsellor in your old treatment centre?'

'. . . No. The pain was so bad I couldn't think straight.'

'There are lots of ways to manage pain. Hot and cold compresses, acupuncture. You had options, Bronte.'

'But you didn't want them,' Harlie said, dripping with judgement. 'You wanted an excuse to go *back on the drugs*.'

'You!' Bronte dripped with disdain. 'You're hardly a—'

'Bronte,' I interrupted. 'How soon after you began taking the medication did the physical compulsion flare back into life?'

'Soon.' Her face was bleached of colour. 'Very soon, really.'

'How did it feel?'

'I—' She clenched her jaw. 'I felt so guilty, but—'

My body was tense. The answer to this question felt important in ways I didn't understand.

'— it was like coming home.'

40

'. . . and then I wanted to get stoned and dance with him on his deck—'

'No!' Brigit cut me off. 'It wouldn't be sexy and lovely, not for you. You'd end up toppling off the deck or passing out in a planter. Something bad would happen because once you start you can't stop.'

'Yeah,' I said, quietly, all of my giddiness leaking away. 'Okay.'

'I'm sorry.'

'No. You're right.'

'But you never have a hangover. You never have to wake up and think, Oh Jaaaaaaaaaayzis, what did I *do* last night? Rach, being you is the best!'

It was, I supposed. I just needed to reconnect with the grateful part of me.

After we hung up, I was in the utility room, checking on the health of my next batch of potted seedlings when Kate arrived home.

'Well?' I asked. 'What did you decide about the party dresses?'

She laughed. 'Seriously. No. The one I liked? The cape dress? Rachel, the *price*. I honestly can't.'

'But—'

'I know. Mum says she has the money. But it costs twice as much as I earn in a month and . . .' She made a face. 'I need some self-respect. Anyway! I met Devin's grandad today. He said to tell you he . . . what was it? "Sends his regards".'

'. . . Is it just me or does that sound slightly threatening? Like when the Mafia man says, "You have a beautiful daughter, it would be a shame if anything happened to her"?'

'He said you're to come to his birthday thing.'

'A birthday thing? But . . . his wife has just died.'

Kate looked anxious. 'All I know is, it's Saturday teatime, at Devin's parents. Pizza and prosecco. So what'll I tell him?'

I was astonished. 'No, Kate. You tell him no.'

What the hell did he want with me? He'd once been my father-in-law—he'd been pleasant, certainly, but it's not as if we'd been close. Even when things were good with Luke, Mr Costello and I had lived on different continents.

And after Luke had left, shame had stopped me from keeping up with the Costellos.

'Oh, yeah.' Kate fished something from her bag. 'Do you need anything from Zara? I've a credit note.'

'How come?'

'I lent Kallie fifty euro. She repaid me with this credit note, it's for six-ty-seven euro. But I can't afford to buy clothes right now.'

I put out my hand. 'Can I see?'

I looked up the item code on the credit note and discovered it was the dress Kallie had worn to the restaurant last night. Trying to make sense of things, I concluded she'd bought it, worn it, returned it and for some reason—maybe because it was obvious she'd worn it?—they wouldn't give her a cash refund.

So . . . Kallie was short of money? She'd wanted a new dress and she'd scammed Zara? It was hard to summon any real outrage about *that*, but to fob Kate off when she really needed cash—that wasn't cool.

'I was looking at a shirt in Zara, I'll buy this off you,' I said.

'You will?' Her face lit with relief. 'Thanks, Rachel!'

Just before bedtime, my phone rang—Luke.

'It's my dad's birthday on Saturday,' he said. 'Sarina is doing a thing in the house—pizzas, cake. Around twenty, twenty-five people. Dad would like you to come. Quin too.'

'But . . . why?'

'To tie up loose ends, he says. You were part of his family, then you weren't.' Defensively, he said, 'That's what he's told me. Make whatever you want of it.'

'It's only been two weeks since your mum died.'

Sounding weary, Luke said, 'Yeah. He's gone a bit . . . Look, we're *all* slightly insane right now. He's adamant he wants this, says it might be his last-ever birthday . . . A dab hand at emotional blackmail.'

Go.

No.

Go!

I didn't know what to do. I didn't know what I *wanted*. All these long-buried feelings and memories breaking the surface was exhausting.

'I'd find it very hard, walking into a house filled with your family. It would be . . .' I blurted, 'After everything, I'd find it humiliating.'

A pause. A sharp intake of breath. 'If it's any help, they all blame me. Everyone's still very fond of you.'

WhatShouldIDo? WhatShouldIDo? 'Do *you* want me there?'

'It would make my life easier. I'd appreciate it, he's driving me up the wall with this.'

'Would Kallie mind?'

He paused for slightly too long. 'Why would Kallie mind?'

Grand, be like that.

'I'll have a think. I'll let you know.'

41

As soon as I hung up, I was flooded with memories. Of an evening, more than seven years ago, when Luke came in from work.

'Guess what!' I called.

'What?' His face flashed white with anxiety.

'No, Ridey-Man, it's good. Guess. Fucking. *What!*'

His eyes widened, then he crossed the room and took my hands in his. 'Are you . . . ?' He swallowed hard. 'Really?'

'I've done four tests, they were *all* positive!'

'Babe! This is . . . Are you sure? How do you know?' He pulled his hands from mine, shaping them around my body. 'Should you be . . . standing? Sit down, sit down, you need to sit.'

Just for the novelty, I let him steer me to the couch. I was a pregnant woman and my husband wanted me to sit!

'Wow,' he said. 'It's hard to believe it's finally . . .'

It had taken a lot longer than envisioned when we'd been starting out. When we'd first gone to see Dr Solomon, I'd naively imagined we'd be parents by the age of thirty-four. But between studying, qualifying, then working two jobs each to pay back student loans, we discovered that somehow we were thirty-six.

The next logical step was to buy an apartment. I wasn't so bothered but Luke said, 'I don't want to be still living in a tiny one-bed rental in the Lower East Side at the age of fifty.' Engaging with the purveyors of New York real estate was a bruising experience and when we eventually bagged ourselves a two-bed in a brownstone in Boerum Hill, we were thirty-seven. (Also, exhausted and with our faith in human nature somewhat diminished.)

Then we were all set to commence our round-the-clock riding when, unexpectedly, Luke got an opportunity to buy his own accountancy practice, which would give more security than we'd ever dreamt of. But we needed a bank loan and by the time we were on top of the repayments, both of us were thirty-eight.

During those years of Waiting For The Right Time, I was mostly happy, often very happy. I loved being clean, I loved my husband, I loved my job, I had a busy, fulfilling life full of great people.

But there were still agonizing spells of doubt. About once every six months, I'd ring Nola and ask, 'Should we not just chance it and hope for the best?'

Her answer—always—was to Golden Key it: if we were meant to have children, we'd have them. 'You want guarantees but that's not going to happen. You have to learn to live with uncertainty.'

'But what if I'm too old?'

'But what if you're not? Dr Solomon says you're looking good—honestly, I feel like I know that woman as well as my *own* doctor—and you've got to remember that you're not like other people. You can probably have everything you want, so long as you wait. If you launch into it all at once, you could bring your whole life crashing down on your head. Too much stress puts you in danger of relapse.'

The mere suggestion that I might ever relapse made me huffy—there was no chance!—but she was right that I didn't want my life to be a bodge job.

Luke tended to agree with Nola. 'Babe, look at our lives! A *lot* of plates are spinning here. If one falls, so will some of the others. If you get pregnant now, you'll have to stop working, at least for a few months, and we just don't have the money.'

If we'd had an accident with contraception, we'd have gone ahead and had the baby. But there were no accidents. And that, in its way, was telling me plenty, I decided.

However, the day did finally dawn when we were both qualified, our college loans had been repaid, Luke had a small but solid business, doing personal accounting, tax returns, etc., and I'd finally been made a staffer in Hope House, a rehab facility in New Jersey.

'Look at us!' I declared. 'Adulting like no one's business!' Then, seized with anxiety, 'What if we've left it too late? What if my ovaries have shut up shop?'

'What if they have?' Luke asked. 'We have a good life. Don't we?'

'Luke . . . if you're having second thoughts, now would be a good time to mention it . . .'

'Not having second thoughts,' he said.

So I came off the pill, downloaded an ovulation app, bought a thermometer and drew up a sex schedule.

Being me, with my penchant for dramatics, I was convinced that it had worked the very first month. 'I feel pukey. And my boobs feel sore.'

'Your period isn't even due for three more days,' Luke said.

'Yeah, but . . .'

He was right, of course. I wasn't pregnant that month. Or for many more. Seven or eight months in, Luke found me crying because—once again—I'd got my period.

'What if it never happens?' I asked him.

Gently he said, 'We can have a good life without kids.'

But by then, I was obsessed. 'We *can't*. I'm going to look into IVF.'

His face became solemn. Shake and his wife Melanie had spent tens of thousands of dollars on IVF which hadn't worked. They had just got divorced.

'In the meantime,' I said, 'the sex will continue until morale improves.'

It had taken over a year of sex that had become more and more stressful but here I was, finally pregnant!

Excitement battled with fear. I wanted to be the best mother there ever was and the thought of failure was terrifying.

'So what do we do now?' Luke asked. 'You should see a doctor!' Then, 'Am I patronizing you? You're not sick, you're pregnant.'

'Hold on there. I'm not sick, no. But . . . like, I'm *pregnant*. I want special treatment. Cushions for my lower back, that sort of thing.'

His laugh was loud. He was so good at pure joy.

'But I guess I have to decide how to'—I quoted what I'd heard other women say—'"take control of my birthing experience".'

Minimizing medical involvement in childbirth was very Brooklyn. Also very NA. Nearly every woman I knew was vocal about their right to choose where and how they'd give birth. Home birthing was popular. My New York sponsor, Olga Mae, had planned to have her baby in a beautiful ceremony with her partner and two children in an orchard in upstate New York, but the day she went into labour, she got stuck in gridlock traffic on her way to Stone Ridge and Baby Carter ended up entering the world in RBS Furniture Liquidators in the Bronx.

Decisively I said to Luke, 'We need a doula.'

'A what-a?'

'A woman. I don't know, she advocates for us, for me. In the hospital. Say if they wanted to do a C-section, well, she'd say no.'

'But what if you needed one?' Luke looked alarmed. Quickly, he changed tack. 'Sorry, no, hey, I get it, you're the one who'll be doing all the work, you get to decide.' But he couldn't help himself. 'Rachel, what if something goes wrong?' He looked slightly sweaty and I felt relieved. While Luke and I had been 'trying', I'd paid lip service to the idea of a natural birth. But now that I was actually pregnant, I was afraid. Pain panicked me. Other women, more evolved than I was, could meet it—'dance with it' as they'd probably say, and good luck to them and all, the weirdos—but as soon as I touched up against it, I'd be yelping for pain relief.

I blurted, 'I'm so happy to be pregnant, but, Luke, I'm scared of the pain.'

'Babe!'

'I want all the epidurals and painkillers and everything but I'm scared I'll be judged.'

'You will *have* all the epidurals and painkillers and everything! Anything you want, *habibti*, anything. And fuck anyone who judges. Remember,' he said, with a twinkle, 'other people's opinions of you are none of your business.'

'Haha!' It was funny when he repeated Recovery slogans back to me.

'So should I say, "We're pregnant"?' Luke mused. 'Or, "My wife is pregnant"? "My wife is pregnant" makes us sound like boomers. But "We're pregnant" makes me sound like an asshole with a man-bun.'

I gathered up his silky hair and held it in my hands at the back of his head. 'You'd be gorgeous with a man-bun.'

'Not my look, babe.' He was brusque.

Indeed. Luke was *so* not a metrosexual. He regarded wearing SPF as a namby-pamby indulgence and he used the cheapest, most depressing shampoo to wash his hair—and even so, it was always glossy and gorgeous.

'You could say, "I'm about to vastly increase my carbon footprint"?' I offered. 'Or how about, "I'm going to be a daddy"?'

'This should be about you. "My dutiful wife is carrying my first-born child and heir."'

'First-born? You're planning on more than one?'

'Oh yeah. Six, at least.'

42

'Dennis? How are you?'

It was Thursday morning, he'd had three days reeling from the revelations from Juliet, Joya and Maudie and it was time to press him. His eyes, as they focused on me now, were like windows in a ransacked house. 'Jez, Rachel, now you're asking . . .'

'It was a fairly thorough going-over they gave you,' Bronte said gently.

'"Twas,' Dennis agreed. '"Tis hard to take it all in . . .'

Poor Dennis, there was so much to freak out about: his wife and daughters knowing about his girlfriend; Juliet saying she wanted a divorce; Joya openly despising him. And the one huge fact that anchored all the others—the likelihood he really was an alcoholic and would have to stop drinking.

'Do you think she meant it?' Dennis asked the room. 'Joya? About me being a terrible father?' He was watching his old friend, Ella, hoping for support. But after yesterday's visit from Jonah and Naaz, Ella was off in her own mini-hell. 'Do you think she meant it?'

'Yeh, but do *you*, like?' Chalkie asked.

'I did everything for those girls.' Dennis produced a burst of defensive ire. 'Anything they asked for, they got. Tickets to Lizzo, Jacquemus handbags, leggings that cost more than my suit!'

In the silence that followed, he asked, 'D'you know what's tearing me asunder? Joya seeing me and thinking I was dead. Doing that to a child is a desperate thing. That used to happen with my own oul' fella. I was forever finding him out cold. Every single time I thought he was a goner.'

'What age were you?' Giles asked.

'He kicked the bucket when I was fourteen, but it had gone on since I was in me pram.'

'So, you were young when you used to find him?' I said. 'That must have been very frightening.'

'"Twas.' His lip shook.

'How were you when he died?'

He stared at his knees, fighting to hold off crying. 'I was heartbroke. But I swore that if I was ever a father, I'd be the opposite to him.'

'And instead you've repeated the behaviour.'

He looked appalled. 'But I didn't mean to! Do you think they'll forgive me? If I promise to be different? 'Tis desperate when people are cross with me.'

'Learn to live with it,' I said.

Miserably he twisted. 'No. I'll ring them and say sorry. Can I do it now?'

I shook my head. 'I know this is hard. You've so little love for yourself that you crave it from others—and this goes for all of you, by the way—but you need to learn to sit with the discomfort.'

'I'm breaking it off with Maudie. I can't believe the neck of the woman, coming in here, acting like she's something special—'

'You asked her to marry you,' Harlie said.

'Shur, how could I do that when I'm already married?'

'You tell us. You're the one who did it.'

'Ah! 'Twas a moment of madness. Probably . . . To tell ye the truth, I've no memory of proposing. The first I knew of it was Maudie bundling me into the car, one morning, for us to go to Athlone to pick out a ring. I'd asked her the night before, she said. But maybe I didn't! Maybe she was making it all up! One thing is for sure, Maudie's for the high jump. What a thing to do to my wife and children!'

'Fuck you,' Harlie said. 'You're the one who cheated, then tried to wife your side-piece! Maudie did nothing wrong, this is all on you.'

Dennis scrambled to defend himself. 'The only thing I can be blamed for is taking up with the wrong woman. Next time I won't pick a mad yoke. Harhar.'

A circle of stony faces stared at him, in silence.

'Harhar?' he repeated, a little sweatily.

When, once again, he was met with impassive silence, real fear passed behind his eyes.

43

'Why does your ex-husband keep inviting you to things?' Quin asked.

'Twice. Two things. And, technically, it was Kallie who invited us to the first thing and it's his dad now. So? You think you'll come?'

'No, Rach. That would be mad. Hey! Don't look at me like that, you know it would. I'm going climbing on Saturday. But even if I wasn't I still wouldn't go to my partner's ex-husband's dad's birthday.'

'Often people are friends with their partner's exes and their families.'

'Thing is, you're *not* friends with your ex.'

Nor could I imagine us ever actually being real friends, I realized. The connection Luke and I had shared had been too intense to survive a transition to something as wholesome as friendship. I wanted other things from him—remorse, atonement. And once I had them, I could let go completely.

'Do *you* want to go?' Quin asked.

'"Want" isn't the word. I feel I *should* go. Like taking liquid iron—it tastes disgusting but it's for my good. I'd like an explanation from Luke. Actually, I'd love one. An apology would be even better. But he's not going to do that off his own bat—if he was, he'd have done it by now. It won't happen unless I kind of . . . *insist*. But you matter to me, Quin, you matter a lot, and I'm not going if it bothers you.'

Frowning, his eyes roamed over my face. 'If it's for your good, then you should go.'

'How much do you mind?'

'I don't know.' His vulnerability surprised me. Then he disappeared behind his macho shell. 'Nah, I'm good, Rachel, do what you need to do. Nola says you're stuck. So get *un*stuck. Get your apology. Destroy the motherfucker! So what's going on with this soup?' He turned to the pot bubbling on my kitchen hob and tasted a mouthful. 'God, that's good. Maybe some more salt?'

I shooed him away. He always interfered when I cooked. 'Open the wine,' I said. 'They'll be here in a minute.'

'Promise there won't be vampires.' Timothy peered at Quin through the steam in my kitchen.

Quin sucked his teeth. 'Sorry, dude. Can't.'

'Brown bears?' Taryn had done her research. 'They really *are* found in Transylvania.'

'We didn't see any last year.' I tasted the soup one more time and decided to call it done.

'We'll be fine,' Quin said. '*Fine.*'

Taryn took a cautious sip from her glass—then a second more enthusiastic one. 'Hold *on*!' She sounded surprised. 'This wine is very drinkable. You're sure it's from Transylvania?'

'Yep,' Quin said.

'Now for the food.' I put the pot on the table. 'Cumin soup, pepper salad and *cozonac*—Transylvanian sweet bread.'

Timothy dived on the bread. He was one of those malnourished-looking creatures who could eat for Ireland. 'This is what they'll feed us?' he asked, his mouth full of food. 'Is it some sort of earthly paradise?'

To date the four of us had done a couple of successful short trips, where no one lagged behind too badly or had bitter arguments over map-reading (a regular occurrence with hikers), so we'd decided to chance a six-nighter to Transylvania.

Quin and I had been the previous June. While he'd have preferred the going to be tougher, we'd both been enchanted, me in particular. There were wildflower meadows, medieval-style villages and tall, spiky castles, truly terrifying-looking at night. The guest houses had ranged from gorgeous to charmingly odd.

But at times I'd been frustrated by the recommended route, suspecting that we were missing out on undervalued gems and overlooked beauties.

So this time, *I* was in charge, tweaking and deviating from last year's itinerary.

'Stick with me,' I said, 'I'll show you the true Transylvania.'

'. . . Aaaand the issue of the brown bears?' Taryn asked politely.

'I'll do my best to prevent us from being mauled to death by brown bears,' I said. 'That's all I can promise.'

44

It was Friday morning and Bronte was reading her life story. I had to admit I was *very* interested. Ireland's small Anglo-Irish tribe was very different to the rest of us. They tended to be big landowners and have strong ties to England, often sending their kids to boarding school there.

Bronte had been one of four children, the youngest by far to 'a third son'—which translated as 'having no money'. She'd been brought up in County Tipperary, on what she called a small farm, which bred horses and 'dry stock cattle'. (No idea, but Dennis briefly emerged from his catatonia to express that this was a good money-making enterprise.)

'Did you live in a beautiful old house?' Trassa asked wistfully. 'With tapestries and lovely curtains?'

'Oh, *no*. A seventies bungalow. Everyone had more money than us.'

'Everyone?' I was looking for context.

'Oh.' She blushed. 'I don't mean the people in the town—'

'—the peasants,' Chalkie threw in.

'I mean our cousins, our friends. We were always the poor relations. It was dismal. Everyone else went to boarding school.' Quickly she added, 'Not everyone in the town, I mean, but—'

'—your cousins, your friends.' Chalkie finished for her. 'The people that count.'

'So you went to the local school?' I asked.

She shook her head. 'Because my family's not Roman Catholic, I went to a Church of Ireland school in a different town—there weren't enough of us to have a school where I lived. But it was twenty-seven miles away so it ended up that I didn't really have friends.'

'The peasants no good to you?' Chalkie asked.

She turned and gave Chalkie a long, cool stare. 'I would have loved to be friends with the peasants,' she said calmly. 'I utterly *adore* peasants.'

Chalkie visibly coloured and Dennis stirred from his torpor to mutter, 'Lads, would ye get a room.'

'But', Bronte said, 'the peasants mistrusted me. They called me "that posho from the stud farm".'

'Any fucking wonder, when your ancestors stole their land?'

'Chalkie,' I said. 'Stop.'

What was clear was that Bronte was the original Outsider. Her own tribe looked down on her while the local people kept their distance. Even within her family of origin she was alone: her father had anger-management problems, both her parents drank a lot and the sibling closest to her in age was nine years older.

But she already knew this. It had been established during her first spell in a treatment centre. I wasn't uncovering anything useful here.

Aged fifteen, at a weekend party with her better-off cousins, she'd had her first brush with drugs. 'Just hash,' she said. 'It was so much fun.'

'"Just" hash?' I asked.

'Compared to heroin, it's "just",' she replied without a flicker.

She was hard to jangle, I'd give her that.

It wasn't until she was twenty-two, in London, that she first took heroin.

'What were you up to in London?'

'House-sitting my great-aunt's mews and working in an art gallery.'

'How d'you get the art-gallery gig?' Chalkie asked.

'My godmother was best friends with the owner's sister.'

'You poshos really look after each other.'

'And how was your first time with heroin?' I asked.

'It was indescribable.' She looked dreamy. 'It was complete elation combined with the hugest, best feeling of love and safety.'

'Yeh, it's nice, all right,' Chalkie murmured.

Bronte's next life event was meeting Eden—also Anglo-Irish but, unlike Bronte, rich and titled.

'He said I had to stop taking drugs, so I stopped. We got married, set up home in Riddlesden Hall, I had my babies, I was working with my beloved horses. Everything was perfect.'

'Yet you suddenly ramped up your drug-taking six years ago? Why was that?'

'Oh. I really can't remember. I'm not really sure . . . I couldn't say.'

I got a horrible feeling that Bronte was just going through the motions here. She'd been through rehab once before, she knew the right noises to make.

Looking for another route in, I said, 'Tell us about your children. You had the first, Freya, when you were twenty-five?'

'Hugo at twenty-seven and Gerald at thirty. Then Eden said there were to be no more, now that he had two sons, an heir and a spare.' She gave a little laugh, which died a death in the room. The rest of them, even Giles, were a long way from an heir-and-a-spare lifestyle.

Suddenly very curious, I asked, 'What kind of relationship do you have with your children?'

'I utterly *adore* them.' She went to say more, then stopped abruptly.

'"But"?' I asked.

'They're at boarding school in England. Well, not Freya, she's on her gap year. I don't see them as often as I'd like. Perhaps . . . five weeks a year. Six? They go to French camp during the summer holidays.'

Jesus. 'What age did they start boarding?'

'Seven. I know it seems young,' Bronte said. 'But it's just what's done. Eden was *five* when he first went. He says it made a man of him.'

That sounded cruel and terrible.

'Before your relapse,' I asked, 'what tended to make you happy?'

'My horses.' No hesitation. 'I'm just a groom, but I adore it. I would do it all day, every day.'

Something was off here and I didn't know what . . . but maybe Bronte was just one of those people who loved animals more than they loved humans?

At lunchtime I drove like the clappers through the Wicklow backroads to chi-chi Enniskerry to get my brows and lashes tinted—Claire's idea. She'd told me I also needed a facial and a blow-dry before tomorrow afternoon—so I'd look 'amazing' at Mr Costello's birthday thing.

'And show up early.' She'd been adamant about this. 'Make sure everyone sees you, then you can slope off as soon as the room fills up. Get the oul' fella a gift, something mind-blowing, maybe a test drive in an Aston Martin. And what're you thinking of wearing? You need to look stunning but effortless.'

She decreed that I wear jeans, a loose, falling-off-the-shoulder sweater and all the jewellery Quin had given me.

I was fully on board. 'Me, swanking into the thick of the Costellos, bursting with "Look at me now!" energy? I am here for it!'

'And you're to be all "Not only did I survive but I fucking thrived! Check out my shiny hair and my glowing skin and my age-appropriate yet very cool clothing."'

'Can I say, "Yes, my jeans *were* cripplingly expensive because they're all about the cut. Yes, my sweater *is* angora, yes I *do* know that this colour does amazing things to my eyes. You think this sort of thing just happens by accident?"'

'Totally! And, "My earrings? Yes, they're diamonds—well excuse *you* and your good eye! Gift from my boyfriend. Boyfriend—oh yeah, of course! Is it serious? Totally." G'wan Rachel,' she urged. 'Ate 'um!'

'"Ate 'um"?'

'The young people are saying it. So now we say it too.'

'Ate 'um,' I tried experimentally. 'I dunno . . .' Then, 'Claire! What's the latest on you and the swinging?' I'd told her about Adam revealing his reluctance to me at BanDearg.

'I'm working on him. Most men would be overjoyed for an opportunity like this. I don't know what's wrong with him.'

'Ah, Claire . . . You and Adam are very lucky. Don't ruin it.'

'Stop worrying, it's all grand!'

45

'I knew she was drinking a lot.' Gemma Kaye held a tissue to her eyes. 'Too much.' This poor woman was the mother of Harlie's friend Tegan. 'But I never thought she would die.'

I cleared my throat; this was extremely painful to hear.

'The guards coming to our door that Sunday morning.' She choked. 'It was the worst moment of my life.'

Who knew what kind of woman she'd been before her life was upended so tragically? But it was clear now that she'd experienced something devastating. She was a study in neglect—her clothes hung loose and her skin was grey and dusty.

'Harlie.' And she was pleading. 'If you can't stop for yourself, could you stop for your mum and dad? I wouldn't want another person to go through what I'm enduring. Darragh—my husband—has been off work since. He's on tablets. I'll tell you now, love, we'll never get over this.'

Harlie's face was as closed as a slab of granite and panic froze me—what if I couldn't get any further with her?

'If I'd been given the choice, I'd have died instead,' Gemma said. 'If it wasn't for Darragh, I would be dead.'

Trassa was openly weeping—and something was going on with Chalkie. His mouth was clamped shut, his eyes bulged and he looked . . . appalled?

'Harlie, you're young,' Gemma pleaded. 'You can't imagine what it's like to be a mother and to lose your little girl. There's nothing worse, I can tell you that now.'

Oh God, now *I* was about to cry.

'I loved her so much, I'll always love her, she'll always be my little girl and this pain will never leave me.'

Abruptly, I stood up. That was enough—for all of us. And it would be cruel to put Gemma through any more. I took her for a cup of tea, and when she was able, I folded her into a taxi and sent her home.

As I came back in, Brianna accosted me. 'Chalkie's looking for you. He's out the back, having a cigarette.'

I found him standing alone in the garden, a cluster of other smokers giving him concerned looks.

'Chalkie?'

Oh my God, the look in his eyes.

'Come with me.' I led him to the nicest of the consulting rooms. 'Sit down.'

'I can't.' His jaw was clenched.

'What's going on, Chalkie?'

'Listening to that woman.' He paced back and forth. 'The way she loved her young one. I started thinking about my ma. She just . . . *fucked* off and left me. I wasn't even three years of fucking *age*, Rachel.'

'You're angry.' And about time.

'I'm fucking . . .' He almost growled, 'If she was here now, I'd fucking kill her.'

'You think she didn't love you?'

'Obviously fucking not.' He was in so much pain that it was difficult to watch. 'If she'd loved me enough, she wouldn't have died.'

'Even though you know how powerful addiction is, Chalkie? When you're in the grip of it, you've no choice.'

'Yeh. That's the sickener—how can I be angry when I'm a junkie too? But I am, Rachel, I fucking *am*.'

'You know you're allowed to feel this way, right?'

He rolled his eyes. 'People—professionals, like—tell me I'm a junkie because of the great big hole where my ma should be.'

'And?'

'Too simplistic. "Looking for home." It's the obvious conclusion, amirite? But today that woman was talking and this feeling was coming—rushing in, like—and I thought I was going to puke.'

'The feeling was . . . ?'

'Rage. I'm fucking raging, Rachel. I want to kill someone. No. I want to walk out that gate, go into town, buy a big bag of gear and whack it into my veins.'

'But you won't. Not on my watch.'

'I'm serious.' He looked frantic. 'I don't want to but I can't cope with these feelings. I have to do something.'

'Okay.' I picked up the phone and called Brianna. 'Find Giles. Bring him to room seven, thanks.'

'Giles?' Chalkie spluttered. 'What do you want that prick for?'

Holding up a finger for silence, I called Waldemar on his walkie-talkie. 'It's Rachel. Can you come to room seven?'

'What's going on?' Chalkie demanded. 'I'm telling you, Rachel, I—'

A knock on the door announced Giles, Waldemar hot on his heels.

'Giles,' I said. 'Chalkie needs your help—'

'—I fucking don't!'

'Waldemar, have you the keys to the gate? And the shed? Yes? Okay, boys, let's go.'

Walking speedily—after all, I had an appointment for a Carboxy Gun Facial I didn't want to miss—the three men scrambled to keep up as I led the way out into the grounds.

Waldemar unlocked the gate to the threadbare pitch and led us into the shed.

'Good Lord!' Giles said. 'It's a gym.'

Ah, it wasn't really. But a giant punchbag hung from the ceiling and a crate overflowed with boxing gloves, tennis balls, skipping ropes and other basic keep-fit paraphernalia.

'What you need?' Waldemar asked me.

'Tennis rackets and balls.'

'Tennis?' Chalkie was incredulous. 'I'm not playing fucking tennis. Especially not with *him*.'

'Come now,' Giles said. 'Who would miss an opportunity to—how did you put it—prance around and yelp, "Deuce".'

I wished he hadn't said that. Chalkie was dangerously volatile—this was risky as fuck.

Briskly, I took a racket from Waldemar and put it in Chalkie's hand. 'Go out there and hit that ball. Giles will show you how. Do it until you're exhausted. Do it until the anger is gone.'

'I fucking won't.'

Tightly, I grasped his wrist. 'Do. It. The anger will come back, it'll keep coming back. When it does, you tell Waldemar or Florian and they'll set you up with the punchbag, or Giles will play more tennis with you—isn't that right, Giles?'

'Absolutely.'

'It's Friday.' I was intent on Chalkie. 'I'm leaving now, but when I come back on Monday morning, you'd better still be here.'

Absolutely furious, he glared at me.

'Okay?'

Still, he wouldn't talk.

'If you're gone,' I promised him, 'I will find you and I will kill you.'

'She hev very particular set of skill,' Waldemar said.

I flinched. This was no time for jokes. But Chalkie hadn't shoved Giles or made for the gate, so I decided to be hopeful.

Back at the house, I told the weekend staff to keep an extra-careful eye on Chalkie, also on Trassa, Harlie, Dennis and Ella—it had been a big week— then left for my facial.

Laughter and squealing sounds met me as I opened my front door. Devin must be here. Unless Kate had started talking to herself. And considering she came from the Walsh gene pool, anything was possible.

No, there they both were, in the kitchen, making something.

'Rachel, hey!' Kate looked so happy.

'Hey!' Devin stuck his head around her.

'Hey.' I smiled into his eyes, thinking, *I don't mind hearing your orgasm noises at ALL*.

'We've made dinner,' Kate said. 'It just needs to go in the oven for an hour now. You'll eat with us?'

'Sure. Lovely. Thanks.' *Shite*.

'Meanwhile, a favour? Granny's surprise party—can I borrow something of yours?'

'Sure! Like, if you can find anything.' I didn't have much call for party frocks.

'Can I look at the vintage stuff in the spare room?'

Calling it vintage was a stretch. They were just old clothes I hadn't worn in years but still had an emotional attachment to. 'There *might* be something in there.'

'Cool! We take a look?' Kate touched Devin and both of them scampered up the stairs.

Not long afterwards, Kate called, 'Rachel? Could you come here?'

In the tiny bedroom, her face was radiant with delight. 'This one!' She held up a vintage cocktail dress in midnight blue—and it actually *was* vintage, from 1980. The boned bodice was strapless and embroidered with metallic planets, the skirt a tulle explosion. 'Can I try it on?' She bent to pull off her leggings—then, prim and pink-cheeked, she ordered Devin, 'Look away.'

'*Now* you're shy?' With a slow smile, he moved to face the window.

'I'll tell you when to look,' she told his back. 'Rach, can you do the zip?'

It whizzed up nice and easy, the sheeny fabric hugging her waist and ribcage, her wavy hair tumbling onto her bare shoulders. She was *gorgeous*. Checking herself in the mirror, she pulled at her bra strap. 'I'll need a strapless bra.'

I'd never bothered with a bra at all. The early noughties had been a different time.

'Dev,' she said. 'You can look now.'

He turned—and his jaw dropped slightly. 'Kitten, you're *dope*. Fire!'

'Yeah?' Her eyes were like stars. 'It still needs . . . something?'

'Scarf in your hair. Big messy hair and a scarf. And maybe stuff around your neck? Crosses?'

Despite his intrusive sex noises and his wasteful carry-on with the shower that morning last week, I was beginning to like Devin. Getting involved with his girlfriend's look with such straightforward enthusiasm was admirable.

'When did you wear this?' Kate asked me.

'To house parties, maybe fifteen years ago, after I'd got clean and moved back to New York. It was The Best Dress in The World.'

Flicking through the hangers in the wardrobe, every new item of clothing triggered memories of another life. Then my fingers landed on a pink slip dress, in slithery satin. I pulled it out, with its matching short fluffy cardigan and ridiculous little handbag.

'Oh my God!' I exclaimed. 'I *loved* this outfit.'

'Cute.' Kate wasn't really interested but I needed to talk about it.

'I wore this at Johnno and Elaine's wedding, around 2006. We'd been so short of money, I'd nothing to wear but Luke sold a record, a rare one—'

'Which was?' Devin asked.

'A Led Zeppelin album . . .' I was trying to remember. '*Houses of the Holy*? Limited Edition.'

'Oi!' Devin winced. 'Serious.'

I laughed. 'You're too young to know about Led Zeppelin.'

'With Luke as my uncle, I can't escape.' He shook his head. 'Selling that must have *hurt*.'

'Yeaaah.' I was still a bit dreamy and starry-eyed. 'I guess.' I stroked the slippery fabric. 'But I made it up to him.'

Emerging from my reverie, I noticed that both of them looked mildly mortified and I burst out laughing. Now they knew how I felt.

46

Rocking an expensive blow-dry, I dropped in on yet another committee meeting. Claire—who was there with Francesca and Molly, her stepdaughter—nodded approvingly at my ripped jeans and deceptively casual angora sweater.

'You look . . .' Helen's head snapped up. 'You're *stealth-glam.*'

'Have you the funny orange earrings on?' Margaret sounded anxious. 'Oh, you have. Well, ah . . .'

'All of that effort because your ex-husband will be there?' Seventeen-year-old Francesca was sodden with scorn. 'Are you not a bit *tragic?*'

'Absolutely not!' Molly declared, kind and diplomatic. 'She's doing exactly the right thing. Also, Rachel, your sneakers?' She made her first finger and thumb into a circle. 'Chef's kiss.'

'To be honest,' I told Molly, 'I *am* tragic. But it's okay. Luke discarded me but there's no need to behave like gone-off potato peelings.'

'So, Rachel?' Francesca interjected. 'You've met this . . . *Devin.* What's he like?'

My eyes flicked to Claire. 'Yeah,' she admitted. 'I invited him to dinner next week.'

'To meet the family.' Francesca's smile was frightening.

Helplessly I said to her, 'I was going to ask you to be nice, but you won't be, will you?'

She shook her head with another of those smiles.

'*I'll* be nice,' Molly said.

'We're so lucky to have you,' I said. 'Right, I'm off to Luke's dad's birthday party.'

'Just a minute now,' Mum said. 'If you're going to Brian Costello's birthday, can Luke come to mine?'

'No!' I was appalled at the idea. 'No, no, no, no, no. Goodbye.'

To my chagrin, even though it was only three minutes past five, several cars were already parked on Justin and Sarina's sizeable, cobble-locked drive.

I rang the doorbell, which bellowed, 'Intruder, intruder!' followed by a wailing air-raid siren.

Moments later Sarina, looking stressed, opened the hefty front door. 'That bloody bell!' She ushered me into the double-height entrance hall for a hug. 'Teenage children with too much time on their hands. I don't know how to reprogramme it.'

'Nice to—ah, see you again.' We'd once been sisters-in-law. Not close, but we'd got on. 'Thanks for having me today and sorry about Margie.' I spoke quickly. I wasn't sure whether to be respectful or celebratory.

Christ, how awkward was this?

'I know it looks weird having a thing but Brian put his foot down.' She shook her head as she led me down acres of limed-oak flooring into a massive modern kitchen, a wonderland of granite and ash. To neutralize my uncomfortable feelings of phenomenal under-achievement, I tried telling myself that it was 'soulless' but it actually wasn't. If I'd done a kitchen like this, it would look as uninviting as a quarry. Some people just have the gift.

The kitchen 'flowed' into a huge open-plan dining and seating area, with sectional sofas in stone-coloured suede and low tables of white resin, lit by statement pendants of glinting glass.

Plenty of people were there: Luke's sister Vanessa, her husband and teenage kids; Kate and Devin, hand-in-hand and glowing with young love. (Kate and I hugged as if we hadn't seen each other in twelve years instead of five hours.) In a low cluster around Mr Costello's wheelchair were three older men.

Oh, and over at the far window, watching me, was Luke.

Our eyes met and the stare went on for a moment too long. Then, in a fluid movement, he pushed himself from the glass and crossed the room.

'Thanks for coming,' he said. 'I'm . . . I appreciate it. No Quin?'

'He already had plans. Rock-climbing. So,' I said, 'I'd better say hello to the birthday boy.' And give him his gift-wrapped socks. (There had been no test drives available in any Aston Martins in Ireland so, instead, I'd gone with three pairs of Argyle-patterned wool-mix socks.)

Luke led me towards the quartet of elderly men. 'Boys,' he murmured to Mr Costello's buddies, who discreetly withdrew.

'Dad, here's—'

'Rachel!'

'Mr Costello.'

'Brian.' He waved me onto a suede cube as Luke disappeared. 'I'm always telling you to call me Brian. I saw you at the funeral. You were very good to come.'

'The least I could do.' I flushed. 'She was once my mother-in-law. She was so nice to me.'

'Is that right?' I couldn't really get a handle on his tone.

'Happy birthday, Mr Cost—Brian.' I handed over the gift-wrapped socks.

'Aren't you very good. Ah, there's Kallie.'

I followed his gaze. Kallie, barelegged in a T-shirt dress and cowboy boots, was swishing her hair at Justin.

'Tell me now.' Mr Costello drew me closer. 'What do you think of her?'

'. . . She seems . . . lovely.'

What *exactly* was going on here?

'Do you think Luke's going to marry her?'

'I . . . Mr Costello, Brian, I'm not the person to ask.'

'I'd love to see him settled down. Happy.'

Oh, for God's sake! Is he for real*?*

'Tell me now, are you off all the drugs and that?'

The cheeky feck! 'I have been for years and years.'

'Good, good, good. It was an awful shame about you and Luke. We were very fond of you.'

'I was fond of you too.' But I was trying to calculate the number of people between me and the door. How easy would it be to leave?

'The thing is, when a baby dies . . .'

'Yep, that's right.' I was scrambling to my feet before the tears began falling in earnest.

'Ah now, Rachel.' He made a grab for my hand. 'I didn't mean to upset you.'

What had he expected? The only way I lived with her loss was by keeping it private. 'Could you excuse me for a second?'

'Justin!' Mr Costello summoned his eldest son. Christ, no, I did *not* want a song and dance.

Blind-eyed, I made for the door, hoping to escape without further ado.

'Justin! Luke!'

Shite. Luke had been alerted and was looking annoyed.

'What?' He stepped forward to block my exit, and saw my face. 'What did he say?' He glared at his father.

'Nothing.'

'Yeah, it really looks like nothing.' Irritably, he scanned the room and plucked at my sleeve. 'Come on.'

He took me down the hallway and opened a door into a smaller, more formal sitting room, featuring prim armchairs and a stiff, starched-looking couch. Shiny fire irons stood by a pristine marble fireplace and on an over-polished table was an artful arrangement of family photos in silver frames.

To my shock—horror, almost—Yara's photo was among them. Luke noticed at the same time and he stiffened in response.

'Shit,' he said. 'I didn't know—'

My floodgates opened. Suddenly there was no fight left in me, not a shred, and everything—the last three weeks, the last several years—caught up with me and I was thrown right back into the past.

47

'Luke! Luke, come here!'

He put his hand on my stomach then looked at me, wide-eyed.

'Can you feel it?' I whispered.

'Yes. It's like a . . . a *fluttering*?'

'That's exactly what it feels like!' I said. 'Like there's a little butterfly in here.'

I had had a dream pregnancy. In my first trimester, I had minimal morning sickness, tons of energy, and most of my time was spent floating around in a state of blissed-out joy.

I gave up my beloved caffeine, bought every vitamin and supplement recommended by the many pregnancy blogs I'd taken to reading and made yet another stab at meditation.

Meanwhile Luke bought *What to Expect When You're Expecting* and consulted it daily.

'This week it's the size of a cranberry.'

'Tomorrow it'll be as big as a blueberry. Our little berry!'

Stopping by Mia's fruit stand at the Farmer's Market became a thing. Luke would hold up, say, a strawberry, telling anyone who cared to hear that this week our baby was that size. Then, 'Sorry, Mia. Manhandling your goods, my bad.'

Mia, whom I knew from my meetings, froze every time Luke spoke to her. Sweet and pretty, she reminded me of a cuddly toy—big brown eyes set in a round face framed by short, messy dark hair.

Then Luke would swerve me away from the cheese stall, glaring at any soft cheese that might have been entertaining notions about being purchased by us. 'Sorry, man,' he called out to Lionel, the cheesemonger. 'Rachel's pregnant! We'll be back in seven months.'

Raw meat was regarded with the horror normally reserved for nuclear waste and Luke kept coming home with random stuff—fresh ginger for my non-existent nausea; a packet of folic acid, even though I'd already been taking it for two years; a three-kilo bag of mixed dried fruit. 'Iron and calcium,' he said, dumping it on the counter.

In my second trimester, my skin suddenly became radiant and my hair grew in great, shiny spurts. But I burst into tears at the drop of a hat. If someone gave me their seat on the train, I cried. If someone *didn't* give me their seat and left me standing for the hour-long journey to work, I also cried.

Everything seemed either *unbearably beautiful* or *indescribably appalling.*

'What if I'm a terrible mother?' I sobbed and sobbed while Luke stroked my hair. 'I'm such a weak, *weak* person.'

As we approached the five-month mark, Luke said, 'Babe, are we having a gender-reveal party? Only Gaz was asking. He says he can do something with fireworks.'

'Oh my God, no! Gaz would probably blow us all up.' Gaz destroyed everything that he touched. His nickname was Shiva. 'Plus, they're so tacky. Gaz has been living in Queens too long. You must remember, we're Brooklyn people, baby!'

At our next scan, the radiologist asked, 'Would you like to know the gender?'

'Oh yeah!' Luke exclaimed. Then, to me, 'We do, right?'

'You're having a little girl.'

There and then, Luke cried. 'Allergies,' he said, wiping the tears away.

Once we got outside, I asked, 'You're not disappointed it's not a boy?'

'No way! Anyway, the next one will be a boy. Meanwhile we need to start thinking about names.'

'Yara.' All business, Luke strode into our bedroom.

'What?'

'Yara. Her name! I was over with Ebrahim and Saira.' The Iraqi couple who ran the corner 'convenient' store. 'I told them about the fluttering feeling. "Yara" is Arabic for "Little Butterfly". It's perfect, right?'

'It is.' My eyes were shining. We had our name.

At seven months, Anna threw me a baby shower at the Williamsburg House. Turnout was exceptionally high—people I hadn't seen in *years*—because everyone hoped Anna would throw in free skincare for the guests.

Thankfully she did, especially as the baby gifts were embarrassingly lavish. There were *mountains* of toys and clothes, as well as vouchers for Baby Yoga and certificates of trees planted in Yara's name (done by some of the crunchier Brooklynites). Several of my glossy Manhattan friends had clubbed together to buy a Baby Jogger City Mini stroller—they insisted that no new mom would be caught dead with yesterday's news, a MacLaren Globetrotter.

'Erm, *thank* you,' I said, 'I had no idea.'

'You should never have left the city, Boo.'

As we headed into the ninth month, I put on my Central Casting Pregnant Woman overalls, tied my hair up in a red bandana, then Luke and I painted Yara's room a pale yellow.

'You've never been so beautiful,' Luke said. 'You're a goddess.'

'Ah, stop!' Then, 'Say it again!'

Yara would sleep in a Moses basket in our room for the first couple of months but we wanted to create a beautiful nursery for her.

We hung curtains patterned with giraffes and monkeys, we assembled a chest of drawers and filled the drawers with teeny-tiny clothes and diapers, then sheepishly Luke produced a white muslin princess canopy which he suspended from the ceiling above her crib.

'I know it's girly,' he said. 'We might be kicked out of Brooklyn for gender stereotyping, but look at it! I can't not.' He was so agonized that I laughed and kissed him.

By the time we'd finished, the nursery was absolutely beautiful.

'I think she'll approve,' Luke said.

'I'm so excited about meeting her,' I said. Then, seized by fear, 'What if I fail her?'

'You won't fail her, you big eejit! C'mon, let's see if she's in the mood for dancing.'

We'd discovered that if we put on music, particularly Luke's beloved Led Zeppelin, she got really lively.

Our latest thing was to watch my stomach. 'Was that an . . . elbow?'

'Or maybe a knee?'

'We could sell tickets to this.'

48

At the thirty-seven-week mark, I was winding down at work; two more weeks before I finished up. Five months' maternity leave was the most I was entitled to—three months of which would be unpaid—but we'd saved money for it.

Hope House was a bit put out about the length of time I'd be away, but said they'd take me back.

When I woke on the Thursday morning of that week, something felt . . . *off*. I realized I hadn't woken once since 2 a.m., and at this stage of my pregnancy Yara usually woke me with her antics several times a night. There had been no activity for hours.

'Wake up, little girl.' I stroked my stomach. 'Come on, play with me.'

There was no response. I stared and stared, praying for a knee or an elbow to jut out at me, but nothing.

'Luke!'

He emerged from the bathroom, half his face covered in shaving foam. 'What's up?'

'She isn't moving, she didn't wake me during the night. Maybe I'm over-reacting, but—'

He put his hand on my bump. In stillness, we looked at each other, both of us terrified, both of us searching for reassurance that the other couldn't give.

'Let's go!' Luke strode to the bathroom, grabbing a towel and roughly wiping away the shaving foam. 'We'll get a cab on the street.'

On the way to the hospital, Luke held my hand tight, while I began to bargain with God. It had been a long time since I believed in a higher power who listened carefully to my specific requests, then promptly actioned them, as if it were a genie which had escaped from a bottle. I *knew*—in my bones, my brain, my soul—that in any situation, the best outcome to hope for was acceptance. Trying to persuade God to pull off something particular never worked. This, though, was different: it mattered too much. *Make her be okay*, I pleaded. *Just this once, I'll never ask for anything ever again, but give me—us—this.*

Isolated by our fear, we watched armies of other people on their way to work and envied them. I wanted to be anyone but me.

Now and then Luke and I muttered hopeful little phrases at each other, flip-flopping between disbelief and terror. Silently, I pleaded with Yara, 'Give me a kick! Make your poor mommy feel stupid for panicking.'

First it was a relief, then it very much wasn't, that the hospital took us seriously. Within a short time I was hooked up to a monitor and, oh, the surge of *joy* when the pitter-patter skip of a heartbeat sounded in the room!

'That's *your* heartbeat,' the technician said. 'Just waiting for your daughter's.'

She pressed buttons then flicked a switch on and off but there was no new sound.

'Try a different machine.' Luke's voice was husky with fear.

But on the new machine there was still only one heartbeat.

Someone said, 'We'll do a scan.'

Things happened fast. In a different room, I got on the table, Luke beside me, crushing my hand. Gel was smeared on my bump and the sonographer began moving the probe around. My breath was held. I was waiting, waiting, waiting for her to say, 'And *there* she is! All good!'

Say it, I prayed. *Say it and make it all okay.*

But a long soundless moment passed, and another, she was still moving the probe and her silence had lasted too long. The panic on her face was undeniable, then I heard her say, 'I'm so sorry.' Immediately every sound became muffled and the room went blurry.

I knew what she was telling me, but I wasn't ready.

'Is she not . . . okay?' I heard myself ask.

She repeated, 'I'm so sorry.'

'But she was fine last night. Tell her, Luke. She was moving and, like, so lively—'

Luke was a picture of devastation.

'Is this real?' I asked him.

Looking stunned, he nodded.

'It doesn't feel real.'

'But it is, babe.'

Ridiculously, I expected Luke to fix this. He was the one who fought my battles when I couldn't. But this wasn't getting us on an overbooked flight or moved from a noisy hotel room, this was something very different and he couldn't work miracles.

'What happened to her?' I asked. 'What did I do wrong?'

A duty obstetrician had appeared from somewhere. Gently she said, 'You most likely did nothing wrong. We'll check for infections but this sometimes happens for no reason at all.'

'What do we do now?' I was reeling from shock and confusion. 'She's still in there.' It made me think of the Chilean miners who'd been trapped underground. How were we going to get her out?

Even more gently, she said, 'You give birth to her.'

'How can I do that? If she's not alive? It doesn't make sense.'

'We induce you, you experience labour and, when she's born, you and Luke get to spend time with her.'

'But—'

'You can dress her, take photographs, take a lock of her hair, we can do impressions of her feet. Make a memory box of her. You and Luke are still her parents, she's still your little girl.'

She made it sound like a good thing. But how could any of this be positive?

As they prepared me to be induced, a pastor appeared, carrying a bible and wearing a performatively 'loving' smile. Touching my hand, he murmured, 'Everything happens for a reason.'

For real?

'God has his purpose.'

Beside me, Luke flared with rage, Luke who so rarely got angry. 'Hey.' He bit out the words. 'Not now, man.'

The pastor looked like he might try to style this out.

'Seriously, man.' Luke half rose.

The pastor beat a hasty retreat.

All the worries I'd had about the pain of labour now seemed silly—I would have endured anything if she could have been born alive.

My strongest memory was of the abnormal quiet. Having a baby had always seemed like a rowdy event, maybe like watching the Grand National, an intense, high-octane dash with lots of different voices shouting encouragement. 'G'wan, good girl! Faster! Harder! Catch your breath, now go *again*! Home stretch now, keep at it. Eye on the prize, Rachel, eye on the prize!'

But my labour took place in almost total silence.

At one stage, I heard myself choking back sobs. Then I realized it wasn't me who was crying, it was Luke.

Even after the birth, no one said anything. But when Yara was put in my arms, a sudden calm descended. There she was, our little girl, miniature and perfect. Her skin was cool when it should have been warm, her eyes would never open but, oh, the wonder of her tiny, tiny toenails, her spiky black eyelashes, her mini-prawn fingers.

'Hello, sweet girl,' I said. 'Hello!'

Luke traced his finger along the curve of her cheek. 'Her skin is so soft.'

'And look at her hair!' There was a thick clump of it on the crown of her head, jet black. 'She got that from you.'

Luke's chin wobbled.

I inhaled the scent of her head. She smelt just like a baby.

Tears were landing on her from both of us.

'We're so sorry you couldn't stay,' I told her.

'But you mustn't feel bad,' Luke said. 'It wasn't your fault.'

At some stage Anna had brought in the pregnancy bag which had been sitting in our hall for the last three weeks. Luke and I chose a supersoft sleepsuit, with a rabbit appliqué and paws for feet, to dress Yara in.

As instructed, we took lots of photos, so we'd remember everything about her. Then one of the nurses suggested she take pictures of the three of us together.

'Let's try and smile,' I said to Luke, 'You're still her daddy, I'm still her mommy.'

In most of the pictures, Luke and I were like a pair of zombies but there was one where our faces had softened with love, where we looked almost happy; then another, where Luke had his eyes closed and his lips pressed to her downy forehead.

We'd been told to spend as much time with her as we needed but eventually Luke said, 'Babe, we should go now.'

'But—'

'Babe.' He stared at me with hollow eyes.

I got it. We couldn't stay there forever: one of us had to be bad cop.

'Can she come with us?'

He shook his head. The hospital needed to keep her to try to figure out what had gone wrong. She would be returned to us soon and we'd get to have a small funeral.

Then we went home without her.

49

The emptiness howled in me. I stood in the cosy, yellow nursery we'd prepared, touched her crib, the smooth texture of the cotton sheets, the delicately knitted baby blankets, so much softness and innocence. In the corner was a plumply upholstered armchair, reassuringly solid, for me to sit in to do the night feeds. Mobiles dangled above her cot and the room overflowed with toys.

Only days before, I'd bought her a little fuzzy elephant—a giddy impulse purchase because I was simply so excited. There had been a lot of that, me buying her stuff, just because. Luke too. The previous weekend, he'd come home with a miniature ballerina outfit—the full works—a tulle skirt, a pair of satin slippers. ('Yeah, it's pink. My bad. Blame Gaz, he's a sap, even worse than me.')

It was all over. So long had been spent in intense anticipation of this wonderful event—an entire new person being born. But nothing had come of it and never would.

My head knew but my heart didn't. And neither did my body—my breasts began leaking milk. Blankly I looked at the two wet patches on my T-shirt. 'What should I do?' I asked Luke.

He lunged for the information we'd been sent home with. 'Ice-packs,' he read. 'Ibuprofen for the discomfort. It should stop in a few days.'

But I didn't want it to stop. It was one way of remaining her mother.

Our phones and laptops were flooded with messages but the words could find no landing place in me, because I couldn't really believe that this was happening—that *I* was the person being told, 'the shock and pain will eventually ease'.

Tragedies could hit anyone, I knew I wasn't immune, but still, to find myself on the wrong side of the divide, to be the object of everyone's pity instead of being the one doing the consoling, felt all wrong.

'Fuck you, man!' Luke was staring furiously at his phone. '"Everything happens for a reason"? Why do they keep saying that? It's bullshit!'

His anger was shocking. It dawned on me that Luke and I were at the bottom of an abyss, trapped with each other. No one else could come in or out. Briefly, it was terrifying.

'Luke. They're trying to help.'

'How can they help? We've lost everything.'

'We still have each other.'

'Yeah.' Wearily, he gathered me to him. 'Okay.'

I wasn't due to finish work for another two weeks but I had to call to say I was taking leave immediately. It was inconvenient for them, but my boss said, 'Take all the time you need.'

She didn't mean it literally, of course. It was just a meaningless thing people said, like, 'Drink lots of fluids.' In a week or ten days someone from HR would call to pin me down to a return date. But I'd worry about that when I had to.

Reminders of Yara were everywhere. In the bathroom, I was shocked by the teeny baby bath sitting in our bigger tub. That wouldn't be needed now. Neither would the neat pile of bath toys, waiting for her to play with. Nor the breast pump Olga Mae had loaned me, or the bottles, sterilizer or drying mat.

Meanwhile my arms ached with emptiness—*literally* ached. I'd heard the phrase a thousand times and thought it was just a saying. But the muscles on the insides of both my arms actually hurt. Worse than that, though, much worse, was a suspicion that this was all my fault. As soon as the first prickles of alarm about Yara had begun, a familiar inner voice had piped up, telling me that I didn't deserve good things. As a person I was too flawed, too defective, to attract and keep anything pure. Or maybe I'd done something in my old life, in active addiction, to guarantee that my body wasn't a safe place for my baby.

On the second day of our new life, Luke said, 'Do you think you should go to a meeting?'

It was the obvious thing. No matter what happens in the life of a recovering addict, good or bad, a meeting is always important to maintain emotional equilibrium.

But I felt strange about leaving the apartment, about going out into the world when I was so altered, so he called my sponsor Olga Mae, who took me along.

Sitting on hard chairs in an anteroom belonging to a church, Olga Mae kept elbowing me to share. Eventually I did, saying the bare minimum.

'My baby died. I'm going out of my mind, but I won't take anything to kill the pain.'

Afterwards, I was besieged with well-meaning types reminding me that other addicts had endured unbearable losses and didn't relapse. They were adamant that I could survive this and stay clean, so long as I asked for help. Over and over I was told, 'Don't forget that you're an addict.'

'I won't.' But their intensity was exhausting.

Back home, in the bathroom, I said to Luke, 'We're going to have to . . .' I indicated the bath, the toys. 'We can't keep these, can we?'

'Sure we can. We'll put them into storage . . . because won't we . . . I mean, we'll have another?'

But how could we have another when we loved her so much? And how would I survive another pregnancy and the certainty that it would happen again?

50

In Sarina's sitting room, I sat on an armchair, my body folding in on itself, getting as far away from Luke as possible. I sobbed and sobbed and sobbed. 'Sorry.' My voice was thick. 'I'm really sorry.'

'I'm sorry too. I'd never have brought you in here if I'd known about the photo.' He was on the edge of the couch, leaning far forward, right into my space, but he didn't touch me.

I just needed to stop crying, then I could leave.

'Stay there,' he said. 'Don't move.' He sprang upright, left the room and moments later returned, tearing sheets off a roll of paper towel.

I pressed them to my salty skin.

'I wish I could cry,' he said.

I met his eyes. 'I wish I could stop.'

We both managed a weak laugh and I dropped my gaze.

'Rachel?' His tone made me look up. 'Just because I'm not crying doesn't mean that I don't feel it.'

'I didn't. I don't think that.'

'You probably think that I . . . I know you must hate me.'

Startled, I said, 'Well. I mean . . .'

'You have to know that losing her changed me forever.' Suddenly there he was—the man I used to know, in pain but recognizable. 'I had no say in any of it. I was powerless.'

'Oh . . .'

'Please believe me.' His look was deadly earnest and the hairs on the back of my neck prickled. This, I suddenly understood, was his apology, the one I'd waited six years for. There was sincerity in his eyes—and guilt. 'If things could have been different . . .' He stopped and began again. 'I wish *I* could have been different.'

The longed-for admission of remorse hadn't gone anything like my wildest fantasies, but he'd given me a credible reason for why he'd stopped loving me.

'I've often wondered . . .' he said. 'You know how it—'

But something was going on outside the window, something that couldn't be ignored. 'Luke. Hold on a . . .' I hurried to shift the sheer curtains. 'It's a rainbow! Come here.'

I turned to him. 'Rainbows are *her*. I see them at important times in my life—I know it sounds mad but that's her, she's *here*.'

'Are you serious?' He sounded surprised. Wrong-footed, almost.

'Totally.'

He frowned. 'So, you don't—'

A gentle knock sounded on the door, then immediately it was opened by—no surprise—Kallie. 'Guys!' she declared. 'Just checking you're both okay.'

Luke had already put several feet of empty space between us. 'Fine,' he said. 'We're fine.'

Kallie grasped my shoulders. 'Fathers-in-law, right! Believe me, Brian is one of the good guys, he just never knows where the line is.'

Flustered, I nodded.

'I would have brought you a glass of brandy but'—she shrugged—'you can't have it. It's too bad.' She turned to Luke. 'How about you, hon? Something medicinal?'

'I'm good, Kal, thanks.'

'We should . . .' I began moving to the door.

Speeding down the hill, as relieved as if I'd done a jailbreak, I rang Quin to tell him I was on my way over.

As soon as I stepped into his house, I said, 'That was the last time. I'm not going to see him again.'

'And why's that?'

'He apologized.' I laid it out for Quin. 'I mean, it wasn't the grovelling that I'd wanted, once upon a time. But it's a realistic explanation. It's good enough.'

'Well. *Great*.' Then, 'Are you okay?'

'Yes. Well, I think I am.'

'Come here to me.' He pulled my body against his.

I had been seeing Quin for several weeks before I told him about Yara. I'd needed to be absolutely certain that he'd get it.

'I can't even imagine . . .' he'd stuttered, visibly shocked. 'I love my kids so much and if anything happened to them . . . I'm not sure I'd ever get over it. Jesus, Rachel.' He'd shaken his head. 'You've really been through it.'

The revelation of his vulnerability had surprised me. Without a doubt, it had bonded us in a more loving way. And although he never tried to involve himself in my grief, he was always solicitous and gentle.

'What would you like to do tonight?' he asked. 'Dr Quin suggests bed rest.'

'Does he now?' I laughed. 'Well, Dr Rachel agrees.'

'Wait now, what *kind* of bed rest is Dr Rachel prescribing?'

'The nice kind,' I teased. 'The good kind.'

Later, lying in bed, we were chatting idly about bits and pieces, when I mentioned the weird business with Kallie and the credit note.

'What?' Quin exclaimed. 'She's a right chancer.'

'I think she's just short of money.'

'Ah now, Rach—that bullshit with the condom? Even if it was true, asking *you* for help was suspect. And she didn't come prepared to pay the doctor. Nor has she paid me back—not that I care, I'm good for it. But to do it to Kate, that's really shitty. Telling you, Rach, Kallie is a hustler.'

'Ah, no.'

'She's likeable, I'm not saying she's not. She's fun. But she's a grifter.'

'. . . Luke wouldn't be with someone like that.'

'Ah, he could.' Quin's certainty was surprising. 'Like, he's not the brightest, is he? Luke, I mean.'

Wasn't he?

Okay, he was nothing like Quin, who was all over hard news and popular culture, consuming everything with an impatient hunger, trying to glean the gist of a thing as quickly as possible. Also unlike Quin, Luke had a tendency to think the best of people until they proved otherwise—well, he had once upon a time, it could be different now. But that didn't make him 'not the brightest'.

However, I kept my mouth shut. Quin was entitled to his opinion. And for me to openly disagree with him, to actually defend Luke, that would be weird.

51

After Yara died, Luke took a week off work, while his deputy Gustavo ran things—then he had to go back. Me, though, I found myself unable to get out of bed. My sadness was unbearable.

It was impossible to stop scanning the timeline of my pregnancy, moving back and forth along the months, searching for the break, the point at which I'd done something that had damaged her. Was it that long-haul flight to Ireland? Even though I'd only been five months gone then, so it should have been safe. Could it have been the chemicals from hair dye? I'd got my roots done just before I knew that I was pregnant—was that when the damage had been done? Or had it been something I'd eaten?

I sobbed and sobbed all day, every day. Luke would come home from work and find me exactly where he'd left me eight hours earlier.

'I'm sorry.' I told him. 'This is terrible but I can't help myself.'

'It's okay.' He was so weary. 'It's okay.'

When the inevitable call from HR came, I said I couldn't come back just yet. 'Can you use the therapist you'd got to cover my maternity leave?'

'Oh . . . yes, I guess.'

But a report from my family doctor was required so Luke helped me into the shower, to wash myself for the first time in six days.

Dr Esposito—Carlotta—had been our GP for about three years and she was kindness itself. After she'd written the report which said I wasn't faking my devastation, she offered me antidepressants.

I was reluctant. 'I don't know . . . I'm not depressed. This is grief, right? Shouldn't I just *feel* it?'

'But look at you, Rachel!' She waved her hand at my swollen eyes, my baggy sweatpants, my grey skin. 'You're not doing well here.'

'Carlotta, you know I'm in NA, don't you? I shouldn't take tablets.'

'Antidepressants aren't addictive. They're not mood-altering—well, I guess they are, but the change is subtle and slow, it's hard to abuse them. They don't get you high. Hey, your call. I'm here if you need me.'

With some information about self-help groups for bereaved parents, she sent me on my way.

As a result of her letter, Hope House gave me three months' leave at full pay and, yes, that was a relief. It would be impossible to return because I literally couldn't stop crying.

Every day I told myself, tomorrow will be better. I'll get up, I'll tidy the apartment, I'll go to a meeting, I'll sit in the park and let the sun shine on my face. But tomorrow would come and I'd stay in bed, choking with tears, looking for the moment when I'd done the thing that had hurt her.

I hadn't been to a meeting since that first one with Olga Mae, and when Nola got wind, she said she was coming to New York. I said, 'Not right now. I'm in no condition to be minded.'

'What do you mean?'

I meant that it would put pressure on me to perform. I loved her too much to let her think she was failing me. But there was more: Luke and I were reeling—we weren't connecting. Having another person in and out of our home would just make it harder.

But I didn't want to worry her, so I promised to go to meetings.

My greatest fear was what verdict the hospital would produce for Yara's death. I'd been wondering—terrified—if the reason was simply *me*. If it had been crazy to expect that a person with my defects could do something as beautiful and loving as give birth to a child.

It was years since that self-hatred had had any real hold but now it was on the rampage. There were times when I wondered if my drug use had somehow damaged my body, making it incapable of keeping a baby alive, but more often, my fear was that the flaw was my personality, my spirit, whatever essence makes up a person.

Fear and shame kept me suspended in a silence that became increasingly difficult to endure and in the end I blurted it out to Luke. 'I think it's my fault. She knew she wasn't safe to be born to me because I'm a fuck-up.'

'That's—' He frowned. 'Crazy. Stop. Don't say stuff like that.'

'I'm just afraid that—'

'Don't!'

I should have been glad that he wouldn't let me diss myself but because he wouldn't actually talk about it, I couldn't shake the horrible feeling that maybe he shared my worry.

And when the nice doctor finally called, the news couldn't have been worse—they'd found no reason for Yara's death.

He was keen to stress that sometimes it just happened. But if there was no obvious cause—no virus, no blood clot—then it was definitely my fault.

Telling Luke was hard. 'I'm sorry,' I whispered.

'For what?'

'I must have done something. Or maybe it's just *me*—' Tears choked me.

'It's not your fault.' He gathered me to him, but not before I'd seen the flatness in his eyes.

Then came the funeral. Luke in a suit. That tiny white coffin. Luke reading the heartbreaking poem.

Remember me when I am gone away,
Gone far away into the silent land;
When you can no more hold me by the hand,
Nor I half turn to go yet turning stay.
Remember me when no more day by day
You tell me of our future that you planned.

I didn't know how I could feel such pain and still be alive.

Everyone reacted in different ways to Yara's non-arrival. Some ghosted me—only one woman from my antenatal group got in touch. Others, people I barely knew, tried to invite themselves round, and offered tone-deaf platitudes when I stalled them.

Deliveries kept arriving at the apartment—elderflower lemonade, boxes of fancy teas, pastries, cool-crates of ice-cream. My colleagues in Hope House had a tree planted in Yara's memory. The Real Men—a sizeable number if you added up all those on the C, D, E and F Lists—donated a hefty chunk of cash to a children's charity.

The best people asked, 'Can you bear to see anyone? Just say no if you can't.' And I always said no.

No matter how kind anyone was, the fact remained that our tragedy had plucked Luke and me from the scrum and set us down on an uninhabited island, where people could see us but never visit.

We were the ones who had taken the hit in order to spare others, as if there were only so many tragedies to go round. People were grateful to us but they were also afraid to get too close, in case the bad luck was catching.

52

Then I stopped sleeping.

The night before what would have been my due date, I was imagining everything that would have been going on, if we hadn't been so unlucky: my waters breaking, preferably in some movie-worthy moment—perhaps on the train home from work?—my contractions starting; the mad dash to the hospital with Luke; the joyous innocence of it all. Even the pain would have been glorious! Me sweating and yelling, Luke encouraging me, the medical staff fluttering in and out doing their checks—and eventually the thrilling miracle of a new life entering the world.

All night long, my head raced with what-might-have-beens and when Luke woke in the morning, I hadn't been to sleep, not even for half an hour.

That day, I slept for a couple of hours in the afternoon, but when night fell and Luke tumbled into bed, clumsy from too much whiskey, my head began racing again, going through it all. For a second night sleep eluded me. After trying progressive muscle relaxation and listening to a guided visualization, neither of which worked, I got up, sat on the couch, watched five episodes of *The Golden Girls* and would have kept watching them into infinity except Luke woke to get ready for work.

'Babe . . . ? You couldn't sleep again? Literally not a wink?' He sat and took my face between his splayed fingers. 'Yesterday, today—these are the worst days. Thinking about what might have been.'

'You're thinking about it too?'

'Like, of *course*. But we'll get through this.'

After he'd gone, I got myself up and washed and dressed—which was impressive in itself—and hit the health store, buying lavender spray, a calming blend of bath oils and sleep-inducing pressure-point plasters.

Again, in the afternoon, I fell into a deep dreamless sleep for almost three hours—and jolted awake into a world filled with loss.

In the three weeks since Yara had died, Luke had been drinking more than usual, staying up late in his shirtsleeves with his bottle of Jack Daniel's. I didn't blame him. I'd never minded his drinking and, even then, I didn't want to get drunk or high, I just wanted to sleep.

Despite drenching my pillow with lavender spray, having a long bath in the scented oils and wearing the pressure-point plasters, a third almost entirely sleepless night followed. Now and again, I'd be drifting off, then I'd remember that Yara had died and, with a zap of adrenaline, I'd bump into wakefulness once more.

The next day I went to an NA meeting but a headache, like a band of copper, had tightened around my skull. A hail of platitudes rained down on me and when the speaker invited me to share, all I could manage was, 'I can't sleep and I really want to. I need the escape.'

As soon as the meeting ended, I was set upon and overloaded with advice. 'Be strong, Rachel. Endure.' Again and again I was told that sleeping tablets were okay for normal people, but not for me.

'I know, I know,' I mumbled, then made my escape because I had an acupuncture appointment.

I told Mr Lee, 'Give me the most intense session possible, so that I can sleep tonight.'

With the aid of Dr Google, I'd identified the cause of my insomnia: Yara had died while I'd been asleep. While I'd been off enjoying myself in the Land of Nod I'd let my little girl die. It made perfect sense. But I couldn't see how I could trust myself to sleep any time soon.

That evening, Luke wasn't home long when the buzzer went. Warily we looked at each other—we really couldn't cope with a 'well-wisher'. Then my phone beeped with a text.

'It's Mia,' I said. 'Downstairs at the door. Fruit Mia. From NA.'

'Oh? Okay. You want her to come in?'

Not really but I felt I should.

'Hey.' She was rushed and apologetic, her cuddly-toy face anxious, her brown eyes huge. 'I'm not here to bother you. Just need to give you something then I'm gone.'

Her candour was hard to resist. 'Come in.'

Already she was fishing something from her ivy-coloured messenger bag, which she wore cross-body over a red leather jacket and what looked like a pair of men's suit trousers. She was an attractive combination of cute and cool.

She stepped into our living room, then saw Luke, his top three buttons opened, his hair mussed. 'I didn't mean to intrude . . .'

'You're not,' Luke said. 'Hey, Mia.'

She nodded at him, her face flushing. 'Hey.'

'Would you like to sit down?' I asked.

'Seriously, no. Just need a quick word.'

This was Luke's cue to leave so Mia and I could speak privately, but he didn't move.

'At the meeting today you shared that you couldn't sleep?' She put a small jar in my hands. 'Melatonin. It's non-addictive, natural. Safe for you and me to use. Might help.'

'Th-thank you.' I was touched and suddenly hopeful. Why hadn't I thought of melatonin? In the past I'd used it for jet lag but hadn't thought about using it for insomnia.

'I'm not good at sleeping,' she said. 'Never really was. Tried everything. As you know, Rachel . . .' Mia had arrived in NA after a dependence on Ambien and Xanax had brought her to her knees. 'I also brought you—' She fumbled in her bag and produced a punnet of dark, glossy cherries. 'Left over from today.'

She held them out and Luke stepped forward to take them.

'I hope the melatonin helps,' she told me. 'But if it doesn't, one thing to remember, no one ever died from lack of sleep.' As she turned to let herself out, she said, with great sincerity, her gaze moving from my face to Luke's, 'I'm really sorry about your baby. It sucks so bad.'

The door rattled shut and she was gone.

For a short while, Luke and I stood in silence, him holding the punnet of cherries, then, with a trace of a smile, he said, 'How nice was that?'

53

In the park, I held my face to the sun and urged its rays to work their magic on whatever part of my brain controlled sleep. Daylight—apparently that was what I needed. With the amount of time I'd been spending in the apartment, maybe it was no wonder I was trapped in insomnia.

No one ever died from lack of sleep, Mia had said. Maybe not, but you could go mad without it. The previous night, my fourth without sleep—even though I'd taken Mia's melatonin—I'd felt trapped, like a rat in my own head, where time kept jumping—I'd forget what had happened, thinking I was still pregnant, waiting to give birth, only to discover that it was all over, but I had no baby, then I'd tumble into horror.

I prayed and prayed for sleep, to not go mad.

This morning, when Luke had brought me tea he'd seemed lighter somehow.

I dragged myself up to sitting, exhausted and queasy.

'You didn't sleep?' He was very surprised. 'Not even with Mia's melatonin? You mean that from midnight to seven a.m. you literally didn't nod off once? Are you sure?' For the first time he had sounded impatient about it.

The heat on my face dimmed—the sun had gone behind a cloud—so I opened my eyes and looked around the park. It was a small, scrappy affair, but it was the closest to our apartment.

In the playground, a man with a weighty little bundle strapped to his chest sat on a swing. Gently he rocked back and forth, talking to the bump . . .

. . . and for a moment I was wondering if that really *was* a baby on his chest? What if he was chatting away with a bag of potatoes or his sweatshirt rolled up in a ball? It was a strange idea, almost funny, and maybe that was the thing about having had almost no sleep in five days—everything felt off, slightly mad, as if I was dreaming.

Then I spotted a baby in a stroller headed towards me. My first urge was to get up and run away—I was afraid of getting too close to what I had lost—but a horrible fascination kept me frozen in place. Closer it got, then closer, the mommy walking jauntily and singing a song.

The baby was near enough now for me to touch. We made eye contact as it passed, it was maybe three months old, squishy and milk-drunk.

In a second or two, the stroller was gone. I watched the retreating mommy in her Birkenstocks, wondering what it was like to be her, with her healthy baby. Did she know how incredibly blessed she was? For a moment I thought I was imagining it but she was deliberately squeezing her buttocks with every step she took. I guessed that that accounted for the jauntiness of her walk. Not happiness, as I'd first thought, but an attempt to 'snap back to her pre-baby body'.

My own body was a far sight from its pre-baby-ness. Maybe the woman would lend me her baby so I could walk and clench my buttocks . . . Out of nowhere I was gripped with fear that the baby in the stroller would die because of having been close to me. That I was, in some way, toxic.

In the playground, the man and his baby were still on the swing. What if that child died too? And that one over there, being breastfed on the grass? And it was all traced back to me? Because it *could* happen. I'd already been responsible for one death.

I knew I was crazy. With so much sleep deprivation, it was no surprise. But part of me actually believed it and that part was terrified.

This couldn't go on.

I stood up and went straight to the drugstore, where I bought a packet of Unisom. I was in dangerous territory here, buying tablets, but I was desperate. Unisom was basically horrible, an antihistamine which would give me a dry mouth and no happy feels, but it might knock me out.

But I couldn't tell Luke. I couldn't tell anyone.

I took it at 10.50 p.m., nodded off—and woke two hours and thirteen minutes later, my mouth like cotton wool. That was it for the night.

Lying in the dark, I was quietly frantic. Where would this end? Seriously?

My mind began tracking back over my day, landing on the baby in the stroller. What if, at home in its apartment, it had developed a high temperature? Or had trouble breathing?

A thrill of terror seized me. Maybe it was already at the hospital, its mom and dad sick with worry?

This was nonsense, I *knew* it was, just down to lack of sleep.

But what if it wasn't?

My mind jumped from the anonymous baby in the stroller to my friend

Olga Mae's little boy, Carter. Thirteen months old and cute as a button. What if he died?

Panic spiralled and I had to leave the bedroom and turn on the TV. That calmed me. But the fear began to stack up again until I was convinced that Carter was in danger.

I should call Olga Mae.

But there was no need—Carter was fine and I just needed some sleep.

But what if morning came and the news arrived that Carter was dead? As soon as I had that thought, I reached for my phone.

'Rachel . . . ?'

'Can you check Carter? See if he's okay?'

'. . . It's five a.m. What's going on?'

'Just check him. Please.'

'. . . Sure.' Then, 'All good. He's sleeping. He's good.'

'Breathing normally? No temperature?'

'His skin feels normal. Rachel, what is it?'

'Nothing. Thank you for checking. Go back to sleep.'

The spike of relief at learning that Carter was safe lasted no time—because suddenly I was worried about Luke. I tiptoed back into the bedroom and to my disbelief I couldn't hear his breathing. I crept closer. He was lying unnaturally still, no rise and fall to his chest.

I put my hand on his stomach, sick with fear that he'd be cold. He was warm to the touch but if he had just died, then he wouldn't be cool just yet . . . Suddenly he jolted awake and when he saw me looming over him, looked terrified. 'Rachel! What the—'

'Are you alive?'

'Yes! What's going on?'

'Luke, did I kill her?'

'What? Babe, no!' He pulled me down into bed with him. 'Of course you didn't. We'll talk about it in the morning. Let's just go to sleep.'

Within moments he'd tumbled back into dreamland.

Our bodies were clammy and stuck to each other and he was snoring softly into my ear, every exhale lifting a lock of my hair. I tried to not hate him but it was hard.

When he woke at 7 a.m., I'd extracted myself from his embrace and was back watching telly. He wandered into the living room, looking at his phone, at the text he'd got from Olga Mae.

'Babe, what's going on?' he asked.

So I told him about my fear that I was dangerous.

'This is . . . so *sad*. None of this is your fault. But this can't go on. You need to go back to Carlotta.'

'What can she do?'

'She's a *doctor*. She must be able to prescribe you something?'

Luke was a lot more innocent than me. The thing was, I *knew* there was no sleeping pill that I could safely take.

Carlotta suggested antidepressants again, which might also help with sleep. 'But I'm not depressed,' I said. 'I'm—I don't know—grieving? Traumatized?'

'I'm not sure the distinction really matters when you're this bad.'

I considered it. But I wanted to see what Carlotta's next offer would be.

'I can refer you to a good grief counsellor,' she said. 'But the work will take time. Because you can't sleep *right now*, how about I prescribe you a short course of Ambien? Used short-term, they're not addictive.'

'Maybe not for normal people, but for me, they . . .' I hesitated. '. . . probably are. I'm an addict. Sleeping pills were part of my thing.'

'Five pills,' she said. 'No more.'

It was so *alluring*. Five nights of blissful sleep. I'd feel so much more normal after them and surely I could manage to not get addicted in five short nights?

My thoughts hovered on a knife-edge. I'd been clean for over thirteen years, an achievement I was grateful for and really proud of. If I took these pills as they'd been prescribed, I'd be doing nothing wrong. Things only got tricky if I started doubling up, messing with the prescribed dose or taking them at times other than bedtime.

I'd be doing nothing wrong.

And, with that, my decision was made.

'Only five,' I said. 'No more, you promise? Even if I beg?'

She laughed. 'Not even if you beg.'

'Okay.' I exhaled, already feeling better.

I walked home, gratefully clutching my five little circles of magic in the drugstore bag. But I didn't want to tell anyone. I'd be afraid of being judged in meetings.

But I had to tell Nola, Olga Mae and Luke. Those relationships were too important.

'What did Carlotta say?' Luke asked.

'You might not like it. She gave me Ambien.'

'. . . Sleeping pills?' Concern zipped across his face. 'Rachel, no.'

In exasperation, I asked, 'What did you *think* she could do for me? Doctors aren't miracle-workers.'

'Was there any other option?'

'Antidepressants.'

'Maybe you *are* depressed?'

'I'm not. I'm . . .' I tried to locate the exact word to sum up my sadness, my shock, my self-blame, my yearning. '. . . grieving. We both are.'

'Sleeping tablets, though. You know you can't take them safely.'

'She gave me five tablets, enough for five nights' sleep. I told her to not give me any more, even if I beg. This is a short-term emergency thing.'

He sat, his head in his hands. 'What if this starts you back into addiction? I don't want to lose you as well.'

'You won't. You know how strong I am. But I swear to you, Luke, I'll lose my mind if I don't get some sleep.'

That first night, it was like a miracle. One minute I was conscious, then the next thing I knew, it was seven in the morning and Luke was getting up for work.

'Oh!' I was full of wonder. 'I slept for eight hours!'

It had been *gorgeous*. No broken sleep, no bad dreams, just a perfect blankness, as if I'd been temporarily dead.

I felt like a new person! Yes, my baby had died, but today I could cope. Especially because I knew for certain that a time would come later in the day when all the pain would stop.

The second night treated me to the same delicious oblivion.

On night three, when I looked at the card, at the three remaining pills—a mere *three*—panic gripped me.

By the fifth night, I was waking up intermittently. If I'd had any tablets left, I'd have taken a second one.

On the sixth night, it was time to try again on my own—and I was still awake when the sun came up.

'No one ever died from lack of sleep,' Luke said, parroting Mia.

But those five nights had changed me. Now I knew the magic the pills could do, I was in thrall to their wonders.

Getting through the day was suddenly far harder than it had seemed before, because today there would be no cut-off point when I could swallow a little white tablet and all the pain would dissolve.

I couldn't bear it. Not when I knew there was a solution. So I went back to Carlotta and flung myself on her mercy.

'You told me I shouldn't give you any more,' she reminded me.

'Yeah, I got it wrong. I didn't understand how bad . . . how deep the damage is. I can't stop asking myself what kind of mother sleeps through her baby dying?'

Her pupils flared with pity. Doubtfully she studied me. 'Can I trust you to be sensible?'

'You totally can. The last thing I want to do is relapse, things are bad enough.'

She exhaled. 'Okay. I'll give you a month's script, renewable by three, to be taken if and *only* if you need them, mmmkay?'

'Of course, of course.' I was breathless with relief.

'And you must start seeing a psychiatrist. You need more help than I can give you.'

I'd have agreed to anything, so long as I could get some sleep. 'Who should I . . . Is there anyone you recommend?'

'It's better if you do the research. It works best if it's a doctor you feel comfortable with. Perhaps someone experienced in addiction?'

I promised I'd sort it out, then left, gratefully clutching the prescription.

But this time I couldn't tell Luke. He'd go crazy.

It was easy for him, he could drink whiskey, he had the option to self-medicate any way he liked. I needed to sleep, I'd go round the bend if I couldn't and I was desperately grateful for the tablets. *I* knew I had no choice and *I* knew this was just temporary, until I'd done some healing. Luckily, I knew enough about addiction to know how to handle this.

54

I was woken by a dream about Yara and Luke. Quin's bedroom was pitch-dark and already the details of the dream were dispersing, leaving just a watery sorrow. It was only 3.20 a.m., but there would be no going back to sleep, not for ages.

Quietly, I slid from the bed.

'Y'okay?' Quin mumbled.

I paused. Quin tried so hard to be kind about Yara but nothing he could say would make me feel okay. It was better to just leave him to sleep. 'All fine, sweetie.'

But downstairs, because his TV was embedded in some sophisticated audio-visual set-up, I couldn't switch it on. Honest to *Christ*, what good was it that I could—in theory—get nine hundred channels in surround sound if I couldn't access one simple episode of *Brooklyn 99* to distract my grieving heart?

I decided to go home. At least there, technology didn't laugh at me.

Meanwhile, a text had arrived from Claire during the night: FYI, the birth-day girl's got the bit between her teeth about inviting Luke to her party.

Ah, no! My fragile acceptance was a long way from happily watching Luke Costello eating mushroom vol-au-vents in the thick of the Walshes, being quizzed by Auntie Imelda on my many failings.

As soon as I got home, I tripped over Devin's boots in the hall—which tumbled me into thinking about Luke again. For a moment I wanted to ring him because he was the only other person on earth who knew exactly how I felt.

Instead, I gathered Crunchie to me. We snuggled under a blanket, listening to Nigel Slater read his *Kitchen Diaries*. I was hoping his calm voice would soothe me enough to doze off again, but not today. Then I remembered there was an NA meeting at seven thirty on Sunday mornings in Bray, I might as well have a shower and go.

The turnout in Bray's parish centre was very small—only eight of us.

'Because the clocks went forward,' someone said. 'The usual crowd will turn up in an hour.'

Oh, right. Summer time had officially arrived. How had I missed it? Because my head was full of the past, obviously.

When it was my turn to share, I did a quick recap on what had happened yesterday. 'I wish I could time travel,' I said. 'To when I was pregnant. And just magically avert whatever made my baby's heart stop beating. I want to go back and rescue the three of us.' Suddenly I was crying so hard, I could barely speak. Tissues came my way from all quarters of the room.

When I could talk again, I said, 'I've been lucky, I've—mostly—accepted it. But seeing Luke again, it's churned up a lot of painful feelings and I'd like to sleep for a month. Or disappear into something like *Big Little Lies*, except I've already seen it twice.'

As soon as the meeting ended, I got a lot of advice—some of it very specific. 'Have you seen *Ozark*? Oh, right, how about *Mad Men*? *The Fall*? *Breaking Bad*? Obvious one, this, but *The Sopranos*?'

I'd already watched everything the man suggested and my eyes were becoming glassy.

'*Tin Star*?' he said.

'*Tin Star* is shit.' An older woman called Loretta had taken my arm and steered me away from Mr Netflix. 'Don't waste your time. Go out into nature today. Spend time with your feelings. Talk to your baby. And don't stick things in your ears and distract yourself.'

'Okay.' Maybe I would.

In the car, I texted Quin: Couldn't sleep. Head a bit melted. Going for a walk on the beach like a woman from a Hallmark movie. See you later xxxx

I pressed send and my very next thought was, *I want to talk to Luke. Shite.*

Today Rachel envied Yesterday Rachel, so certain that she didn't need to see Luke again. The thing was, of course, that the only other person in the world who'd loved Yara was Luke.

My phone was still in my hand. I looked at it. Kept looking. Was I really doing this? Calling him?

He *had* apologized. My anger and hurt weren't entirely gone but I could get past it. Right now I felt I needed him—and I was curious to see if he'd make himself available.

'Hey.' He answered immediately, sounding as if he'd been waiting to hear from me.

'Ah . . . hey. Listen . . . sorry about this, but are you okay today? I dreamt about her last night, like a lot, and—'

'So did I.' He sounded relieved. 'It was yesterday? Seeing her photo? Talking about her?'

I was afraid I might cry again. 'It's stirred up a lot of memories.'

'Yep.' After a moment of silence, he asked, 'How often do you think about her?'

'Every single day. I talk to her, in my head.'

'About what?'

'*Every*thing. Anything. And she talks back. We have conversations. She wants the best for me, but she's also fun.'

He seemed interested. 'It's not like that for me. But she's nearly always my first thought when I wake up. On the days she isn't, I'm kinda relieved because maybe it means I'm getting better, then I feel guilty. I don't want her to think I'd forget her.'

'She knows you'd never do that.' My voice was fierce. 'Does Kallie know about her?'

'Of course. But I don't talk about it.'

'To anyone?'

'Nobody else went through it.'

'I did.'

'Yeah, but you and me . . .'

I let the silence last.

'Should we—' he asked. 'Would you like to get coffee? Today. Like, now.'

'I was going to go for a walk. To the beach. The sound of the waves, it calms me.'

'Can I come?'

YesNoMaybeFuuuuuuuuck.

'Okay.'

Even though the morning was dry and striving for sunny, Pebble Beach was deserted. Luke was already there, lounging on a low wall, his hands in his pockets, the salty breeze whipping his hair.

His face was raised to the try-hard sun but at the sound of my car, he looked for me. From a long way away, his eyes met mine. The impact felt physical.

By the time I'd parked, he'd walked over. I opened the car door into a rough breeze. Overhead, seabirds circled, their cries harsh.

'Hi.' Luke hadn't shaved. Dark bristles shaded his jaw and shaped his mouth. Up close, in the glassy light, occasional strands of silver flashed in his hair. They were new. At least, new to me.

Out of nowhere, the ground felt unsteady. This was a mistake. Too soon.

'What?' He'd noticed something was off. 'You've changed your mind?'

'No, I . . .'

His eyes scoured my face.

'Sorry,' I said. 'Forgot how weird this all is. I think I got over-confident.'

'Over-confident?' I couldn't read his tone. 'O-kay.' Clenching his jaw, he stared towards the water. Then, 'So? We staying or going?'

'Might as well stay. You've driven all this distance.' All seven kilometres.

'Sarcasm?'

Sudden fury surged in me. 'Yeah.'

He slanted me a glance; he seemed unimpressed.

I began walking along the blue-grey shingle, my boots on the stones sounding like coins rattling in a jar. Luke followed, then caught up.

'Thanks for calling me today,' he said.

'. . . Um, sure. It made sense—you're the only other person on earth who knows how I feel. No one can help us the way we could help each other.' Then I wanted to add, *And, finally, you're talking to me.* But with incredible restraint I contented myself with, 'We never got the chance to do it before.'

'And whose fault is that?'

Surprised at his tone, I said, 'We *know* whose fault it is.' Puzzled, I watched until his glower faded.

'Yeahhhhh.' He sighed. 'Does Quin know where you are?'

'Yes.' I mean, he knew *where* I was. But he didn't know who I was with. 'Does Kallie know where you are?'

'Of course.'

Although I had no real clue what to make of Kallie, it seemed important to bury any signs of jealousy. 'I like Kallie,' I heard myself say. Then forced the words, 'A lot.'

Watching the waves, he said, 'So do I.' He turned to look straight into my face and emphasized, 'A lot.'

Hearing it felt surprisingly painful.

'Are you planning to . . . have kids?'

The idea twisted something terrible in me. But I had to admit that another child of Luke's in the world could only be beautiful.

'No.' He sounded shocked. 'Kallie is great, but I've always been honest with her. I'm not available . . .' He cleared his throat. 'That thing of surrendering my life to her, of . . . of stopping just being me and becoming an "us", I'm not able. But I care about her. She's lovely to be around. *And*,' he added, 'I wish I could offer her more. But my life happened the way it happened and this is the way it left me. I'm grateful that there's plenty I can still enjoy.'

'Like smoking weed on the deck with her. That must be good.' There was a sudden lump in my throat.

'Don't do that, Rachel.' He stopped walking. 'I never missed it when I was with you.'

His gaze tracked over me. I was the first to look away.

'How's your dad?' This was a fairly weak attempt at conversation.

He shook his head. 'Deliberately acting up because he doesn't want me to leave. But spending time with him feels right. I'll need to get back to Denver soon but . . .' Staring out to sea, he said, 'I wish I'd spent more time with Mum.'

With genuine sympathy, I said, 'It's not easy living so far from your family.'

'Tell me about it. Is that why you decided to move back here?'

All sympathy disappeared. Was he for real? 'My baby died. My husband left me.'

He wheeled around. 'Seriously? That's your'—he made air-quotes—'"reason"?'

Astonished, I said, 'No, Luke. It's my *reason*. Like, what the hell else would it be?'

Yesterday he'd been not exactly friendly, but willing to move forwards. Today felt like we'd taken a step backwards. I didn't know what had changed.

He returned to watching the waves. 'She'd be almost seven now. In July. What would she be like?'

I needed a moment to gather myself. 'She'd look like you. She had your hair.'

He shot a look my way. 'But those Walsh genes are *strong*. Sooner or later, she'd have turned into you. She'd be losing her baby teeth . . .'

'Cute and gappy.'

'The Tooth Fairy would come.' His jaw clenched. 'That's . . . wow. Could you imagine?'

I couldn't speak. The thought was too painful.

Our eyes met. He looked appalled. 'God, Rachel, you were right,' he said. 'This wasn't such a great idea.'

Small patches of blackness were floating at the edge of my vision. I needed to sit.

'Have you eaten today?' he asked.

'Yes.' I hadn't.

'I can give you a mint?' He offered me the packet and we sat on the shingle. I flipped a mint into my mouth and lay back, letting the sweetness flood in, listening to the rush and crash of the waves. For a moment, the universe held me, free from pain.

'What are you thinking about?' He asked.

'Ahhh. That the fizzing noise the small waves make, in their last gasps, just before they run out of steam, sounds like Alka-Seltzer dissolving in a glass.'

'Never not thinking about drugs . . .'

Was he trying to be funny? I sat up. 'Just in case you're in any doubt about it, I'm *clean.*'

'You'd hardly be working at the Cloisters if you weren't. Head therapist. Wow.'

'Luke? What are you—'

'I'm glad you're clean.' But 'glad' wasn't how he sounded. 'Can you be around kids?' he asked, with another of those whiplash conversational segues. 'Or does it hurt too much?'

'It depends on the day.' My voice was tight.

'Is this too hard?' he asked. 'Should we stop?'

'But it's why we're doing it—to try to make it more bearable?' A drop of rain splashed onto my hand and I decided to ignore it. 'Mostly I love being around kids.'

'I love them too.' He stared out over the water, his expression dreamy. 'Their possibility . . . When I first moved to Denver I just wanted to sit in the playground and watch them on the climbing frames and the swings . . . But the moms called the cops on me.'

'Seriously? God. And how are you with kids these days? Any better?'

'Only so much healing can be done. It would be wrong to be cured. I saw a person, you know, a counsellor, in Denver. I thought if I went for long enough, that the weirdness would stop. I feel like . . .' He gestured with his hands. 'Like one of my legs is shorter than the other. Moving through life,

I feel . . . *off*. I thought the counselling would make both of my legs the same length again.'

'It didn't?'

'But I can still walk. The loss will always be there but these days I don't notice as much that I'm different from everyone else. And you, Rachel? You seem okay. Quin seems like a good guy.'

'Quin is great.' Because Quin *was* great.

'What have you done with your share of her ashes?' Luke asked.

'I planted a small tree in my garden.' Another drop landed. Several dark dots were visible on the stony ground. 'A cherry blossom.'

'Wait, you're a *gardener* now?' Then, 'Is it raining? It was sunny thirty seconds ago.'

'Oh?' Suddenly I was far too angry. 'It doesn't rain in Denver?'

'Hardly ever.'

'Well, you're in Ireland now. Anyway, it'll stop in a minute.'

Irritatingly, though, it didn't. The Irish weather had decided to show me up. As the unexpectedly cold rain began to tip down in earnest, I said, 'Let's go.'

He turned up the collar of his coat, I slung my scarf around my hair and we began crunching back the way we'd come.

'You know what just happened?' he demanded. 'I felt anxious. About your hair going frizzy in the rain.'

'It's not your responsibility any more.' Technically it had never been, but back in the days when he'd loved me, my concerns had been his.

'Shows how deep the programming goes,' he muttered.

As we said goodbye at my car, I blurted, 'Luke, the memories aren't all sad. Remember us painting her nursery? We were so happy then. That was real.'

He blinked and put a hand on the crown of his head. 'God. Just got a . . . déjà vu or something.'

'I know what came after was horrific, but we need to remember the good parts as well as the rest.'

He nodded. 'And I'm glad you're okay now. Really glad.' Startling me, he took my chilled hand between both of his and pressed his lips into my palm. His eyes met mine—then he stuttered, 'Sorry.' Letting my hand drop like a stone, he said, 'More déjà vu. I don't know what I was . . . Sorry. Thank you for today.' He turned towards his bike, got on and roared away.

Mystified, I watched him disappear, the heat of his mouth still warming my skin. What had *that* been about? Maybe that was how they said goodbye in Denver? Like, obviously, though, it wasn't.

It was all so confusing. Yesterday he'd seemed willing to accept blame but today he'd been angry. Right up until he'd done the Denver Goodbye.

Now I was exhausted. *Now* I was ready to fall asleep on the spot.

The moment I got home, I slid gratefully into bed and slept until 5 p.m.— and woke up to discover that an Emergency Committee Meeting had been called in response to Mum's threats to invite Luke to the party.

55

Immediately I rang Claire. 'She can't do it.' I was adamant. 'Absolutely not.'
'I know, babes.'

'The thought of Luke showing up at a Walsh family party is making me feel sick. Having to stand around eating cheese-on-a-stick in a function room in a three-star hotel while sixteen of Mum's bitchiest sisters say, "No wonder he ran away." I can't!'

'Got your back, babes.'

But red-faced and bullish, Mum held the line. 'Yesterday you went to Brian Costello's birthday party! What's the difference?'

'Luke wanted me to go. I *don't* want him at your do.'

'Why not?'

'Because! Could you *imagine*. Auntie Imelda taking note of all the ways Kallie is better than me! It would be horrendous.'

'If that fucker comes,' Helen said, 'I'm throwing a glass of red wine all over his white T-shirt.'

You see, this is what people didn't appreciate about Helen—she had many positives, including dogged loyalty.

'And how do I know he'll be wearing a white T-shirt?' Helen continued. 'Because he's a Basic who got stuck in his look three centuries ago.'

Another of Helen's attributes was her tendency to speak unpalatable truths.

'But he'd be company for Angelo,' Anna called, via Mum's tablet, from New York.

'Angelo's a grown man!' I exclaimed. 'He doesn't need a buddy.' I turned to Mum, 'Wouldn't you be embarrassed in front of your sisters? To have my ex-husband there? With his new girlfriend?'

'No! We're a blended family—'

'That's not what "blended family" means.'

'It would show that we're all friends again. That would put Imelda in her box.'

'Please, Mum. Have you no loyalty to me?'

'It was a long time ago. I heard he apologized yesterday—'

I glared at Claire, who mouthed, *Sorry, babes.*

'—and you're fine now.'

'Why do you even want him there?' Helen asked.

'I was fond of him. He was part of the family. It was hard on all of us when they separated.'

'Admit it, you fancy him,' Helen said.

'Maybe I do.' Mum went an even darker red. 'But it's not my only reason.'

'Hold on, please.' Claire was sharp. 'I'd like a look at him. *And* Kallie. I'm a shallow person, that's hardly news. But if Rachel doesn't want him there, he shouldn't be there.'

'Hard agree,' Helen said.

Margaret had been very quiet to this point—and her take was always interesting. 'What do you think?' I asked.

Carefully, she said, 'I know an early miscarriage probably isn't the same as what you went through, Rachel—if I'm saying the wrong thing, I'm sorry. But when I miscarried, and afterwards . . . the only person who was as devastated as me was Garv.

'What Luke did to you was . . . but people do terrible things when they're off their heads with grief. He's here, he's talking to you now. He apologized. I think it would help you if fences were mended. So I'm in favour of inviting him.'

'Me too,' Anna called. 'For sort of the same reasons. You can't avoid what the universe wants for you.'

'Let's do a show of hands,' Mum said, raising both of hers.

Mum, Margaret and Anna were in favour of Luke coming to the party; Claire, Helen and I were against.

'It's my party,' Mum said. 'I have the casting vote.'

'It's Rachel's ex-*husband*,' Helen yelled. '*She* has the casting vote.'

'I'm the oldest person here, *I* have the casting vote.'

'Yeah, you *are* the oldest person here.' Helen was savage. 'And clearly gone in the head. Crunchie the *dog* should have the casting vote instead of you.'

'Fine.' I'd had enough. 'Invite him. But if you do, I'm not coming. And I don't make idle threats.' Like, of *course* I did, all the time, but this once I actually meant it. 'I'm leaving now, going over to Quin's, so we can make plans for Saturday week, when you'll all be at the party. Enjoy yourselves.'

Amidst a hue and cry, I exited the living room—and promptly stumbled over Dad, who was lurking in the hall.

'Jesus!' I yelped. 'What are you doing?'

'Has anyone any interest in what I think?' he asked.

'Are you not dead?' Helen asked him. 'Could have *sworn* . . .'

'Come in here.' Mum was watching him appraisingly. 'Say your piece.'

Nervously, Dad stood in the middle of the good rug. 'Their baby died, then they split up, so they never had a chance to talk about it.' Helplessly, he let his hands drop and met my eyes. 'People need to talk about things.'

'You heard him, Rachel,' Mum said. 'Your poor father—'

'—back from the dead—' Helen threw in.

'I'm not dead!' he squeaked. 'I'm the head of this family—' The rest of his sentence was drowned out by a storm of laughter.

'Thank you, Claire, thank you, Helen.' I threw on my coat. 'The rest of you, you're insane and very mean. Bye.'

Breathless with hurt and fury, I flung myself into my car and headed for Quin's.

Quin stared hard at me. 'Last night you said you wouldn't see him again. Twelve hours later, you spent half the day with him. Rachel? Should I . . . be worried?'

'No. Not at all. Quin, can I try to explain? Since yesterday, all these feelings about Yara have suddenly come out of . . . wherever I've managed to stash them for the last six years. I'm grateful for the chance to talk about her.'

'You can talk about her with me.'

'I know. And that's lovely of you.' I was trying to find the right words and, at the same time, avoid hurting him. 'But talking about her with the one other person who loved her like I did . . .'

'I understand that,' Quin admitted. 'It's just . . .' Suddenly infuriated, he exclaimed, 'I never get to feel sure of you.'

'But you can! Quin, I haven't done anything wrong.'

All of a sudden, he looked exhausted. My heart twisted with frustration, then softened with pity for him.

'Just . . .' His voice was weary. 'If anything changes, be honest with me.'

'It won't change. I'm mad about you. We're together.' *I love you* hung in the air, unspoken. But to say it now, in response to his insecurity, would have felt wrong.

'I'm completely serious,' he said. 'I can cope with anything except being lied to. "Protected from the truth" is the worst thing you could do to me. Even if you know you're going to hurt me, I'd prefer the facts.'

'Okay. But—'

'Do you swear?'

'Yes, but honestly, Quin—'

'Let's leave it there.'

56

It was something I kept to myself but I actually *liked* Mondays. My little duck-lings were in such a process of constant change that it was exciting to sit in the Abbot's Quarter and see what might have developed over the weekend.

But this Monday, as I hurried along, hoping for a good chair, dread had me in a chokehold. I felt spacey, slightly disconnected from reality—hardly surprising, considering all the turmoil of the weekend—and braced for something bad.

Which I narrowed down to *an outburst from Luke.*

Sometime during last night's broken sleep I'd seen that he was angry with me. Despite his mixed messages—the Denver Goodbye showed he was trying to be nice—his anger had kept leaking out.

He had never actually *said* that he blamed me for Yara's death—but it was clear that he had. And probably still did.

He was going to accuse me, *that* was what I was dreading—hearing those terrible words. The irony, though, was that I no longer blamed myself. I hadn't, not since the meditation weekend where I'd met Quin.

Quin hadn't known me from a hole in the ground but our strange con-nection during the LovingKindness exercise had absolved me. It was the greatest gift I'd ever been given.

No matter what Luke still thought, Yara's death hadn't been my fault. I had to remember that.

My phone rang, making my brain bounce off the ceiling of my skull. God, I was in *bits*. But it wasn't Luke, as I'd expected. Instead, it was Bronte's husband, brusque and bossy. 'Our eldest child, Freya, is flying in from San Francisco tomorrow morning. Just for the day. She's coming in to confront her mother.'

Is she now? Is she *indeed*?

That wasn't how it worked—he didn't get to decide Bronte's schedule. And had he forgotten there were six other people in Bronte's group? There could be countless things already tabled for tomorrow.

Coolly, I said, 'I need to check the agenda, there may not be an opportunity for Freya to—'

'She's catching a flight back straight after her session. We'll be with you at ten a.m. Leaving at eleven.' And he hung up.

The high-handed fucker!

As it happened, tomorrow morning could be freed up. But I'd get no chance to interview Freya, to brief her. Her written testimonial had been worse than useless—she had nothing but lovely things to say about Bronte. And was there any point in her coming if she wasn't capable of a tough conversation?

Switching off my phone, I got the best seat in the Abbot's Quarter and watched my ducklings file in. Trassa was first. God love her, she was carrying so much pain, but she'd had a peaceful weekend.

Dennis, however, seemed buoyant as he swaggered in. *Too* buoyant, actually. I suspected he was engaged in high-wire cognitive manipulation, convincing himself that, despite all the evidence, he wasn't an alcoholic. This wasn't my first rodeo.

Apparently, Ella had spent the weekend stomping around, badmouthing Jonah and Naaz, but she was still here, so she obviously didn't completely believe she was innocent of all their accusations.

Giles, leaving today, radiated wisdom and compassion. You could find it irritating, if you were that way inclined.

Speaking of which, here came Chalkie. He'd smashed a tennis racket on Saturday, another one yesterday and he'd hit the punchbag so hard it fell down, bringing half of the shed ceiling with it. All excellent stuff!

At least *some* good had come out of poor Gemma Kaye's visit—because Harlie still hadn't cried. In a small, quiet way, I was actually starting to panic. She had only two weeks left and if she stayed locked into anger for much longer, I'd have failed her.

Sometimes it happened—that a client only got so far in the process, and stayed stuck. Not often but when it did, it sort of *killed* me.

Here came Bronte, cool and slightly inscrutable. She was a challenging one, no doubt about it, very skilled at protecting her addiction. Probably because she already knew so much about it.

Her relapse was interesting. It was undeniably hard when an addict had to re-engage with medicine they'd once been addicted to. In so many ways it was easier to be an alcoholic—you just didn't drink. There was never any reason for medicinal vodka (no matter what Claire might tell you).

Bronte had exaggerated the pain of her broken ankle, I was fairly sure of that—but I was just as sure that it genuinely had hurt. That's what made it so tricky—the fact that it had been *real*. Same as with me, when I hadn't been able to sleep. And in those situations, the right doctor was vital.

Carlotta had been so kind to me. So too had Dr Gagnon—the psychiatrist I'd found, on her orders.

One of his reviews had described him as: 'A doctor who really gets it, who knows what real insomnia looks like.' When I'd read that, my heart lifted in relief. Immediately, I'd picked up my phone to make an appointment.

I'd sat in front of him and told him my terrible story. I didn't have to exaggerate—I really was broken.

'Oh boy,' he'd said, 'what a trauma. So, acute insomnia? You know about sleep hygiene? No electronics in the bedroom? Wearing glasses to reduce blue light?'

'I already do all of that.' I gasped, suddenly terrified he was going to recommend warm baths and camomile tea. 'I do mindfulness. Yoga. Eat a banana at bedtime. I do absolutely *everything* everyone recommends.'

He frowned. 'It also sounds as if you're experiencing anxiety.'

Well, I certainly was then, as a recommendation to start Yin Yoga (most boring of all the yogas) looked increasingly likely.

'But you're finding the Ambien helpful?'

'A lifesaver.' Once again I wasn't exaggerating.

'Taken as prescribed, they're non-addictive. Even for a person, such as yourself, with a history of addiction.'

'Yes. Absolutely.' For over thirteen years I'd thought differently, but the previous few weeks had changed my mind.

'Should I add an anti-anxiety medication into the mix?' he said. 'How are you with Xanax?'

Suddenly nervous, I said, 'No, please don't.' I didn't *need* tranquillizers but I might have taken them anyway. Having them felt dangerous. 'Just sleeping tablets.'

He seemed surprised. '. . . Okay.'

Next thing, he was printing out a prescription, scribbling a signature and handing it over. 'You can pay outside.'

It appeared it was time for me to leave. 'When should I come back?'

'In a month.'

The reviews had said he was brisk—and he was certainly that. Also expensive—my insurance wouldn't cover all of his fee. But he'd listened to me, he'd heard me.

I was back out on the street before I saw that he'd doubled Carlotta's dosage—and I was surprised. But also very grateful. I remembered, then, one of the reviews which had criticized him for 'throwing pills at the problem'.

But sometimes that was exactly what the problem required.

At the end of group, Dennis danced over to me. 'Rachel, *a chara*, could I have a wordeen?'

Oh, here we go . . . 'Sure. Now suit you?'

'Down to the ground. And further! Right through to the centre of the earth and . . . out the other side.'

In a consulting room, he perched on the edge of the chair, fixing his bright eyes on mine. 'I was thinking about Trassa. About . . . That's a desperate thing that happened to her, you wouldn't wish it on anyone. But, Rachel, wouldn't I have had a trauma or something?'

'Maybe you have?'

He perked up. 'Was it the time Patch won the egg-and-spoon race out from under me nose? There I was, thinking I was coming home to a hero's welcome and, at the last minute, the little feck whips certain victory from me grasp.'

Steadily, I eyeballed him.

'But, Rachel, being serious, like. If that's the worst thing I can think of, there isn't anything there.'

'What are you trying to say?'

'That, well, it makes sense, doesn't it, that Trassa would get addicted to something. Cause and effect, like. But with me, there's no cause. So no effect.' His curls bounced as he sat up and announced, 'So I can't be an alcoholic!'

'Oh, Dennis.' In less tragic circumstances, it would actually be funny. 'Trassa is Trassa. But everyone is unique. People are addicts or alcoholics for all kinds of reasons and some for no reason at all. No obvious one, anyway.'

He cocked his head. 'How d'you mean?'

'Sometimes a trauma can occur when the person is too young to remember. Other times there genuinely isn't any trauma, just excuses and justifications.'

'How's that now?'

'Addicts are great at hard-luck stories—their parents didn't love them enough or their boss doesn't value them or their wife isn't grateful—and that's why they have to drink or use. But, Dennis, you'd drink even if you had no excuse. All that matters here is that you're an alcoholic and you need to get well.'

He looked crestfallen. In a small voice he said, 'I don't want to be an alcoholic.'

I nodded. I knew. 'Dennis? When you used to find your father passed out, looking like he was dead? What did that do to you?'

He dropped his head. 'How do I know?' he muttered. 'You're the expert.'

'I'd imagine being a little boy of six or seven discovering his daddy and thinking he had died would have been devastating.'

His head remained bowed. Then he cast a furious look at me. "'Twas,' he choked, his eyes wet. "'Twas.'

He curled inwards, making himself smaller. Roughly rubbing his face with his hands, he became a little boy before my eyes.

Well, that was easy, a lot easier than I'd expected.

I let him cry. He had a lifetime's worth to catch up on.

'There are probably worse crimes I've committed.' It was Giles's last session in group and he was in giddy good form. 'But this memory is the worst I can think of.' In a fruity voice, he asked, 'Are you ready, children? Then let us begin. One night, after a right old time of it, I thought I was having a heart attack, so I went to Emergency. I wanted an ECG. The picture in my head is me standing in the waiting room, yelling at all the sick and injured people, "I am having a cardiac arrest! *I!* Giles Freyne! And you know who I am!"'

'Holy fuck,' Chalkie muttered. 'Morto for you, bud.'

'The security guards were trying to catch me but I was sprinting around the place, whisking open the curtains around the cubicles. At one, I told the woman in the bed to get out, that I needed it. Then I said I had a gun.'

'And had you?' Chalkie asked.

'Where would I get a gun?'

'No? Okay. As you were.'

'I tried to pull the drip out from the woman's arm,' Giles said. 'Then the police came and arrested me. I told them I'd gone to school with the minister for justice and they'd be directing traffic for the rest of their careers. *That's* the sort of thing', he said, 'I want never to repeat.'

'You don't have to,' Trassa said. 'So long as you go to your meetings and aftercare.'

'Of course.' He twinkled his eyes at her, acknowledging that, along with Chalkie, she was now one of the group elders. 'I'm looking forward to not feeling ashamed. Or having to remember which lie I told to whom. And being relieved of all that *planning*—where I could get cash, when I could do a line, how to hide that I was buzzed. It was *really* hard work.'

'And remember, Giles,' I said, 'addiction is a parasite that never quits. Nail that to your heart. The second it spots weakness, it's right back in, as strong as ever.' Briefly, I had a moment of strange confusion, something like déjà vu, then reality returned. God, I was really stressed. 'You need to work on your firewalls every single day. You can never drop your guard. Okay?'

'Okay!'

I stood up. 'Time for cake.'

Sadly, no homemade Gateau Diane for Giles, he hadn't been popular with the catering staff. But there was a long-life Victoria sponge from Spar and a healthy turnout to heckle him.

'Six weeks ago, I could not *believe* that I was a patient in such a dreadful place!' He was up on a chair, delivering his farewell speech. 'The only reason I was here was to get my job back . . .'

Approaching from behind, Brianna grabbed my arm and hissed, 'Drama. His first wife has turned up to take him home. So has his third wife. They're both up in the office, looking like it's Staplers at Dawn. What'll I do?'

'Nothing.'

Giles could take care of it. Telling the two women that actually he'd be living with his second wife could be his first clean and sober challenge. Hit the ground running, as it were.

When he climbed down from the chair, people lined up to hug him. It always made me teary that despite every harsh word said in here, at the end of it all, everyone wished everyone else well.

I watched him hugging Trassa, then Dennis, people the likes of whom he'd probably never crossed paths with before.

Oh, and here came Chalkie. He and Giles faced each other and, for a moment, neither man moved. A tense energy pulsed between them, then they fell into a tight bear hug.

'Stay safe, bud,' Chalkie said with a sly smile. 'Go to your meetings.'

'You go to *your* meetings.'

'If we both go to our meetings, we'll probably run into each other. Imagine that. You and me, hanging out, having the chats. Jaaaaaayzisss.'

'Or,' Giles twinkled, 'we could have a game of tennis?'

'Ah, Gilesy man, that's enough to send me back on the gear.'

57

Switching my phone on after work, I'd expected a missed call from Luke—but nothing. I should have been relieved but waiting for the other shoe to drop was unbearable. I'd rather get it over and done with.

However, Helen had texted, asking if I wanted to get what she described as 'evening food'.

I assumed she meant dinner but that the word 'dinner' was on her Shovel List. God only knew why, but it wasn't as if any of her pet hates were rational.

I rang her and, after a long time, she answered. 'You couldn't have texted?'

'It would have taken too long. But here's what I would have texted: Yes, thank you, Helen, I would like to get "evening food" with you. I'm going to a meeting in Stillorgan at eight o'clock, so a place nearby would be good. I've taken a quick look and there are three restaurants with tables available at six thirty, which is when I'd arrive—'

'—but not a place with an Early Bird Menu! That *boasts* about it. Rachel, I couldn't! I'd be too irritated to eat.'

'Way ahead of you.' I was smug. 'See you at Chopping Block at six thirty.'

Of course, there was always a chance that Chopping Block might be on her list for some other reason—perhaps the name was infuriating? Or misleading? Perhaps because it wasn't an *actual* chopping block?

To my relief, she said, 'Okay!' Then, 'Why can't everyone be as reasonable as you, Rachel? This is why you're my favourite sister.'

'I *am*? Thanks.'

'Apart from Anna, like.'

At Chopping Block, I found her deep in conversation with a waiter. I guessed they were discussing coleslaw. Helen liked coleslaw. Cheese and coleslaw sandwiches were about all she ate.

'Howya!' she cried when she saw me. 'Sit down. This is Ultan, he's sorting me out with cheese and coleslaw sandwiches—and a pint of Diet Coke. Did I say that, Ultan?'

'You did.' He consulted his pad. 'Room temperature. No lemon or lime or any fruit, especially no pears, cranberries or kiwis.'

'Good man. But Rachel will order normal food.'

'Fine.' Ultan gave me a menu and skedaddled off to do Helen's bidding.

'So?' I asked her. 'How are things?'

'Do you want to know why I suggested this?' she asked. 'Us, meeting for evening food?'

'Something's wrong?'

'No.' Then, with a great deal of pride, she said, 'I'm checking in on you.'

'Oh! That's . . . ah . . . nice.'

'Yep. Trying to behave like a normal person.' She was so *very* delighted with herself.

'Checking in, in case I'm upset about you and Artie tryi—' I stopped myself. 'Sorry. I nearly said the "trying" word there.'

'Good job you didn't.' And both of us laughed.

'In case I'm upset about you and Artie *hoping* for a baby? Because I'm fine about it.' Well, *almost*, and that would have to do.

'Not just that,' she elaborated. 'I was thinking about you seeing Costello again, after what went down with your little girl. And now the old woman and her bullshit about the party. I'd say it's a lot for you, like.'

Very surprised, I said, 'Thank you.'

'You've had it rough. I get it, now that I'm . . . *broody* myself. Thing is, I'd probably be fuck all use to you. I'm bad at sympathy . . .' She paused, her mood suddenly darker. 'So I've been told. Or is it empathy? Maybe it's both.' Brightening again, she said, 'But if you were stuck, I'm . . . yeah, here for you.'

'Thank you,' I repeated.

'You've been good to me,' she said. 'When I get the Mads, you don't make it all about you.'

I found this admission almost unbearably touching.

'Nearly everyone else does,' she said. 'They can't help it, I suppose. But you're different.'

I swallowed hard. 'And how are you? With everything that's going on?'

'It's a pain in the hole, isn't it?' She sounded exasperated. 'Wanting a baby. There's so much more to lose. I was better off when I wanted nothing and loved nobody.'

'Oh, Helen, no. That's no way to live.'

'But it's safe.' Her anxiety was suddenly very evident. 'Rachel, what if I can't get up the duff? And I go mental again? Or what if I have a baby and then get the Post-Baby Mads? Because that can happen to'—she spoke in a dorky voice—'"women with a history of depression".' She rolled her eyes and stuck out her tongue. 'Which is me. Fuck's sake! Or what if—and I'm sorry, Rachel—but what if I do get pregnant and then lose it? It'd be straight back to the nut-house for me.'

Christ.

The thing was that any of those scenarios *could* come to pass. Though the chances were small, the prospect was terrifying. A frantic need to protect her surged in me.

'I'll tell you something,' she said. 'I wish I had meetings to go to, the way you do.'

'But there *are* self-help groups for people with depression.'

'Yeah. I went one time.' More eye-rolling. 'But the others annoyed the living bejesus out of me. They were so . . . *moany*. I didn't go again.'

When I got home after my meeting, I was exhausted. Slowly climbing the stairs to bed, I knew I'd have no trouble sleeping. And, oh God, my *gratitude*. Even now, the very thought of insomnia threw me back into those terrible weeks after Yara died.

The world had shifted on its axis and nothing would ever be the same again. A whole new dimension of sorrow had opened for me. It was only once I'd got a regular supply of sleeping pills that I could bear it.

Waking up every morning to live another day without Yara was always a shock. Surviving each individual minute was gruelling. But knowing that at 10 p.m. I could stop enduring and disappear into delicious oblivion gave me strength.

The only thing was, it didn't take much to build up a tolerance to the pills. So it was no real surprise that after a week or so of taking them, I began waking after five hours, then four. For a couple of nights I tried waiting it out, hoping to go back to sleep, but it was hard, especially knowing there was a small stash of pills nearby, rolled into a pair of socks in my chest of drawers. On the third night, I tiptoed over and tried to pull out the drawer without making a noise. But with a squeak, the wood caught and Luke shifted in the bed.

'What are you doing?' he mumbled.

'Nothing,' I whispered. 'Go back to sleep.'

I pressed the pill from the card, placed it on my tongue, slipped back into bed and soon I was carried off to pain-free nothingness.

After that night, I kept a second tablet hidden in my pillowcase for when I woke at 2 or 3 a.m.

In an awful development, daytimes seemed to be becoming more painful. It was about seven weeks since she'd died, the initial devastation had shifted and the full weight of my—our—loss was starting to settle. Instead of the wide-open expanse of love and happiness Luke and I had been primed for, the life we were left with seemed small, stunted and very sad.

Then *he* went through a spell of insomnia. After one morning too many when I woke to find him hollow-eyed and exhausted, I suggested he go to Carlotta. My hope was that if we were both taking sleeping pills, he'd understand how helpful they were—and I could tell him I was still taking them.

But he said, 'I'll just tough it out. Your sleeping got back to normal.' Then, 'Didn't it?'

I couldn't be sure, but I thought his eyes flicked to my sock drawer and I went cold. If he found out about them, he'd make me throw them away and I couldn't—they were the saving of me.

When he left for work, I gave it twenty minutes, just to make sure he wasn't coming back to catch me, then I retrieved my precious little stockpile—three cards, twenty-seven pills remaining. They needed to be broken up and hidden around the apartment, so that if Luke found some, at least there would still be plenty left.

As I cut the cards into quarters, I felt ashamed, then resentful. Why did he have to be so difficult? If only he'd take on board that this was a very temporary thing and as soon as I was stronger, I'd stop.

The bathroom seemed too obvious, that was probably the first place he'd look. But it seemed safe to slide some pills into the pocket of a coat I no longer wore. In the kitchen, my hand rummaged down low into a bag of basmati rice we hadn't touched in years and I buried four tablets. So long as Luke didn't take it upon himself to do a kitchen clearout—and that was wildly unlikely—they'd be safe.

My focus narrowed in on the three photographs hanging on the living-room wall: smiley, happy pictures of Brigit and me on a night out with the Real Men, a thousand years ago. They'd been there for so long that Luke and I no longer saw them.

I took them down and as I was sellotaping tablets to their backs I got a glimpse into how insane this was. Like, it was *mad*. Shouldn't I just tell Luke? There was nothing dodgy about taking these pills, they'd been prescribed by a doctor. Well, two doctors actually. Carlotta didn't know that Dr Gagnon had given me a prescription and Dr Gagnon either didn't know or wasn't interested in Carlotta's script.

But they were *prescribed*. Admittedly, I was taking more than either doctor had given me, but that was just to get me through this awful time. For all that Luke had freaked out about the initial five Ambien from Carlotta, he was forgetting that I was the least likely person to relapse. I knew so much about myself *and* so much about addiction that I would make sure it would never happen.

58

I woke up to a series of texts from Claire.

Devin Costello a BIG hit. Luka and him in bromance! Even Francesca stopped being bitchy after a while.

Then:

No effing job, though. Do any of them ever have jobs? Us Gen Xers keep the world turning then they make us feel guilty for buying clothes. Not cool.

Then:

I'm barely Gen X. Almost young enough to be millennial lol. They're happy enough to take allowance from us though and let us pay for stuff.

Then:

Doesn't really look like Luke. Would have been weird if he did. He seems mad about Kate. Never liked that Isaac.

Then:

What you up to this evening? Luka and me having mother-son bonding time. Going shopping. Proves my earlier point. Then going for Mexican food. Teenage boys obsessed with tacos.

Well. It was good news for Kate that they liked Devin. That was about as much headspace as I could spare for it. Then I went to work.

At ten past ten, Freya Tollemarche hurried up the steps, her bossy-pants father, Eden, behind her.

I'd expected Bronte's daughter to be a fey, fine-boned blonde but instead she had lots of thick, russet hair, barely contained by a knitted utility hat.

Her face was long and thin with prominent teeth but she was gorgeous, with fresh bouncy skin and glowing eyes.

Eden greeted me by bellowing, 'Today must be all about Freya.'

'Excuse me?' Cheeky fecker, telling me how to run my sessions.

'I can be here whenever you command. But as Freya is visiting for just one day, she must have the floor.'

'We'll see.' I gave him a thin smile and turned my attention to his daughter.

Emotionally, she was all over the place, smiling non-stop while on the verge of tears. The poor little thing, she was only eighteen.

'Rachel.' Gingerly, she double-kissed me, as if we were meeting socially. 'We're so grateful for your help with Mumma.' She plucked at my sleeve. 'Your jumpsuit is heaven.'

She flashed an anxious grin while tears made tracks down her face. From the pocket of her chocolate-coloured twill trousers, she pulled out an actual cotton handkerchief and used it to dab her eyes.

I have to say, her look was *mesmerizing*. On her long, narrow feet was a pair of dark brogues polished to a high shine. A glimpse of a vest in vivid green appeared under a boxy-shouldered serge jacket, topped off with a crossbody satchel which looked like a family heirloom. She could have come straight from the Margaret Howell catwalk *or* from the All You Can Wear for a Tenner from her local Oxfam.

'Jumble?' Bronte asked, faintly, at the sight of her daughter. 'Oh! It's really you!'

'Mumma!' Freya and Bronte fell into each other's arms, Eden hovering behind them.

'I'm so sorry you're in this place,' Freya said.

'Jumble, no.' Bronte was dotting Freya's face with little kisses. 'Please don't fret. They're all terribly nice. But . . . how are you here? Have you left San Francisco?'

'Just for today. I fly back tomorrow.'

'You've come for one day? Because of me?'

'Yes!'

Then they were both laughing and crying into each other's faces.

All of the others were *gripped*.

Freya said to Dennis, 'May I?' And indicated his chair, which was beside Bronte's.

'You certainly *may*.' He hopped up and crossed the room to sit next to a stony-faced Eden. Nervously, he gave him a nod and muttered, 'Grand day for it.'

Freya was stroking Bronte's hand and Bronte was smoothing Freya's hair—literally *grooming* each other. They needed to be separated if I was to get any sense out of Freya, so Dennis was despatched back to his original seat.

When everyone had settled, I began. 'Freya, you were thirteen when your mum went to rehab for the first time. What was it like growing up with an addict parent?'

Freya was all angles, an earnest arrangement of knees, elbows and long expressive fingers. 'What you must understand is that Mumma is the sweetest soul. We knew she had gone to rehab but I don't remember her ever being . . . whatever the word is—out of it? Stoned? High?'

Ah here. 'Ever?' I asked.

'Sincerely, no. She was so much fun and so sweet, always. I've always felt very loved by her. So have Hugo and Gerald. We adore her.'

Funnily enough, I believed her on that.

Bronte blew kisses across the room. '*Bisous*,' she said, tears in her eyes.

'What-oo?' Dennis whispered, leaning sideways into Chalkie.

'French word for "kisses".' Chalkie rolled his eyes.

Not everyone with an addict for a parent was messed up. Maybe Freya was damaged in less obvious ways but I was certain that she loved her mother.

'I'm horse-mad,' Freya offered. 'We both are. We—she and I—Our horses are the loves of our lives.'

'Will you get to see Bubble while you're here?' Bronte interrupted.

'Yes!' Freya squeaked, suddenly animated. 'I'll pop home for a little love-in if there's time after this.' She glanced at Eden, who nodded.

He'd told *me* they were going straight to the airport from here.

'Give her a kiss from me,' Bronte said.

'Of course. And I'll visit Merryweather, shall I?'

'Oh, please!'

Something about all this horse-love made me wonder about Freya's career choice. 'In San Francisco?' I asked. 'You're working in a bank?'

'Investment bank. Just for a year, before I start uni.'

'Are you planning on being a banker? Wouldn't you prefer to work with horses?'

'Yah, yes. But no.' She flicked a furtive glance at her father. 'It's not a career.'

'Isn't it?' Surely there were all *kinds* of jobs in the horsey world?

'No, not financially. No.'

I wanted to press her further but she wasn't my client, it wasn't my business. 'How did you feel,' I asked, 'when you heard your mum had relapsed?'

'I—' Freya's Adam's apple bobbed up and down.

After a long silence, I asked, 'Were you surprised?'

'Well, yes, because I'd never seen her . . . what should I say? Being an addict? But she's fragile. I think she finds life more painful than others.'

'Do you want her to stop using heroin?'

After another pause, she said, 'I want her to be happy. Hugo and Gerald also want it for her. Above anything.'

'Freya.' I tried to be gentle. 'You love your mother, you want to protect her from pain. But heroin is a very dangerous drug, with a high fatality rate.'

This really wasn't fair, Freya was young and innocent. But I'd been hoodwinked by Eden, who'd made Freya fly five thousand miles to say unpalatable truths so that he wouldn't have to.

Poor Freya was in agony. 'Well, then she must stop.' Her tears began again. 'I'm sorry, Mumma, we love you too much. You must stop.'

Bronte looked stricken. This was the key to her, I suddenly understood. This was what I'd missed: she *adored* her children.

59

As soon as I'd seen Freya and Eden off the premises, I made for the office, *itching* to focus on the timeline of Bronte's relapse. I was nearly certain I had it figured out—then Brianna intercepted me with a dense little package. 'I'm guessing it's from another grateful customer.'

I should have kept going but Brianna was keen to see what it was—a giant hunk of nougat, as it transpired.

Brianna recoiled. 'I've a literal phobia of that stuff. Aren't you worried it'll pull out all of your teeth?'

'No. I love it.' But I knew someone who'd love it more—Nola's husband Harry. Nougat was his thing.

I was *so* fond of Harry. Obviously, he'd never know me as well as his wife did because Nola knew literally *everything* about me. But simply by opening his front door to me dozens of times a year, an affectionate warmth had built up.

It must be strange being the partner of a sponsor, seeing people arrive at your home, in all kinds of states, good and bad—but not being privy to any of the details.

It had been the very same for Luke. Like the time I'd been sponsoring a lovely woman called Jessamay. She'd been doing very well, then suddenly relapsed three times over five months. Her girlfriend, Britt, threatened to leave if she did it again. Then it actually happened—Jessamay slipped and Britt left.

Jessamay rang me in a terrible state and I told her to come to my apartment. Somehow Luke got to the door first and Jessamay flung herself against him. 'Oh, Luke! I relapsed! Britt left me! Could you talk to her, please, tell her—'

Looking terrified, Luke cut his eyes to me. 'I'm sorry to hear th—'

'Jessamay.' I took her hand, led her into my bedroom and tried to calm her. We talked for a long time and then went to a meeting. Afterwards, I walked her back to her apartment.

When I finally got home, Luke hopped up off the couch, full of anguish. 'Is she okay? Has Britt really left her?' Then, 'I know. It's none of my business. You can't tell me. But that was hard to see.'

I compressed my mouth, trying to stop the words from jumping out.

'I know you can't tell me,' Luke repeated. 'But has Britt really gone? What if she doesn't come back?'

'Maybe it's for the best.' That wasn't an actual divulgence of facts, I told myself. It was a hypothetical answer to a hypothetical question.

'What? Rachel, no!' Luke seemed offended. Upset, even. 'Why?'

'Listen to me, you romantic sap. How often have I told you that if an addict doesn't lose something, they've no incentive to change?'

'Right.' But he didn't like it.

'In fact, if—and it's not going to—but *if* I ever relapsed, you couldn't stay with me.'

'But what if I wanted to?'

I laughed. 'You wouldn't want to. I wouldn't be me. And you wouldn't be helping me, you'd be doing the very opposite.'

He shook his head. 'This is all very tough love. I don't like it. I don't like it one bit.'

When I cracked Bronte's timeline, I was so gleeful, I literally rubbed my hands together. As soon as we were back in group after lunch, I launched in.

'Bronte? You were happy to see Freya?'

She lit up. 'I was *bouleversée!*'

'What-ee what-*say*?' Dennis asked.

'French word,' Chalkie said. 'Means "bleedin' delighted".'

'I *adore* her,' Bronte said. 'I adore all three of my children.'

'So how do you reconcile being a loving mother with using heroin?'

'But they weren't there.' She sounded surprised. 'They were away at school. I never took drugs around them.'

Really? Well, *maybe.* It fitted with Freya's version of events. 'When you got married you—for the most part—stopped using heroin? But you began again about six years ago? Yes? Why?'

'I'm not really sure . . .'

'Your youngest child is thirteen? What age was he when he went to boarding school?'

'Seven.'

'Which was how many years ago?'

'. . . Six.'

I let that sit with her for a while.

'Eden sent you to rehab five years ago? And you got clean and stayed clean, until eight months ago? Yes? Before you broke your ankle, how were you doing with your life? Was anything different? Any changes? Big or small?'

She widened her eyes. 'Not that I can remember.'

'Let's track back. It was June when you had your accident. What else was going on last June?'

'Mmm. Most of the dams had foaled—'

'Anything going on with your children? Freya? She'd done her A Levels, left school and come home? For how long?'

'Two weeks.'

'You had expected her to stay for longer?'

'I thought she was home for good. To study Equine Science at uni in Dublin.'

'So what happened?'

Bronte's face became pinched. 'Eden got her an internship in a bank. In San Francisco. It came as a huge shock to Freya. And to me. When her year in the bank ends, instead of going to uni in Ireland, he says she's reading economics in Durham.'

'How did you feel about that?'

'It was devastating.' Her voice was faint. 'We—Freya and I—had such wonderful plans, to work together with our horses. We were both so excited. It had been agony being away from her, from all three of them. But I'd stayed strong because I knew better times were coming. Then I discovered that the end of her schooling meant she'd be more gone from me than ever.'

'So you fell off your horse.'

Startled, she said, 'Are you suggesting I did it on purpose?'

'Did you? Put it another way. You'd waited a long time to have a proper relationship with your daughter, only to discover that that special mother–daughter time you'd been yearning for was never going to happen. You felt . . . ?'

'Desolate.'

'Then you fell from your horse. I don't doubt that you were in a lot of physical pain. But the drugs they offered you were old friends. You knew they would numb your anguish about Freya. There were many ways of relieving the agony of the broken bone. But only one way to muffle your loss about Freya.' I shrugged. 'Heroin.'

Dennis actually gasped. In fairness, though, they were all awestruck, thinking I was some sort of a witch.

'So it's Eden's fault?' Bronte asked.

'You're the one who takes heroin.'

'But Eden's so—' She stopped abruptly.

'High and mighty?' Dennis offered. 'Bossy?'

'Autocratic?' Chalkie said. 'Overbearing? Dictatorial? A pain in the hole?'

'I thought he was lovely,' Ella murmured, giving Bronte a poisonous look.

'Enough,' I said. 'This isn't about him.'

'Ah, Rachel, I was enjoying that,' Chalkie said.

Eden Tollemarche did seem like quite the tyrant, but the Cloisters wasn't a reinvention heaven where under-the-thumb women came to get their groove back. Bronte could sort out her marriage further down the line—or maybe not, who knew?—but, much as I would have loved to wade in there and give her all *sorts* of life advice, my only job was to help her to get—and crucially, *stay*—clean.

60

When I switched my phone on, it beeped: a missed call from Luke, then a terse two-word text: Call me.

My stomach fell down a well.

He answered after half a ring. 'I need to see you. We need to talk.'

'. . . About what?'

'Something we have to get straight.' His voice was calm, measured, furious. 'On Sunday, at the beach, you said I left you, but that's not how it was—'

Stunned, I said, 'You absolutely *did*. You hired a van, packed your stuff, moved to Denver—'

'Rachel, *you* left *me*.'

'Luke, are you . . . okay?' I was confused. 'You sound a bit . . .'

'You were already long gone,' he said. 'You and your sleeping tablets. Off in a place where I couldn't reach you.'

'But . . .' I didn't know where to start. 'You know why I had to take them. And why are you ringing about this, two days later? Why didn't you say anything on Sunday?'

'Because . . .' He paused. 'Because I feel—felt—bad about, yeah, the end, how we . . . ended. But I woke in the night, like a bomb had gone off in my head. Rachel, you can't put all the blame on me. We need a serious conversation.'

'We needed a serious conversation six years ago but—'

'I had a lot of serious conversations with you, Rachel, back then, *plenty*, and you know how much good it did me? None. So I'll be finished with Dad in about an hour, I can come to—'

'I can't this evening.' In the morning Quin was going back to New Mexico for a few days. Tonight we had plans for a movie. 'Tomorrow night?'

'No.' Then, 'What time? I'm taking Kal to the airport—'

'She's leaving?'

'She's got a gig on Friday night. I could be with you by eight-thirty, nine-ish? Too late?'

'It's fine. The Huntsman?'

'A pub?'

'It's halfway between both of us.'

What I didn't say was that I could get up and walk away if it got too much. This—Luke's rage, his conviction that events had been different to the way I remembered them—had shot a swirl of dread through me, making the whole world seem inky and ominous.

The movie was no multiplex blockbuster but a documentary about a young mountaineer who climbed giant rock-faces without any safety gear.

Hurrying into the Irish Film Centre, the calibre of tonight's patrons almost made me laugh—mostly men, they were sinewy and serious, sharing tales of high-altitude bravado. As I looked for Quin, fragments of conversation reached me: 'The weather came in, we decided not to push it . . .' '. . . carrying forty K of kit . . .' '. . . massive whipper, but it held . . .'

There he was, with Murph and Golden, the three of them dressed to the nines in their technical clothing. It was probably subconscious, the way Anna and I had got labelled up to see *The Devil Wears Prada*.

Quin's arm shot out and he pulled me to him for a kiss, then I said hello to the other two—Murph (a man) and Golden (a woman). Along with two other men, they'd all been friends since junior school. Together, they'd been on countless climbs.

Golden openly disliked me and, uncharacteristically, it caused me no angst whatsoever.

For at least ten years, she'd been in an epic on-again-off-again with one of the other men, Prosser. In the off-again phases, she slept with Embury, the fourth man in the group. But at various stages, over the years, she'd slept with all of them—Prosser, Embury, Murph, even Quin, before his marriage to Shiv. I suspected she thought of them as her personal property.

'Would you like anything?' Quin nodded towards the café. 'We had carrot cake.'

There was no popcorn or pick-n-mix, it wasn't that sort of cinema. And it wasn't that sort of night. The clientele were *serious* about their climbing, *serious* about their nutrition.

. . . Except for cake. I'd noticed that climbers liked cake. Although they only seemed to eat it with other climbers.

To my surprise, the movie was great.

'Did you *really* like it?' Golden asked, afterwards, in the Nepalese restaurant. 'Or are you just saying it? To make us feel okay about you taking Embury's ticket?'

I looked at Quin. 'Did I . . . ?'

'This was booked weeks ago.' He shrugged. 'But I'm away tomorrow until Saturday, I wanted to see you tonight. He did me a favour.'

'*So* obliging of Embury.' I smiled at Golden, who sent daggers from her pale blue eyes. 'Things off again with Prosser?'

Her face reddened. Although it was fairly red to begin with.

She looked like a weatherbeaten cat.

'Fuck you,' she muttered, which made me laugh.

Next to me, Quin shifted. 'Don't blame Rachel,' he told Golden. 'Blame me.'

'Whatever. Shall we order?'

It was late by the time we got home and Quin and I were both relaxed and giggly. It would have been so easy to say nothing.

But that would have been all kinds of sneaky.

'Quin, tomorrow night I'm meeting Luke.' I spoke quickly. 'The way we split up, the reason, he sees it differently to how I do. It would be good to . . . untangle it.'

After several moments of silence, he asked, 'Is something going on?'

'Not the way you mean. But—'

'What if you "untangle" that you still love him?'

'That's not going to happen. But I'm hoping to get some peace.'

'Rach?' His tone was surprisingly scornful. 'Something you should know: your ex-husband is just a man. An ordinary man that, despite how he treated you, you've idealized. I've met him and I can tell you he's not a French sauce that's been reduced and reduced until it's . . . fucking . . .' He waved his hands, searching for the right phrase. '. . . food of the gods. And I'm better than cheesy fries from Jo Burger. A lot better. I know it. I wish you did.'

'I should never have said that, Quin. I can't tell you how sorry I am. Please forgive me.' I felt breathless. 'Maybe it was what I thought in our early days. But it was mean and stupid and *wrong*. Things are different now.'

'What way?'

'Well, they are. Aren't they?'

'Yeah. Whatever. Can we go to sleep now?'

He turned his back to me, then switched out the light.

61

In the weeks and months after Yara's death, I still went to NA meetings but nothing like as often. For the first time, they'd stopped giving me comfort. My loss was too huge; it had separated me out from everyone else and set me down on an island of one.

Everyone was as lovely as they'd always been, so supportive and encouraging. Over and over, they promised me that I could get through my loss without relapsing. But their fervour exhausted me. They didn't—couldn't—know how bad I felt so they had no right to tell me how to cope.

And if they knew I was taking tablets to help me sleep, they'd probably freak out, worrying that I might relapse.

My higher power had always been the meetings but I no longer believed. Not in anything, really.

Every morning Olga Mae, my sponsor, sent comforting recovery texts: Just for today and This too shall pass. But when they beeped onto my phone, all I felt was guilt.

Mia had taken to popping by at around six in the evening, bearing a box of heritage tomatoes or a punnet of blackberries left over from her day on the stall. It became another thing to dread—having to drag up words from my depths, to thank her for food I had no ability to eat. Eventually, I left Luke to deal with her.

Carlotta had urged us to try out self-help groups for bereaved parents, but I wanted to go to one that was only for women. However terrible Luke's pain was—and I guessed it was appalling—mine, because of my corrosive shame, had to be worse. It was the most natural thing in the world to give birth to a healthy baby, and I'd failed. Maybe if I could talk to other women who'd failed in the same way, I'd get some comfort?

But when I tried explaining, Luke was hurt. Huffy, even. 'You're shutting me out, babe.'

I didn't have to. We were already doing it to each other. I couldn't take care of him and he couldn't take care of me.

And as it happened, even in a group of bereaved mothers, I felt isolated. After only two sessions, I bowed out.

Claire's way of showing support was to send links to stories of celebrities making shows of themselves. Two or three times a day, State of this eejit! would pop up on my phone. And to be fair, a couple of minutes reading about another person's meltdown *was* distracting.

Anna visited most weekends, usually bearing expensive skincare—at times including some for Luke.

'So this is a . . .' Dutifully, Luke would read the box. 'An overnight skin-cell renewal serum. That sounds . . . cool. Thanks, Anna.' I'd watch him struggling to be light-hearted. 'Next time you see me, I'll look twenty years younger.'

'And twenty times hotter!' We'd all laugh awkwardly, then Luke would slide from the room.

Anna was the one who tentatively suggested that Luke and I might try to have another baby.

'It's too late,' I said. 'I'm forty already.'

'Forty isn't old!' she cried. 'You've every chance of getting pregnant again.'

I almost smiled. It was such a New York way of thinking, that science could make nature dance to its tune.

'I'm too . . .' I tried again. 'Anna, I don't think I was meant to have this.'

'You can't give up,' she said, little and fierce. 'You need to have hope.'

'Anna . . .' It was so difficult to say the words. 'Luke . . . he blames me. For her dying.'

'No! He doesn't—'

'It's true. He hasn't said it out straight, but the way he looks at me, it's awful.' I choked. 'I'm so ashamed and—I'm afraid. Me and him, it's not good, we're not being nice to each other.'

I'd been reading about couples who'd lost a baby. How, often, they blamed each other. How, frequently, the relationship broke and ended. It felt as if it was happening to Luke and me. Previously it had been unthinkable, we'd been so close, so very much a team. But when Yara died, something had ruptured.

I hadn't noticed it straight away, because we'd been lurching around, appalled and disbelieving. But now that some time had passed, the landscape was starting to look more settled—and very different from how it had been previously.

I'd catch Luke watching me, almost evaluating me, as if I were a puzzle he needed to figure out.

He was distant. Irritable. At times cold.

And I felt . . . Well, all I wanted to do was sleep.

We needed to talk but if he admitted that he thought Yara was my fault, we might never get past the damage.

There was a morning when I tiptoed into Yara's room to find Luke sitting on the floor, holding a small teddy bear and full-on sobbing. I was so shocked—so *ashamed*—of the pain I'd caused that all I could do was stare, then back away.

We lost our dreams when we lost our baby and now it looked like we were losing each other.

62

'Morning,' Brianna said. 'Your new client is in room three.'

'Thanks.' I needed to get my head in the game and focus on Lowry Cooke. He was thirty-nine, cross-addicted to alcohol and cocaine and had been persuaded in here after his life had fallen asunder: his girlfriend had left him; his friends had walked away and he was being sued by a pair of newly-weds for ruining their wedding.

I opened the door and there he was, good-looking in a lanky, loose-limbed, slightly grimy way, waxy jeans hanging loose on his hips, dark hair flopping over his forehead.

'Lowry? I'm Rachel, your therapist.'

He blinked, doing a theatrical double take. 'Wow.' A slow smile spread across his face and both of his hands closed around mine.

Oh God no, not one of them! A pathetic flirt-monster who won't rest until everyone fancies him.

He was a photographer—high-end, but dressed like an indie-band singer, in a fashionably washed-out Karen Carpenter T-shirt and embroidered cowboy boots. Friendship bracelets and other nonsense festooned his wrists, tattoos ran up and down his arms, an army dog tag hung heavy around his neck and his collarbone was inked with 'Dead on Arrival'.

'Please sit down,' I said.

He lounged low in the chair, manspreading like no one's business, his long limbs and even longer boots stretching almost to the far wall.

'So?' I asked.

'So?' He smirked, as if we were on a first date.

'Why are you here?'

'This place has a good rep. A boot camp for the mind. You guys need to sort me out.'

'What do you mean by that?'

He took a breath. 'Depression. Bad. I've had it on and off for years. It's the reason I drink and get high. But you guys get to the root cause, right?' He produced a pack of cigarettes from his jeans, flipped one into his mouth and mumbled, 'Okay if I smoke?'

'There's a smoking area in the garden.'

'Wow.' Radiating woundedness, he replaced the cigarette in its box. 'So yeah,' he said. 'Once you discover what went wrong for me, I won't need to drink as much.'

This was a regular thing—addicts showing up, convinced that all that ailed them was a forgotten trauma. They expected that we'd forage around until we'd plucked it out, like an ingrowing hair, then they could resume their drinking or whatever their poison was and everything would be dandy.

But ten times out of ten, our foraging revealed that the reason they felt depressed was *because* of their heavy drinking or enthusiastic drug consumption.

Still, I had to be clear with him. 'This is a rehabilitation centre, not a hospital. There are no doctors. We treat alcoholics and addicts. If that's not what you want, you should leave.'

'You've got me wrong. I'm not an alcoholic.'

'Lowry, you were employed to take photos of a wedding. Someone's special day. You got so drunk that most of their photos are unusable. You fell into an ornamental lake. You knocked over the wedding cake and stood on it—'

'I didn't mean to—'

'You vomited on the wedding car. You made a pass at the bride—'

'Hey—'

'Then made a pass at the groom's father.'

He waved a hand. 'Love is love.'

'It sounds more like alcoholism to me.'

'Yeah, okay, I wasn't my best self that day. But that's why I'm here. When I find out why I drink, this sort of thing will stop happening to me.'

'"Stop happening to you"? The alcohol didn't magically infiltrate you, Lowry. You drank it.'

'Only because I felt so dark. It was the only way to get through that day. My girl had left me . . . Shooting a wedding with a broken heart, that was *hard.*'

I could have laughed. Lowry Cook couldn't have been more of a classic alcoholic if he'd *tried.* Firmly bonded to his stance as a victim, refusing to own his actions, insistent on justifying anything shameful.

'That day,' he said. 'The way I drank. It wasn't usual.'

I referred to my notes. 'But you'd received a caution for drunk and disorderly the previous month—'

'Rachel, the break-up with Sienna hit me right here.' He touched his chest. 'The crazy drinking, that out-of-control stuff . . .' He shook his head. 'It's not who I am.'

Again, I could have laughed. If only he knew what a cliché he was. Hopefully he would stay long enough to find out.

63

The door of the Huntsman opened and there was Luke, his silhouette—height, hair, shoulders—unmistakeable. He scanned the room, his eyes searching, then made his way through the clusters of chairs and sofas.

Standing over me, he unzipped his leather jacket, shrugged it off his shoulders and threw it on a seat. 'You okay for a drink?'

I indicated my water and he strode to the bar, returning soon after with a pint of something. Clattering it onto the table he said, 'So. I left you?'

His mood? Not overtly angry. But far from friendly.

'You know you did.'

'And you left me. We left each other.'

'I don't really—'

'Can you just let me tell it from my side?' He paused, his eyes intent on me. 'Please?'

It was the *please* that did it. 'Okay.' But I was full of dread.

'So. It started when you said you were awake all night every night. But I wasn't sleeping so well myself, either. I used to check on you. A lot of the time you were asleep.'

I stared at him, wondering why he would say this.

'When you told me Carlotta had given you enough pills for five nights, that was the last time you were honest with me.'

'Wait—'

'*You*, wait.' There was a flash of anger. 'You got another prescription from her and more from at least two other doctors and not only did you not tell me but when I asked you straight out, you lied.'

'Hold on, Luke.' He was trying to distort the facts. 'I was going insane from lack of sleep. A doctor prescribed me sleeping tablets. But you were so against me taking anything, *ever*, that the only solution was to keep the truth from you.'

'"Keep the truth" from me? That's just a fancy way of saying you lied. As soon as you started doing it in secret, you were in trouble. You know that. You're the authority on addiction.'

'It was only secret because you'd have stopped me—and, Luke, I needed them.'

'Would you *listen* to yourself. If a client told you that, you'd reef them out of it. You didn't need them, you wanted them—'

'You're wrong. I—'

'Can you imagine how scared I was? Our baby had died and now I was losing you. When you said you'd taken nothing'—he bit out the next words—'I. Can. Not. Tell. You how much I wanted to believe you. But I'd been there with you before, back in the day. I knew the signs. Soon after you started on those tablets again, you were taking more than you should. And during the day as well as bedtime. *And* in the middle of the night. But whenever I asked, you lied.'

I was trying hard to hold on to what I knew to be true. Admittedly, I *had* taken more than the prescribed amount, and there had been mornings when the pain of a day without my baby was too much. But taking the tablets had always been a choice. I was always in control.

Luke's version was a distortion. But the solid ground of my conviction was slipping from beneath my feet and I was confused.

'One evening you were completely bombed, it was fucking horrible, you were slurring and stumbling—'

No. 'Sometimes I was groggy when I woke up—'

'It was worse than that. So I went through the apartment and found pills hidden everywhere. Rachel . . .'

I remembered and even now it made me feel sick. I'd woken to find an array of Ambien laid out on the kitchen counter and Luke pacing in a cold fury.

'In the box of teabags.' He'd held up two tablets. Pointing at others, 'In the freezer. In your coat pocket. Sellotaped to the back of those photos. Have I missed any?'

'The rice, the basmati rice.' I rummaged until I found the four pills, then surrendered them to him.

'That's it?' he asked. 'That's all?'

I nodded. 'That's all. Sorry,' I whispered. 'I love you, I'm so sorry.'

He'd pulled me onto his lap, then I buried my face in his neck and gave in to the despair. I cried for our baby dying and me being a worthless fuck-up and the horrible suspicion that I was losing everything.

I'd thought my essential brokenness had healed years earlier—how had I ended up back here again?

'It's okay,' he'd murmured, kissing my hair. 'It's okay.'

But it wasn't okay. Because I hadn't told him about the ones stashed in the lid of my foundation bottle or in the jar of folic acid or at the back of the drawer with all the old chargers. He didn't understand, he'd never understand because the only person who could get me through this hell was me.

'That day,' he reminded me, 'you cried in my arms and swore you'd stop. But you didn't. No wonder you were so good in the escape room with Quin—you knew how to find things because you know how to hide them!'

That rocked me to my core. It was such a mad way of looking at things and maybe . . . Luke wasn't wrong?

I guess it explained why he had been so weird and alert when Quin had praised my escape-room skills.

'You know I'm right,' Luke said. 'I can see it in you.'

'No . . . not at all . . . you don't see it.' But I was scared—I'd had a brief insight that there were two ways of looking at one situation. In the first, my baby had died, my grief was temporarily unbearable and I needed to sleep. The other was that I was an addict who had used her symptoms to legitimately get her hands on sleeping tablets—and then took more than she should have.

Could both be true?

'Luke, I . . . I don't know what to think. I'm . . . It's all a bit much . . . I'm scared.'

He watched me carefully. 'You'll be okay.' He sounded definite about this. 'Take some time. Let all of this settle.'

'Luke . . . listen. I'd better go home. I need to . . .'

'Sure. Of course. But should you be on your own? Will Quin be there?'

'He's in New Mexico. I'll be fine, though.'

But as we walked towards the door, my sanity returned. After everything he'd done, Luke had somehow managed to convince me—briefly—that I was entirely to blame.

'Luke?'

Outside in the indigo night, he towered over me.

'Luke.' Now I was angry. 'You can't put all the blame on me.'

He blinked. 'Don't you get it?' He looked shocked. 'I spent nearly six months trying to help you to quit. There was literally nothing else I could do. I had to leave.'

'. . . That wasn't all you did.'

There was a pause that went on for too long. I watched understanding—and something else, something less pleasant—arrive in his eyes. 'You mean Mia?' I nodded.

'Oh yeah,' he said. 'I nearly forgot. I slept with Mia.'

I gulped. At the time he had denied it—denied it again and again. But I'd always had my suspicions. To have it confirmed—even six years later—was excruciating.

He lowered his face to mine, strands of his hair brushing my skin. 'Fuck you, Rachel,' he said. '*Fuck* you.'

Wheeling away from me, he swung across the tarmac, vaulted onto his bike and, with the angry roar of an engine, drove off into the night.

64

Shakily, I leant against my car. Six years ago, Luke had sworn nothing was going on with Mia. He'd full on gaslit me and knowing now that I was right was no comfort.

This shouldn't have made things worse. Mia or no Mia, he'd still left me. He'd still spent several years blanking me.

And even so, I'd survived; I'd made a new life and was happy with Quin. Whatever Luke and Mia had got up to back then shouldn't matter now. But, stupidly, it did.

I checked the time. God Almighty, it was only twenty past nine—how was it still so early when so much had happened? Quin was on a plane and Nola was at the opera so I rang Claire. 'On my way,' she said. 'Be with you in ten.'

Claire's 'ten' was closer to twenty-five when she finally hurtled into the parking lot. Stopping with a skid of gravel, she ordered, 'Get in. I'll drop you back later.'

She had a lot of make-up on—was she wearing *lashes*?—and a black leather dress.

'It's vegan,' she said. 'My dress. Just in case you were thinking of schooling me.'

'. . . I wasn't. But . . . you're looking very glossy for a Wednesday night, at home, doing nothing.'

'Just how I roll, babes.'

She drove like she did everything—fast and focused. But when the turn-off for her house came up, she kept on going.

'What's going on?' I cried. 'Where are you taking me?'

'Town. The club. Someplace quiet to talk.'

Her house was really that noisy? Hmmm . . .

Then my phone began ringing and both of us leapt with shock.

'Oh my God!' Claire said. 'Who's dead?'

'No one. It's Luke.' I hit decline.

'He *rings*? Who rings when it's not a fatality! Total *Luddite*.' Then, 'What are you doing?'

'Sending a text.' I clicked out, Stop calling me.

Then a second one: Never call me again.

'Now I'm blocking his number. See how he likes it.' I took a bitter pleasure in doing what he'd done to me, then threw my phone back in my bag.

'So. Tell me,' Claire said when we were in a plush booth, in a low-lit lounge. Then, 'Large Ardbeg,' she rattled off to the hot, beardy waiter. 'In a warmed glass. Just-out-of-the-dishwasher warm. And my sister here will have a—'

'—glass of tap water,' I said.

'No, you won't.' Claire looked disgusted. 'She'll have a Silver Mountain.'

'It's mineral water,' she informed me when the young man had departed. 'Horrendously expensive. So, go on, tell me.'

'I was right about Mia.'

'Oh, *babes*.' She clenched my hand. 'I'm so sorry. The fucking *fucker*!'

'But he tried to make it my fault. Said that I was out of my head on sleeping tablets the whole time.'

'So what if you were?'

'Yeah, but I wasn't.'

'But who'd *blame* you?'

Wait, though. This was confusing. 'Claire. Remember after he left me? And you came to New York? How was I?'

'In absolute bits.'

'But was I . . . coherent? I mean, did I seem . . . you know, like I'd been taking sleeping pills?'

'Oh God, yeah.'

'I don't just mean at night—'

'Yeah, yeah, I know, you were taking them round the clock. But your baby had died, your husband had left you. Wouldn't anyone?'

Oh. Kay.

'He was the worst,' she mused. 'He used to ring me—this was before he left you—complaining about you taking too many tablets. And not just me, he called Anna, Brigit, your friend Nola.'

'I remember.' Because soon after Luke rang the person, they then rang me and I'd have the job of putting them right. 'You know Luke,' I'd say. 'Mr Straight Arrow, freaks out over me taking literal aspirin.'

'Until then,' Claire said, 'I never knew he was so judgy.'

In the silence that followed, I heard myself ask, 'After he'd left me, were you ever . . . *worried* about me?'

'Of course! Your baby had died, your—'

'I mean, worried that as well as the sleepers, I might . . . slip back into taking other drugs?'

'Or that you'd overdose? I mean, yes, but we talked about it. You explained.'

'What did I say?'

'That you knew everything there was to know about addiction. That you needed the Ambien until the worst pain about Yara had passed, then you could stop. And then, what—a month or two later?—you *did* stop. Point proven. Oh, would you look at who it is! Piet! Hi!'

Ah, for the love of *feck*! Piet the Swinger, here obviously by appointment.

Claire hopped up and she and Piet kissed on the cheek, then exchanged a smouldering, silent stare.

Eventually Claire remembered that I was there. '. . . Ah, you know Rachel? My sister?'

And cover story, I wanted to say.

Poor Adam at home, thinking his wife was out ministering to the needy. When, in fact, his wife had *kidnapped* the needy, whisking them to a members' club, a thirty-euro taxi journey away from their car, to provide a paper-thin veneer of plausibility for a meet with a slightly thuggish, shaven-headed, sexy-in-a-sinister-way man.

By way of a greeting, all Piet got from me was a smile-free rise of my chin. For a moment he seemed to be considering coming in for a double kiss but I killed it with a look.

It wasn't that I was pissed off with Claire—I mean, Claire was Claire, great in countless ways but this stunt was straight from her playbook. The problem was that far too much was going on in my head. I simply wasn't able to ignore the simmering sexual tension and soldier on with the production of small talk.

I managed to endure almost seven minutes of the bullshit before I left and got a taxi back to my car.

65

Thursday morning dawned bright and blue. On my drive to work, clumps of yellow daffodils blew in the breeze and newborn lambs were literally springing in the fields. The world looked sparkly clean and hopeful—but my head was dark.

So much had happened last night and the worst thing, the most worrying, was Claire saying I'd been taking tablets day and night. I mean, yes, I *had*—for a very good reason. But for the first time I could see things from Luke's perspective: I'd been taking sleeping tablets, more than the prescribed amount and at the wrong times.

I saw my side and I saw Luke's side.

I was in the right, but maybe he hadn't been in the wrong?

Then I remembered Mia and changed my mind. He had definitely been in the wrong.

That whole episode had been horrible. The first inklings had come late one night, when Luke sauntered in home, giving off an unusually defiant energy.

'Where were you?' I asked.

'With Mia.'

'*Mia?*' That was a surprise. 'What were you doing?'

'Me and Mia?' He swung off to the kitchen and, uneasily, I followed. With an insolent smile over his shoulder, he said, 'Talking.'

'Talking?' I was startled.

He'd got a block of cheese from the fridge, then slapped a couple of slices of bread on a plate.

'You and Mia were talking?'

He looked up from the sandwich he was making, stared me in the eye, literally stuck his tongue in his cheek and said, 'Oh. *Yeah.*'

'What are you . . . Luke?' What was he telling me? 'Is there something going on? With Mia and you?'

His giddy mood of mutiny vanished. 'No.'

But it wasn't long after that I saw them together—staring into each other's eyes, Mia tenderly stroking Luke's hand, neither of them even pretending to hide it. I almost vomited in the street.

When I'd called him on it, Luke had looked me in the eye and sworn that nothing was going on. I hadn't been sure whether or not he was telling the truth. For the longest time, even years after we'd split up, I'd flip-flopped back and forth over the line, shifting from believing him to hating him. The combination of humiliation, grief and doubt meant it was the one thing about my marriage that I'd never told Quin.

And last night, I'd finally got the truth.

At work, I stared out of the office window, worrying that Caleb, Harlie's ex, might not show. It had been such a triumph to have persuaded him in here and if he let me down—hold on! Someone was walking up the long drive; please God, let this be him.

Even from a distance, his clothes looked ridiculously fashionable, from his bang-on-trend Harris-tweed peacoat to the four inches of bare ankle between the bottom of his trousers and the start of his shoes.

In the entrance hall I met him as he shouldered the door open. He was huge.

'Rachel?' His smile was nervous.

Such *grooming*! His eyebrows were boy-band tidy, his teeth were dazzlingly white and his hair obviously got a lot of love. *So* much in common with Harlie.

In the drawing room he refused tea and biscuits. 'I have this.' He indicated his black Myprotein shaker. His hands trembled. 'It's good she's in here.' He was talking too fast. 'It's been a nightmare, though. It all got so dark, so fast.'

'Save it for when we're in the room.' I felt desperately sorry for him.

He stood up. 'Can we start? I just want to get it done.'

When we walked in, everyone stared, wondering who this good-looking man belonged to.

Lowry Cooke—who'd obviously just understood what was going down—was gleeful and alert, practically rubbing his hands together in anticipation. *Yeah, well, enjoy it while you can.* Wait until Sienna, his ex-girlfriend, was here to spill the beans on *his* antics!

'So, shithead?' Harlie said to Caleb. 'What the fuck are you doing here?'

Caleb was waxy with pallor. 'Your ma told me,' he stuttered. 'I wanted to help.'

'I don't want your help.'

'Harlie . . .' I silenced her with a look.

Caleb took his chair. 'Can I . . . ?' he asked, and began removing his jacket, revealing huge shoulders and bulky biceps which strained against his sleeves. We were all rapt.

Caleb was objectively hot, but his oversized biceps made me sad. It was bad enough that women angsted about all the ways their bodies were wrong. But now it seemed that the young men were getting in on the act, going to the gym, living on raw eggs and boring on about ketosis, God love them.

'I'm Harlie's ex-husband,' Caleb said. 'We're still married, but separated—'

'—I haven't seen him or heard from him in eleven months,' Harlie said. 'Packed up his stuff when I was at work, told me nothing about it—'

'—I told you—'

'—I came home, everything was gone. He wouldn't answer my calls. Went round to his mum's and she wouldn't let me in. Went to his work. Same.'

Gently, Trassa shushed Harlie. 'Let the lad tell his side of things. Go on,' she instructed Caleb.

In a husky voice, he said, 'I met Harlie when I was twenty-five. She was twenty-four. First night I met her, that was it, I was *done*.' To my relief, he was picking up confidence. 'She was my dream girl. Gorgeous, a great laugh, great dancer, hard worker, ambitious. Like me, she was into her fashion, her fitness. We both wanted kids, two, but not for a few years.'

'Her drinking?' I prompted.

'Like, she *drank*. But so did everyone. Five years ago, weekends were party central—everyone got messy. Monday to Friday though, I'd go to the gym, eat clean, focus on work. I was living with my ma, and Harlie was at home with her pair. Once or twice a week she'd come over and stay. She'd always arrive with her quarter-bottle of vodka but, you know . . . I thought it was one night a week, not every night. Like, not a problem.

'So we got married two and a half years ago, and bought a house. Suddenly we had a mortgage so we were on a budget, we didn't have the same money for going out on the lash, but it was grand. Me and Harlie were together, we had our new home. I was training in the Drill, a Korean fitness model—we were hoping to buy the Irish franchise and set up on our own. We were buzzing, really excited, like, we had a *plan*. Except Harlie kept buying vodka—'

'—I *didn't* keep buying—'

'But you did.' He sounded so forlorn that it silenced her. 'At the start, money was my worry. But . . . I don't drink vodka. So the two of us were knocking around the house on a weeknight, ironing our work clothes or whatever, Harlie drinking vodka and me on the Kinetica Recovery. It was *weird*. Drinking is for when you go out. But I kept making excuses for her. She said her job was stressy, she needed to relax—'

'It *was* stressy and at least I'm not addicted to the gym, like you.'

'My job was stressy too—'

'Caleb, you're not the one in rehab,' I said. 'You don't need to explain yourself.'

'Oh, okay. Thanks.' He looked heartbreakingly young and grateful. 'So. Harlie got drunk. A lot. Often by bedtime she was out of it, like slurring her words and making no sense—after an evening of watching *The Sinner* and eating turkey stir-fry, you know? Like, it didn't *fit*. So I helped her get a new job, one with less pressure.

'But nothing changed, except the quarter-bottles became half-bottles, became full bottles. Then there were two on the go every evening, the "official" one in the fridge, the "secret" one under the sink. Even when I showed her that I knew, it didn't stop her.'

This was a familiar story but still horribly sad.

'Weekends became a total shitshow, Friday night, Saturday night, you'd never know what was going to happen. Fights. Like, actual fists, with strangers. Or she'd disappear and not come back until the next day. Then she, Tegan and some of the other girls started this brunch thing on Sunday. Harlie would come home at like, one a.m., in absolute *tatters*.' He flinched at the memory.

'She said she was depressed so we went to her doctor and she got tablets. I really wanted to believe her reasons for drinking because it meant there was a solution. But nothing worked and everything was going to hell. We were behind on our credit cards and we hate owing money—well, she used to hate it . . . She'd stopped going to the gym. She'd lost all interest in buying the Drill.'

Even though I knew how this story ended, listening to the inexorable downward spiral had my stomach clenched in knots.

'When did you realize she was an alcoholic?'

'Took a long time. Like, she's beautiful and young, always looked after herself, her hair and clothes. Nothing like old men on benches in the park. And I didn't want it to be true, I admit that. A few times she quit weekday drinking, maybe for three or four days, she said it proved that she wasn't an alcoholic because alcoholics drink every day.' With a shrug of the gigantic shoulders. 'I guess that's not true.'

'It's not,' I said. 'So you loved Harlie?'

'I loved her so much. Like, I mean it, no one else ever came close.' He paused and took a breath. 'She loved me too. For a while we were happy, really happy.'

There was a lump in my throat. Addiction destroyed so much that was good and pure.

'Why did you leave her?'

He folded in on himself; it was clear he was ashamed of this. 'Everyone was telling me I was making it easier for her to keep drinking, because I did stuff like ring her work when she was "sick". They said if I left it might shock her into getting help. But it was hard. She was my best friend.' His jaw clenched. 'I kept hoping . . . I kept giving it one more week, hoping things would go back to the way they'd been. Everything was mixed up and fucked up. This amazing girl, beautiful and *going places*, and now she was a tragic mess. Even though the person I loved wasn't there any more I felt so guilty for thinking about leaving. I worried about her all the time, anyway, I knew it would be worse if I went—and it was. Leaving her was the hardest thing I've ever had to do and I watched my dad dying of Parkinson's.' He seemed utterly tormented. 'But I wasn't helping her.' He had started to cry. 'I left her because by staying I was making everything worse.'

Everyone was focused on Caleb—everyone except me. I was watching Harlie and holding my breath. Her head was bowed, then I spotted movement in her shoulders, a rhythmic shaking. But she could just as easily have been laughing.

But no! Wait! She was rubbing her eyes. Then she straightened up, searching for the tissues and I got a proper look. She was crying. *She was crying!* Thank you, God!

66

After work, I spent three hours sitting in a hairdresser's chair, getting a major job done on my colour. I'd put it off for as long as I could but the forthcoming trip to Barcelona had made it suddenly seem *vital*.

At some stage, Claire rang. It took about ten minutes to fight my way through the rustly forest of tinfoil to get the phone to my ear. 'Sorry about that,' I eventually said. 'I'm at the hairdresser.'

'Can you talk?' she asked.

'Like I said, I'm at the hairdresser.'

'So. It's all planned. The'—she hissed the word—'*swinging*. Saturday night. We've booked a hotel. This will be an Easter to remember!'

'Fair play.'

'Do you mean that?'

'No.'

'Am I doing the right thing?'

'No.'

'How do you know?'

Actually, I didn't. I wasn't Claire. 'Look. If it's what you want, then enjoy yourself.'

'Do you think I will?'

'You might.'

'Do you *really* think it?'

'No.'

When, *finally*, I was released from the tinfoil, I came home to an empty house—Kate was doing a night shift. I wished she was here. I couldn't stop thinking about Luke and I wanted distraction.

I hated him. Absolutely hated him.

Was he upset that I'd blocked his calls? I wondered. I fucking hoped so. In fact, I hoped it so much that I wanted to know. So I *un*blocked his number.

Within minutes, his name lit up my phone. I snatched it from the table and snapped, 'What?'

'Are you at home?' he asked. 'Can I swing by?'

'Yes,' I said. 'And absolutely not.'

'Please, Rachel. I'm not asking to come in, I don't deserve to, but please may I see you.'

'It's late.' It wasn't that late, only nine thirty, but I was so angry.

'It'll just take a moment,' he said. 'And I'm five minutes from you.'

'. . . Okay.'

'Thanks for unblocking my number.'

I took a moment. '. . . Horrible, isn't it? When you're desperate to talk to someone and—'

'I'll be with you shortly.'

I locked Crunchie in the kitchen—she was too cute and this conversation would be strictly business. Then I put on my coat—it was dark and far from warm out there.

Moments later, the bell rang. Luke was leaning against the door jamb. In the lamplight, he looked shattered.

'I didn't sleep with Mia,' he said.

'Yes, you di—'

'—and you know I didn't. It was a story you told yourself to make me your enemy. So you didn't have to listen to me begging you to stop the tablets. But I'm really sorry I swore at you last night. That was . . .' He shook his head. 'Out of line. I'm deeply sorry.'

'You *behaved* like you were sleeping with Mia—so . . . smirky and—'

'—yeah. I was an arse that one night. Angry and mean, a bit drunk. I felt so hurt, I wanted to hurt you back. I'm sorry, Rachel.'

'But I saw you with her.'

'In Coffee Express, in full view of, like, *fifty* other people, most of them from NA. They knew me, they knew you. Mia had managed to kick sleepers, so I was asking her advice about how to help you. That's all.' He exhaled, long and weary. 'You know this.'

'So why were you holding hands?'

'We weren't. She was touching my arm. Out of pity.'

'She fancied you. You encouraged her.'

His face twisted in exasperation. 'She didn't fancy me. I didn't encourage her. I am not that man. I never was.'

Frustration flared. 'How could she not have fancied you?'

'Why would she? And even if she had—which she didn't—I loved you.'

'But we were barely speaking to each—'

'I still wouldn't have fucked another woman.' He bit out the words. 'I was not that man. I played it straight. I didn't have the imagination to be a player. Remember, you told me that?'

A memory flash-flickered, of an argument we'd had. He'd found more tablets and was threatening to leave. I was defensive, then scornful . . .

Perhaps he hadn't slept with Mia? Hard to know for sure, because the man I'd once thought I knew had vanished—metaphorically and literally. But he'd always been surprisingly traditional—quite judgy about cheaters.

'At the time even my wife didn't fancy me.'

Who—? Oh *me*. Didn't I?

'You don't remember. Of course not. But there was a night.' He shrugged.

Wait, no, I did remember.

'I hoped we might . . . reconnect,' Luke said. 'You weren't interested.'

Another of those freeze-frame memories flared, of candlelight and scented oil, of—dear God—Luke taking my face in his hands, the hard heat of him pressing against me through his jeans.

'I remember.' I was embarrassed. 'But I was afraid.'

'Of *me*?'

'Of getting pregnant again. I wasn't safe to have a baby, I'd never been safe. I was too . . . toxic. Fucked up. Whatever the word is. You thought so too.'

'What? I would *never* . . . Rachel, we were unlucky, that's all.'

Hardly daring to breathe, I watched him closely. 'You *did* think it.'

'That's insane.' He seemed adamant. 'I didn't. I wouldn't. You said it a few times but I thought you were just trying to guilt me.'

'Into what?'

'Feeling sorry for you. So you could take your tablets without any hassle. I didn't think you actually *believed* it.' He wheeled away and muttered, 'God, this is the worst.'

Returning to face me, he said, 'If it's true, you must have gone through hell.'

'It was true, but I don't any longer. Quin "cured" me.'

Something flickered across his face. 'That's good. Great.'

'Can I ask you something? The morning when Kallie needed Plan B. You know, the morning-af—'

'I know what it is. And you're going to ask if it was a set-up by Kallie? My answer is, I don't know. We . . . had . . . the night before, we'd—But I hadn't known there was an accident.' Obviously ill at ease, he looked away.

'Sorta thing you'd think I might have noticed. Only found out when I got home that evening.'

'Would Kallie make it up?'

'Maaaaybe.' He seemed somewhat entertained by this, if his small smile was anything to go by. 'She's . . . sort of . . . she's determined. Kallie wants what Kallie wants, you know? And she wanted to meet you.'

Abruptly, he stopped. 'I mean no disrespect to Kallie. She and I . . . I'm a different man now, my relationships are gonna be different to the one you and I had. Kallie suits me. We work.'

'I didn't say anything.'

'Yeah. But. Okay, sorry.' Making an effort to change his tone, he asked, 'Is Quin back?'

'No, he gets in on Saturday morning, about five a.m.'

'Ouch.'

'Yep. Saturday's my stepson's birthday, he's going to be thirteen. We're making a big deal of him becoming a teenager. My in-laws are throwing him a little party. Nothing huge, just family.'

Finley wasn't my stepson. Vivi and Roly weren't my in-laws, I wasn't part of their *family*. But I wanted to wound Luke. I actually believed him about Mia, but his defence of Kallie, his admiration for her maybe-lie *hurt*. He'd let me get away with nothing when we'd been together.

'On Saturday evening,' I went on, 'we're going to Barcelona. Just Quin and me.'

'Well . . . nice one. Barcelona, Texas, right?'

'Haha. Yeah. For our anniversary. So when is Kallie . . . ? Is she coming back to Ireland?'

'No.'

She'd left without saying goodbye. Not even a text. Unexpectedly, it hurt.

'Money,' he said. 'Or the lack of it, I should say. She's trying so hard to make a go of her music that she's had to drop most of her CPA work. Another flight here would be just too much.'

Well, that explained why she'd given the Zara credit note to Kate. I still didn't approve, but at least I understood.

'Anyway, I'm going home to her some time in the next week.'

That *also* hurt.

But what had I expected? That Luke and Kallie would never leave and, along with Quin, we'd go round in a tight-knit foursome, visiting middle-of-the-road restaurants, gorging on boiled potatoes and over-buttered carrots?

'You've found a carer your dad likes?' I asked.

Luke shook his head. 'Never gonna happen. But Dad's got two other sons, a daughter and four adult grandchildren in Ireland—there are enough of them to look after him. My life is in Denver, I've a partner there, a business.' He shrugged. 'I don't have to stay here and I don't have to feel guilty about leaving.'

Something in his tone suddenly reminded me of the terrible morning he'd left.

It was late January, dark and freezing. I'd woken abruptly, alone in bed. My phone said it was 3.43 a.m. Outside the bedroom were furtive, shuffling sounds. Fuelled by an adrenaline spike, I shot across the room, yanked open the door and found Joey and Luke in the hallway, looking stressed and sweaty.

'I'll take this—' Joey was picking up a box—then he noticed me.

Luke whipped around at the same time I saw that the sealed boxes, accumulated in the living room over the last day, had disappeared. Did that mean . . . ? They'd already been moved to some sort of car or van?

'You were trying to sneak out?' I couldn't believe he'd do something so cruel. 'Without saying anything?'

'Typical,' Luke said. 'That today of all days you're not comatose.'

Joey muttered, 'I'll wait in the van.' And off he scarpered, hefting the final box.

A jingling sound made my nerves flare—Luke's wedding ring. He'd taken it off and discarded it on the hall table. With the clatter of dropped metal, he said, 'And here are my keys.'

I hoped that this was some sort of stunt—but the conviction that it was real was winning.

'Luke, please, I'm begging you.' Frantically, I placed my hands on his chest, trying to get him to hold still. 'I love you so much.' My laboured breaths were humiliatingly loud. 'We can fix this, we'll go for counselling, whatever you want.'

Eyes as cold as slate, he peeled my hands off him and held me at bay.

I was reduced to a state of desperation, a ball of terror. But he slung on his jacket, picked up his bag and swung out of the door. Fuelled by panic, I grabbed the keys he'd just abandoned, shoved my feet into a pair of Uggs and followed him down three flights of stairs, out into the sleety street. In my leggings and fleece, I tried to keep up as he strode to a van.

When he opened the van door to vault up beside Joey, I flung myself at him. 'Don't,' he said, cold and unknowable. 'Please.'

Shocked, I stepped back, hearing the grind of metal as the door slid closed. The engine fired up and the van jerked out into the thin flow of traffic and moved away.

I stayed in the street for a long time. I still thought—hoped—they'd come back. It was the cold which drove me back inside, where the first thing I did was call him—but my number had been blocked.

Fumbling with terror, I called Joey, who said, 'You can't talk to him, Rachel. Any bills, official stuff, come through me and I'll pass them on. I'm turning my phone off now. And listen, mind yourself, would you? Sort yourself out.'

Stunned, I'd sat on the floor, wondering if this was actually real. Then I swallowed a sleeping tablet and waited for merciful oblivion to take me.

In the lamplight at my front door, I realized that Luke was watching me. 'What?' He sounded wary. 'What have I done now?'

Overwhelmed by memories, fresh rage flooded me. 'Just remembering the day you left me.'

'Oh God, that was—'

'You cruel, cold-hearted monster,' I spluttered. 'You mean, heartless . . .' I could hardly find the words. 'You ice-cold—'

'I hated having to do it.'

'*You* hated it?'

'Rachel, please. Listen to me. *Please.* My baby died—she was my baby too. And my wife, the woman I adored, had relapsed—'

'—I hadn't—'

'—I was broken, the loneliness was killing me and you were gone, Rachel. You might as well have been dead too.'

'However bad it was for you, it was worse for me.'

He pulled in a deep suck of a breath. 'I believe you. But you'd always told me that I should leave if you relapsed.'

'But I hadn't *relapsed.* That's not the word—'

Ignoring me, he continued speaking. 'For the longest time I couldn't imagine it—you were so committed to staying clean. Then it happened and it was a fucking nightmare. How often did I beg you to quit? And you just lied.' His face spasmed. 'All your girls—Claire, Anna, Nola, Brigit and Olga Mae, I rang them so often, they stopped taking my calls. I kept doing sweeps of the apartment and finding more stashes of the pills. I was wondering about cancelling your cards—'

I'd have found the money somewhere.

'—but forcing you to stop wouldn't have gotten you clean. You had to be the one who decided. It took me nearly six months to face it, you didn't love me enough—'

'Of course I loved you!'

'You loved the pills more. That's a fact, Rachel. I couldn't cure you. Just by being there, I was allowing it. If nothing in an addict's life changes, they won't change—how often had I heard you say that? If I left, I hoped it might shock you into getting clean.'

'Wait, now—' This was so confusing.

'But I couldn't move just eight blocks uptown. I wouldn't be able to stay away from you.'

'You really wanted to get far, far away from me.'

'I didn't want to leave you at all. But, you know, Rachel, I wasn't exactly *sane* around then.'

He looked so distraught that suddenly that was easy to believe.

'In the years since, it's obvious I overreacted . . . But at the time it seemed like the only choice left to me. I'd run out of road.'

For the first time I had a sense of how he might have felt.

'To do it right, you had to be out of reach. And I was terrified, Rachel. My life was in Brooklyn with you. At the best of times, I hate change. I picked Denver because I knew two people there—two more than any other place. I had to start a new job, find a place to live and get up every morning and go through the motions like a dead man walking. No one wanted to hang out with me, not even Johnno and Elaine after a while, I must have been too . . . depressed, whatever the word is. I couldn't connect with other people, their lives seemed so stupidly light-hearted . . .' He looked at me, a shiny-eyed glare. 'That morning I left, I'll never forget it, the way you pleaded, it tore me to shreds. I nearly gave in.' He clapped a hand over his mouth. 'I didn't want to go, but I felt I had to.' The words were muffled. 'Because—'

To my shock, I saw that he was crying.

'—by staying, I was only making everything worse.'

67

'Luke!' I moved towards him.

'No.' He swung away from me. 'Don't.' Stepping well back, he wiped his eyes with a rough swipe of his jacket sleeve. 'I'm fine. I'll leave now.'

'Don't. Please. Wait a moment. Just until you're okay.'

'I'm grand.'

It suddenly seemed wrong to be carrying out this intense, emotional discussion on my doorstep, on a dark, chilly night. 'Luke, hey, would you like to come in?'

He met my eyes. He looked worn out—and something else. Unlikely as it seemed, he might have been amused. 'Yeah,' he said, hinting at irony. 'Yeah, Rachel, I would.'

I stood aside. 'Come on then.'

With a small smile, he shook his head. 'I should go now.'

. . . *What the hell? Yes? No?*

He was definitely leaving, backing away towards the big motorbike parked on the kerb. Baffled, I watched him.

Over his shoulder, he clicked his key fob and the bike behind him chirped into life. 'Bye, Rachel,' he called, his voice carried by the night air.

Inside, I tried FaceTiming Quin but he didn't answer. I felt desolate—his common sense, his lack of sentimentality, was very grounding.

Because I didn't know what else to do, I went to bed. Just as I was drifting off to sleep, a question jolted me awake: *If you hadn't asked Carlotta for sleeping pills, would you still be married to Luke? With another child?*

Had that one request triggered a domino effect which had completely altered the path of my life, of Luke's life?

But who ever knew what was in store for us? And considering that we'd lost a child, it was remarkable that both Luke and I had gone on to rebuild good lives and be happy again. It wasn't what we would have chosen but we were okay now.

It was all fine.

68

'Harlie Clarke?' Hector said. 'Been crying nonstop since yesterday afternoon. Didn't want any dinner. Went to bed early. Chalkie came down around 1 a.m. and complained that the crying was keeping them awake.'

'Excellent,' Ted said approvingly.

'Good stuff.' There was general agreement around the table.

'Ella has been very quiet, Dennis is in good form again, Chalkie is still raging, Bronte seems calm and happy, Trassa the same, and Lowry, your newbie, has been telling everyone his sad stories—cruel father, ungrateful girlfriend, you know how it goes.'

In the Abbot's Quarter, Chalkie was already there, surrounded by a force field of fury. Then in came Dennis.

'Bee-soo, Rachel.' He blew me a kiss. 'Bee-soo, Chalkie.'

Chalkie glanced up. 'Bee-soo yourself, you fucking loon.'

'Oy, oy, *oy*!' Dennis recoiled. 'No need for that sort of talk. I'm smartening up my act. Bronte has inspired me. She's classy, so she is, *fierce* classy. And here's the woman herself! Bee-soo, Bronte.'

Bronte seemed startled, then began to laugh—the first time I'd seen her do that. '*Bisous*, Dennis, *bisous*.' She blew kisses at him, he returned fire and they grinned at each other.

'See,' Dennis said to Chalkie. 'It's nice to be nice. Here's Harlie. Bee-soo, Harlie.'

Harlie was weeping openly.

'Ah, now, now, *now*.' Gingerly Dennis patted her on the back. 'Still crying about your man? Jez, who'd blame you, he's a hunk, that lad, a hunk and a half. *Any*wan'd be boolie-versay about him.'

That just made Harlie cry more and as soon as everyone was settled, I started with her.

'We were really in love, me and Cal,' she said. 'You know how you see other couples and they don't even *like* each other? But me and Cal were best buds.' As the tears seized her once more, she squeaked out the next five words. 'He was my best friend.'

We let her cry.

'I'd always wanted to meet the perfect man,' she said. 'And he was it. But he still wasn't enough.'

'What do you mean?'

'I thought he'd turned into this boring fucker who interfered with my drinking. But I was the one who had changed. I preferred drinking to him. And still, I *hated* him for fucking off and leaving me. I thought he was really selfish. Now I sort of get it.'

'What do you get?'

'He left me because he thought it would help me.'

All the downy hairs on my arms stood up—this was exactly what Luke had said to me last night. If I believed Caleb—and I did—surely I should believe Luke?

If my ducklings thought they'd get an easy afternoon because it was Friday, they were in for another think: Ella's boss, Boyd Heffernan, had arrived.

Late thirties, dressed in a suit and tie and already balding, he was a very different proposition to Ella's boyfriend Jonah.

From the couple of chats we'd had, Boyd struck me as a man who'd expected great things from his life, only for it all to veer off into tedious mediocrity. Whatever dysfunctional thing he had going on with Ella, he was hanging a lot of hope on it.

When I led him into group, Ella's head snapped up and visible sweat popped on her skin. From the looks of her, there was a real chance she might faint.

I asked Boyd to introduce himself.

'I'm Ella's line manager at work,' he said. 'We're also in a relationship.'

An audible shock moved through the group and Dennis blurted out, 'What about the other lad?' Then, with a mortified squeak, 'Sorry, son, don't mind me.'

'Are you talking about Jonah?' Boyd asked. 'Because they've finished. She's just waiting for the right time to leave.'

I was certain that that would have come as news to Jonah.

Boyd looked at Ella, waiting for her to back him up, but she was slumped and floppy, unable to speak.

'Has she ever asked you to get sleeping tablets for her?' I asked.

'Um, yeah. You know she was mugged and then she couldn't sleep? So about five months ago her own doctor cut off her supply.'

That wasn't true but I let it pass for the moment.

'About five months ago, wasn't it, hon?' Boyd consulted Ella, who managed a dazed nod.

'She couldn't cope without the tablets—she asked if I could get some. I went to my GP, said I couldn't sleep, got a two-month supply. Gave them to her. I know it sounds wrong, but she was suffering and I could help. I'm okay with it.'

'Did you do it with other doctors?'

'No . . .'

'"But"?' There was something there that I hadn't expected.

'. . . not in Ireland. But I travel a lot for work, often to cities in the US. There are doctors who take care of hotel guests and they're okay about giving out prescriptions for sleeping pills.'

Out of nowhere I went hot-cold. 'How, erm . . . ?' Panic flashed through me. 'How often did you do this?'

From a long way away, I watched Boyd shrug. 'I think, five times.'

'Those doctors . . .' I had to clear my throat and start again. 'Those doctors are expensive, though?' I was freestyling now, we hadn't rehearsed this. And whatever was going on with me *had* to be parked for the rest of this session; my duty was to Ella.

With an enormous effort, I pulled myself back into my body, back into the room.

'Who paid the doctors?' I asked Boyd.

'Ah, yeah, I did.'

'Did Ella pay you back? No? Why was that?'

Everyone turned to Ella, who said, 'Mmm, I don't . . . Boyd, did you ever ask me for the money?'

'I don't know.' His cheekbones pinkened. 'Maybe I forgot.'

I couldn't help but feel sorry for him. He was crazy about her. She had no interest in him but as long as he continued to be useful, she'd keep sleeping with him. The most painful part was that he suspected it himself.

'Boyd, you did several things of dubious legality.' Now I was back in my groove. 'Which cost you a lot of money. Why was that?'

'Because I love her. We love each other. She was in a bad way and I was able to help. It was a no-brainer.'

'Ella was taking pills which hadn't been prescribed by her doctor. No single doctor knew the quantity she was taking. She could have accidentally over-dosed. Weren't you worried?'

'I was more worried about what would happen if she didn't have the tablets. She talked about suicide.'

'Boyd, you're under no obligation to answer.' I tried to be gentle. 'But are you married?'

'Y-yes.' He cast a look at Ella. 'Yes. But I'm leaving my wife.'

'When?'

'When Ella is . . .' He watched Ella, searching for a sign from her. But her eyes remained downcast. 'When Ella is . . . ready?'

Which would be precisely never, if I'd understood this properly.

It was absolutely horrifying. Poor Boyd, poor Boyd's wife, poor Jonah, poor Ella. So much damage, so much shame, so many secrets.

As soon as I'd seen Boyd off the premises, I went to a consulting room, and locked the door, as I tried to breathe through a stabbing pain in my ribs. When he had started talking about visiting hotel doctors, a memory—appallingly vivid—had landed wholesale in my head, of a time I'd gone to one of those doctors.

What was astonishing was that until now I'd managed to forget it completely.

It had been some time during those terrible months after Yara—late autumn, probably. I remembered how cold I'd been. My supply of Ambien had run low at an alarming speed and I was in a panic, wondering how to get more.

I couldn't ask Carlotta, it was too soon for yet another visit to Dr Gagnon, but then I remembered a doctor that Dad had visited a few years earlier when he'd been visiting New York with Mum. Dad had had an upset stom-ach—like I said, something *always* happened—and he'd gone to a nearby GP who serviced the hotels in midtown Manhattan.

In the speediest consultation of all time, the doctor had given Dad a prescription for several strong drugs, relieved him of a couple of hundred dollars and bounced him back out into the street.

With the aid of Google, it was remarkably easy to track down the doctor and even easier to bag an appointment for later that day. Getting showered and dressed was a bit of a big deal, but I'd caught the subway into the city, sat in the chair and told the doc I was visiting New York for five weeks. 'The jet lag has triggered my insomnia. And I need to be on top of things for my job.'

'That's too bad.' He was all unctuous sympathy, as well he might be, considering how expensive he was.

'I've used Ambien in the past,' I said. 'It's always worked well.'

'Okay.' He scribbled something on a pad. 'Five weeks, you said? Should I also give you some Xanax?'

A powerful longing seized me, but very quickly, I said, 'Oh no. No thank you. No.'

I couldn't let sleeping tablets be a gateway to any other drugs. Staying clean was *vital*. The Xanax—or Valium or any kind of benzo, really—would have taken the hard edges off the world. I couldn't truthfully say that I wouldn't have enjoyed it but I didn't *need* it the way I needed Ambien.

As I handed over my credit card—issued from a New York bank, not that the doctor was in any way bothered—the high cost almost cancelled out my relief.

Because I was a 'tourist' it couldn't be claimed back on my insurance and I wondered what to say to Luke if he saw it on the statement. Maybe I could pretend it was dental work? Or . . . Botox?

He'd freak out at Botox.

But not as much as he'd freak out at Ambien.

Even so, I'd managed to make the whole thing small and not important: I'd needed to sleep, I'd been resourceful.

But sitting in the Abbot's Quarter, quizzing Boyd, the memory of what I'd done suddenly astounded me. I'd gone to a doctor—the third doctor I'd seen in perhaps two months—and lied.

Even at the time my crappy, bullshit story had embarrassed me, and it was obvious that the doctor hadn't believed it either. We'd both come away sullied by the charade.

Luke had asked me what I'd think if a client told me my story. I had to admit that visiting more than one doctor, lying to them and hiding it all from my husband was addiction 101.

As the knowledge settled, my whole body went cold. Goosebumps broke out on my skin.

Back then, I'd taken my sanctimonious spurning of the offer of Xanax as proof that I was in control. Certain that if I simply *decided* to not get addicted to sleeping pills that I wouldn't.

But I had.

. . . or had I?

69

I couldn't think about it. Not now. I was going to Barcelona with Quin, I needed to be *together*. I'd think about it when I got back. I'd worry about it then.

Although maybe there wasn't anything to worry about. Maybe everything was fine.

At home, Kate and Devin were all glee and hilarity because Crunchie was wearing a bonnet.

'She *wanted* to wear it,' Kate insisted. 'She pulled it out of the drawer.'

Crunchie seemed happy enough, which was a relief because Kate and Devin were babysitting her for the weekend and I didn't want them treating her as a dressing-up doll. 'Are they laughing at you?' I asked in my special Crunchie voice. 'Are they making fun of you?'

'We're totally not,' Devin said. 'She looks like a wise woman—'

'—from a Jane Austen series,' Kate finished.

'Yeah!' Devin high-fived Kate.

Maybe she did. Crunchie's brown eyes were very kind and *perhaps* shrewd. Or, much more likely, I was just biased.

Up in my bedroom, I finished packing, throwing a couple of short, going-out dresses and a pair of teetery-heeled shoes into my wheelie case. The night at Jake's Place, when Quin had complained that he never saw my legs, I'd felt bad for him.

There was no harm in being nice, especially at the moment.

Which was why I also flung in some expensive knickers and bras.

'Crunchie! Let's go!' She came running for her last walk of the night. 'Let's just take off that fecking bonnet.'

Out in the woods, the flashlight lighting our way, Crunchie and I in perfect harmony, my head suddenly said, *You relapsed and ruined everything.*

Terrified, I tripped over a root. Even after I'd steadied myself I still felt like I was falling.

I needed to get home.

But once I was there I didn't want to stay. So I made the impulsive decision to surprise Quin by being in his bed when he arrived home at 5 a.m. I had a key, the alarm code and an open invitation, so why not?

Keen to leave, feeling slightly panicky, I threw the last few things into my carry-on, said goodbye to Crunchie, Kate and Devin and off I went.

But it was strange, being alone in Quin's house. Every time a floorboard creaked or a pipe banged, I thought it was a burglar or a ghost—something bad anyway.

I'd want to get used to it, though. This could be my home soon enough. Which was *good*. Proof that no matter what had happened with Luke—even if I *had* relapsed—I'd survived and built a new life. Quin's noisy pipes, possible burglars, these were real, tangible markers of progress.

When I'd got into bed and was switching off the light, I suddenly realized that if my life were a movie, Quin would tumble in, in a few hours' time, in a mad, snoggy, semi-undressed clinch with another woman. Who would transpire to be . . . ? The flight assistant from the plane? Shiv? Golden?

My money would probably be on Shiv.

The idea made me feel . . . bad. I couldn't narrow it down to individual feelings. Just weird. Bad weird.

But I was too tired to get up, get dressed again and go home. If, in five hours' time, Quin fell in here with his ex-wife, I'd just have to deal with it.

The bedroom light clicked on and I woke up, blinking against the brightness.

'Hey!' Quin looked confused. 'You're really here. I saw your car but—' Dropping his luggage he declared, 'Well, this is great,' and, making me laugh, planted big, smacky kisses on my forehead, my eyelids, my ear.

'How come, though?' he asked.

'A surprise.'

'I'm so here for this sort of surprise. Okay, let me brush my teeth and all that, then we'll get some sleep.'

Moments later, he came out of the bathroom, naked and smelling of toothpaste. 'Budge over.' He slid into the bed. 'I mean, budge *nearer*.'

He hit the light and into the darkness said, 'How come I arrive home and find you in my bed?' He still seemed uncertain. 'I mean, I'm happy and all—'

'How happy?'

'. . . That's a bit of a leading question.'

'Let's see.' I slid down his body.

'What's . . . . going on?' Then, 'No. Don't answer that. I'm just ecstatic it's happening.'

70

Thirty-two floors up, high above the sea, blue light streamed into a cool, white bedroom, the huge windows suggesting vast space beyond. I slid from the bed, dying for my first look at Barcelona in the daylight.

And it was spectacular. Far below was a teeny pool, a miniature strip of sand and, stretching to infinity, endless sea and sky.

I was in Quin's shirt—I'd woken during the night, chilly from the aircon. But I could spend every second in this room naked because no one could see us.

'Oh, Quin,' I said. 'The *view*!'

From the bed, he said, 'I'm looking at it.'

'Haha!' I pulled down the shirt so that it fully covered my bum.

'Get back in here,' he said.

'I didn't come to Barcelona to spend my time doing . . . *that*.' I swept my hands in the direction of his groin.

'I'll be *real* quick,' he promised, a gleam in his eye.

'Hold on.' I picked up the phone. 'I'm ordering our breakfast. Yes, I am. Shush!' After giving all the details, and supplementing them with extra requests from Quin—'Do they do detox juices? Yeah, great. But no papaya, Rach, tell them, no papaya.'—I hung up. 'It's being delivered in fifteen minutes.' I pulled off the shirt. 'Your time starts . . . *now*!'

We'd landed in Barcelona late last night, into Saturday-night frenzy—bumper-to-bumper traffic, horns blaring, music pulsing from competing venues. And it was *warm*. Palm trees lined the streets and it was a thrill to discover that our hotel was right next to the beach.

Quin had fallen asleep on the plane. After his middle-of-the-night homecoming, he'd managed about four hours' sleep before getting up, unpacking, *re*packing and then driving five kilometres in Saturday-morning gridlock traffic to pick up twelve bottles of orange wine from Fincas de Azabache, an iconic South Dublin wine store where Audi-driving Rugby Dads regularly engaged in shouting matches with other Audi-driving Rugby Dads over parking spaces.

Said orange wine was for Finley's birthday brunch at Vivi and Roly's, which was surprisingly enjoyable, even though both Shiv and Golden were present. Shiv, being Finley's mother, kind of *had* to be there. And Golden was Finley's godmother.

But the beauty was that Shiv and Golden had history, so long running that it was barely concealed. (Among other things, they'd fought over Quin, a grant from the Irish Enterprise Board, and an old picnic rug Roly had been throwing out.) This meant that their attention was focused on each other, leaving me flying beneath the radar, having a surprisingly pleasant time.

Mostly with Vivi and Michelle, who engaged me in book talk, but whenever I sat up straight and declared, 'Oh, I *loved* it,' they frowned and used words like 'specious' and 'mendacious'.

It happened so often that we ended up laughing uncontrollably. 'You must think we're impossible-to-please snobs,' Michelle said.

'And you must think I'm a halfwit!'

'But at least you try,' Vivi declared, inadvertently glancing at Shiv, then colouring at her faux pas.

My heart filled with warmth for Quin's clever, cultured family. Okay, they weren't over-burdened with empathy but they were great company and meant *so* well.

No matter what you did wrong, everything worked out in the end.

At the airport, Quin fell asleep in the fancy frequent-flyer's lounge, then again on the plane. But Barcelona woke him up. 'Hey.' He was suddenly animated. 'Let's go out.'

Though it was gone midnight I was on for it. Parking all the emotional shifts and insights of the previous week and being here, present, with Quin, was important. I was keen to do anything he wanted. Except, 'Not a place with a pool.'

'Why's that, then?'

'Saturday night, in a party city? Me, shy and stone-cold sober, watching beautiful young things, out of their heads, misbehaving in the water? I have my limits, Quin.'

Briefly, he went tight about the mouth, then looked around. 'Where's the concierge? Oh, it's a she.' He engaged her in intense chat, quizzing her on nearby pool-free bars and making her laugh. 'Okay.' He was back with a booking. 'Five minutes from here, on the oceanfront. Sounds good.'

After a quick change into more glitzy clothes—me in spindly-heeled sandals and one of my short dresses, him in a casual suit—off we went.

The bar was *gorgeous*. Three walls were open to the balmy night, revealing a sophisticated space with a hint of salt and sea.

Panels of aqua glass formed clusters of intimate seating—and what seating! In my first seven seconds I saw two Eames loungers, a Barcelona chair and a marshmallow sofa. A transparent bubble chair swung from the ceiling, shifting back and forth, looking slightly saucy.

'Great music,' Quin said.

'And not too loud!'

We were led to a pair of low-slung lounge chairs, set in a circle of mellow light. Hiding behind my menu I took a cautious look around. To my relief, the clientele seemed ordinary enough people—perhaps slightly better-looking than average—instead of the coked-up, yacht-jumping Eurotrash I'd feared.

I squeezed Quin's arm. 'We're not even too old!'

'Speak for yourself, Grandma.'

Then I opened my menu . . . 'Yikes. This buzzy, mellow vibe does *not* come cheap.'

'Don't, Rach.'

'Don't what?'

Quin shook his head. After a moment of silence he touched my knee with the toe of his shoe. 'So what's the sexy dress about?'

'Must it be about anything?'

'Not because you wore a dress for the night with Kallie and Luke and I complained I never saw you in one?'

'Well . . . I mean, you had a point.' Then, 'Quin? Are you okay?'

'Yeah. Sorry. Probably just tired.' Making a visible effort to be nice, he said, 'So. How are things with your ex-husband?'

Shoving down a thousand confusing feelings, I said, 'Kallie's already gone back and he'll be off in the next few days.'

'And? Are you okay?'

'Yes . . . But . . .' Suddenly the chance to unburden myself to Quin was hugely attractive. He cared about me, he'd listen. 'Things with Luke weren't as black and white as I'd once thought.'

'What do you mean?'

'I mean that maybe he wasn't entirely to blame.' I forced myself to say the unsayable. 'Quin, I think I might have relapsed after Yara died . . .'

'Um . . . what? You "think"? Isn't a relapse sort of a yes or no situation?'

'I'm not . . . exactly sure. I couldn't sleep and my doctor gave me tablets.

They were legal. Prescribed. I started taking more than I should have. I went to a second doctor, then—'

'But they were legal? You were hardly texting your dealer?'

'No, but—'

'And you're not doing it now, right? *He's* the arse who moved to Denver and blocked all contact.'

I took a breath. 'I'm still trying to figure everything out—'

'Rach!' he interrupted. 'Are we really doing this? Spending our time in this amazing city talking about who was to blame in a marriage which ended six years ago?'

'. . . No.' Then, 'Of course not.'

Internally, I began pressing down the thoughts and feelings again. This wasn't the time. Which was a strange relief.

Except . . . what would we talk about now? I threw a look around the bar and noticed a woman wearing an amazing neck cuff, the sort of thing Claire would wear. 'Oh God!' I'd just remembered. 'I wonder how Claire and Adam are getting on?'

'Yeah. Good on them.'

'. . . Mmmmm.'

'Oooooh? You're very judgy.'

'I'm not.' I sounded snappy, because I genuinely wasn't judging anyone. 'Just worried Claire isn't being honest with Adam.'

'Calm down,' Quin said.

'Okay.' I took a breath. 'Sorry.'

After a couple of extremely pricey drinks, we strolled back to the hotel along the boardwalk, the sucking and crashing of waves reaching us from the darkness.

'It's ten to two,' I said, 'And I know that's only ten to one in Ireland, but I still feel glamorous. Debauched, nearly!'

The heat had faded, the breeze had got stronger and Quin took off his jacket and put it around my shoulders.

'Like we're in a perfume ad! What should it be called? The perfume? "Mini-break"?' I whispered it a couple of times in 'the voice'.

'It needs to be an emotion,' Quin said.

'Amourrr,' I whispered. 'Sssssexxx. Loversssssss.'

'Trrrreachery,' Quin said.

'Nostalllllllgia.'

'Betrayalllllll.'

71

'Mum says we're not to go to Las Ramblas. That we'll get mugged.'

'We're *not* going to Las Ramblas.' Oh, such *scorn* from Quin. 'It'd be as tragic as visiting London and going to Oxford Circus.'

You relapsed and ruined everything.

'The boardwalk where we were last night', I read from a blog, 'is "a popular place for a romantic stroll"'. C'mon, Quin, let's stroll romantically.'

My phone pinged and Quin's head jerked up. 'Text from your ex-husband?' His tone was acidic.

'. . . From Claire.'

'Well? How did the swinging go?'

It was a fucking disaster.

'Oh God, no!' I said. 'Poor Claire.'

I was JEALOUS. Of Adam and Beatriz.

Then:

Adam was into it. I wasn't!

Then:

I've gone too far this time.

'This is what happens,' Quin said obliquely.
And I had enough sense to not ask him what he meant.
There was a final message from Claire.

Mum invited Luke to her party. He said yes.

'Quin? Mum's invited Luke to her party, apparently he said yes.'
'So we're not going?'
'That's right. Come on, let's see Barcelona.'

Outside the day was blue and yellow and all go. Tanned, muscular hotties were running at speed and visored cyclists, bent low over their bikes, came at us like attacking insects.

'Exsqueeze me!' I said as three roller-skaters whizzed by, whipping the air around us. 'Trying to stroll romantically here!' I smiled at Quin but at that exact moment, he was twisting his head away from me.

On the busy beach, golden young things were playing volleyball or doing slow, graceful movements that might have been t'ai chi.

On the other side of the boardwalk was *real life*—a quaint-looking neighbourhood of four- and five-storey apartment buildings, separated by dim, narrow streets. Laundry hung on tiny iron balconies or on lines strung between buildings, and squat, pretty palm trees—more like palm shrubs—sat at regular intervals.

An elderly woman was having a shouted, balcony-to-balcony conversation with another woman, who could have been her twin. Clusters of older men sat on rough chairs, talking energetically.

I asked, 'Can we take a look?'

'Rach. It's not a theme park.'

Oh. Kay. 'Quin . . . are you . . . ?'

'Fine. Just—locals live there, it's their home.'

'Sure.' There were other people, obviously tourists, strolling through the narrow streets but no way was I risking an argument when we still had thirty-six hours trapped with each other.

He exhaled. 'Sorry, Rach, of course we can. It's why we're here.' He led me into the small streets. 'Until the 1992 Olympics, it was just a poor fishing port, then they gussied it up. But it's still a real community.'

Men sat at tiny zinc tables, playing a board game. 'Dominos,' Quin said.

Everyone seemed to know each other and the whole place was vibrant, teeming with life.

Just as I wondered if any kids lived here, we came upon a playground filled with them, climbing, jumping, calling to each other. Watching children was always bitter-sweet but the balance had greatly tipped in favour of joy.

I'm happy now, so is Luke, everything is fine.

'You sure you don't mind doing this?' I asked Quin. 'You've seen it all before. We could do something else.'

'All good.'

After lunch in a low, pokey traditional restaurant—'a Barcelona secret', according to Quin—we went back to the hotel for a quick rest before hitting the beach but we accidentally slept all afternoon.

I awoke, without a clue where I was. I lay, staring at nothing, trying to get it together, when a memory ambushed me. It had been a morning in New York. Early. Too early to start living through another day where my baby was still dead, so I'd slipped some magic tablets into my mouth and got relieved of the feelings for a little longer.

Some hours later, groggy and confused, I'd woken again. This time, I'd got out of bed. Beneath me, the floor felt unsteady. I stood, waiting for it to become more solid, when Luke appeared in the doorway.

Suddenly wary, I'd said, 'I thought you were at work.'

'I know you did.' He watched me, the way he always watched me then— analytically. Detached.

It was three weeks, maybe four, since he'd discovered my hidden pills. Since then I'd done a good job of taking them in secret.

Moving into the bedroom, he pulled me against his chest and held me tight. I relaxed against him, suddenly grateful for the hard heat of his body. Then, very quietly, he whispered into my hair, 'You have to stop.'

Back in the now, in Barcelona, sadness rushed in, different layers of it. *You relapsed. It was your fault.*

Every time that thought arrived, a bolt of fear shot through me and every time it went a little deeper.

I shifted, looking for Quin. Stretched across the bed, he was still conked out. I put a hand on his shoulder and his eyes snapped open.

'We fell asleep.' He sounded stunned. 'What time is it?'

'Ten to eight.'

'Okay . . . I need coffee.' He stumbled around the room, then into the shower. When he came back, he was awake. 'So tonight? Food? We can pick up something casual out there.' He nodded towards the sea. 'Or.' He paused. 'I've booked two places at a pop-up in a villa belonging to a Catalan noble-man, a *comte*.'

I'd have quite happily gone back to the boardwalk and some unscary, touristy place, but it was obvious Quin was lobbying for the nobleman's apartment. 'The pop-up sounds interesting.'

'Interesting' was one of the things I loved about Quin. An 'opera supper' on a boat in Helsinki harbour had been a total shambles but we'd had such a laugh. However, you needed to be in the whole of your health for his adventures and tonight I wasn't.

Wearing the second of my sexy dresses, we headed to an eerily quiet network of leafy, residential streets which reeked of old money. Imposing villas, their windows dark and shuttered, snubbed us with their haughty façades as we hurtled past in an Uber, trying to catch glimpses of house numbers.

'I think this is it,' Quin said as the driver stopped outside a pale-pink, five-storey villa, and said things to us in Catalan, the gist of which seemed to be, 'Get out.'

Framed by palm trees and uplighting, the villa was set behind metal gates which were unnecessarily tall. Clambering onto the pavement, I tipped my head back to see the top and had to wonder at what point the extra metal became just *showing off.*

Quin is great and my life is good.

'Is that the Comte?' Quin asked as a balding, irritated-looking man beckoned us to the front door. 'I thought he'd look more . . . noble?'

Once it was established that our names were on the list, we were led up stone stairs by a harried woman into a dimly lit room where perhaps twenty other people milled around, drinking red wine from large goblets. From what I could see—admittedly not much—they looked as if they'd come straight from a very fashionable evening wedding. There were a lot of feathered hairpieces, thick purple lipstick, dark red tartan, spiky jewellery and gold platform shoes.

The fashion people, who turned out to be Italian, greeted us with delighted cries. Lovely, of course—but it was only then that I understood tonight would be a communal experience.

Sometimes I'm *fine*, meeting twenty new people in a pitch-dark room in a villa in Barcelona, when everyone else is crazy-drunk but I'm stone-cold sober and haven't eaten in eight hours, while bothered by awful suspicions that six years earlier I relapsed into drug addiction and ruined my marriage. *Fine.*

But the language was a problem. Quin and I spoke almost no Italian and the fashion people, though smiley and charmingly affectionate, spoke no English.

'I thought it would be just you and me,' Quin said. 'I didn't know we'd have to *socialize.*'

'We can pretend it's just us,' I said.

But they wouldn't leave us alone. Two drag queens, both wearing platform ankle boots which looked like goats' hooves, made a stab at a conversation. We established that the whole group was from a town called Messina and tonight was a birthday party for someone called Giuseppina. But it was hard work for the four of us, and eventually the duo said something to each other in Italian, along the lines of, *Ah, fuck this, Vera,* and went back to their friends.

'I'm hungry,' I said to Quin. 'Scrap that. I'm *hangry.*'

'Oh no,' Quin muttered as two more fabulously attired fashion types materialized, grinning, from the gloom and the excruciating attempts at chat began again.

Quickly, though, they tired of us but our relief was short-lived, as two fresh ones showed up, black-toothed and garrulous from the wine.

'They've done a rota.' Quin looked as though the misery might kill him. Then both of us began to wheeze with laughter while attempting to apologize to the Italians.

For the next hour, new companions continued to join us every ten minutes, until they burnt out, and replacements popped up in their stead. In normal circumstances, I'd have said, 'Hey, Quinster, I'm having the worst night of my life, can we cut our losses?'

But circumstances weren't normal.

Eventually we were led into another room—just as dimly lit—for dinner. There was a scramble for places at a dark-wood table as long as a runway and Quin and I found ourselves shunted right down at the end. It was for the best.

It was no surprise that not a single one of the browbeaten waiters knew anything about my pre-ordered vegetarian meal. Quin, who was normally very good at complaining—calm but effective—was all set to weigh in but I sensed nothing good would come of it. 'It's fine, it's fine, I'll just eat the non-meat bits.'

'Or we could leave?' he said.

'No!' Bailing early would stamp the evening as an Abject Failure and we needed some sort of a win.

The menu was delivered in loud Catalan by the maybe-Comte. The Italians seemed to understand but Quin and I hadn't a clue and there was no written menu to translate. However, when the first course arrived, our new friends did their best to demonstrate. From their flapping, it seemed to be a bird.

'Chicken?' Quin was deep into Google translate. '*Pollo?*'

'No, no, no!' They did bombing motions.

'A bird of prey? Seriously?' Quin was looking up words on his phone. '*Falco?*'

'*No!*' some of them said, but just as many others exclaimed, '*Sí!*'

'*Aquila!*' a voice yelled from the gloom.

'*Aquila?* Is that not Spanish for "grandmother"?' I remembered it from watching *Dora the Explorer* with JJ.

'That's *abuela,*' Quin said.

The others overheard this and took up the cry. '*Abuela!*' they declared, pointing at their plates and laughing their heads off. '*Abuela!*'

God, this was hard. It was too dark to distinguish which bits on my plate weren't meat, so it wasn't safe to chance eating anything. Then Quin discovered that '*aquila*' was Italian for 'eagle' so it was official that our new friends were laughing at us.

Next thing, two of the fabulous women opposite us began kissing each other, in a very 'perform-y' way. I turned to Quin. 'I'm too hungry for this.'

'Okay.' He was already standing. 'We're off.'

Our departure triggered a riot of hugs and yelling and the whole place felt moments away from descending into an orgy. I felt sad and ashamed, a non-wine-drinking, non-eagle-eating, non-orgy-attending failure.

Quin and I didn't speak until we were side by side in an Uber, halfway back to the hotel.

'I'm sorry,' I said.

'*I'm* sorry.' Then, 'We can get room service. Or anything you'd like.'

'Quick is all that matters.'

'We'll go to the marina. There are stalls there, they'd be fast.'

The car dropped us at the seafront, where we sat on a wall and had churros and hot chocolate from a stall. Because the night was once again breezy, Quin put his jacket around my shoulders, the way he had the previous night, but this time, neither of us mentioned our perfume.

72

'. . . for an actual moment, I wondered if I was dead?' Quin said, laughing. 'If this was hell? Having the chats with friendly Italians for all eternity.'

After the churros on the marina wall, we'd slept heavily and had woken up in a better mood.

'To me,' I said, 'it felt more like a zombie movie. The black teeth, the eyeliner . . . And as soon as we got free of one lot, another popped up in their place.'

'Seriously, though.' He rolled over in the bed and looked up at me. 'I'm really sorry.'

'No *way*, Quin. It was a risk and this time it didn't pan out. But if you play it safe all the time, nothing exciting happens.'

'And playing it safe is the most dangerous thing a woman like you can do.' He said that to me a lot. I loved it even though it wasn't true, not even remotely.

'So, this morning, the Gaudí house?' I said. 'And then the airport?'

'And if we've time, I'd like to drop in on someone. There's a man here, deals mostly in furniture, but he's always got beautiful, interesting pieces, things with a story. I like going along, just to see what he has. You'd like it.'

'Okay. Great.'

'Oh my God, I'm in *love*,' I said to Quin, turning in a circle in one of the rooms in Casa Batlló, letting the colours from the stained glass wash over me. 'Like, he didn't hold back, did he? Gaudí? Not a man for restraint? I'm getting my house redone soon as we get back. Make it wavy! All of it, the floors, everything!'

I was genuinely mad about this beautiful house but I was overdoing the delight. My unsettling memories from six years ago were casting a long shadow. Pushing back against it, desperate to reach baseline normal, was hard work.

Finally, I let myself admit that for a lot of this weekend I'd been impersonating my happiest, most carefree self. Because Quin deserved it. He'd put a lot of thought and effort—and money—into these few days.

But there were other reasons—I needed touchstones. Things being good with Quin *mattered* because it was proof that, Yara aside, my life had worked out. The facts were: I was clean today; I was good at my job; and I'd met a lovely man.

I smiled at Quin. 'Is being in this house like being underwater?' I asked.

'Yeah!' He was pleased with me. 'See how the ceiling looks like a whirlpool? And the effect this glass has . . .'

'You're a *great* tour guide.'

The walls were curved, the windows were wavy, even the ceiling undulated. 'There are no straight lines, are there? Not a single one.' Laughing, I said to Quin, 'I bet you hate it.'

'It's not how I'd do my home but I can appreciate it.'

'Well, *I*—I grabbed him by the shirtfront and leant close—'am enchanted!'

His smile was wide, he seemed genuinely happy and my heart lifted, even if it didn't get as high as it needed to reach.

Each room, right up to the roof, revealed new delights. The wall mosaics, the shapes of the doors, even the ventilation system was gorgeous. 'This is a dream world,' I declared.

When we reached the roof, I looked around, then asked, 'What's next?'

'That's it,' Quin said. 'You've seen it all.'

'I have? Oh no!' It was like a bubble bursting. This magical house had kept me cocooned from harsh reality. I wasn't ready to return to my suspicions and fear. *You relapsed, you ruined everything.*

'What time is it?' I asked. '*What?*' We'd been there for two and a half hours. 'Oh, Quin, what about the man you want to see?'

'Was worth it to see you happy. Anyway, there's still time.'

'Okay. So. Let's go.'

As we walked, Quin made a call. 'Mr Navabi? Nick Quinlivan here. We're on our way, we'll be with you in fifteen minutes.'

'You've to make an appointment? Go on, tell me about him.'

'His name is Omid Navabi. From things he's said, I think he's from Iran. Sometimes his stuff is a bit wack but it's always interesting.'

Down a narrow side street, at an anonymous door, we were buzzed in and went to the first floor. Mr Navabi was a handsome, suave, well-tailored twinkler. 'Nicholas, my old friend, come in. And the famous Rachel, how are you enjoying the Minerva bracelet? I can offer you *orxata*? *Vermut*?'

The showroom was styled like an apartment straight out of *Mad Men*—no wonder Quin loved it here. There were Knoll sofas, a peekaboo coffee table, a modern piano in rosewood and lamps so gorgeous I wanted to buy them all.

A louche drinks cart featured a sleek rounded whiskey decanter and matching tumblers. Atop a sectional sideboard was a chrome-and-walnut cigarette dispenser.

On a wall of open shelving were all kinds of charming, probably useless things that you could only call *objets*: an old camera in a battered brown leather case; a Lucite Rolodex; vintage sunglasses; toy sports cars.

'Look in the bedroom part.' Quin pointed me to a space further along.

God, it was gorgeous—hand-tufted rugs, *more* beautiful lamps and a bed with a cartoonishly padded headboard. I opened the wardrobe to discover Pucci kaftans, a silver Courrèges coat, dresses from Biba and a stack of Hermès luggage.

'All vintage,' Quin was behind me. 'Have you seen the jewellery? There on your right, on the dressing table.'

I looked—and gasped: there were bangles, pendants, earrings and cuf-flinks. All in precious metals and stones, winking and dazzling on a velvet backdrop.

'And.' A short pause followed. 'There are rings.'

. . . The back of my neck prickled. God almighty, he wasn't about to—? I turned to see him holding a large green ring towards me.

Panic surged. *No, Quin, no, Quin, no, no, no, no, no, no, no, no.*

Inadvertently, I'd stepped away from him—and only then did I notice his confusion.

'What, Rach?'

His gaze moved from my stricken face to the ring in his hands. I watched understanding dawn on him. 'Jesus.' He sounded shocked. 'Did you actually think . . . ?' In disbelief, he spluttered, 'I wasn't asking you to *marry* me, Rachel.'

'Ah. One of my favourite pieces.' Mr Navabi appeared. 'Green tourmaline and diamond. A cocktail ring.'

'A cocktail ring?' I managed.

'Worn for special occasions. I'm available if you need any information.' Discreetly, he slipped away.

The ring was still in Quin's hands. 'So you're certain you don't want to marry me?' His tone was sarky. 'Quite certain, I'd say. Yeah, *no* room for doubt there.'

'Quin. I'm sorry, I don't know what . . .'

I'd hurt him terribly. I'd even managed to shock myself.

And we'd been doing so well.

We left for the airport, checked in, endured security, had a seventy-minute wait in the lounge and got on the plane, all without exchanging a word.

About two hours into the flight, Quin suddenly uttered, 'I don't know why you thought I was *proposing*.'

'I don't either.' I genuinely hadn't a clue. But what was clear was that, in that moment, the thought of a long-term commitment to him had been terrifying. So much so, I hadn't been able to hide it.

'If it had ever been on the cards,' he said, 'not that it was, you have my word that now it never will.'

'Quin, I'm so sorry for hurting you. I don't know what—'

'I need you to stay at your own place tonight.'

'*Quin.*'

'I'll drop you at mine,' he said. 'Your car is there.'

'Quin—'

'I don't want to talk to you.'

I bit my lip and stayed silent. By now I thought I understood where my wild overreaction had originated. Quin and I had had a tense few days. He'd resented the soul-searching I'd been doing about my past, about Luke.

And I'd resented him for resenting it.

Our glamorous weekend had done heroic work trying to conceal the strain, but our mutual grievances had kept breaking the surface.

At Dublin Airport, we got into his jeep and drove, in silence. When we reached his house, he yanked my carry-on from the trunk and clattered it to the ground. With an angry beep, he locked his car, then rattled his front door open and slammed it shut behind him—leaving me outside in the cool night.

Feeling sad and foolish, I hung around, hoping he'd return. I watched the lights go on inside his house, then watched them all go out again. When the last one disappeared, I had no choice but to go home, already worried about what tomorrow would bring.

Whatever it was, I sensed it was going to be bad.

73

And sure enough, at 6 a.m., when I jolted awake into heart-pounding anxiety, the truth *finally* caught up with me and landed intact: Luke had left me because I'd started using drugs again. *Ab*using. I'd plunged right back into addiction and become totally unreachable.

There was no more uncertainty, no more flip-flopping. The knowledge snapped into place, then clicked, turning on lights, *flick, flick, flick*, illuminating everything with a grand sweep.

Nothing had changed but everything was different.

The reality was there, hard and clear: as soon as I'd seen there was a chance of getting sleepers from Carlotta, I'd relapsed into addictive thinking, then addictive behaviour. In so deep I hadn't even known I was in trouble.

No wonder he had left.

Not because he blamed me for Yara. Not because he'd stopped loving me. But because I was, once more, an active addict.

Now that I knew, it was laughably obvious—and yet, the shock was enormous.

What also landed was the understanding that, in a way, I'd always known I'd relapsed. It was as if, when I'd started abusing drugs again, a part of me had sliced itself off from the main track and run on a parallel path. I had worked very hard to ignore that phantom self but now and again, I'd catch a glimpse of it—a glimpse of *me*—almost keeping pace.

Now that I knew, it was hard to believe how I'd managed to blind myself.

But that was addiction, that was denial. There was nothing special about me. Day in, day out, I saw how hard addicts worked to hide their shame-filled behaviour from themselves. When they finally ran out of road and went careering smack-bang into the truth, it wasn't that they remembered things they'd conveniently forgotten. They'd always known the facts, but some shift happened which recontextualized them.

I was no different.

I called Nola, who sounded as if she'd been expecting to hear from me. She said, 'Come over when you finish for the day.'

Then I rang Quin but it went straight to message. I asked him to call me, then went to work—where I had to listen to Bronte describe my own delusions, almost word for word.

'I thought it was fine to take the tablets,' Bronte had said. 'Because a doctor had prescribed them.'

'But,' I said, going through the motions as best I could, 'as soon as you started, the craving for more and stronger would kick in?'

'It did. I admit it.'

'You had other options? You knew you had? And you still went for the dangerous one?'

'Yes. Yes. And yes.'

'But you're educated,' Trassa told Bronte. 'You know French words and the names of Greek gods. You'd got free of heroin years earlier so why would you do something so stupid?'

'Education makes no difference. I forgot I was an addict. No, that's wrong, I *decided* to forget.'

'Why, though?' Poor Trassa was trying to understand. 'If your life was good?'

'But it wasn't.' She bit her lip. 'Rachel was right. When Freya was . . . when Eden changed Freya's plans, it felt as if I had no reason to live. I had managed to stay hopeful for a long, long time because I'd expected good things would come to pass.'

'I don't get it.' Lowry was scornful. 'Okay, you're upset about your daughter and your horses but you'd kicked your habit. That's a big deal. Why would you take drugs that would lead you back to smack?'

Bronte gave him a cool stare. 'Because we addicts'—she twirled a finger around the room, ending by pointing it at Lowry—'at our core, we want an excuse to relapse.'

'Hold on now,' Lowry piped up. 'I'm not addicted to anything—'

'There were two versions of me.' Bronte cut across him. 'The one who wanted to be well and one who wanted to disappear into the drugs again. There will always be two of me. No matter how many clean years I have, the addict in me is always waiting for its chance.'

'That sounds desperate.' Trassa was distressed. 'I want to be able to stop.'

'You can stop but addiction is never cured,' Bronte said. 'It's just under control.'

'Jesus, Rachel.' Chalkie gave me a sly smile. 'Is Bronte applying for your job?'

But I was in no mood for bants with Chalkie. Once again I was faced with the realization that, like Bronte, I had had other options: I could have taken Carlotta up on her offer of antidepressants that helped with sleep. But I'd known that they weren't any fun.

Deep in grief and self-loathing, I'd wanted the delicious balm of sleeping tablets.

Next up was Ella, whose body was folded in on itself, like a puppet whose strings had been cut.

Going for the jugular, I asked, 'What did you like about being out of it for days on end?'

After a long, tense wait, she said, 'Everything.'

Lifting her head, she stared me in the eye. 'Every fucking thing. But mostly not being afraid. I'm always afraid and I'm so tired of it.'

Well, this was a surprise. I hadn't expected a capitulation *quite* this soon.

'Cheers for that, Rachel.' Ella vibrated with anger and sorrow. 'You broke me and you've ruined my life and I fucking hate you.'

'Your life isn't ruined,' I said. 'That's a promise.'

'Oh, fuck off!'

At lunchtime I switched on my phone, hoping to hear from Quin. There was nothing so I called again. Same as before, it went straight to message. 'Quin,' I said. 'I'm so sorry for hurting you. Can we talk? Please? You matter very *very* much to me . . .'

A text had arrived from Claire so I rang her.

'You around tonight?' she asked. 'I really need you.'

'I'm seeing Nola after work, can I ring when I'm done?'

'Grand. Except we can't talk in my house *for obvious reasons*. And we can't go to my club *for obvious reasons*. And we can't meet in public in case I cry. It'll have to be your place but Kate is to know nothing about . . . what went on.'

'Okay.' With a heavy sigh, I switched off my phone. I'd try Quin again after work. Now it was time for afternoon group, where we got Lowry's life story.

His opening line was, 'Everyone I've ever loved has abandoned me.'

Chalkie actually chortled. We'd decided to keep Chalkie for another few weeks because he was too angry to be let out into the world.

In Life According to Lowry, everything was always someone else's fault. He'd shown real talent—'rare talent' according to himself—as a photographer, but his parents wouldn't pay for the expensive school in New York. 'So instead of producing actual *art*, I take cheesy shots of weddings. It's the main reason I'm depressed.'

'But who's stopping you from producing art?' Trassa asked. 'Do you have to be in the artist's trade union or something?'

Under his breath, but loud enough to be heard, Lowry muttered, '*Fuck's* sake.'

'I'm not trying to be a smart alec,' Trassa said gently. 'I honestly don't know.'

'No one is stopping me. As *such*,' Lowry said. 'But—okay! Let's be real here—the money for the weddings is good. I got used to it, I like it. So shoot me.'

Dennis and Chalkie exchanged a look and Dennis sniggered.

'What?' Lowry asked. 'I'm meant to be ashamed of earning a living?'

'Keep reading,' I said.

Sienna had broken up with him because she 'couldn't accept me as I am'.

'How are you "as you are"?' Bronte dripped contempt.

'Too much of a free spirit.'

'Hah!' Chalkie was scornful and delighted. 'Which translates as "can't keep your lad in your jocks". Amirite?'

'Hey, smackhead.' Lowry stood up.

'Sit. Down,' I ordered. Jesus Christ, fisticuffs were the last thing we needed. Lowry was a lot taller than Chalkie but my money would have been on the little guy.

Lowry made a show of reluctantly sitting back down again, while Chalkie lounged in his chair, eyeballing him. 'You're a joke,' Chalkie informed him. 'A fucking joke.'

'We can't all come from central-casting deprivation. Okay, so my mum didn't die of a heroin overdose but my feelings are as worthy as yours.'

'Lowry, you crossed a line. Apologize to Chalkie.'

'Jesus, Rachel, I don't need his meaningless, middle-class apology.'

'But Lowry needs to do it.'

When group ended, I powered on my phone. Still nothing from Quin. Feeling sick, I rang him and once again it went to message. 'Quin? Please can we talk? I can come over later.'

Because I didn't know what else to do, I typed up my daily notes, said goodnight to everyone and ran down the steps, out into the evening light.

Then—surprising me—Quin rang. 'I'm out tonight. Pints with Golden, some of the others. Planning to climb Denali in May.'

This was the first I'd heard of *any* of it—pints, climbs—but I was being punished and this was how Quin wanted to do it.

'Could we see each other afterwards?' I asked.

'Nah. Could be a late one.'

'Tomorrow night?'

'. . . Don't think so.'

'Quin, please—'

'Maybe later in the week. Depends.' And he was gone.

74

Nola sat me in her conservatory, draped me in a soft, silky shawl, made me tea and insisted I eat a scone.

The soft wool around my neck was a comfort. 'Is this a Tibetan prayer shawl?'

'It is not, they're only cheap muslin. That's your finest lambswool from Takashimaya in Osaka. So tell me what's going on, pet? A rough idea.'

'Is Quin breaking up with me?' I asked.

'Park Quin for the minute. You've hurt him, he needs time. Meanwhile, you've bigger things to think about.'

'Like . . . ?'

'Rachel . . .'

'So.' I took a breath. 'I think . . . after Yara died I—I . . .' It was so painful to say the word. '. . . relapsed.'

Nola nodded, not even remotely surprised.

Then, neither was I. 'Of course you knew.'

'How could I not, pet? How many times did poor Luke ring me that winter? Asking me to talk sense to you? Dozens. And you insisting he was punishing you for letting your little girl die—'

'—I thought he *did* blame me.'

'A terrible thing happened to you, but it doesn't mean you didn't relapse.'

'Nola, I didn't know. I was in such pain and I couldn't sleep and I *needed* to and . . . I took sleeping pills. More than I should have.' *Fuck*. 'I lied to doctors. To Luke. To you, Nola. To Claire and Anna and Olga Mae.'

'And yourself, while we're about it.'

Oh God. For six years I'd had my version of how things had played out and I'd been wrong.

'Nola, I've been back in Ireland for years, why didn't you say it before now?'

She laughed sadly. 'Every time I broached it, you reminded me that your baby had died. That's where we always got stuck. Rachel, what you went through with Yara would break anyone's heart but you used it to justify your capers.' Gently, she said, 'How often did I tell you that you and Luke needed to talk?'

'And I told you he'd blocked me on everything and I'd no address for him.'

'So I told you to Golden Key it. It took six years but Luke is here, you're talking to each other and you're finally facing the truth. I've a question for you,' she said. 'Why don't you mark your NA anniversary?'

'Because the important thing is to stay clean *today*.'

'Baloney. You used to love the cake, the medallion, all the fuss. After you relapsed you stopped. Because despite all the lies you were telling yourself, you *knew* that your original date twenty years ago no longer counted.'

'No, I . . .' Whenever I thought of my anniversary date, my head filled with a sort of fog. I hadn't been consciously denying anything. It was more like I *couldn't* think about it. But now I saw the truth and it was very painful. 'My clean time was—is—so important to who I am. I was proud of getting clean and staying clean. Without it, I feel lost. The me I thought I was, *isn't*.'

I'd seen other people come back into recovery after a relapse and I'd pitied them.

'Mourn it,' Nola said. 'Do your best to make sure you don't do it again. Then embrace your actual recovery date.'

I had a clear memory of the morning in New York, a couple of months after Luke had left, when I'd decided to stop taking the sleepers. I'd woken very early—and felt inexplicably calm.

It was more than eight months since Yara had died and the frenzied storm seemed to have finally blown itself out.

I wasn't okay, not cured—nothing like that. My appalling loss was still sharply defined but the thrashing agony, the anguish I just couldn't accept, had eased. My little girl was gone, I was changed forever, there would still be terrible times but, finally, I could acknowledge the facts, even submit to them, and my soul was quiet.

I opened the bedroom curtains. Beyond the window, the first glimmers of dawn were lighting the sky. My window was wet, it must have been pelting down earlier. As the sun continued to rise, a ray caught on a raindrop on the glass and broke into the seven different colours of the spectrum, becoming smudged stripes of transparent colour on the wooden floor, right in front of me.

Experimentally, I moved my fingers in the arc of colour, spellbound by the different shades on my skin.

Seeing signs wasn't really my thing but the same weird calm I'd woken up with was insisting that this was a message from Yara, saying that she was always with me, but that it was time to start living again.

Another certainty settled—from that day forward, I'd be able to sleep. There would be no more need for tablets. I went around the apartment, gathered them all up and flushed them away.

'How come I just decided to stop?' I asked Nola. 'All by myself?'

'Are you stone mad, girl? Two months earlier, your husband had left you. Into the bargain, the likes of myself and Olga Mae were blue in the face begging you to have sense. The question I'd be asking myself is: What took me so long?'

When she put it like that . . . 'So what do I do now?'

'We'll get busy soon enough, you and me. You need to do your steps all over again.'

Oh God. Having to do a deep-dive on my various dishonesties and fuck-ups was hard, painful work. It needed to be done, though.

'. . . I need to apologize to Luke. I told everyone he was a terrible person but I was the one in the wrong.'

'Lord save us, I'm blue in the face telling you that.'

'I feel sick about my job, Nola. What kind of an addiction counsellor am I? I've been carrying around a huge big sack of my own denial. How could I have helped other addicts?'

'But you know that you've helped. Unless you've been lying about the thank-you cards and Jo Malone candles? And all your promotions have only been a cock-and-a-bull story and you're really working in a carwash, which would at least explain your'—Nola waved a hand at my jumpsuit—'rig-out.'

The steady stream of cards from ex-patients was real. As was the fact that the high-ups in the Cloisters—Ted and the board—had, over the past five years, in several steps, promoted me from deputy counsellor all the way to head counsellor.

'Maybe . . .' I chanced, 'because I was an addict in denial, I was actually *better* at my job?'

'Arra, now . . .' Nola wasn't having that.

'My past isn't the past I thought it was.' I was trying to articulate my exact fear. 'This new knowledge, is that going to impact the present?'

'In what way?'

Tentatively, I sought the right words, trying to assemble my precise emotions. 'I feel this mad relief that Luke didn't blame me for Yara. Except I'm also incredibly sad.'

'No doubt about it, this is big stuff. But it's already happened and you've survived. Your feelings just need to catch up with the facts.' Then, 'Listen to me now. Two important things, Rachel. Make your amends to Luke. And keep Quin in the picture every step of the way.'

'Okay.' I froze with unexpected fear: what if Luke had already returned to Denver?

As soon as I left Nola, I texted him. You still in Ireland?

He replied instantly. Can you take a call rn?

Yes.

My phone buzzed in my hand. 'Luke?' I answered.

'Hey,' he said. A pause. 'I'm still here.'

Intense relief swept over me. 'Do you think . . . Could you meet me? Can we talk?'

'. . . Sure. Now?'

'I can't tonight, I'm sorry. How's tomorrow?'

'Any time after two is good. Devin's spending the afternoon with Dad, I'll be on the doss.'

'I can finish work at about five thirty.' Since the clocks had gone forward, the evenings were suddenly a lot brighter. 'Can you come to Wicklow? We'll go to Morrigan's, she's open till sevenish.'

'Morrigan's?'

'A café near my house. It's beside a little river. A secret only locals know about. I'll drop you a pin. I can be with you about ten to six, or as close as possible.'

Then I rang Claire. 'I'm leaving Nola's now. See you at my house in forty minutes.'

'It wasn't sexy fun.' Claire couldn't meet my eye. 'It was nothing like a fantasy. Everything was too real. Look, are you able to hear this?'

'Totally.' It was easier to join in with Claire's soul-searching than do my own. 'Why don't you hold Crunchie? She's very comforting.'

'I'm disappointed in myself.' Claire ignored my offer of my dog. 'I thought I was more evolved than this. I was actually *jealous*. Of Adam . . . liking . . .' She cleared her throat. '*Liking* other people.'

'But that isn't . . . abnormal.'

'Seeing him with another person . . . with two other persons—' She stopped. Then, 'Okay. I have something to tell you. We were all getting along . . . grand. Everyone having a good time. Thennnnnn, it sort of became clear that Piet was more into Adam than he was into me. And . . . Beatriz was more into Adam than she was into me. I don't exactly know what went on, it just went strange and I was . . . left out.' She swallowed convulsively, trying to not cry.

'But that's terrible, Claire. That's not meant to happen, it's meant to be equal, surely! Or at least with your agreement?'

'Rachel, I'm mortified. The four of us were supposed to discuss it afterwards, to check that we felt safe and seen and all that blah but I left early. I took the car keys. Adam was still asleep. He arrived home *five* hours later, in a taxi.'

'And . . . how was he about the whole thing?'

'Adam? Oh, Adam had a great time. Adam wants to do it again.'

It was after eleven when Claire left. I rang Quin, but his phone was switched off and there was no point leaving a message.

It was time to go to sleep but I was afraid of lying in the dark, my messed-up head churning. In a last-ditch attempt to calm myself, I tried a quick fifteen minutes of meditation. Crunchie joined in but it didn't work for either of us. My upheaval was too huge. And Crunchie? Well, Crunchie, though well intentioned, was only a dog.

75

'Six weeks ago, I thought ye were all stone mad.' Wobbling slightly, Trassa was up on a kitchen chair, looking down on a roomful of smiling faces. 'I'd only come in so my son would pay off my debts. But thanks to Rachel there, and all of ye in my group, I know now that I'm addicted to gambling.'

Amused and scornful, Lowry squinted up at her.

'It broke my heart, so it did, seeing that I had to stop. But it had made a prisoner of me. And now, finally, at the age of sixty-eight, I'm free.'

Whoops and cheers greeted this.

'I've plenty of work to do on myself and a lot of trust to win back from my family, it won't be easy, but, one day at a time, I'll do it. Now let's see if I can get down off this chair without making a show of myself. Chalkie! Dennis!'

To a rowdy round of applause, Trassa was helped back to terra firma. As everyone else dived on the cake, Trassa came to me.

'Thank you for asking me that question.' Her mouth trembled. 'You know . . . that day.'

'Thank *you*.' She'd never know how grateful I was to her: that despite my relapse, I'd still been able to help her.

'You'll go to regular meetings?' I checked. 'You'll make friends with other people in recovery? Take on a service commitment and find some sort of higher power?'

'I will.' She nodded vigorously. 'I certainly will.'

I'd let all of that fall away in the days and weeks after Yara had died. No wonder things had gone sideways.

'You've been unbelievably brave,' I told her.

We hugged each other fiercely, then I had to leave—to try to make things right with Luke.

*

It was almost six by the time, following the babbling stream, I broke through the trees at Morrigan's. Luke was at a wooden bench, spotlit by sunlight. Dappled shadows of branches shifted over the table.

When he saw me, he got to his feet.

'Sorry I'm late.' I was *so* anxious—keen yet afraid to admit my failings. 'Work.'

'It's really okay.' He actually smiled. 'It's beautiful here. Peaceful. Sit down. Make sure you're in the light.'

'July in the sun,' I managed, 'January in the shade.'

'What would you like?' He gestured towards the café interior. 'Mint tea? Something to eat?'

I shaded my eyes to look up at him. He was in dark jeans and a loose white shirt which seemed to be missing half of its buttons. 'Just mint tea.'

The angst, fury and sorrow of our last conversation outside my house seemed to have gone.

This will be okay.

A cup and a plate arrived on the table. 'I got you a rocky road,' he said and swung back into his place opposite me.

Right. Off you go.

'Luke, I want to apologize. What I mean is, I actually *am* apologizing. I'm deeply sorry. I see it now. I relapsed, with all the dishonesty that goes with it. It was hell for you.'

He seemed slightly stunned. 'Oh. I see, I, ah, thank you . . .'

'It was my fault,' I said. 'You leaving—it was all my fault. But it's only in the last day or so that I've seen it. I honestly thought that because a doctor had prescribed the pills, they were legitimate.'

He was still and focused, listening intently.

'I knew the facts. I did, Luke. But the picture they formed wasn't a problem: my baby had died and I couldn't sleep. I thought it was a temporary thing, taking the tablets. That I'd stop when the loss got more bearable. I genuinely thought it was a choice . . . it sounds mad but I never saw it as a relapse.'

'Ahhh, okay, just give me a—' He took a breath. Then another. 'I've spent so long waiting to hear this and now I don't know what to say . . . Okay, answer this—why did you think I left you?'

'I thought you blamed me for Yara.'

'How could you—'

'Because *I* blamed me, Luke.'

'God. Okay.' A long pause followed. 'Thing is,' he eventually said, 'I'm sorry, too. I was too hard on you. When I left I was so angry and like, *hurt*, that you'd choose drugs over me. But I'd forgotten how powerful addiction is. After I'd been gone—a year? More?—long enough to get some distance on it I started wondering, if I hadn't been such a mess over Yara would I have handled things differently?'

Oh?

'My first couple of years in Denver, I was drinking too much. Then it stopped working, I couldn't get any relief. There was one night, I remember thinking, I'd give anything to make this stop. I should have got it then—how it had been for you. You were in agony, there was something that eased it and you took it.'

'No. You're being too nice. And I believe you about Mia—'

'I'd never have done that. You know what I was like. So, I dunno, *square*.'

'"Steady", I was going to say, Luke. Or "loyal". You were a decent man.' My heart felt swollen and sore. 'I'm sorry, Luke, we were happy and I ruined it.'

'But our baby still died.' Gently, he shook his head. 'Nothing could fix that.'

'Maybe we could have got past it? People do.' I stopped because thinking that way wasn't helpful.

Again, he shook his head. 'You've got to play them as they lay.'

After several long moments of silence, Luke asked, 'How are you now? Right now?'

'Still in shock, I think. I swear to God, during all this time, I never thought I'd been in the wrong. Before your mum's funeral, my life was good. Now it's been upended, you know? It's confusing to feel heartbroken about a time that I've already got over.'

He nodded.

'It will all sort itself out, though,' I said. 'And worse things happen to people. Far worse. Like, I'll never stop being sad about Yara but I can live with it now. How about you?'

'Same. I'm not angry with you now—knowing that your version of reality matches mine, that's a big help. Even though we didn't get to know Yara, I'm still so thankful for her.'

'Oh God, me too.' My voice became watery. 'I'd never change that.'

'And I'll always be glad that you and I were together.' His voice was husky. 'You were the love of my life.'

My breath caught in my chest. 'And you were mine.'

'But we've still got plenty of our lives to go. Still young. *Ish.*' With a dazzler of a smile, he said, 'There will be other loves of our lives.'

I nodded, impressed by his—our—wisdom, our mature perspective.

'Rachel?' His tone changed. 'What made you stop? Taking the pills?'

'I know this might sound insane but I think Yara . . .' I shrugged, almost embarrassed. 'I think she wanted me to. There was one morning, about two months after you'd gone. I saw a rainbow. It was more than that, it was almost as if a rainbow came into our apartment—the colours were on our bedroom floor. Remember at your Dad's party I told you that I've always thought that rainbows were messages from Yara—'

'I remember.' He seemed sad. 'But have you forgotten that we'd talked about her, about rainbows, about a week before I—before I . . . left? I'd been seeing them, I was sure they were signs, messages, whatever you want to call them. You and I were having a . . . conversation about your pills, when a rainbow popped up outside our kitchen window. I told you my theory, you liked it and said you were definitely stopping. I was convinced you'd be okay, *we'd* be okay. But then you—'

—kept on taking the tablets. I remembered, then facepalmed with regret.

'Hey,' he said. 'It's okay. Stop. Please.'

The sun was low in the sky, the warmth of the day had abruptly vanished. I rubbed my chilly arms, wishing I'd worn more than a T-shirt and jeans.

'You know your mum invited me to her surprise party?' Luke said. 'So? See you there?'

'Aaaahhh, I'd been thinking of giving it a miss . . .'

'What? Why?'

'The idea of all my aunties laughing at me because you did a runner—'

'Hey, look, I won't come.'

I thought about it. 'You can come. It's okay, I don't feel as . . . humiliated. You *had* to leave me—not that I'll be explaining that to Auntie Imelda.'

'I'm not going if you won't be there. You and Quin.'

'Grand.' Surely Quin and I would be okay again by then? 'We'll be there.'

Morrigan's was closing up. 'Time to leave,' I said.

Luke grabbed his jacket and we stood. 'I came on the bike,' he said. 'It's out on the road.'

'I walked here.'

As we made our way back out through the trees, he asked, 'What you up to this evening?'

'Committee meeting for Mum's party. Last one before the big night. Hey.

358

Luke. Can I ask you something?' I said. 'When Joey rang to tell me about your mum, did he do it off his own bat or—'

'I asked him.'

'Why was that?'

He stared into the middle distance. 'Because even at my most angry, I never stopped wanting you to be okay.' He went quiet. 'I'm going to tell you something now and you might be . . . This is creepy. Stalkery. But I asked Joey to keep an eye on you.'

'"Keep an eye"?'

'Yeah. Look. I needed to know you were okay. Still alive, mostly. Not small details, I'm not that bad. But the big things like you moving back to Ireland. Getting a job in the Cloisters—from that I figured out you were clean again.'

A snarl of emotions seized me—humiliation, deep interest, offence and, again, *interest*. So he'd still cared?

'How did Joey do this?'

'Instagram, mostly.'

Well, he'd have had a job of it. For a couple of years after Luke had left, I'd barely posted anything. Even now, about 90 per cent of my content was Crunchie being adorable.

'Why did you do that?' I asked.

'Because I loved you. That didn't stop straight away.' After a hesitation, he said, 'I knew about Quin.' His look was mischievous. 'Now *that* was hard. What? I wasn't macho enough for you?'

'You're a fine one to talk. You and your Kallie.'

'Yeah, look at us.' He smiled. 'We survived. We rebuilt our lives. After what we'd lost, we should be proud. Thankful, anyway.'

We reached his bike and stopped walking.

'I go up that way.' I pointed to a turn off the road. 'There's a shortcut through the fields. Luke, do you think we could try being friends? Even if it's just to talk once a year on her anniversary?'

'Sure. Absolutely. We could give it a go.'

I remembered another question I wanted the answer to. 'Luke, the other night, whenever it was—Thursday?—at my house. Why did you say you'd come in, then leave immediately? What did I miss?'

'I didn't say I'd come in, I said I'd *like* to.'

What?

'You can figure it out, Rachel.'

Could I? I ran the sentence through my head again.

Oh. Seriously?

I could hardly speak. 'But—'

'My mother died less than a month ago. The past, the present, it's all mixed up in my head. I'm a mess, babe.' He stopped, mortified. 'Old habits. Sorry for calling you . . .'

'Babe.' The one word brought back a multitude.

'That.' He took a breath. 'Rachel, you need to know that even though I was very angry when I left New York, it soon changed to guilt. And, God, I *missed* you.'

'Luke . . .'

Out of nowhere, the air felt thick.

I blinked, trying to break the tension.

His eyes were fixed on mine. Shimmering between us was the irresistible attraction we'd once shared, powerful and familiar.

I didn't want this, it was dangerous. But all of my old responses were activated.

Startling me, he slid his hand around my waist, his index finger under my T-shirt, on the bare skin above my jeans. In one fluid movement our bodies were touching.

Overwhelmed by the intensity of my sudden longing for him, I watched his face, looking for clues on what to do. To my disbelief, I felt him begin to unfurl, then harden against me. Holding my gaze, he knew that I knew. Almost suffocating from such intimacy, I stopped breathing.

'Fuck!' He stepped back and spun away from me. 'Rachel, I'm sorry. I forgot, I—'

Dazed, discarded, I managed, '. . . It's okay.'

I was breathing again, and the oxygen wasn't coming fast enough, I had to fight the urge to pant.

'Just for a moment there'—he was able to look at me now—'I was confused.' With an awkward laugh, he said, 'I could never behave myself around you. And with Kallie not here . . .'

What . . . did *that* mean?

That because Kallie wasn't there to put out, anyone would do? Even someone as repellent as his junkie ex-wife?

I went cold. 'I'm leaving now.'

He seemed wrong-footed. 'Uh. Sure, yeah. Take care—'

Fucker.

Sleazy fucker.

I walked *fast* through the field, trying to put distance between me and that creep.

My *God*, he'd changed. He'd once been a good man but now he was—

'Rachel!'

I turned. In the encroaching night, his outline advanced.

'What?' My tone was sharp.

'I'm sorry.' He was short of breath. 'I didn't mean it the way it sounded. Like I was saying that if Kallie isn't here to . . . *deal* with me, I'm a liability who'd ride anything.'

I was still waiting for an explanation.

'Being in Ireland,' he said, 'seeing you, it feels like no time has passed. I'm a *state*. Kallie kept me anchored to the life I have now. But since she's gone back I'm . . . I've so many emotions, mostly from the past but it's like they've just happened. I don't know which end is up and I shouldn't have touched you . . . I'm very sorry.'

'. . . It's okay. Really.' I meant it. I'd been affected just as badly. So much so, I had to get away from him. 'Don't worry. See you on Saturday.'

'Okay, see—Hey! Do you have far to go?'

I turned once more towards him.

'It's nearly dark,' he said. 'There's no light out here. Come down to the road, I'll take you home on the bike.'

No. After what had just taken place, I was frightened. 'There's no need.'

'I'll walk with you then.'

'But how will you get back to your bike?' Then, 'Okay. It's easier to say yes than to spend fifteen minutes arguing in a field in the dark.'

He laughed, a proper burst of delight. It was a surprise to hear him so light-hearted, but maybe it shouldn't have been—once upon a time he'd always been that way.

At his bike, he insisted I wear his helmet. Again, it was easier to just go along with it. I was being torn in two—desperate for him yet terrified by my *want*. The sooner I got on the bike, the sooner I could get off.

He climbed on first, swinging his leg over with easy grace, then I clambered up behind him.

'Okay? Hold on tight.' He kicked off the stand and we roared away.

My arms in a cautious circle around his waist, we sped through the narrow roads until a sharp swerve pressed me against him. The heat from his body was too hard to resist and I let myself relax, leaning into his back, inhaling the smell of leather.

If I moved my hand even four or five inches lower, I could cup his . . .

The graphic vision arrived in my head from nowhere. The thought—and it was an actual memory—of him hardening in my hand made me swoony, then very ashamed, then even more fearful.

Wanting this—him—was much too much of a complication. I was still dealing with my damage from the past. If I started fancying him again, I'd also ruin the present.

Outside my house, he stayed on the bike, his feet on the ground, the engine still throbbing. With fumbling fingers, I untied the helmet. 'Thanks for the lift. See you Saturday.'

The movements of his hands, as they fastened the clasp on the helmet, had me somewhat hypnotized.

Bye, he mouthed with a smile I didn't understand, and as soon as he was gone I missed him.

Crunchie was waiting by the door and, instead of her usual wild, barky delight, she greeted me with enquiring kindness. 'I'm in bits,' I told her.

It's to be expected.

'I feel like I've cheated on Quin.'

Random thoughts about Luke's 'region' isn't cheating.

'What about emotional cheating, though?'

You're hardly doing that. Some of your old feelings have got jumbled up with more current ones. The confusion is understandable but nothing to worry about.

'You're sure about this?'

Yes. Well, probably. Obviously, I can't know for certain. I'm not Esther Perel, I'm only a dog.

After I fed Crunchie, I checked on my seedlings and eventually trailed up the stairs. I'd really need to get moving, the committee meeting was scheduled for eight thirty and it was already almost eight o'clock. Instead, I shut the bedroom door, kicked off my sneakers and lay on my bed, thinking about Luke. I knew I shouldn't but my body was so full of longing for him.

Putting my hand on my waist, I pretended it was his. And that he hadn't stopped when he had.

Behaving like this was insanity, it would only make things worse, make them *real*. But the feelings were too strong.

Until, making every nerve in my body flare, my phone beeped with a text. From him.

I can't stop thinking about you.

Staring at it, the rush of elation had me paralysed. I read and reread the six short words, shocked and grateful. Then the text disappeared. It just . . . disappeared. Stabbing at the screen, I hit refresh, trying to find it. Nowhere. It was gone.

Unable to stop myself, I texted, Did you just message me?

Sorry. It was meant for Kal.

Slowly, I lowered the phone to the bed and curled on my side. *I am pathetic. Utterly, utterly pathetic.*

Moments later my phone began to ring—him. 'Sorry about that text,' he said. 'My clumsy fingers. Listen, wanted to tell you, flight's booked, I'm going home Sunday.'

'Oh-kay.' This upset me a ridiculous amount.

'We're having Mum's one-month mass on Saturday. I'll stay for your mum's party Saturday night, then fly back Sunday.'

'. . . That makes sense.' I made myself say. 'Thanks for telling me. You didn't have to.'

'Yeah. But I did. Well, I wanted to. We're going to try being friends, aren't we? Well, we *are* friends?'

'Sure.' I didn't know what we were.

He must have picked up on my desolation because his tone changed to Let's Cheer Up the Poor Sap. 'Hey! How about you and me hang out on Saturday? Maybe go for a walk. I'll see you and Quin at the party but that'll be crazy, like. No chance for the chats there. But Saturday? Anytime you like, just you and me?'

It was all soooo Pity Poor Rachel. 'That's sweet of you, Luke, but it's going to be *insanely* busy on Saturday. Mum, Anna, Angelo, everyone, you know?' I made myself laugh.

'Cool, cool.' He sounded *so* unbothered. 'Listen, what present should I get your mum?'

'God, I don't know . . .' With a nervous giggle, I said, 'A photo of you.'

A moment of startled silence followed before he spoke. 'Estée Lauder Night Repair.' He'd decided to behave as if I hadn't just been really weird. 'That's what my mum always asked for. So, ah, see you there.'

76

Say what you like about Claire, she was *organized*. Despite her setback with the swinging, she was still all over Mum's party. Every single task was allocated to someone—*plus* a back-up person, just in case the first one had a nervous breakdown.

There was a spreadsheet and multiple parallel timelines.

People's phones were set to ping to remind them to . . .

Leave their home.

Eat something.

Yell, 'SURPRISE!'

I was twenty minutes late when Dad met me at the front door. 'You're always on time,' he said. 'What kept you?'

Too overwhelmed to lie, I said, 'I was out with Luke. It did my head in.'

'Ah, now.' Tentatively, he patted my back. 'Now, now, now.' Then, 'Now. Now, now, now.'

'That fucker Costello?' Helen called. 'Where'd you go?'

'Morrigan's.' I stood in the sitting-room doorway. They were all in there.

'Aaaand?' Helen asked. 'What d'you get up to?'

'Gave him a hand job by the stream.'

'*Must* you?' Mum demanded.

The answer was yes. Acting coy was the worst thing you could do with this lot. Invent an outrageous scenario and they were far more likely to lose interest.

'Are you okay?' Margaret asked.

'No, but I will be.'

'Do you have any noise-cancelling headphones? JJ needs to borrow a pair.'

'I have. I'll drop them in tomorrow after work.'

'Now that you've sorted out your son's headphone needs . . .' Claire was a little sour and it was hardly fair to take it out on Margaret, but when were emotions ever rational? 'This is the plan for Saturday. At fifteen hundred, I will arrive at the SugarLoaf Inn—'

'"Hours",' Helen, who was stretched out on the floor, said. 'Fifteen hundred *hours*.'

'At *three p.m.*,' Claire countered, 'accompanied by Francesca, Luka, Molly and . . .' She barely faltered over his name. '. . . Adam, I will arrive at the hotel. There I will meet Kate and Devin and check us all in.'

Although the SugarLoaf Inn was only twenty kilometres from central Dublin, lots of people were staying the night, so they could drink themselves comatose at the free bar, without worrying about getting home.

'After a fortifying glass of champagne, I'll join forces with'—she pointed at Margaret—'your husband and children, then we'll dress the room. This means that Holly and JJ will blow up the balloons. Garv, along with Luka, Devin and . . . Adam . . . will pin the ceiling with streamers. I'm in charge of the table place-names, *the* most important job—one wrong move and we could be looking at an outbreak of slobberknockery. That means "brawls" but you could probably guess from the context—'

'Goody bags,' Mum interjected.

'I'm getting to them.' Claire was brusque. 'At approximately seventeen fifteen—'

'Hours!' Helen said.

'At *a quarter past five*, after a light meal to line our stomachs, hair and make-up arrive, then we change into our party finery.'

'The goody bags?' Mum pleaded.

'Could you wait! At seventeen forty . . .' She paused and yelled, '*Hours!*'

That Helen had broken her so quickly was an indication of how far off her game she was. Taking a moment to rearrange her neck, then square her shoulders, she carried on. 'At seventeen forty hours, Rachel picks up Anna, Angelo and the eighty goody bags. Their ETA is eighteen fifty. *Hours*. Rachel does the drop-off and leaves.'

'Yeah, no, I might be staying. I'll let you know.'

'You might want to hurry it up, it's only three days away,' Helen said.

'I can handle it,' Claire said darkly. 'Oh yeah, good old Claire can handle anything. Any. Fucking. Thing. Right! Where was I? Yeah, so Anna and Angelo will check the place-names, just in case I made a mistake, which I never do, but it'd be sod's law. When Artie arrives, I'd also like him to take a quick look. He's good at detail.'

'Not all he's good at,' Helen murmured from her supine position. We ignored her. She only said those things to distress Mum.

'At nineteen hundred hours, all the guests, including Helen, Artie and

Helen's Best Friend Bella Devlin, will assemble in the party room and undergo several practice rounds of yelling, "SURPRISE!"'

'What if my sisters are late?' Mum asked anxiously. 'And they miss the practice?'

'They won't be late.' Claire was confident. 'Old people are early for everything.'

'They're probably lining up in the parking lot already,' Helen said. 'And we're still seventy hours out.'

'*And* they won't get any champagne until they've proved they can do it properly.' Claire gave a grim laugh. 'Oh, they'll be there.

'At eighteen thirty hours, Margaret will pick up Mum and Dad. Five minutes out from the hotel, Margaret sends a WhatsApp, everyone assumes the positions we've practised, Dad will lead Mum in, we all yell, "Surprise!" And we're off to the races!' She cocked an ear. 'Whose phone is ringing?'

'Mine.'

'Luke Costello the Luddite again?'

No. It was Quin and I didn't pick up. A minute later, a voice-note beeped.

'Not talking to me?' He sounded sheepish. 'Fair dues. So. I'm over my sulk. Come by tomorrow. I'll cook.'

As the final committee meeting broke up, Helen collared me. 'I'm checking in with you.'

'I—'

'Oh, Christ.' She could see it in me. 'Costello?'

'Yeah. I—' I couldn't find the words to convey just how much I wanted him.

But she nodded. She got it. 'Makes sense. After what you both went through. That bond . . .' She sighed. 'I guess it's *adiós* Dr Spork. Pity. I liked him. Him and his weirdo presents.'

'No! No. That's not what I . . .' I stopped. I didn't know what I wanted.

'So? A night of mad sex with Costello? Draw a line under the whole business?' She shrugged. 'Could work. And remember, even though I'm woejus at both sympathy *and* empathy, I'm here for you.'

77

A night of lucid dreams followed: a vivid movie reel of pictures and sensations where I was pregnant with Yara. *But she died.* No, she was right here, under my hand, still in my body! She shifted, tumbling me onto my side and everything was all okay. *Thank you, God.* Suddenly I was giving birth, the pain worse than I remembered but it was what I deserved. I heard Luke crying—except it was actually Quin and, oh! Here was a full box of Ambien! Then Luke was gone and I was cold and alone. But a man was in bed with me . . . Quin? He must have let himself in with his key. Except this *could* actually be a dream? Clenching my muscles I discovered that a man was definitely with me and in my body and perhaps it wasn't Quin, but Luke? *That* thought made my body obediently orgasm and I couldn't keep doing this, not with Luke and—

I jolted awake, flung into the day on a surge of powerful emotions, to realize that Quin was trying to FaceTime.

Still trapped in my vivid, jumbled dreams, my body was shaking. Incapable of speaking to Quin, I watched my iPad until the noise stopped. Soon after, he sent a text. Now I'm worried. You coming to me tonight?

If I replied immediately he'd know I'd ignored his call. But it felt wrong to wait, say, half an hour, because that would mean we were in the realm of lies.

But Quin and I were already in a different place, he just didn't know it yet. How had we moved so far off course, so quickly? Picking up my phone, I quickly clicked, I'll be with you about 7. Got to drop headphones off to JJ first. x

After work I went to Margaret's lovely, calm house, with the headphones. It had been a hard day, spent obsessing about Luke while feeling torn apart by guilt about Quin.

'Are you okay?' she asked. 'Seeing Luke again? After . . . everything.'

A long time ago, she'd had two miscarriages, so she had some sense of what I'd lost.

'I'm in bits.' It was a huge relief to spill it out. 'Last night, I dreamt I was still pregnant. It's been a long time since that happened. And now . . . I fancy Luke. To put it mildly.'

'That's no surprise.' Margaret paused. 'Unless he's aged very badly?'

I shook my head.

'Isn't it normal to want to reconnect in a physical way?' she asked. 'Like, you're trying to pretend to yourself that you could have another baby?'

You see, that was what I loved about Margaret—her essential pragmatism. Her theory *could* make sense. It also absolved some of my guilt about Quin.

'I'd like one night with Luke,' I admitted miserably. 'Not even a night—just to sleep with him one last time, as a way of saying goodbye.'

She looked concerned. 'But remember, his mother has just died, he's vulnerable.'

She was right about that. Luke had been mortified when he'd touched me and his body had reacted as it had.

'And you're vulnerable too.'

Right again. I was a shambles.

'*He* doesn't want to.' I told her about the mis-sent text. 'He really cares about Kallie.'

'And you really care about Quin.' Then, 'Don't you?'

'But it's not stopping me from obsessing about Luke. Which I'm ashamed of. But he's leaving in three days, going back to his real life, and that'll be it, I might never see him again. I'm freaking out because my window of opportunity is closing.'

'You didn't even do the inverted-comma fingers around "window of opportunity",' Margaret said. 'You must be really upset.'

'I am.' I heaved out a huge sigh. 'And now I'm going to see Quin.'

For the first time in over a year, I rang Quin's doorbell instead of letting myself in.

'It's you!' He was cheery, confident, smiley. 'Why didn't you use your key?' He went in for a snog and I stepped away.

'Quin? We need to talk.'

The colour leached from his face. 'About what?'

I felt like the worst person on earth. 'I promised I'd be honest with you . . .'

He pointed me towards the kitchen where, looking like a sleepwalker, he turned off the hob. 'Your ex-husband?'

I nodded. 'Yesterday we went for coffee. You know how I've always thought it was his fault we'd broken up? It was mine. Having to rearrange all my memories, the stories I've told myself, it's confusing.' I cleared my throat. 'Quin, I'm so sorry, but I've got feelings for him.'

He flinched, as if I'd slapped him. 'What about me?'

'I care about you so much, Quin. You're really, *really* important to me. But Luke is leaving on Sunday. I want to go to Mum's party because he'll be there.'

'Last I heard, you and I were boycotting it *because* of him.'

'If he's going to be there, with all of my family, I want to go too, as a sort of full stop, if that makes any sense? It might draw a line under everything.'

'So what exactly are you asking me for?'

'Well . . . nothing. You asked me to be honest and I'm trying to be.'

'Are you going to act on these "feelings" of yours?'

'Luke wouldn't want to.'

'And if he did?'

Our eyes locked. Quin could see what I wanted. 'Right.' His voice was flat. 'You'd sleep with him?'

I took a breath. The answer was yes but saying so felt too cruel.

'Your problem is you want to time travel,' he said. 'You think if you sleep with him, you can pretend you didn't fuck everything up in the past. But it won't change anything. Except fuck up the present.'

There was nothing I could say. He was probably right. And it still wasn't enough to quench the want in me.

'Is this because of Monday?' he asked. 'To get back at me because I haven't wanted to see you?'

I shook my head.

'Okay.' He sounded as if he'd reached a decision. 'Go to the party, sort out whatever you need to . . .' In frustration, he flung up his hands. '. . . *sort out.*'

'What does that mean?'

'Rachel, for God's sake!' His eyes were full of pain. 'Don't make this harder for me—'

'. . . And if something happened? If I . . . ?'

'I don't know.' He looked at me. 'I've no clue. But right now I don't want to be around you. Can you please leave?'

I couldn't blame him but I felt afraid and so terribly ashamed.

'Claire, I'm going to the party. Can you put me at the same table as Luke?'

'Is Quin coming?'

'No.'

'I have questions.'

'And I don't have answers.'

'Got it. But be careful.'

Me be careful? She was a fine one to talk.

78

'What's arugula?' Mum sounded panicked.

'Rocket.'

'What's *that*?'

'Fancy lettuce.'

'For the love of God! We're in the supermarket trying to get the stuff on Anna's list—'

'And I've just arrived at the airport to pick them up—'

'We should never have let her go to New York. There was a time she was happy to live on cornflakes. But now she has *notions* and your father and I—'

'Bye.'

Because Anna and Angelo always flew business class, their plane had barely landed when the Arrivals double doors swished open and out they strolled, giving off low-key, big-city glamour, in dark glasses, Loro Piana sweats and sleek Thom Browne carry-ons.

'There she is,' I heard Angelo say.

'Rachel!' Anna flung herself at me, and I wrapped my arms around her narrow ribs and soft, luxe clothing. 'Thank you for coming.'

I had a wild urge to say, *Thank* you *for existing*, but I managed to keep it together. Of my four sisters, Anna was the sweetest. I'd leant on her a lot in the months after Luke had gone. I *loved* her and seeing her now, with all that had been going on with Luke, made me want to cry.

Angelo whipped off his shades and kissed me on the forehead—which was fully on-brand for his sexy guru vibe.

'The car is five thousand miles away.' We were a far cry from Quin and the private terminal. But thinking about him was too confusing and awful, so I made myself stop.

'Hey, did the goody bags arrive at Mum's yesterday?' Anna asked.

I nodded. Three giant boxes of spendy skincare were squatting on the sitting-room floor, blocking out the daylight.

'We'll have to assemble them later.'

As I headed for the M50, Angelo said, 'I hear my man Luke Costello is coming to the party.'

'Yep.'

'How is that for you?'

I settled for, 'Weird.'

'*I'll* say.'

Mum's first question to Anna was, 'What are you wearing to my party? Put it on, givvus a look!'

'Now?' Anna asked. 'Seriously? Now? When I'm just off a plane?'

'Yes. Good girl.' She turned to Dad. 'And you go and put on your new suit.'

'Do I hav—'

'Yes!'

Anna went off, then returned in a super-tasteful beige sheath. Stunning in a phenomenally boring way, to be honest. That was her look these days.

'Alaïa,' she said. 'From Rent the Runway. I didn't actually buy it.'

'You've been in New York for too long!' Mum accused. 'You've become Good With Money!'

'You look great,' I said.

'Do *I* look great?' It was Dad, shy in his new suit.

'You totally do!'

'Hardly seems worth the money,' he said. 'I'll be dead before I get the wear out of it.'

'So wear it lots,' I urged. 'Around the house, watching the telly. Or on the other hand, just don't die.'

'That's what I'll do,' he said, seeming pleased by his decision. 'I just won't die.'

79

My phone rang *again*—Francesca, for at least the fiftieth time, looking for an update on my location. 'Mum's freaking out!' She was on speaker in my car. 'She wants proof of life of the goody bags.'

'We'll be with you in ten minutes,' I said, hoping it might be true. These roads were more narrow and twisting than I remembered.

Wild yelling sounded in the background and, apologetically, Francesca said, 'Mum says to tell you that you should be here now.'

'She's going as fast as she can,' Anna called.

'Everybody be cool.' Angelo was crouched in the back seat with fifty of the goody bags. 'These roads are twisty little mofos. We'll get there when we get there. And how about that!' he declared as the hotel appeared on the horizon. 'We have eyes on you! See, all good.'

I turned in off the road, looking for a parking spot and a couple of people, looking like Zombie Glamazons, lunged from the shadows, yelling about goody bags.

One of the glamazons was seventeen-year-old Francesca. With modern, slick-backed hair and a *very* short black Balmain masterpiece, she looked stunning. 'Jesus Christ.' I regarded her architectural shoulder pads and bare legs with wonder. 'Is the dress . . . *real*?'

She winced apologetically. 'Mum made me. Quick, the goody bags!'

The other glamazon was Molly—long-legged and elegant in a red one-sleeved, body-con dress.

'Tom Ford.' Another apologetic wince. 'Claire made me.'

And here was Claire herself. In a strange black dress over a strange acid-green bra over even more strange ivory-coloured trousers. And yet she wore it with such confidence that it worked.

'You look—'

'Thank you. Supriya Lele. Nearly bankrupted me. But I couldn't stop myself, it was literally like being *possessed*. Luka, c'mere and carry these boxes!'

Fifteen-year-old Luka, as long and lean as a whippet, darted towards the car, dressed in a dark, silky tracksuit. Claire had obviously persuaded him into some expensive outfit for the night. What could you do? Only admire her.

'Give me a look at you.' Claire inspected my professionally made-up face, my—very natural-looking, I must say—fake eyelashes, my costly blow-dry, my fabulous dark green dress, my black nail varnish and my high sandals. She sighed. 'You're an utter *babe*.'

Before I knew what she was doing, she'd slid her hand up my thigh.

'Claire,' I squeaked. 'For the love of—'

Her hand met bare skin and her eyes met mine. 'You went with the hold-ups. And why might that be?'

'I—'

'He's inside, looking absolutely fucking gorgeous. One of the first to arrive. The best of luck to you, babes, I hope you get whatever you need from this. Okay, let's go!'

The noise in the reception room hit like a roar. They were all there, Mum's sisters, her cousins, her golf friends, their respective spouses. The women were generally brightly coloured and shiny while their spouses were sombre in suits, many of them leaning on sticks. One or two even had their legs up on chairs. 'Hip-replacement season has just ended,' Claire said, then marched away, with Anna and Angelo in tow.

Adam grabbed me. 'Hold up there, missy.' He inspected my outfit. 'You look *amazing*. That dress! The Vampire's Wife, right?'

'How do—'

'—I know? From doing my wife's many, many returns to Net-a-Porter, Mytheresa, and . . . what's the Italian one? Luisaviaroma? That's it.'

'You look pretty amazing yourself.'

Adam's look tended to be classic but never dull. Tonight he was in a dark suit, which at first glance seemed discreet. But the cut was faultless, the fit was perfect, the fabric was alluringly touchable and the whole shebang had probably cost about a million euro.

'He's over at the window.' He nodded across the room and there was Luke, smiling slightly, in a black reefer jacket, the collar up. Surrounded by my fucking aunties. 'Moody and beautiful.' Adam sighed heavily. 'I'm sure you heard about the shitshow with Piet and Beatriz?'

I nodded.

'She told me to keep an open mind!' Adam hissed. 'I only did it because *she* wanted to.'

'But she felt sidelined.'

'How am I meant to know the rules? Nobody *explained*. All I knew was she said if I didn't enjoy myself, she'd laugh at me. So I did what I was told, I *did* enjoy myself and now she's furious. Jesus, he's taking the coat off.'

Luke was shrugging his jacket back from his shoulders, revealing dark jeans and a black, fitted shirt.

'Very . . . lithe, isn't he?' Adam asked. 'Is that the word I mean?'

I didn't know but my heart hurt with how much I wanted him.

'Like, you'd swear he'd practised that jacket thing. I hear he goes horse-riding these days.' Bitterly he said, '*Figures*. I'll be honest, Rachel, I wasn't *happy* you broke up, that would be going too far, he was *nice*—well, before he wasn't—but I was never comfortable with him. I don't get his look and we've nothing in common. Quin is much more my type.' He glanced around. 'Where is he?'

'Not coming.'

His glance flicked to Luke and back to me, then he exclaimed, 'You're fucking *joking*.' He looked horribly concerned. 'Because of *him*?' He nodded across at Luke.

'No. Well . . .'

'I can't,' Adam managed. 'I really can't.' He'd spotted a roving waitress with a tray of champagne and dived at her. 'Thank you,' he whispered, gratefully accepting a glass. 'You're very kind.'

'What's up with him?' Helen had appeared in a tight little black dress. Flanking Helen was her Best Friend, Bella Devlin.

'Bella,' I said. 'How lovely to . . . You look . . .' I couldn't find an adequately effusive word for her fair, pale-skinned perfection. 'Beautiful.'

To be accurate, Bella looked as though the air she breathed was the purest oxygen, that she only drank water from melted glaciers and that her every thought was good and loving.

'Rachel.' Bella took my hands between hers—her social skills were impeccable. 'You're breathtaking.'

'You're more. You're breathtaking to the moon and back.' Sooner rather than later, I usually let myself down around her. 'Tell me about your dress.' Because there was always a story. Bella Devlin would never say, '*This* fucking thing? Karen Millen! Two years ago. There was a tear in the hem so I got twenty euro off.'

'It was my mum's wedding dress,' Bella said.

But of course it was—the dress was red and, apart from a mandarin collar, super-plain.

'Dior,' Bella Devlin said. 'Crêpe de Chine. Vintage.'

'*Vintage* vintage,' Helen clarified. 'It was vintage when Vonnie got married. So now it's vintage squared.'

Another tray of champagne flutes appeared and Adam, who'd devoted himself to swigging down the glass he already had, once again made a lunge.

'Have you anything non-alcoholic?' I asked the server. 'Tap water is fine.'

'And for me,' Bella said. (She didn't drink, even though her parents said she could.)

'It's *not* fine for me,' Helen said. 'Water, please, but the fanciest you have.'

'I'm grand with champagne.' Artie, in jeans and a shirt that could definitely have done with an iron, had joined our cluster.

'Good of you to dress up, bro,' Adam said to Artie.

With a quiet smile, Artie said, 'Always.'

Very cool, Artie was. *Impossible* to rattle.

'So three waters?' the server said.

'Er, before you go.' Anxiously, Adam lunged at her tray. 'I'll take a second glass for my . . . because I drink quickly. Anna! Hey! And Angelo! Hello!'

Poor Adam was almost as uncomfortable around Angelo as he was with Luke.

Into my ear, Anna said, 'One of us should go over and talk to Luke. This can't be easy for him. When I say "one of us", I mean you, Rachel.'

It was actually a relief to get an order to approach him. It didn't make me as tragic as if I'd decided off my own bat. Not that he'd know the difference. 'Okay. Going.'

Nervously, I infiltrated the circle of aunties, stood next to Luke and said, 'Hey.'

He jumped and turned around. 'Hey!' His face shifted from serious to an unexpectedly sweet smile. After a speedy scan of my dress, he said, 'You look gorgeous.'

'No need to sound so surprised.' Quickly, I added, 'I'm joking.'

'Where's Quin?'

'Not here.'

'Is he . . . okay?'

'I . . . Just . . . I don't really know . . .'

He didn't speak, just stared, appearing troubled.

A shift in energy pulled my attention away—Kate and Devin! Kate in the midnight-blue dress, the boned bodice figure-hugging and narrow, the skirt a tulle explosion, Devin in an eighties-style suit in the same colour. They'd come as a matching set and they were *dazzling*.

As they moved through the room, people were doing second takes, wondering why this duo was so captivating. *Oh, I* see, *they're young and in love. Well, isn't this a beautiful thing to witness.*

Luke frowned. 'Is that . . . one of your dresses?' He looked upset. 'I remember when you used to—'

'No, don't, please,' I said. 'Let's not be sad. Just for tonight?'

'I don't know if I can.' Then, 'Okay, I'll give it a try—Angelo! My man!'

'Heeeeey!' With man-hugs and backslaps, Angelo annexed Luke. Back in the day, they had been matey.

'And Anna!' Luke took Anna's knuckles and kissed them, then they hugged each other. Of all of my sisters, Anna was closest to Luke, probably because they'd both lived in New York. Oh, and here came Claire, looking for her piece of the Costello action.

Suddenly, my phone buzzed—Mum was five minutes out! Claire, Anna and Helen had got the same text and nervous energy infused us all.

'Positions, please,' Claire called, sweeping through the room and herding aunties into graduated ranks. 'Taller ones at the back! Phyllis, *Imelda!*' She snapped her fingers. 'That means *you.*'

'Uncles-by-marriage—Donagh, Dónall, Deaglán, Diarmuid and Daithí— kneel in the front row. Molly, Luka, help them kneel!'

As Molly and Luka desperately tried to cajole octogenarian men riddled with arthritis into a kneeling position, Francesca called, her voice laced with panic, 'Time's running out! Just kick the sticks from under them.'

'Remember.' Helen patrolled the aunties as if she were a sergeant inspecting her raw recruits. 'If *any* of you don't shout "SURPRISE" loudly enough, *none* of you will get your New York goody bag, each with a retail value of over three hundred euro. We're *watching!*'

Then, 'Sssh. *Sssh!* She's outside. She's coming. She's . . . . SURPRISE!!!!'

Balloons flew, whistles were blown and everyone really did yell loudly. Mum did an excellent job of looking shocked and delighted.

Afterwards she was asked, again and again, 'Did you really not suspect anything?'

'Not an iota!'

Gazing around the room, I searched for Margaret, who, despite the vital role she'd played in this drama, was getting no thanks. I found her standing with Garv. Tenderly, he touched her face while she smiled and fiddled with his tie—and, frankly, she looked incredible.

Her gleaming hair was tousled and cool—but, oh my God, her dress! The stone-coloured midi dress was deceptively plain. But from the supple sway of the skirt to how the scooped neckline revealed her collarbones, it was perfect.

'Margaret.' Maybe I shouldn't have interrupted whatever intimacy was going on but feck it, she and Garv lived together, they could share moments whenever they liked. 'You look *beautiful*.'

She swung herself and her amazing hair around to me. 'But wait!'

'Yes!' Garv exclaimed. 'You must see the best part!'

'Look.' She slid her hands along her hips. 'It's got . . . *pockets*!' Her smile froze. 'Oh. Hi, Luke!'

'Sorry for cutting in . . .' Respectfully he kissed Margaret's cheek and shook Garv's hand. 'So good to see you both. Just wanted to congratulate Margaret for delivering your mum here. And on time too. Not everyone could have pulled that off.'

'Oh, ah, you know . . .' Margaret was all set to go full-on self-deprecation but Garv interrupted, 'Nice one, Luke, she doesn't get celebrated enough. To my wonderful wife!' He held up his glass.

The other people at my table were Anna and Angelo, Kate and Devin, Auntie Dolores, the least worst of Mum's five sisters, with her husband Daithí—and Luke.

I was seated between Angelo and Devin—and directly opposite Luke, who was between Kate and Anna.

With surprising efficiency, we got our starter—and it was borderline edible which is a lot more than you'd usually get on a night like this. But when the beef arrived, it was no real surprise that my vegetarian meal didn't.

The waiter said he knew nothing about it but he'd enquire.

'Seriously,' Anna objected. 'It's not as if you're asking for pixie dust!'

Not one other person at the table was a vegetarian. Oh, more *flexi*tarians than you knew what to do with, everyone giving it, 'I eat red meat twice a year, and then only if it's grass-fed, organic and locally sourced.'

'Start,' I said as their dinners cooled before them. 'Mine will be here soon.'

Daithí and Dolores were already horsing into theirs. Seeming uncertain, Devin and Angelo picked up their knives. 'You sure?'

'Absolutely.'

But Kate, Anna and Luke held off.

'Please,' I begged. 'This is making me feel bad.' Scanning the room, I thought I spotted our waiter down at the far end, dancing attendance on other people.

The whole business was curiously humiliating.

Luke was getting to his feet and throwing his napkin on the table. 'Is that the guy?' He indicated the man I'd been scoping.

'I think so—'

'Stay where you are.'

He wove his way through the tables and, watching the twist of his narrow waist, I felt almost sick with want. At the end of the room, he collared the waiter and engaged him in chat, pointing towards me. Next thing, both of them went to the swingy door that led into the kitchen—and disappeared.

I'd never see either of them again, I was convinced of it.

However, in an unexpectedly short time, they re-emerged, the waiter bearing a plate which, with some ceremony, he carried the length of the room and placed before me.

'Thank you,' I murmured, keeping my eyes low.

Luke's kindness felt crushing. As if my lovesickness was so pitiable that hunting down my risotto was the charitable thing to do.

As soon as it was decent, I'd scarper, I decided. I'd go back to my house and lie low, waiting for everything to settle, my feelings to get back to normal, then I'd resume my life—which had been *fine* before all of this. Better than fine, actually. Lovely, it was *lovely*. Apart from the dearth of vintage Chanel handbags, I'd had no complaints.

In double-quick time the dinner plates were being whipped away and replaced with the gold-leaf dessert. Next thing Dad was up on a small stage, nervously holding a mic. He began thanking people, a phenomenal number of them, for making tonight possible. Then it was time for Mum's speech, which had a lot in common with Father Ted's lengthy, score-settling address when he won the Golden Cleric. And we were *getting there*. Soon everyone would be so drunk that I could slip away unnoticed.

I was surprised by a tap on my shoulder—Artie. Directly into my ear, he said, 'Helen needs you. She's in the ladies.'

Quickly I got up.

In the frilly powder room, Helen was alone, sitting on a pink velvet pouf. She looked tearful—and Helen never cried.

'Rachel. I'm not pregnant.'

'. . . Did you think you were?'

'Yeah. My period is only a day late but, yeah, I did.'

'. . . This is your first month of trying?'

'I know. But I thought . . . I was hopeful. You can hug me if you want.'

Carefully, I wrapped my arms around her—and then she *did* cry.

'Helen . . .' I felt helpless. 'I was the same. Every month I thought this was the one where it had actually worked. And in the end it did.'

From the way her body stiffened, it was clear she'd remembered what had followed.

'That won't happen to you,' I said.

'How do you know?'

'I just do.'

But I didn't. I couldn't. And my worry was that if Helen didn't get her desired outcome, it could kick-start another descent into the darkness.

'You've got to remember,' I said, 'that trying to get pregnant when you're not sixteen is a marathon, not a sprint.'

'A marathon, not a sprint,' she repeated. Then, with a scornful look, 'I can't believe you just said that.'

She was obviously fine again. 'Come on, we'd better go back out there.'

I was hoping that Mum hadn't noticed our absence. But up on the dais, with her elevated overview, of *course* she had. As I scurried back to my table, her laser eyes burned a hole in my back.

Luke mouthed at me, *Everything okay?*

Embarrassed by his pity, I gave an abrupt nod, then turned my head.

Behind Mum, an actual, real-life band was setting up on the small stage. When, *finally*, she surrendered her microphone, the band leader announced they were kicking things off with an old-timey waltz set—which generated a veritable trickle onto the floor. Mum was out there with Dad. Uncle Donagh, showcasing his new knees, had Auntie Phyllis in a hold. Imelda and Philomena were dancing with each other and they all looked joyous and jolly which, despite everything, made me smile.

. . . Except something was going on with Claire and Adam. I watched her yank him by the tie into a hungry clinch. In the parlance of our culchie cousins, she was 'ateing the face off him'. *Devouring* him. From a distance it could have been mistaken for passion, but to me it was clear she was in a blind fury. If someone could die from being snogged, Adam would have been a goner.

I was about to get up and intervene when abruptly Claire desuckered her face from Adam's, shoved him away and stalked off, only to fall into the hands of Anna and Angelo, who garlanded her with concern.

Meanwhile, at our table, Auntie Dolores was on her feet, trying to pull her husband out to dance. He batted her away. 'Stop. No.'

'Daithí, *please* dance with me.'

'I don't want to.'

Red with humiliation, she sat down and lunged for her glass. Next thing, Luke was out of his chair and extending his hand. 'Come on, Dolores, why don't you and me show them how it's done?'

'You mean . . . ?' Dolores's face lit up. 'Right, let's go!'

As soon as Luke led her out into the middle of the dance floor, there were a few ribald whistles. Suddenly, a small knot of aunties, cursed with refusenik husbands, were alert and interested. When Dolores rotated to face them and Luke couldn't see what she was at, she flapped her tongue towards her chin in a suggestive manner.

Mum had spotted them! Still waltzing with Dad, she covered a huge amount of ground at great speed and muscled in, fobbing Dolores off on Dad and sailing away with Luke.

'I'm next,' I heard Auntie Peggy say, smoothing down her dress and advancing with conviction.

Out of nowhere, several aunties and cousins—even those with dancing husbands—were forming an impromptu line. 'Thirty seconds,' a voice said. 'Everyone gets thirty seconds!' There seemed to be an accord and when the time was up, they ousted their predecessor, sliding into Luke's arms, to take their place.

Auntie Dolores returned to our table, drained her glass in one grateful swig and looked around, desperately searching for a waitress.

I stood up. 'I'll get you a drink.' Then I'd check on Claire and leave, I decided. Nothing was going to happen with Luke, I was delusional to have hoped that it might. 'What would you like?'

'Large brandy,' she said. 'A settler. Although I don't know if I'll ever be right again.'

Cutting across the dance floor, en route to the bar, Luke lunged into my path. 'Two seconds, Imelda,' he said, over his shoulder. Then to me, 'When do I get to dance with you?'

Miserably, I flicked a glance at the impatient line up. 'Ha!' I forced a laugh. 'They'd eat me alive.'

'Rachel,' he said, softly. 'Dance with me.'

My mouth went dry.

He was suddenly extremely still, his dark eyes on mine. 'That text the other day? It was for you. I lost my nerve.'

My lips formed a silent 'Oh'.

'The only woman I want to dance with,' he said, 'is you.'

For a long moment, I searched his face. He was so very serious about this.

'Not here,' I said, and surrendered him to Imelda.

Ten minutes later he cornered me.

I was back at the table, desperately trying to concentrate on a conversation with Angelo when Luke materialized on the chair beside mine. One second he wasn't there, the next he was. When I saw him, I jumped.

Intent on me, he asked. 'Where, then?'

'Luke, I shouldn't have said—'

'Where?'

Silently, I shook my head.

He stared at me.

I took a ragged breath. 'My house. Come home with me. Just for tonight.'

He nodded, his face giving nothing away. 'Thank you.'

Drive safely, I reminded myself, again. *Drive safely*.

Out in the countryside the roads were narrow and dark. The headlight of Luke's bike, directly behind my car, lit my way.

We were the only two vehicles on the road.

It felt like the only two vehicles in the world.

I thought about Quin, of course I did. He would be very hurt and we might not survive, but there was an inevitability to this. It wasn't exactly about desire, at least not for me, it was about saying a final goodbye.

And Kallie? No, I couldn't do this to myself. Kallie wasn't my responsibility.

The houses around mine were in darkness, everyone in bed, asleep. I watched Luke get off his bike. Even in the dark, he was unmistakeable. As he approached, I felt as if I were dreaming.

Then, suddenly, I landed back in my body. This was real.

By the circle of light thrown by the porch lamp, he hesitated. 'Rachel, what *is* this?'

'I don't know. Yet. Do you?'

'No. But it's not nothing.'

My relief was brief. 'Luke, what about Kallie?'

He took a breath. 'What about Quin?'

Warily we watched each other and came to an unspoken agreement: this wasn't something to be proud of but we knew what we were doing.

When we tumbled into the dimly lit hallway, Crunchie barked at Luke, but within moments was rolling over and displaying her belly. Luke got down on one knee, petting her, then he glanced up, that familiar dark gaze. 'Does she need to go out?'

'Benigno next door took her earlier.'

Crunchie was trying to lick him to death. *Yeah, you and me both.*

But enough of Crunchie. I whistled and pointed towards the kitchen. 'Sorry,' I whispered to her sorrowful face, shutting the door firmly and turning around—straight into the heat of Luke's body.

He pressed me against the wall, shifting his feet, adjusting his stance so that his hips were level with mine. Cradling my face between his splayed fingers, he whispered into my mouth, 'Babe.'

His breath, his lips, his warmth, his sweetness—as the kiss intensified, relief flooded in, filling me up.

'Rachel.' His mouth still on mine, he groaned, 'You are *gorgeous.*'

Desperate to reach his skin, I was pushing his jacket from his shoulders. It hit the floor, then I began to unbutton his shirt.

'I've wanted you so badly,' he breathed. 'Tonight has been hell.'

Together, our hands fumbled over his buttons. 'Watching you,' he said. 'Wanting you. Worried that you'd leave and—'

Parting the dark cotton, warm from his body, his skin released a fragrant fug, an intense distillation so musky and sweet that I moaned. 'You smell like *you.*'

He laughed, his teeth flashing in the semi-darkness. 'Who else would I smell like?'

'The night you came over, raging about Kate and Devin, you were different.'

He flinched. '. . . That night. I'm sorry.'

'No. Shush.' Pulling his head down to kiss him again, my fingers got tangled in his curls. 'I've missed your hair,' I whispered.

'I've missed your everything.'

Stroking the smooth skin of his stomach, I slid my thumb along the line of silky dark hair that arrowed downwards from his belly button. Arriving at his waistband, my fingertips moved to his belt buckle and as they slid over the scratched metal, his sharp hiss of breath was audible.

Suddenly anxious, I looked up at him. Maybe he'd misunderstood this. Maybe *I* had?

'Oh God, Rachel.' His voice was husky. 'Don't stop.'

'If this is just because you're horny . . . Then don't do it. Please.'

Holding my gaze, his hands worked on something. There was the click and jingle of his buckle. Glancing down, I saw that his belt hung open and his top button had been popped. 'I'm yours.' Then he added, 'If you want me.'

I could have laughed. 'Do *you* want me?'

He indicated his body, the thick bulge, listing to the right, beneath his zip. 'Not much point denying it, is there?'

The heat of his hand was on my thigh, sliding under my dress and upwards. When his fingertips touched the bare skin at the top of my hold-ups, he flinched. 'Jesus, Rachel.' His voice sounded choked. 'Can we take this upstairs?'

I wanted to laugh with delight. I loved when he said things like that, stuff that was borderline cheesy.

In my bedroom, the lamp gave off a mellow glow. I lay Luke, shirtless, on my bed. 'Let me do this. Please.' I slipped my hands along his satin-smooth shoulders and the tangle of silver and braided leather around his neck.

With deliberate care, I undressed him. His boots first, then I moved to his jeans. Propped on his elbows, he watched with grim anticipation. 'Rachel.' His voice was low and urgent, his jaw clenched. 'You couldn't hurry things up? I'm dying here.'

'This will be my only chance. I want to remember everything.' I unzipped his jeans and inched them from his body, savouring his hair-roughened legs, the paler skin at the tops of his thighs, then all the drama of his crotch, as his erection sprang from his underwear.

I couldn't stop myself from burying my face and inhaling the musky fragrance. 'If only they could bottle it.'

He laughed, suddenly appearing light-hearted—then vaulted from the bed. 'Babe, I'm sorry.' He reached for me. 'I've been patient long enough.'

It was like ballet, the ease with which he unzipped my dress. It fell to the floor and I stepped out from it, sensation flaring as my bare skin touched off his.

But when his fingers reached the clasp of my bra, he paused. 'Rachel? Are you sure?'

'This isn't sex,' I said. 'It's the only way to express our feelings.'

'It *is* sex.'

'You know what I mean,' I said. 'Well, *I* know. Yes, I'm sure.'

Still he wavered, so I repeated, 'Luke. I'm sure.'

Almost under his breath, he asked, 'Why am I even arguing?' And with three or four deft hooks and sweeps of his thumbs, removed the rest of my clothes.

He arranged me on the bed and the second his lips touched the inside of my thigh, my body remembered everything. The response was as intense as it had ever been. In moments, with short, breathy gasps, I was pulsing into the heat of his mouth.

Staying until the last of the ripples quietened, he laughed softly. 'Well.' He seemed ridiculously happy. 'That was easy.'

'Like riding a bike.' I was floaty and dazed. 'Come here. Before . . .'

His angry-looking erection appeared about to explode.

'Wait!' He clicked his tongue as he remembered. 'My jacket . . .' Was downstairs on the hall floor, where we'd flung it.

'It's okay.' I was already opening a drawer. 'In here.'

He removed a foil square, tearing it open with his teeth, unrolling and smoothing it along his length. Transfixed, I watched his hands move in ways that were familiar and wildly erotic. And, oh God, the heft of his body, the grace of it as he shifted and slid into me. I clenched around him, almost choking from so much sensation.

'I know,' he whispered, his eyes so dark they looked black.

Welded together, locked the length of each other, his gaze fixed on mine—and still it wasn't close enough. Slowly, tenderly, every movement was meaningful, every breath felt sacred.

Our movements gathered speed until, without much warning, his breathing became harsher, more urgent. 'Rachel—' His voice was hoarse. 'I can't—' Then he was shuddering against me, goosebumps popping on his skin.

For the longest time, we lay stunned and wordless. I could have stayed, my face to his chest, inhaling him, forever.

Eventually, he spoke. 'I'm sorry it was so quick.'

Light-heartedly, I said, 'You must really fancy me.'

'Nothing new there. But it's not like I haven't been—' Abruptly he stopped.

'Haven't been what?'

'Oh, you know.' He rolled over and grinned into my face. 'Since—what day was it? Wednesday? The place by the stream. You, behind me, on the bike.' He squeezed his eyes shut. 'Christ.'

'Seriously?'

'Seriously.'

'. . . Tell me.'

'I dropped you home, went back to Justin's, barely got into my room. Just about got my jeans open . . .' He shrugged. 'Every time I think about you, I go hard. And the problem is I can't stop thinking about you. I haven't been like this since I was fourteen. I'm *sore* from it.' He hesitated. 'Does that make me pathetic? Disgusting? I told you, the past, the present, it's all mixed up. I'm a mess.'

Oh.

Hearing that he'd spent the last few days as affected as I'd been filled me with joy. But the implication that he only fancied me because his emotions were all over the place?

I was disappointed. Far *too* disappointed.

It was a reality check though, one I should be grateful for.

'Me too,' I managed. 'A mess, like.'

Sometime in the pre-dawn, drowsy and heavy, we woke, our limbs inter-twined. With one slick move, he was inside me, and my body was already in flames even while I was still marvelling, *Oh my God, it's Luke*.

Afterwards we lay in bottomless silence, my head on his chest, his arms hard and tight around me. In my soul and in my body was a deep peace. Here, in this bed with him, even the loss of Yara was lighter.

Outside, the chirping of the first birds began and light was creeping under the curtains.

'Are you okay?' Luke spoke into the room.

I shifted, in order to see his face. 'Better than okay. I'm really grateful to . . . the universe? Well, whoever's in charge, for this.'

'Tell me,' he said. 'How's your sleep these days?' But there was compassion in his voice, not judgement.

'Still my weak point, the first thing to go when I'm upset. I'll never be one of those lucky people who're out like a light the moment their head hits the pillow. But I'm okay most of the time.'

After a while, I sent him downstairs for water. 'In the fridge,' I said. 'Bring up a bottle. Mind Crunchie doesn't lick you to death.'

Even though we were alone in the house he pulled on his jeans. He'd always been an odd mix of raunchy and modest.

While he was gone, I had to tell myself over and over again, *This is real. This is real. This is real.* Luke was genuinely here and it was as if those years apart had never happened. But for a few strange seconds, I decided to terrify myself with thoughts that I'd imagined everything, that I was all alone—and oh! He was back, carrying a green bottle. Bare-chested, his hair a disordered tangle, he stood at the foot of the bed, watching me thoughtfully as, idly, he rolled the bottle back and forth across his torso.

'What?' I asked.

'Never not gorgeous, are you?' Then, 'Just . . . so I'll remember.'

He put the bottle down. His eyes on mine, he unzipped his jeans—underneath he was naked and already erect—and slid them off. In one fluid movement, he was halfway up the bed, climbing towards me with intent.

'Again?' I asked.

'Oh God, yeah. Again, Rachel.'

*

We fell asleep once more and I woke at just gone eight. He'd have to leave soon.

He opened his eyes. 'It really is you,' he said faintly. 'This feels like a dream.'

'It's real.' I ran my hand across his stomach. 'Still flat. How? Don't tell me you've started going to the gym?'

'We—' His voice stumbled. '*I* go horse-riding.'

I'd made him remember Kallie.

'I know,' I said immediately. 'We shouldn't have done this.'

'. . . Yeah—'

'But it wasn't really sex,' I said. 'It was part of our healing.'

In silence, he looked at me and suddenly my shame was overwhelming.

'Kallie won't agree,' I said, feeling even worse. 'I can only imagine if Quin told me he'd slept with Shiv—that's his ex-wife—but everything was fine because it was grief, not, like, lust. Luke, I'm so sorry. I hope she'll forgive you.'

'Wait now, no one put a gun to my head. I wanted this. But what about Quin?'

'He's . . . He gets that humans are complicated.' I struggled to find the right words. 'He'll be hurt. And angry. But he might understand.'

'Rachel, that sounds . . . delusional.'

Now he'd said it, I realized he was right. It was like snapping out of a trance.

'Oh my God.' As the extent of the possible damage hit home, I stuttered, 'I'm sorry. We shouldn't have, *I* shouldn't have—at the time, it made sense but . . . we have lives. It took us a long time to rebuild them—'

'Those lives are still there,' he said. 'It's okay. This was a one-off. It won't happen again.'

'But I want us to be friends.' I was adamant. 'Can we try to forget about . . . this?'

'Totally.'

'You'll take care of Kallie?' I was remembering my devastation when I thought he'd cheated with Mia. 'I'm so sorry for causing her pain.'

'Of course I will, Rachel. But you mustn't—'

'Luke?' I insisted. 'You promise?'

He took a moment. 'I promise. So now will you show me Yara's tree?'

Out in the garden the air was fragrant with early-morning dewy grass and damp earth. Luke, barefoot, wearing a woolly sweater Devin had left behind, looked around, taking in all my flowers. 'You've done this? It's incredible. Wait! You have a *shed*?'

'You don't know the half of it. I obsess over spades. And compost. This way. Over here.' Yara's cherry blossom was only about six feet high and the tiny, tucked-up buds were a long way from flowering. 'It doesn't look much today,' I said. 'But by mid-May it'll be'—I waved my arms for emphasis—'this riot of pink petals, they look like confetti, it's so pretty, it's so *her*.'

'I'll have to come back,' he joked.

Then he went silent and I let him have his moment. There was a stillness to his focus and a slight twitch to his lips—was he praying? Because I'd noticed, amongst the other hardware around his neck, a tiny silver cross on a thin silver chain.

He'd always had tendencies that way—it looked like they'd got stronger?

He noticed my scrutiny and, slightly embarrassed, he laughed. 'Whatever gets you through.'

'Hah!' I said. 'I'm hardly one to judge.'

'Even without the—what did you call it? The "riot of pink confetti petals"?—it's a beautiful tree.'

'I'm so glad you said that!' His approval mattered. 'It helps me. Seeing that, in a way, she lives on, as something beautiful.'

Out of nowhere, a blanket of sorrow dropped—all that we'd hoped for and all that we'd lost. Warily, we watched each other, thinking about the little girl who didn't get the chance to live. As tears spilled from his eyes, he was in my arms, and I cried with him. It was sad, it was *terribly* sad but we were grieving together and that was right and good.

Eventually we wandered back into the house and Luke put his jacket on, readying to leave. The impulse to fix his collar felt automatic, but I resisted. There would be no more of that, and it was okay.

'Safe journey.' My heart was swollen with gratitude, regret, sorrow, acceptance—too many emotions to know.

'Thanks. I'll . . .' Luke shifted awkwardly. 'We'll . . . ?'

'Be in touch?'

He nodded. He smiled. His hand twisted open the lock on the door. And I let him go.

You know it's not an either or? It doesn't have to be Quin or Luke. You can have a very happy life without either of them.

80

'. . . I swapped my regular Wednesday night meeting for pregnancy yoga, so I was getting to just two meetings a week . . .'

The alarm on my phone pinged and, with a long exhale of relief, I stopped typing. Wasting no time, Nola had me doing my Twelve Steps again, making me focus long and hard on what had been in play, when I'd talked myself back into taking the pills.

For the past fortnight, I'd been getting up an hour earlier than usual to do the writing before work. Currently on step four, I was examining my behaviour when I got pregnant. Complacency was the biggest culprit—I'd been clean for such a long time, I'd let my attention shift entirely to my expected baby. Basically, I'd sort of forgotten I was an addict. When the opportunity for sleeping tablets reared its head, there was nothing in place to protect me.

The process was teaching me new respect for my addiction, for its patience, its stealth, its dogged determination.

And now, to my relief, I had to go to work. Self-examination was *faaar* harder than my actual job. It was so much nicer to be looking at the delusions of others rather than my own.

But I was doing okay, especially considering all that had shaken down in the sixteen days since Mum's party.

Almost as soon as Luke had left my house that Sunday morning, I'd had the most thorough shower of my life, washing away every single trace of him. Then I unmuted my phone, ignored the twenty or so messages from Claire and went directly to Quin's.

He would only admit me as far as the hall. 'You had sex with him?'

I'd nodded. 'I'm sorry.' Hurting him was horrible.

'And . . . ?' His voice was husky. 'You're back with him?'

'It was a one-off.'

'But . . . ?'

'. . . It brought up a lot of stuff from the past, I'm sort of all over the place.'

'Yeah. Me too.'

His defiant tone made me focus on him more carefully.

'Yeah.' He shifted in a pretence of awkwardness. 'Me and Golden.'

Maybe it shouldn't have, but it knocked the breath from me. '. . . Last night?'

'The night after we got back from Barcelona.' Then, defensively, 'What did you expect, Rach?'

Now that he'd said it, it was clear that even before I'd spent the night with Luke, Quin and I were done—the mortifying exchange with the ring in Mr Navabi's showroom had seen to that.

He refused to look away, slightly ashamed, a lot more defiant, glad I knew and angry he'd told me. Reluctantly, he said, 'I'm sorry.'

'And I'm sorry, Quin. I'm so sorry.'

In painful silence, we watched each other. I couldn't think of one other thing to add—shockingly, our two-year relationship appeared to have been dispatched in moments. As I moved towards the door, he said, 'Don't.'

'. . . Quin, you want me to. Isn't that why you slept with her? Why you told me?'

'And now I want you to stay.'

'If I did, you'd change your mind again. I'm sorry, Quin, this is all my fault.'

'Hey!' A flash of fear lit his eyes. '*I* decided. This was *my* decision.'

'Sure. Absolutely.' Winning mattered a lot more to him than to me, he could have his victory.

Unsure of what to do, I went home again and FaceTimed Claire, who was still in bed in the SugarLoaf Inn, a mess of smeared lipstick, dishevelled hair and wonky eyelashes.

'Hey,' I said cautiously. 'You look . . .'

'Yeah.' She groaned. 'A good time was had by all. What's up? What about you and Luke?'

'Well, nothing really. He's still with Kallie—'

'—but you *did* sleep with him?' Claire all but shrieked. 'Don't tell me you didn't!'

'Claire, calm down, take it easy! We did. But that's it, that's all. We're done. In a good way.'

'No,' she said. 'No, no, no, no, no, this is a disaster. What about Quin?'

'It's over.'

'Christ.'

'Yeah, but . . .' I hadn't believed it last night when I'd been up to my oxters in delusion, but this morning I'd been prepared.

'Lookit, I've to go. Need to puke. Debrief in Mum's around five. Be there. She's rewriting her will.'

I slept for the rest of that day, then went to Mum and Dad's. Not because I cared about my 'inheritance'—Mum was forever rewriting her will, reallocating her gold-plated watches and miraculous medals. No one cared apart from her. But I liked the post-mortem of a party as much as the next person.

Throwing on some clothes, I tentatively probed my emotions—there was a mountain of shame for hurting Quin. *And* huge amounts of guilt about Kallie.

Quin having slept with Golden also burned, but in a peculiar second-hand fashion, as if a layer of cotton wool protected me. Perhaps the pain would come later.

The strangest feeling of all was about Luke. A calmness hummed in me, a sense of completion, as if a storm had blown itself out, revealing a world both peaceful and benign.

I rang Nola. Brusquely she ordered me to start writing my steps again. 'Start step one tomorrow,' she said. 'An hour a day. Make it a priority.'

'Okay.' Then I left for my parents' house.

In Mum's Good Front Room the mood was subdued, all four of my sisters pale and quiet, curled on the couches, their clothing pyjamas or pyjamas-adjacent. Claire seemed to be wearing an actual duvet.

'I'm sorry I bothered getting dressed,' I said.

Mum, by far the most strung-out, was horribly, nervily jubilant. 'Wasn't it a great night?' Underneath her left eye, a slight twitch was hopping.

'A total triumph,' I said. 'I'll just say hello to Dad.'

'He's watching the golf.'

In the TV room Dad and Angelo were happily side by side, facing the telly, each eating a bag of Monster Munch. Poor Dad, he was so *happy* on the rare occasions he had male company.

'Everything okay here?' I asked.

'Gooch.' Angelo winked.

'What he said.' Dad nodded. 'It's short for "Gucci", he tells me.'

All very amiable.

Moving from their wholesome harmony back to the smoking-ruins vibe of the Good Front Room, Anna, delicious in a silk kimono, was asking, 'Should I get the gin?'

'Jesus Christ, *no*.' Margaret, in blue tartan pyjamas, twisted her head to one side.

'Let me guess,' I said. 'None of you are ever drinking again?'

'Oh shut up!' Mum cried. 'You smug lump.'

'Hey!' Helen's voice emerged from the depths of a black hooded dressing gown. 'She gets one night a *century* to be smug, let her have it.'

'Is there anything for an upset stomach?' Margaret asked Mum.

'Look in the kitchen. They're in the fruit basket.'

'Bring painkillers too,' Helen called after her.

'What do you need?' Claire opened up her handbag. 'I've got them all.'

Margaret had returned with the fruit basket, which contained an apologetic handful of fly-spotted grapes, one shrunken kiwi fruit and a veritable cornucopia of pills. 'Okay. Who needs what?'

'Something to stop the gawks,' Helen said.

'Motilium?'

'Anything stronger?'

Margaret rummaged. 'Stemetil?' She read from a box. 'They're on prescription. They'd be good.'

'Rachel.' Mum's face loomed at me, alarmingly close. 'You don't think they thought I was showing off?'

'Who?'

'Anyone. Everyone.'

'She has the Fear,' Claire said. 'So do I.'

'And me,' said Margaret, then Anna.

'Me too,' Helen said.

'But you weren't even drinking.'

'Yeah. But . . .' It was the stress of trying to get pregnant. I understood.

'Any tranquillizers in that fruit basket?' Claire asked.

'Diazepam?' Margaret asked.

'That's Valium,' Claire said. 'Give me two. No, make it six.'

Mum cut in. 'How d'you know I've the Fear?'

'Describe your state of mind.'

'. . . Tremendously ashamed. Even though I'm not sure what I did wrong. Like everyone was secretly laughing at me, at all the money we spent on the steak and the gold-leaf—'

'—that's definitely the Fear—'

'—and nobody likes me. So I'm deleting them all from my will. I think someone must have told them I only got a C in History in my Leaving Cert, even though I always said I got a B.' Her mouth twitched. 'And everyone thinks I'm too tall—'

'You are.' From Helen, of course.

'—and my nose is too fat. And—'

'Ah, stop,' I said. 'Last night you drank a lot and used far too much adrenaline, leaving you with a huge deficit today. It's simple science. None of those thoughts are true. Keep your will as it is.'

Mum shifted her attention to me. 'What about *you*? Claire says that Captain Spork broke it off.'

'*Dr* Spork!' From Helen.

'Well, we both agreed that—'

'Are you back with Luke?'

'No, but I'm okay.'

'How, though?' Mum was distraught. 'Now you've no boyfriend!'

'Because I feel . . .' I couldn't find the correct word. 'It's over with Luke. And it's over fully, properly. The way it should be.'

A sea of baffled faces was watching and suddenly I had the perfect analogy. 'The door on my spare room, the crappy lock never fully catches, not even when I slam it. It *almost* closes, it *seems* closed, but I'm always tense, because I *know* it'll slip free.'

The same five faces were fixed on me, one or two looking somewhat concerned.

'But once in a blue moon,' I said, 'the right thing happens! The *click*.' I clicked my fingers to demonstrate. 'Click!' I repeated. 'The lock does what it's supposed to—it catches and it's genuinely closed. Do you get me? Click!'

Helen glanced at Claire. 'You restrain her and I'll ring the ambulance.'

In a gentle voice, Anna asked, 'What exactly has "clicked"?'

'Luke and I ended a long time ago, but it never felt . . .' I sought the right word. 'Real? Done? Now it is. Click!'

'Uh-oh,' Margaret declared, literally rolling up her sleeves. 'I know what's going on here.'

She didn't often make those sorts of pronouncements, so I took notice.

'All of us, at some stage, we've had a tooth out?' she said, 'For a while your mouth doesn't hurt and secretly you're proud of your high pain threshold. But it's only because the anaesthetic hasn't worn off.' She shrugged.

'Then it does and you're crying on the couch, eating cloves like they're M&M's. Sorry, Rachel.'

'Bang on,' Claire said. 'Rachel, you're high, literally *high,* on all that Costello man-lurve.'

'Exactly this.' Margaret was earnest. 'The phenomenon has been well documented. The Costello man-lurve has generated oodles of dopamine in you.'

'I adore Angelo,' Anna stated, seemingly apropos of nothing. 'But I wouldn't say no to a night of Costello man-lurve.'

'And there,' Mum muttered, 'I'd have to agree with you. 'Tisn't many a woman who'd turn down a night of Costello man-love.'

'*Lurve.*' Helen corrected, then with savage scorn: 'I'd turn it down. *State* of him.'

'Tell me.' I was interested, almost amused.

'His hair is too long, his jeans are still too tight. He's preposterous.'

'Ahem-*hem.*' Margaret coughed apologetically. 'In the interests of balance, I always liked Luke, but I didn't fancy him.' Quickly she added, 'I don't think he's preposterous either. Just . . . not for me.'

'In all seriousness,' Claire said. 'You need to be careful, Rachel. You're going to crash and it won't be pretty.'

Suddenly I was very nervous.

'But we'll rally round you,' Claire said. 'Won't we?'

'Of course!' From Margaret.

'I'm not much of a rally-er,' Helen said. 'But I'm willing to try.'

Mum gripped my arm. 'You'd be better off without her.'

'Um, I fly back to New York on Tuesday.' Anna was apologetic. 'But obviously I'll rally round in spirit. I can ask Angelo to do distance reiki?'

'Perhaps you shouldn't be on your own.' Margaret was thoughtful. 'Why don't you stay with us for a few days?'

'I'm fine.'

Grimly, Claire shook her head. 'You're a breakdown waiting to happen.'

Out of the blue, Mum asked, 'What's going on with you and Adam?'

'I hate him,' Claire said.

'You were kissing him. Ateing the head offa him, more like. And then you gave him a shove where he nearly landed in the next county.'

'I hate him.'

'But—'

'We're having a lot of hate sex.'

After a startled silence, Anna murmured, 'All part of life's rich tapestry.'

81

Despite the grim predictions of my sisters, I got through that first night without going off the rails and when I woke the next morning, I still felt . . . *fine*.

Okay, so it was a challenge to switch on my laptop and begin writing my step one, all over again. Detailing every single way I'd been 'powerless over drugs' six years ago wasn't exactly how I wanted to start my week, but I gave it a shot.

When the hour was (finally) up, it was no bother to have a shower and get ready for work. But I was in the thick of dopamine, absolutely *saturated* in the stuff, it was vital to keep sight of that.

While drying my hair, my phone buzzed with a text. When I saw who it was from—Luke—the adrenaline rush had the tips of my fingers fizzing.

Hey. Hoping you're good? Just letting you know I got back in one piece. L x

Clenching the phone, staring at the words—in particular the 'x'—an almost irresistible longing seized me, to call him, simply to hear his voice. But it would be a mistake to think that our night together had been the start of anything. It had been the end. A proper end this time.

Abandoning my hairdryer, I began constructing a breezy, just-dashed-off text, taking forever to get the tone right: warm but in no way flirty; intimate but devoid of innuendo. Eventually I produced:

All good here. Hope you're okay too. It must be strange being back in
Denver for the first time since your mum passed. Try to be kind to yourself x

Seconds later, Luke replied.

And remember there are no wrong feelings ☺ x

Wha—Oh! It had been said to Luke and me over and over, in the days after Yara's death.

Totally, I replied. And everything happens for a reason. Double lol. So now I better go to work x

So . . . Don't forget to send me photos of Yara's tree when it's got all its flowers x

Sure! In maybe 6 or 7 weeks' time it'll be at its best x

Looking forward to it. And we're gonna talk on 3 July? x

The third of July was Yara's anniversary.

Thank you, I'd really appreciate that x

Of course. No bother. Talk to you then. Hope you have a good day today. L x

You too x

It looked like the 'x' was definitely bedded in. And it was . . . nice? Friendly? Yes, friendly.

Because we were going to be friends.

That Monday passed without me crashing and burning. Tuesday, same. Then Wednesday. And so on, until it was Saturday morning, a week since Mum's party and—as part of Operation Rally-Round—Claire was marching up and down outside my house. We had a hike planned but I was distracted by her gym gear, which gave off a sheen of extreme costliness.

'How on earth'—I checked her out—'can plain black Lycra look stomach-turningly expensive?'

'Dunno.' She wasn't interested. 'Have you heard from Quin?'

'No.'

'Luke?'

'Nothing since the text last Monday. And there won't be, until I send those photos.'

'C'mon, let's get moving. Need to keep my heart rate up. My Fitbit gives me an electric shock every time it falls below a hundred beats per minute.'

'What? Seriously?'

'No. But it's actually a good idea. An electric shock would be a great oul' motivator.'

'Claire . . .'

Crunchie barked and tried to escape out the front door.

'No!' Claire said. 'That dog is not to come. I need to *stride*. That shortarse just wriggles on her belly.'

I persuaded my little doggie back inside and Claire and I set off.

'Give me an update on your crash-and-burn status,' she said.

'No sign of it yet—'

'—but it will. You're still high on Costello man-lurve.'

'I'm very sad about Quin, though. It's difficult for him, he's not used to rejection. He's more vulnerable than you'd guess.'

'Are you angry about him and Golden?'

'More . . . hurt. Not really surprised, though. It's Quin, it's how he rolls.'

'I'd say he'll "reach out" to you.'

I shook my head. 'He's all bravado. Not going to happen.'

'But . . .' Claire was thoughtful. '. . . because of that self-same bravado, I could see him swaggering in and declaring, "Giddy up, girlie, your luck just changed, I'm taking you back." Right?'

'Maybe.' On balance though, I reckoned he'd stay gone.

'Would you get back with him? If he did that?'

'I don't . . . know. Not "in this moment". I'm not sure of anything. It all needs to settle.'

'Because you still love Luke?'

'. . . not. I don't. No.'

'You don't sound very sure.'

'Claire. That night with Luke, it was . . . amazing.' To put it mildly. 'But I've no idea what he's like now, not really. He could be a Trump supporter—'

'Rachel!' she hissed.

'Who knows? Six years is a long time. These days he rides horses. He's more holy than he was. And they're just the externals. The person he once was, the things I loved—his sunny nature, his openness to life—they might be all gone.'

She was getting it now; I could see it. Perversely, that upset me.

'He told me several times.' The words tumbled from my mouth. 'He said things like, I'm not the man I used to be, and, These days my relationships are different. Like, he *told* me, Claire.' My voice had begun to shake.

'But he *seemed* the same,' she said. 'Dancing with the aunties. Being sweet to everyone.'

Suddenly exasperated, I asked, 'Claire, why aren't we talking about Kallie? Luke has a partner! He cheated on her! How "sweet" was that?'

That silenced her. There was no way that could be reconfigured into something acceptable.

'Do you think he told her?' she asked. 'About sleeping with you?'

I nodded.

'That's the vibe I'm getting,' she said. 'Every few days she posts on the socials about her music—yeah, I spy on her, got your back, babes—but Luke has been back there nearly a week now and she hasn't posted a single "Me and My Hot Man" shot.'

Yes, I'd been also spying on Kallie. Mostly because it was impossible to spy on Luke—there was still no sign of him on any platform.

However, I hadn't been spying on Quin. I'd quietly unfollowed him on Instagram. *And* Golden. Even Shiv. If Quin was with Golden, I'd feel bad, but if he was on his own, I'd also feel bad.

The difference between my interest in Luke and my interest in Quin was fantasy versus reality. Luke was thousands of miles away on another continent. There was almost nothing I could do to influence events. But with Quin, if I got overwhelmed with missing him, or seized by sudden fury about Golden, I could—in theory, anyway—turn up on his doorstep. And I knew enough to know that I knew nothing. Not right now. I had to wait this out.

'From what you told me,' Claire said. 'Kallie's mad about Luke. They'll work through it. Soon as she's back on her feet, the photos will resume.' Suddenly Claire pivoted. 'Or maybe she *won't* forgive him. Okay, I'm going to say something here—maybe he doesn't want to be forgiven! Maybe you and he have a future?'

Hotly, I said, 'Do you really think Luke would break up with Kallie, sell his practice, sell his home, upend his life and relocate to Ireland after one night with me?'

Coolly, Claire raised her eyebrows. The seconds ticked away as her silent appraisal began to feel uncomfortable. 'Do *you*?' she asked. Then, in more urgent tones, '*Do* you, Rachel?'

'I don't think it might ever be . . . anything. It was a one-off. Knowing I've probably caused Kallie untold pain, I'm *ashamed*. But I still wouldn't change that night with him.'

'Why? Apart from the obvious?'

'It's fixed something. My bitterness is gone. It's changed how I feel about Yara. I can't describe it exactly because the loss is still there but it's not as . . . ugly?'

'Is that what you meant by "the click"?'

'Exactly. The price is high, it means doing without Quin. And living with a hefty side order of guilt and shame about him and Kallie. But . . .' I let my hands fall. 'Not all is lost. Luke's trying to be my friend, I'm trying to be his. I'd like to give that a go. Tell me, how are things with Adam?'

'I hate him. He hates me. I fancy him more than I have in decades. We keep having sex. It's angry. It's horrible. But sexy. I've always wanted to have angry sex and now I'm having it.' Doubtfully, she said, 'Which is good.' Then '. . . I guess.'

82

Work was as intense as ever and while I was there, I managed to give it my all. One by one, my ducklings left. Trassa had been replaced by an obscenely wealthy young coke addict called Kael. Three days later, Harlie departed; in her stead we got Celeste, a gilet-wearing alcoholic, armoured with weapons-grade respectability. Dennis had been next to go. And today, three weeks later than originally scheduled, my beloved Chalkie was off.

My phone beeped with a text—from Taryn, my 'hiking friend'. Rachel, when would be a good time to call?

Oh *God*. The holiday Quin and I had booked to Transylvania, with Taryn and Timothy. I'd been putting off dealing with it . . .

But I needed to be an adult so I took a breath and picked up my phone. 'Taryn?'

'Rach. Quin sent a message,' she said. 'I'm so sorry you've broken up.'

'Thanks. I know, it's—'

'How are you doing?'

'I'm okay. Honestly. I guess we need to talk about the—'

'—trip. Quin says he's giving you custody. He means he won't be going, but that you still should.'

Suddenly it hurt to breathe. I felt such sadness for Quin, for both of us, that all that affection and connection had just . . . collapsed.

'Rach . . . ?' Taryn asked.

'Just. Let me take a moment . . .'

Here were the facts and they were unpleasant: we'd already paid half the cost. It was non-refundable. More importantly, this trip was my project. I'd blithely gone ahead and booked our accommodation in daringly out-of-the-way places—I couldn't abandon Taryn and Timothy.

And I had wanted to go—in a way, I still did. Ted probably wouldn't let me change my dates off—our annual leave got locked in *early*—so I might as well spend it in the stunning beauty of Transylvania instead of sitting at home, the curtains drawn, watching *Below Deck* with Crunchie.

'On paper, this seems awkward,' Taryn said. 'But I think the three of us would still get a lot out of it.'

'You're absolutely right,' I said. 'The three of us are going and we will have a magical time.'

Buoyed by that positivity, I switched off my phone and took Chalkie to an interview room for our last one-to-one. And it was *so* encouraging. He'd gleaned a huge amount of new information about himself during his time here; somehow he'd gone way deeper than he ever had before.

After we'd role-played some situations where he'd have to manage his anger or grief, we stood to say goodbye.

'You know how fond of you I am,' I said. 'But I do not want to see you ever again.'

'But', he said, with a sweet twinkle, 'you might.'

At my startled silence, he prompted, 'Right?'

In my five years in the Cloisters, this had never happened before.

'You're in recovery, amirite?' he prompted.

I laughed. 'Yeah.' There wasn't much point denying it.

'Down through the years, a lot of good, hard-working people have tried to help me. You're the one who broke me open.'

'Just doing my job.'

'Na-ah. You go the extra mile.'

For a moment I thought my heart would actually crack with gratitude. Despite my many mistakes, Chalkie was saying that there was a reason for me.

He spread his arms wide. 'Is this . . . okay?'

I stepped into the hug. Silent tears slid down my face for Chalkie, the little lost boy.

'Thank you,' he said, his voice thick.

'Oh my God no, Chalkie! Thank *you*.'

83

'Yara . . .' Helplessly, I pleaded with my cherry-blossom tree. 'Sweetie? Where are your flowers? It's the middle of May, what are you *doing* with them?'

Turning, I caught sight of Devin's face at the kitchen window. He looked concerned.

'All grand here,' I called at him. 'Just talking to . . .' My dead daughter? A tree? Take your pick.

'Okay.' As if he were on castors, Devin retreated from view, seeming even more freaked out.

Once he'd gone, I resumed the chat. 'Seriously, what's the story?' I gestured at the tiny beige buds. 'Is it more rain you're waiting for? Warmer temperatures?'

But Yara's voice—or the voice that I 'heard' in my head—remained silent. And it was very frustrating because, until this tree bloomed, there was no excuse to contact Luke.

In the kitchen, Kate asked carefully, 'Are you okay?'

Funnily enough, I *was*. Sometimes, for no obvious reason, the universe decides to cut us some slack—because six weeks on from Mum's party, despite my sisters' gloomy predictions, I hadn't crashed and burned. Undeniably, emotions were coming at me from all directions and it was a lot, but I was coping.

As I was in good form, I decided to check in on Kallie's Instagram. I'd been keeping a casual eye on her page, trying to not obsess. Recently, there had been a *lot* about her music: she'd done back-up vocals on someone's demo and spent a week at a song-writing bootcamp. But nothing about Luke.

Every day without a picture of him, I exhaled a little more.

But this morning was different.

This latest shot was a selfie, with Kallie's pretty face in the foreground. Several feet behind her was Luke, next to a huge, dark horse. He seemed to be speaking soothingly to it. The caption was 'Playing hard to get'. Followed by several laughing emojis, then a red heart.

Frozen in place, I stared and stared, shocked by how jealous I felt, how deeply disappointed.

Steeling myself, I clicked on her stories. There she was, sparkly-eyed and pretty. 'Hi guys!' she carolled. 'So! Yeah, that was a meaningful "so".' She laughed. 'I'mmmm . . . yeah, hoping for some good news. Some . . . positive changes in my life. It's too soon to go public on it, just in case it . . .' She presented her cupped hands to the camera, then divided them. '. . . falls away. I'm asking for your prayers and positive energy. Whatever you got, send them my way!'

I watched it five or six more times, wondering what the hell this positive life change could be. Moving in with Luke? Getting married to Luke?

Jesus Christ.

And here came Claire. In the six weeks since the commencement of Operation Rally-Round, a Saturday-morning hike had become a thing.

'Were you on Insta?' she asked.

I nodded. 'What good news is she hoping for?'

'Fuck alone knows.' Claire wasn't putting a positive spin on this, which was a worry.

'And what about the photo?' I asked. 'Who was playing hard to get? Kallie?'

'I don't know, babes. Could be Luke. Could even have been the horse.'

It *could* even have been the horse. The *actual* issue, the only thing that was truly important, was that my feelings for Luke hadn't settled yet. Not even close. The Costello man-lurve dopamine had mutated into some sort of tragic crush. Late at night, when I couldn't sleep, I let myself indulge in all kinds of fantasies where somehow Luke and I were together again.

But I *knew* it would never happen.

Or so I'd thought. This morning, Kallie's photo had shown me that I'd got far too attached to the idea.

The insane thing was that I also missed Quin. He'd been my buddy as well as my boyfriend and I bumped up against his absence every day.

But my life was far from empty. Helen checked in on me regularly. That was what her texts actually said: It's me. Checking in on you regularly. Are you okay? Yes? No? A one-word reply is fine. No need to write War and Peace.

During the last month and a half, I'd never had so many invitations. In between redoing my steps, I'd helped Murdo paint his new flat, spent an auntie-and-niece afternoon with Holly (manicure, volunteering), got sunburnt on a chilli cook-out with Brianna and her neighbours, had a glorious weekend of Atlantic squalls and dazzling sunshine with Brigit and tried a woodcarving class with Margaret. (It wasn't for either of us.)

Despite my many activities, I was lonely. But it was my doing. No one had *made* me sleep with Luke.

And I wasn't broken the way I'd been when Luke had left me, six years ago.

'Rachel,' Claire said as she strode up the side of a hill, 'no matter what you think, your life isn't over. You probably won't be alone forever.'

'I'm not alone. I love lots of people and they love me.'

'Yeah, but . . .' She hesitated. 'Nieces? Sisters? People you work with?' She shook her head. 'Nah.'

'For a so-called feminist, you've some worrying ideas.'

'Just being honest, saying what everyone else thinks but is afraid to. Equal pay? Thanks very much. Ridey men? Thanks, I'll have them as well. What about Murdo? He's single now. That's why he moved into the new apartment.'

'Leave poor Murdo out of this. Anyway, my life has no room for men.' Tongue-in-cheek, I said, 'I'm doing work on myself.'

'I know you're being funny, but, Rachel, what *exactly* does that mean? I hear people say it and, honestly, I haven't a clue.'

'It means I must feel my uncomfortable feelings and not numb them.'

'But what's the actual "work"?'

'Feeling the feelings is the work.'

'It's that passive? They always make it sound like they're, I dunno, rummaging around inside themselves, moving their spleen two millimetres to the left, having a good look at their pancreas. Not numb my feelings? That's easy!'

Not for everyone. She was a character.

'What age is Murdo?' she asked.

'Too young.'

'Does that mean you fancy him?'

'I don't.' Murdo *could* have been sexy, I didn't know—because he had those giant pierced earlobes, so big you could pass a carrot through. They were immediate dealbreakers.

Thoughtfully, Claire said, 'My Spidey senses tell me that if you went to Quin and *grovelled*, he'd probably take you back.'

'And he could just as easily have got *married* to Golden. Or met someone else. He probably hates me.'

'Do you hate him?'

'No.' At her quizzical look I said, 'I feel almost . . . *sorry* for him.'

'For *Quin*?'

'Claire. I know he seems confident and, I guess, privileged? In some ways he is. But in others, he's insecure, he's easily wounded. I don't hate him at all.'

'Even though he slept with your one with the red face?'

'That was . . . hard. But hurt people hurt people.'

She shook her head. 'Christ, Rachel . . . I'd want to fucking kill him.' Speaking of which . . . 'How are things with you and Adam?'

Claire paused, one hefty hiking boot planted on a rock for stability, and smiled. 'Me and Adam . . . yeaaaah. He's . . .' Another dreamy smile. 'Great.'

'So you don't hate him any more?'

Sharply, she said, 'I *love* him.'

God's sake! It was impossible to keep up.

'It wasn't for us, the swinging,' she said. 'Things were quite dicey there for a while. But we're back on track—sex three times a year—and at least we tried.'

84

The next morning, it wasn't even 7 a.m. when I woke. A Sunday, I'd a busy day planned: first a sunrise yoga class, then an NA meeting, then Margaret's birthday brunch, even though we shouldn't call it 'brunch', Claire said, because what were we, a Shower of Basics?

While I pulled on my yoga leggings (which were the same as all my other leggings), I went to the bedroom window and once again looked down at Yara's tree. 'Bloom,' I begged her. 'Please. What is *taking* you so long?'

Suddenly it hit me that I'd made peace with not having had other children.

It was the gardening, I realized. Over the past few years, those long hours where I'd been fixed in one place, with no distractions from my own thoughts, paying witness to life, death and a form of resurrection, had forced me to grieve, then eventually—slowly, gradually—to heal.

My gratitude was immense, so much so that it made me dizzy. I lay back down for several minutes, in order to absorb it.

Eventually I got moving again and was rummaging in my drawer, hunting for anti-slip socks, when my phone beeped with a text—someone was awake early.

> Just checking . . . that you haven't forgotten to send me photos of Yara's tree. L x

As if. I'd been standing at the tree, almost muttering incantations, to bring on the flowers.

> Haven't forgotten, but it's taking forever. Maybe next week? Fingers crossed ☺ x

Breathlessly, I watched the phone, waiting for a reply.

> Send a pic today anyway? x

K. Or I could FaceTime you rn? Give you not-very-exciting action shots? x

Do it! X

As I raced down the stairs and out into the garden, desperately pressing icons, Luke's face appeared on screen.

'Hey.' I was thrilled by the sight of him.

'Hey, yourself.' He looked shy. 'Is this okay?'

'It's perfect. What time is it there?'

'Just gone midnight.'

'Last night?'

'Yeah.' He laughed. 'Last night. Is that Crunchie?'

Crunchie, picking up on my mood, was barking and racing around in excited circles. 'You remember Luke?' I showed her the screen. 'You liked him.'

'I liked her too,' I heard Luke say.

'So.' I moved around the tree, displaying the little buds from all angles. 'There isn't much to see right now. But another week or ten days should do it. I'm sorry, it's slower this year. So I'll do some shots or . . . I could call you?'

'Call me! That would be great. Hey, I'm not . . . holding you up, am I? You need to get going?'

'Not at all.' Feck the yoga class . . .

'So . . . stay and talk to me? For a few minutes?'

'Um. Sure.' I sat cross-legged on the grass, Crunchie head-butting her way onto the screen.

'Having a good weekend?' Luke asked.

'Busy! Yesterday morning Claire and I went for a hike, then I planted nasturtiums, poppies.' I stood up and walked towards a flower bed. 'I'll show you. See. Cornflowers. These here are sunflowers, not so impressive today but they will be at some stage. Today I've an NA meeting, then Margaret's birthday brunch. You?'

'Just . . . stuff.' He went a little cagey. Kallie stuff, I guessed. It hurt.

Don't be like that.

Yara was right. So, in a place deep down in me, a transaction took place: I had no right to feel jealous of Kallie. Luke had offered me friendship and it was something I wanted.

It was no real surprise that I was caught up in fantasies about him—those nine hours with him had been transcendent. But . . .

. . . *it will pass.*

'Tell me', he said, 'all about you being a gardener now!'

I sat again, Crunchie bounding into my lap. 'It was a total accident. When I was staying with Garvaret—'

'Who?'

'Garv and Margaret. I lived with them after I left New York.' I'd said the words and, crucially, said them without bitterness—this friendship thing with Luke was *working*. 'Garv is a great gardener, he showed me the magic.'

'And the magic is?'

'Protecting my seedlings, watching them emerge from the earth, be beautiful, then die, then for more to grow in their place. It's taken time for me to see it, but it helped me to live with her loss.' Suddenly curious, I asked, 'Did anything help you?'

'Horse-riding.' His certainty was unexpected. 'Seriously, it saved me. Sometime during that second, awful year in Denver, I gave it a go. Straight away, I knew I'd found my thing.'

'I'd assumed you started because of Kallie.'

'Other way round. When I met her, I'd often spend whole weekends on the trails. She said she never saw me. She was right. But I was too . . . selfish, I guess, to compromise, so even though she was nervous of horses, she took lessons. Now she's great.'

'Wow. She's determined.'

He laughed. He sounded warm. 'She's certainly that.'

'Luke.' I made myself say it. 'It's hard to think of you as selfish. That's not the way you used to be.'

'Aaah. Life.' He looked sad. 'Comes along and changes us . . . So. Who'll be at Margaret's birthday party?'

'No men, just all the Walsh women. The five of us, plus Mum and Kate, Francesca and Molly. And Margaret's friend, Emily.'

'And Holly?' he asked.

'Too young.' But I was touched that he remembered her.

'And Helen's Best Friend, Bella Devlin?'

I burst out laughing. 'How d'you know about her?'

'Met her at your mum's party.'

His eyes flicked away. There was a second, a hiccup of discomfort, as we remembered that night, then we proceeded.

'So tell me, Anna's in Ireland *again*? She visits . . . how often?'

'Every couple of months, sometimes more often if she's in Paris for work.'

'Does she ever think about moving back? With your parents being . . . ?'

'Old? It's okay, Luke, you can say the word.'

'Elderly? Does it bother Anna?'

'I don't think so. Her life is in New York—her job, her apartment. And I couldn't see Angelo living here. Anyway, she's here a lot. Air travel, ya know? How are you feeling since your mum . . .'

'Say it, Rachel.' He was smiling. 'You can say the word.'

'Since she died.'

'It's still early days. But I'm doing okay. It hasn't made me hate everyone . . .'

'That's how you felt after Yara?'

'Yeah.' Such a heartfelt sigh. 'With their bullshit platitudes and their *pity*. I didn't know how angry I was. You?'

'Well, we all know how I "coped".' Then, 'I'm so sorry, Luke.'

'Stop. Please, Rachel.' Even with the awkwardness of the screen, our eyes seemed to meet.

'How's your dad?' I asked.

'A pain in the hole.' He laughed. 'He is *not* going gently into that good night.'

'He's only—what? Seventy-eight? He's young.'

'Well, he wants to see the world. "While he still can." I mean, fair enough. Next month we're taking him to Vegas and Palm Springs. After that he's talking about Cuba. But I'm glad to get time with him.' Suddenly sombre, he said, 'Mum's death has certainly changed my perspective . . .' Then, 'So! You need to get to your meeting and I should get to bed!'

'. . . Luke, are you okay?'

'Yeah. Just . . . sorry, I guess, that I didn't visit my mum more often. Time I'll never get back now. But we can't know until we know. And we had a great relationship, there's nothing left unsaid there. But yeah, it's something I'll have to live with.'

'Luke . . .'

'So you'll give me a heads-up about Yara's tree? You're thinking a week? More?'

'Let's say a week. Any time of the day that's better for you to talk? Mornings? Evenings? I mean, with the time difference?' This was a sneaky attempt to find out about his routine with Kallie.

'Any time is fine.' This gave me no information. 'I mean it. Any time is good. Take care, Rachel.'

'. . . You too.'

With a blooping noise, he was gone.

*

It's me. Checking in on you regularly. Heard you've started having the chats with trees. Are you okay? Yes? No? A one-word answer will do. No need to write Game of Thrones.

Yes, I replied.

'Welcome to Bottomless Brunch.' A young server with pigtails and a cute hat slung menus our way.

'Lunch,' Claire said firmly. 'It's almost two o'clock. It's lunch.'

'Claire . . .' I side-eyed her. 'Let it go.'

'Yeah, sorry.' She waved away the jug of mimosa. 'None of that bottomless crap for me, I like my alcohol to contain actual, you know, *alcohol*. I'll have a negroni, thank you.'

'Hey!' Margaret's friend Emily had arrived and we got up to hug her. Francesca and Molly were next to appear, then Helen and Kate and, finally, Mum and Anna.

Turning to me, Claire muttered, 'I don't know which is worse. That it's "brunch" or that it's a "girlie brunch".'

'It's Margaret's birthday,' I hissed. 'She can have whatever she wants.'

'Hey,' Helen said. 'I've a question. If my baby is a girl, would it be weird to call her Bella Devlin?'

'Yes,' Claire said. 'You fucking lunatic. They'd be *sisters*.'

'And she'd be called Bella Devlin Devlin.' This from Kate.

'Anyway, what baby?' Anna asked.

Suddenly, electrified with understanding, we were all staring at Helen. '*What* baby?'

She shifted awkwardly. 'Yeah.' She was sheepish. 'Yeah. Six weeks.'

'Why didn't you tell us!?'

'I don't know. I could be in shock.'

'What does Artie say?'

'I haven't told him yet.'

'Helen!'

'Anyway, it's six weeks, which actually means only four. That's nothing. It's no guarantee of—' She looked unexpectedly stricken.

Her gaze flicked to mine. Locked in a terrible embrace, fear squeezed my heart.

Sometime later, when we were all leaving, I grabbed her. 'Helen'—I was insistent—'if anything ever feels weird to you, *anything*, ring me, tell Artie, do something. But don't ignore it. Do you hear me?'

'Yeah, okay. Thanks.'

'Even if it's something tiny. Don't be embarrassed by how small it might seem. Take it seriously.'

'But with you, there *were* no signs?'

'There might have been, though. Maybe I just didn't notice them. Don't make my mistakes.'

'Oh, Rachel!'

85

Liberty and Finley had been playing on my mind. All of the Quinlivans had. But I reckoned that Quin's parents and siblings would be better equipped than his kids to process my abrupt disappearance from their lives.

In view of how things were playing out, it was probably a blessing that I'd never assumed a proper parental role. We'd got on, though. I was very fond of them and it felt wrong to just disappear without an explanation.

But I wasn't sure of the protocol, especially because I didn't have a clue what Quin had told them. Was I 'a cheating bitch'? Or had he spun the break-up as entirely his decision? Indeed, was Golden currently ensconced in Quin's black-and-white tiled kitchen, drinking tea from 'my' mug, helping him find the tahini?

I *really* didn't like that thought but it was impossible to extract my dislike of Golden from the whole scenario, to establish my precise feelings.

Several times I'd started composing emails to Quin, asking if I could write to his kids. But the memory of that last morning in his front hall, both of us 'fessing up to having cheated, cast a long shadow. There had been such rancour that I was reluctant to contact him, for fear of getting more of the same.

Something else was holding me back: I had no clue if things were done forever with Quin. Every single day I was surprised—almost shocked—by his absence. Did that mean I loved him? Enough to get past what we'd both done?

The only thing I knew for sure was that I knew nothing.

'Well, thank you!' It was Wednesday morning and Yara's flowers were finally beginning to blossom. On Sunday evening, after Margaret's brunch, I thought I'd detected the *tiniest* relaxing of the tightly clenched buds. Monday not so much. Or yesterday. But overnight, big changes had taken place.

Tell him.

Luke, the flowers have started. Looking good for the weekend. Does it suit if I FaceTime on your Saturday night, approx 11.30? Too late? X

Not too late. But very early for you to be getting up? 6.30am? You want to make it later? It's good with me? L x

All good with 11.30pm. Talk then x

By Saturday evening, the tree was an explosion of pink petals.

'Stay that way,' I warned Yara. 'You better be *perfect* tomorrow morning.'

I will be. Then, *Lol.*

So much for Luke offering me a later time—I was awake at 5 a.m. Still, it gave me plenty of time to fiddle around with my hair and skin and basically *obsess*.

Fresh, that's how I wanted to look. Likeable.

Loveable, actually. I might as well admit it. It was the wrong thing to yearn for but the heart wants what the heart wants.

Out in the garden, the tree looked perfect. Six thirty rolled around and, almost breathless with anticipation, I made the call. And there he was, smiling.

'Hey.' I had to fight an urge to hug my iPad. 'How are you?'

'Okay. Great, really. So! Let's see our little girl's tree.'

For a moment, the breath caught in my chest, the sorrow was so intense. But as I turned the camera, my grief made room for a certain pride. 'Exquisite, isn't it?'

'Totally. But of course it is. *She* was exquisite.'

Thank you.

After circumnavigating the tree twice, I turned the camera back to me. 'I'll send you tons of photos. And would you like some of the petals?'

He seemed surprised. 'Yes! I'd *love* them.'

'Send me your address, I'll post them!'

'Okay, thanks. So how was your week?'

An image of Helen flashed in my head and a second too late I answered, 'Fine.'

He went still. 'What?' he asked. 'Rachel? Is something wrong?'

Should I tell him? 'My sister Helen, she's pregnant.'

'Hey. God almighty.' He blinked. 'That's . . . is the world ready? And you feel . . . ? Babe, it's okay to be jealous.'

'It's not that. I'm worried that it'll all go wrong for her.' Since Helen had announced her pregnancy, anxiety had set up camp in my chest.

'Is there any reason to think it might?'

'None. The chances are tiny. Just that I know it happens. I mean, I *know* it, in my body, if that makes sense?'

He sighed. 'Yeah. Hopefully it'll be grand.'

'Luke . . . What's this about feeling jealous? Do you feel that way?'

'Me? Nah!'

We both laughed.

'Just.' He shook his head. 'Sometimes. There's Joey, spawning kids left, right and centre . . .'

'How many has he now?'

'Four. I know, it's hardly a multitude. But he barely even sees his eldest . . . There are times I want to . . .'

'Speak sternly to him?'

'Yeah.' He smiled. 'Very sternly. But it's okay. It hurts but it's okay. That's about as good as it'll get.'

'How are you feeling about your mum?'

'Doing grief counselling.'

'You *are*?' I didn't know why I was so surprised, after all, he'd told me he'd seen a therapist when he'd first moved to Denver.

'Oh yeah! This is me now, Rachel! Owning my stuff.'

I laughed. I couldn't help it.

'What else is going on for you?' he asked.

'Visiting Brigit the weekend after next.'

'Oh, amazing! How *is* the Brigit of Madison County? Still in that incredible place?'

'Even more incredible now.'

'Rachel, would this be weird? Could you FaceTime me from there?'

'Well, sure. I can show you some of the changes. They've converted the old cow house into a studio, for yoga workshops or painting schools. Residential ones, like. Brigit's new career, hopefully. There's a painting school later in the summer. I'm working at it.'

'Doing what?' Luke seemed confused. 'Counselling?'

'Excuse me! I have other skills too, you know.'

'Oh, I *know*.'

'I'll be helping Bridge. Cooking for the guests.'

'What?' he spluttered. '*You?*'

'Hahahaha! Yeah! Things really have changed. I can cook now.'

Over-dramatically, he blinked. 'I can't even.'

Back in the day, neither Luke nor I could cook. Because we managed the occasional stir-fry, we thought we could, but when it mattered we discovered we couldn't.

Suddenly I said, 'Do you remember the night my managers from Hope House were coming to dinner—'

'—do I remember? Oh my God!'

I'd been angling for a permanent position and fear had made me embark on a menu which was far too ambitious. Luke had been my assistant and we were both fathoms out of our depth.

'You were yelling instructions from the book,' Luke said. 'What was it you kept saying? "Thinly sliced! Luke, these shallots aren't thin enough!"'

'And you said, "They're so thin, they're fucking invisible."'

'Then I tore off my apron—'

'—which I'd made you wear—'

'—threw it on the floor and announced, "I QUIT!"'

We both got a wild fit of laughing at the memory. I was helpless, so was he and the release was joyous. Every uncomfortable emotion held in my body, from the very pit of my stomach, up through the clenched tension of my chest, just spun away. It was gorgeous.

Wiping my face, I picked up my screen. My eyes met Luke's and I said, 'I QUIT!' And it began all over again.

When we had regained control, Luke said, 'I can't remember the last time I laughed like that. So, I should go to bed, you need to get on with your day. And we'll talk on her anniversary?'

'Yes. Yep.'

'Try to not worry about Helen.'

'Thanks.' I smiled, still on a high. 'Take care.'

And he was gone.

Had I imagined it?

Or *had* he actually been flirting?

When he'd agreed that I had skills other than counselling? The twinkle in his eye? The way he'd said, 'Oh, I *know*'?

Had I imagined it?

Or was this what friendship with him was like?

86

The last ten minutes of the drive were always the most beautiful. On both sides of the bumpy boreen were theatres of green-grey rocks or fields that plunged and rose steeply.

Overhead, a massive expanse of mauve-coloured sky threatened rain—torrential, by the looks of things. But in seconds, the clouds had changed to a less ominous grey-blue, and just as I arrived at Brigit's house, the sun was blazing.

I'd been here with Luke and I'd been here with Quin and now I was here alone.

You know it's not an either/or? Suddenly Yara was very loud and clear in my head. *It doesn't have to be a choice between Quin and Luke. You can have a very happy life without either of them.*

Okaaay. I had to sit for a moment, to absorb her wisdom.

Here Brigit came, running in jeans and a rough sweater, her arms open. It was shockingly lovely to see her.

'You're early!' She caught me in a close hug and we half danced, half wrestled in her front yard.

'I'm not. But you know my theory.' Which was that ex-big-city girls went overboard embracing the whole fey Connemara time-is-elastic thing. The blow-ins were always the worst offenders.

'What's going on with your hair?' I asked.

'Got one of those spray-in Krazy Kolours in Dealz, they only had carmine. It runs in the rain. You'll probably see it in action later. So come in, we'll all have lunch, then go to Femke's to pick up a jar of rose harissa.'

Whenever I visited, most of my time seemed to be spent in the passenger seat of Brigit's jeep, traversing the townland of Maumtully, dropping things off and picking things up. It was a billion times more enjoyable and bonding than any contrived spa days or afternoon teas.

'Femke is the lovely Dutch woman in the mansion?'

'That's the one.'

Into the glassy dream house, where I had hugs with Colm and the four kids: fifteen-year-old Lenehan, sweet and straightforward; fourteen-year-old Sully, a confident charmer; ten-year-old Ree, chatty and cheeky; and nine-year-old Queenie, suspicious and hilarious.

Brigit put a sturdy loaf of bread on the table. 'Treacle and walnut.' Then a heavy ceramic saucepan. 'Vegetable soup.'

'Did you make this?' I asked.

'Are you *mad*? Remember Arthur Ankles?' A Welsh ex-footballer who'd had a breakdown and retreated from the world. 'He's working in the hotel now, doing lunches. Great at soups and breads. And, oh my God, his flapjacks!'

Outside, in the sunlight, the greens were a sharp emerald, then the light dipped and the landscape became a muted sage.

'It's ridiculously beautiful here.'

'Try saying that on a November day,' Colm said. 'When it's been raining for a week and a half and the Lidl wine lorry is late.'

'Haha. You're only saying that because you're embarrassed by how wonderful your life is.'

As soon as we'd eaten, Brigit directed me towards the mud-spattered jeep and we set off at speed down the bumpy track. At the turn of the peninsula, a vast beach appeared, grains of white sand blowing in the wind. Beyond was a flat expanse of silver-grey diamonds.

'Tide's going out,' Brigit said, veering sharply inland towards the town. On Main Street we passed a lanky man outside the hardware store. Brigit exclaimed, 'Padraig!' and pulled in suddenly.

'Just need to return his wetsuit.' She jumped from the jeep. 'Two seconds.'

I followed her because I knew that a two-second handover of a wetsuit would become fifteen minutes of intense chat. All fine with me, I was on my holidays.

Padraig was full of news: there had been a 'ruckus' in the creamery; the hotel had offered Arthur Ankles a contract until Halloween and 'the powers that be' were worried about some 'young fellas coming from Dublin' for the August bank holiday. Apparently they didn't 'want a repeat of last year'.

About five minutes into the chat, when the drizzle began, neither Brigit nor Padraig noticed. My theory was that when you'd lived here for half a year, you grew a water-repellent coating. Not fully waterproof—you wouldn't survive a dunking in a rain barrel, say—but light precipitation no longer penetrated.

After we—eventually—said goodbye to Padraig, we got cash from the ATM, filled a prescription for Ree, picked up a plug for Brigit's father-in-law's haybob, then went to Femke's mansion, where we were offered hot drinks from a machine designed by Dolce & Gabbana.

Driving back on the old bog road, I suddenly said, 'Bridge? Have I ever thanked you for saving my life? Twenty years ago?'

'. . . Yes.' She looked surprised. 'Lots of times. Why?'

'I just wanted to say it again.'

'Okay. You're welcome. It's being in contact with Luke, isn't it? Bringing back memories?'

'So I'll be okay?'

'You already *are* okay. Look at all the freedom you have.'

'You're right, Bridge!' Suddenly it hit me. 'I can do anything with my life.'

'Like what? Go on, Rachel, tell me.'

This was what we used to do when we'd shared an apartment—construct beautiful futures for each other.

'. . . Okay,' I said. 'I'd go to London, where I'd befriend some posh old lady, living in a grace-and-favour apartment, whatever they are. She has a giant stash of fabulous vintage handbags—Chanel, Hermès, Goyard, more Chanel . . .'

'And she gives them to you?' Brigit gasped.

'Ah *now*. This is a fantasy but nothing is that easy.'

'I have it! She's down on her luck, I don't know, a dispute with her son, or something. You propose that she sells some of the bags—'

'—but she'd be mortified by going along to the local designer exchange, so I'd set her up online, running the whole show, loading the images to the site, setting up her PayPal account, dealing with all the admin—'

'Colm could help, if you had any IT issues—'

'That's handy, thanks. So the old lady—'

'What's her name? Some posh thing. Persephone?'

'Perfect. So Persephone would be impressed. But she doesn't want to pay me—'

'She's stingy? Posh people are often stingy.'

'Well, no, she's *skint*. Because of the dispute with the son. But she gives me one free handbag in exchange for every ten I sell.'

'Ah, not ten, Rachel! Every eight.'

'Let's make it seven. Six, then. And I'd always take a Chanel.'

'I cannot believe there was a time when labels mattered to me . . .'

'You're an evolved being, Bridge—'

'—but I'm still happy for you.'

'*Any*way, at some stage, Persephone will die and I don't want to be sad . . .'

'Maybe she wasn't very nice? She hated the Irish? Only let you into her apartment because she thought you were Scottish?'

That made me laugh a lot. 'Then I'd discover she'd left me all the unsold bags in her will. I'd feel a little guilty. Although I did go to her funeral—'

'—the only person other than her chiropodist—'

'But I'd own fifty Chanel bags and how could I be anything other than gloriously happy. Bridge, I will be fine!'

Back at the house, after a short savage downpour, the sun came out again, the whole world appearing squeaky clean.

'Now would be a good time to ring Luke,' Brigit said. 'Before the next shower.'

It was eleven in the morning in Denver but Luke answered, seeming smiley and delighted. 'Hey.'

'I thought you might be out horse-riding,' I said.

'Nope. Sitting here all morning waiting for your call.'

I laughed. 'Here's Bridge for you.' I passed her my iPad.

'Luke.' Her voice was weepy. 'I'm so sorry about your mum. I sent a card to your brother's address . . . you got it?' Tears were flowing freely down her face. 'Oh, I'm fine,' she said, and now she was laughing. 'Just an attack of nostalgia. It's so *nice* to see you. You'll always be my favourite seventies throwback.'

'Setback,' Luke replied.

'Paperback.'

'Hunchback.'

Brigit barked with laughter and replied, 'Horseback.'

'Niiiiiiiiice,' Luke said.

'You should come visit. Some weekend when Rachel's here. We'll have a reunion. We're middle-aged now, that's what middle-aged people do. Reunions. Will you come? Seriously?'

'Brigit!' I stood up, and took the iPad from her.

'Sorry about that,' I told Luke. 'Don't mind her.'

'So I'm *not* invited?'

God, at times all of this 'light-hearted' banter was so draining. At times it actually made me sad. 'Take it up with her. So? Would you like a tour of the changes here?'

'Yeah. Great.'

Crossing the uneven, bumpy land to the converted cowhouse, I showed him around, then took him along the boundary line.

'What about our lake?' He asked. 'Do you have time to go there?'

Abruptly, Kallie's hints about her life-changing good news popped into my head and punctured any remaining positivity.

I didn't want to reminisce about the magical lake because, although it was where he'd asked me to marry him, in the end we'd got divorced.

Unable to fake light-heartedness, I said, 'It was only our lake briefly.'

'Okay.' Luke also seemed dispirited. 'Talk soon.'

87

My mood stayed low. Almost as soon as I got back from Brigit's another photo of Luke popped up on Kallie's Insta. Elbows resting behind him, on the top bar of a high gate, he was in jeans, a plaid shirt and sunglasses. Next to him were two giant horses and the caption was, 'Always my happiest, hanging out with these sexy animals.'

It wasn't a posed shot, Luke was looking away. But still.

'It's ambiguous,' Claire said. 'She might have taken a sneaky shot of him, like the mad bunny-boiler yoke she is—'

'Claire, she honestly isn't—'

'Look. Why don't you just grow up and ask him if they're still together.'

Because if he was, I didn't think I could bear it.

'At least she hasn't done any more of that "Good news coming soon, send me your thoughts and prayers" bullshit,' Claire said.

But the very next *day*, up Kallie pops on her stories, all glee and sparkle. 'Hi, guys! Oh boy! I need *all* of your positive energy. I'm super sorry I can't tell you guys yet! Just trust me that fin-al-ly there's a lot of good stuff maaaaybe happening. A lot, a *lot*. It's super-hard to not tell you but I gotta do this the right way.'

After watching it another nine or ten times, I was no better informed. Would she be putting this up on her stories if she was talking about moving in with Luke, knowing that Luke might see it?

Maybe Luke wouldn't see it, though? He wasn't on Instagram.

Oh my God, I was so *tired* from all the uncertainty. Maybe Claire was right and I should just talk to him.

But I did nothing about it. It was far nicer to exist in an imaginary place where all things were still possible.

About a week later, on a warm June night, Luke texted. Sorry if this is a bad time. Can you take a quick call? FaceTime? X

Barely able to hit the keys, I replied, FaceTime me right now x

Moments later, my iPad starting bing-bonging. 'Luke?'

'Wanted to run something by you. In a few weeks' time, I'm coming to Dublin. Just for two days, I've a couple of meetings. I'd love to stay longer but I need to get back. Would you have time—Could we . . . see each other?'

I took a breath, caught up in several conflicting thoughts. On the surface, this was a tangible opportunity to demonstrate our transition to friends, to discover that that one night together had been genuinely healing.

But while we remained separated by seven thousand kilometres, Luke and I were suspended in a fact-free bubble where I could fantasize about us being together again and nothing could contradict me.

When we met in person, the either/or would have to stop.

'What dates?' I asked.

'Monday the ninth of July, I have to fly back the eleventh.'

'Oh.' There was a sudden sinking feeling, which was also a relief. 'I'll be in Transylvania.'

'Transyl-what?' he said. 'The Dracula place?'

In my head, I heard Quin's voice. *Rach,* this *fucking hayseed!* This *is the guy you think you want?*

'There aren't actual vampires, Luke. It sounds more exciting than it is, but I can't get out of it. Long story, Quin and I booked months ago, with our friends Taryn—'

'Hey. It's okay. Calm down. I'll get you next time I'm in town.' Then, 'Vampires, eh? The best I could give you was the redneck Riviera.'

'But it was beauti—'

'Stop.' He was gentle. 'I was kidding. We'll talk on her anniversary.'

88

'The bootees she wore in the hospital.' I held up the minuscule socks to the camera. 'A lock of her hair.' Taking care, I produced items from Yara's memory box, all of them so fragile and precious. A sheaf of photographic paper turned up. 'Every one of her scans. And remember this?' The rabbit mobile for above her crib. 'And these? The satin ballerina slippers you bought her, remember?'

'Oh, God, yeah.' His voice was choked.

'Luke, you could have taken some of these when you left.'

He shook his head. 'I already felt too guilty. I had my share of her ashes, it was enough.'

'Have you done something with them?'

'Not yet. I'm still waiting for the right place.'

'I don't know if you remember but the nurses took impressions of her feet. A few years ago, I got a jeweller to reproduce them. Look.' I displayed two tiny silver versions of Yara's beautiful little feet, sweet and weighty in the centre of my hand.

'Oh God.' Luke looked teary.

'I'll get a pair made for you! And copies of the scans. I'll post them as soon as they're done. It might be a while, though. The jeweller took around two months to make these.'

'Thanks—'

'No, Luke, thank you. It's . . . I appreciate having someone to share this day with.'

'What have you done other years?'

'Worked in the garden. Got out the memory box. Cried.' I half laughed. 'You know yourself. You?'

'Saddled up Shadow, went to the mountains. Being out there, in the vast emptiness, I guess it puts things more in perspective.' Then, 'What sort of person do you think she'd have been?'

'Like you, I'd have hoped. You're so good at being content—well, you were. Maybe you're different now?'

A long silence followed. 'God, I don't know how to answer that.'

'You don't seem dissatisfied? Narky? Always looking for better?'

'. . . I'm not always looking for better. If I have something good, I'm grateful.'

'There you are, then. You know, Luke, I didn't want her to be like me. I was worried that she'd be an addict.'

'But if she was, she was. People have to go their own path.'

'I didn't want her to go through the pain of it. And I didn't want to cause you any more worry, you'd already been through enough with me.'

'Hey.' His voice was gentle. 'It wasn't that bad.'

'Oh, don't. I caused you so much misery that you ran away to Denver.'

'You couldn't help it.' Luke seemed distressed. 'I was thinking . . . Maybe next year you and I could meet in New York? In Brooklyn?'

It felt as if a hundred daggers had been plunged deep into my lungs. 'Luke, I absolutely couldn't . . .' It hurt to take a breath. 'Honestly, that's the saddest thing I can think of. Being back there with you, where we'd once been so happy . . .'

'Sorry.' He was alarmed. 'I thought it might help.'

'I'm okay. Really. But those years, before it all went wrong . . . It sort of horrifies me that I didn't know it, at the time, how ridiculously happy I was. On my deathbed, I'm sure it will stand out as the best part of my life.'

'Same,' he said. 'We had no clue how blessed we were.'

Tentatively, I asked, 'What was it that made it so . . . special?'

After a thoughtful pause, he took a breath. 'Not the obvious stuff. I fancied you, Rachel, I always fancied you, you know that, but it wasn't about fireworks. It was the opposite. What you gave me was . . . I guess the word is *relief*. Remember as a kid if you lost your dad in a crowd, just for a moment. You start freaking out—then you'd spot him. Remember that, like, *whoosh* of relief?'

There was a lump in my throat.

'Other people like drama—look at Joey. Actually, don't. Dude's a train-wreck. But you calmed me.'

'I did? That's very . . .' It was difficult to speak. 'But now that you've said it . . . Whenever I saw you, before my brain even registered it, my soul was going, "Everything's okay because Luke's here." You're quite . . . moral. More, I guess . . . inflexible than some? I always knew where I was with you. I loved it.'

Luke had been an uncomplicated man and with him, I'd walked towards safety again and again.

'Weren't we lucky?' he said.

'So lucky.'

'Don't cry that it's over—'

'—smile because it happened.' My voice faltered.

'About "that night".' He hesitated over the words. 'You were right about it being healing. I'd come a long way anyway, but I feel more, I guess, peaceful now.'

'Me too. Losing Yara, it's always there, like a . . . a spiky ball of torn metal, in my flesh. It's part of every decision I make and every relationship I have. But recently it's got . . . smoother? Smaller? I'll always love her, but her loss is starting to fold into my story.'

'We've a lot to be thankful for.'

That was the right way to look at things.

'Enjoy Transylvania,' he said.

89

I *did* enjoy Transylvania.

Sort of.

Taryn and Timothy were great company, the hills and lakes were stunning, the people and food were delightful but I experienced two parallel versions of everything. One was the reality, but in the other I was accompanied by an invisible hologram of Quin, who offered opinions, thoughts, contradictions and directions.

Every step I took, every bite of food I ate, he was with me.

So much so that, on the second last night, lying on the strange sheets, in a strange guest house, in a strange, beautiful land, I got up out of bed and, suddenly *certain* I was doing the right thing, sent an email, asking if he'd meet me when I got home.

I was blurry about what exactly I hoped for—maybe just to check that he was okay?—but, feeling calmer than I had in a while, I slept well. The next morning I lunged for my phone, hoping he had replied—but there was nothing.

It was still early though—maybe he hadn't woken yet.

On that day's hike, as we moved in and out of coverage, I kept checking. Still no reply from him. He could be away working. Sometimes his job was so intense that everything else got parked.

But by the time my plane landed at Dublin Airport, I had to face it: I wasn't going to be hearing from him.

Deflated and confused, I was no longer sure that that was even what I wanted. I felt as if I missed Quin more in Romania than in Dublin—which made no sense, other than to demonstrate that, over three months on, I still hadn't a clue what was right for me.

It wasn't all bad, though. Since marking Yara's anniversary with Luke, there was definitely a deeper healing. The loss had softened and all of my bitterness towards him had evaporated.

There were even fleeting moments when what I secretly called My Important Thoughts and Feelings shrank down to nothing. Looked at in a cosmic sense, my life wasn't remarkable or important, it simply was.

In those glimpses, everything appeared exactly as it should be: beautiful and bad; painful and good. Wanting things to be different would change nothing. I'd been given what I'd been given and my only job was acceptance.

. . . But there were other times when I went on Kallie Lampart's Insta, poring over every post, looking for clues about Luke and her.

I had an ally in Claire, which wasn't necessarily healthy. This became clear the day after my return from Romania, at Molly's birthday tea party. Claire, in a performatively over-starched "garden party" type of dress, greeted me with cucumber sandwiches and a cheery, 'Three weeks since the last photo of him and a horse!'

'What's this now?' Helen's antennae had pricked up. She lumbered towards us, her hand on her lower back, as if she were two years pregnant instead of fourteen weeks.

'Nothing.' I was hasty. She had nothing nice to say about Luke. Ever.

But, too late, Claire was explaining, then Helen was scrutinizing Kallie's grid.

'Costello doesn't like having his photo taken, *that's* obvious,' she said. 'But there's nothing here to say they're not together. This Kallie is a Tragic who'd post a shit ton of "Me and my gal pals out drinking strawberry daiquiris" whenever she gets dumped—'

'You know nothing about her,' I protested.

'I'm only pregnant,' Helen declared hotly, 'not blind! The evidence here says she's still Costello's girl.'

The thought made me want to cry. 'They're probably out on his deck,' I admitted. 'Smoking hash, dancing to the Doobie Brothers, having a great old time.'

'The Doobie Brothers?' Helen was already googling. 'Who are they?'

Next thing, her phone was playing 'Long Train Runnin'', attracting startled looks from across the garden.

'Fuck, yeah!' Helen was in stitches. 'I can *so* see Costello out there, grooving away to this shit.'

Don't say that. Please.

But later, when almost everyone had left, she took me aside. 'I shouldn't have said Costello is still with that Tragic. I was trying to be tough for you, but that wasn't what you wanted?'

'Well, I—'

'Thing is, I . . . yeah . . . tend to *hold a grudge*.'

No kidding.

'You say you relapsed and it wasn't his fault he left you. That's too complicated for me.'

'Okaaaay.'

'Here's the facts: I enjoy grudges, I don't like giving up on them. But even though I'm an excellent private investigator, I can't be sure what's going on with the pair of them. Those photos could be misleading. Rachel, I . . . I apologize.'

An apology from Helen was quite the event. But it made no difference because I was accepting it was time for me to move on.

The man of my fantasies wasn't the current real-life Luke, but a different one from long ago, before I'd got pregnant, before I'd relapsed, before life had twisted and reshaped us into less innocent versions of ourselves. The irony was that the Luke I was hung up on wouldn't have slept with me, not while he had a partner.

My crush had lasted too long. Now it was just making me miserable. It was time to cop on, to be grateful for all the good that had come from meeting Luke again, from him being my friend.

90

About a week later, when his name popped up on my phone, my heart soared. Yeah, so Rome wasn't built in a day. Next time I'd do better.

'Hey,' I said to him.

'Hey, yourself!' And there was his beautiful face. 'So I'm coming to Ireland again for a few days.'

'Oh. Right. Great.' Or maybe not. Time would tell.

'Could we meet? I'll be there from the fourteenth of August to the seventeenth.'

'Oh, I'll be with Brigit! Working at her summer school.'

'Are we ever going to see each other again?' He strove for a jokey tone but he sounded genuinely exasperated.

'There's no chance you could change your dates?'

'No. It's legal stuff, involving other people.'

'Your mum's will?'

'Wha—? Oh, no.' Then, 'Nothing like that.'

An odd little pause followed.

Did he want me to ask for details? I sensed he did, but what if I was just projecting? How excruciating would that be?

'So . . .' I said. 'Will you be in Ireland for Christmas?' As conversational gambits go, this was poor stuff: Christmas was five months away.

But, surprising me, he said, 'We're going to Malta, all of us. First one without Mum, no one wants to try to recreate Marjorie's Christmas dinners, not this year anyway, it's too sad. We're going to the sun instead. Dad's idea. He's put Vanessa in charge, God love her.' Then, 'Would you like to come?'

'Haha.'

'Seriously. There are dozens of us. Devin and Kate are coming. So is Mattie's son's girlfriend and Vanessa's daughter's fella. No one would notice an extra person.'

Is Kallie going? Are they still together?

'So many people have confirmed, then pulled out, then confirmed again that there's bound to be a spare bed.'

Ask him, Yara yelled. *For the love of all that's holy!*

'Haha,' I repeated dully.

'Well, think about it . . .'

This time I didn't even bother with my fake haha. 'Listen, I've seen the jeweller, she'll have the two little pieces ready in maybe seven weeks. So I'll mail them to the same address as I sent the petals?'

'Ah.' He seemed startled. 'No, Rachel. No. Let's see . . . Could you send them to Justin's? That's probably the safest.'

'They can go FedEx if you're worried about them getting lost in the post?'

'No. Ah . . . no. Just . . .'

'Oh?' Then something made me brave enough to ask, 'Are you . . . moving house?'

'Yes.'

In with Kallie?

Ask! Him!

Rachel, for the love of God, ask him!

After a long, awkward pause, he said, 'How's Helen?'

He always asked—and I appreciated it. No one else seemed worried.

Although, why would they be? Helen was fine.

91

'Hi.' I smiled at a woman who looked vaguely familiar.

I had dropped into a Thursday evening NA meeting in Blackrock. It wasn't one of my regulars but it was as good as any.

'Kitchen's that way.' Someone pointed to the side of the room.

After I'd made a mug of camomile tea, I was looking for a chair when I *felt* something behind me. I turned to see a knot of radiant faces—to my astonishment it was Chalkie, Bronte, Giles, Roxy and Lowry.

'Rachel!' Bronte declared. 'Is it really you?'

'What . . . ?' Giles looked stupefied with shock. 'Why are you here?'

I glanced at Chalkie, who discreetly drew an imaginary zip across his mouth. Clearly, he hadn't told the others about me being in recovery.

'Same reason as you,' I told Giles.

'Is this a new development?' Roxy was absolutely stunned. 'Or . . .'

'Not new.' I smiled. This was funny. Lovely. I was delighted to see them.

But almost my first thought had been, Are Chalkie and Bronte a *thing*? It was hard to tell just from looking at them.

'Are we allowed to talk to you?' Lowry asked.

'Course we are, ya cretin.' This from Chalkie. 'We're all equal in NA.'

'And *outside* of NA,' Giles said.

Chalkie slanted him some reluctant approval. 'We'll make a socialist of you yet.'

'You absolutely won't.'

I beamed around at the five of them. 'Every one of you looks great.'

'Clean and serene,' Chalkie said. 'That's us.'

'How come you're all together tonight?'

'We do it all the time!' Roxy said.

'Touring,' Lowry said. 'Keeping it fresh. Trying out lots of different meetings.'

'We're friends,' Chalkie said. 'Good friends.' Then, watching me, he mouthed, *Just*.

Okay. Good. That was the right thing for both of them.

'Are you in touch with . . . ?' Then I wished I hadn't asked. At least one of the recent ducklings wouldn't have made it.

'Dennis and I text,' Bronte said. 'He'll be *bouleversé* when he hears about us meeting you.'

'I'm in contact with Trassa,' Giles said. 'She's doing well. *Very* well. And Harlie's good. Sober. Going to AA.'

An awkward silence followed.

'Ella, though . . .' Chalkie said. 'She . . . ah. Went back on the tablets.'

My heart slid towards my toes.

But it happened. Not everyone who went to rehab was ready or able. Or willing. Maybe Ella's time would come in another year or so.

And maybe it never would.

That was addiction, the ugly truth of it. Some addicts would never recover.

Meanwhile, there were five people here tonight who were getting well and I'd played a part in it. There was a lot to be happy about.

'Sit in here with us.' Chalkie urged me into the middle of their cluster of chairs.

'All that time you were running group,' Bronte mused, 'you were in recovery?'

'We were terrified of you,' Giles admitted.

'And kinda *obsessed*,' Roxy said. 'Wondering what you did when you weren't scaring us shitless.'

'If you had a cat?'

'A boyfriend?'

'A girlfriend?'

'Where you bought your sneakers . . . ?'

'No wonder you were so good at it.' Bronte was still chewing over my dual identity. 'Are all the counsellors in recovery?'

'In the Cloisters? I think I'm the only one at the moment. But the woman who was my counsellor when I was there—'

That made them squeal. 'You went to the Cloisters too!'

'Yes.' They were so cute. '*She* was in recovery.'

Sister Josephine. The greatest of them all.

Almost ten years ago, she'd died, having helped literally hundreds of us get clean and sober. She was still my inspiration every single day.

92

Four nights later—a Monday—I zipped into the Dundrum parking lot, heading for Aldi. I had twenty minutes before it closed.

Hurrying past Marks & Spencer, making for the top floor, the over-lit mall was almost deserted. Someone had once told me this was the very best time to do your weekly shop.

Behind me, a person called, 'Rachel?'

I turned. It was—of all people—Quin. 'Hey!' Spontaneously, I gathered him into a hug. Smiling into his face, I declared, 'It's so *nice* to see you.'

In less excitable but still friendly tones, he said, 'And it's so nice to see you.'

We stood, grinning at each other—which was strange because our last encounter had been absolutely horrible.

'How *are* you?'

'I am . . .' He had to think about it. 'I'm okay. You? What are you up to?'

I slid my hands from his shoulders, I shouldn't be pawing him. 'Going to Aldi. You?'

'Going in here.' He pointed at Marks & Spencer.

'Of course you are.' I'd just remembered who'd given me the tip-off about the Monday night shopping—Quin! Who else?

'Have you time for a drink?' he asked.

'Sure. Where should we go? Oh, you'll know somewhere fabulous.'

He cast a hunted glance around the glaringly bright concourse. 'The best I can come up with is the café in House of Fraser. Jesus, I can't believe I just said that.'

'Haha, come on, let's go.'

'I'd honestly prefer to sit in a shop doorway and drink bottles of Buckfast. There has to be someplace better . . . Got it. Five-minute walk outside. You up for that?'

'Sure.'

Escaping the glass and chrome monolith, we made our way along Dundrum's original small-town streets.

'In here, Rach.' Quin pushed at a low door on the main street and ushered me through a tiny pub to a flower-filled courtyard beyond. Very quiet—not many takers on this summer night.

'It's gorgeous,' I said. 'Why am I even surprised?'

'Obviously spending time with the wrong sort of men. Drink? Fizzy water?' In moments, Quin was back with a bottle of IPA and a glass of water. He sat opposite me.

'Thanks, I—'

'So?' He interrupted. 'You and your ex-husband?'

God. No pleasantries, just straight in? Okay.

'He went back to Denver. It was just a, you know, a one-off.'

A shock of sadness lit Quin's eyes. 'So it was all for nothing.'

Not exactly. Luke and I didn't pick up where we'd left off all those years ago, but some good had come from our night together.

Quin cleared his throat, then he fixed me with a look. 'You sort of . . . broke me, you know?'

'I didn't mean to. I'm sorry. I was—am—incredibly sorry for hurting you.'

'I missed you badly. It was . . . hard going for a while. I loved you, you know. Did you ever . . . feel . . . ?'

'I *did* love you.'

'But?'

'I wasn't ready. To commit, fully. I was stuck, as Nola kept saying.'

Silently, we both stared at the table. I began circling a knot in the wood with my thumbnail.

Quietly, he said, 'I'm sorry, Rach. In a lifetime of dick moves, sleeping with Golden was the most dick of them all.'

'Quin, no. It was *my* fault.' The business with Golden had shocked and wounded me. But as far back as our first night in Barcelona, Quin had intuited what I was unable to face: that I'd fallen for Luke again. Quin had been thrashing about in pain, he hadn't been able to help it. 'I should have stayed away from Luke. Anyone could see it was dangerous and I did it anyway.'

He sighed heavily. 'I was trying hard to be Mr *So*-Not-Bothered.'

The tip of my thumb was moving in furious circles on the tabletop.

His head bowed, Quin spoke quickly. 'I was okay for the first week or so that he was around, then I began to feel the way I had during the weeks, months, whatever, when Shiv had stopped loving me and I was trying to not know. When you wake in the middle of the night and you know you're *right* to be scared—'

'Quin, I'm sorry—'

'—when you said you wanted to sleep with him, it was almost a relief.'

Carefully, I said, 'No judgement here but . . . you'd already slept with Golden by then?'

He winced. 'Got my retaliation in first, just like I did with Shiv. As if that was ever going to work. Have I learnt nothing?'

'Next time,' I said. 'You'll get it right then.'

'I dunno. Old dog, new tricks . . .' He laughed and shook his head. 'If the ex-husband hadn't reappeared, do you think you and I would have gone the distance?'

This was something I'd given a lot of thought to. 'I do. It's obvious now that I wasn't fully . . . available, I suppose the word is. But we all have baggage and, despite mine, I was very happy with you.'

'So why did you do it? The lure of the bland food? The "outdoorsy" life?' He shook his head. 'Nah. It was those fucking leather . . . thighs?'

I couldn't help smiling. 'I got the chance to tidy up a lot of my past.'

And in doing so, I lost Quin. But everything comes at a cost.

I wondered if Quin and Golden were still a thing? 'What about you and—' I asked, at the same time as Quin said, 'Is Bland Man still with the Grifter?'

'Who—oh, you mean Kallie? As far as I know, yes.'

'Seriously? Wow.' He shook his head. 'Respect. That was one risky game she played.'

'How was it a game?'

'Rach.' He seemed incredulous. 'Her! Checking you out! To see how you rolled, all the better to ensnare Mr . . .' He waved his hand with contempt. '. . . Leather-Pants-Love-God.'

'She wasn't that cynical.'

'Rach, she was a *right* chancer. I'm still waiting to be paid back for that doctor's appointment.'

I faked a frown. 'Maybe give her a quick text? Just a nudge?' And we both managed to laugh.

'Seriously, though,' I said. 'She was putting all her spare cash into her music career. Have some sympathy.'

'Oh?' he said, 'I didn't know . . . I'm sorry.'

The irony was that Quin had been the person who had played a risky game. When the threat of Luke appeared, he had stepped forward to meet it. It was Quin who had booked that doctor's appointment for Kallie, Quin who had convinced me to have dinner with them. Betting—incorrectly—that the more I saw of Luke, the less I'd idealize him.

'So what you're saying is', Quin said, 'you backed the wrong horse.'

Quin wasn't getting that, for me, it had been much more than a simple choice between two men. Luke had crashed back into my life as a catalyst, opening my eyes to complex truths, then leaving all kinds of dust to settle in new ways in new places.

'Thing is,' Quin said awkwardly, spreading his hands on the table, 'I moved too fast to end things. Because I was ashamed of being the loser.'

I waited.

'If—on the day after your mum's party—*if* I could have coped with you having been with . . . ah . . . *him*, would you have given it a go? With me?'

I waited some more. 'Have you forgotten that you'd already slept with Golden?'

That stymied him, but only briefly. 'So we both fucked up. And now we're quits.'

Things were very simple from Quin's perspective: I'd hurt him, he'd hurt me back, and the counter was automatically reset to zero. But I was no longer the person I'd been before that night with Luke.

And right now, I wanted to know if Quin was still with Golden? Or someone else?

'How are your sisters?' he asked.

'Helen's pregnant! Sixteen weeks!'

'Holy fuck! That's . . . terrifying. Is she the first pregnant woman in the history of the world?'

'No one has ever had morning sickness before. Or an ache in their lower back. The actual birth will be reported on the news like it's a natural disaster.'

'And Claire?' He sighed. 'I miss Claire.'

'She misses you too. They all do. But everyone's fine. What about Liberty and Finley?'

He brightened. 'Liberty's good. Going through a happier phase. And Fin is great. Does nothing but eat.'

'That's my boy. And your mum and dad? Michelle? Robert?' He could feck off if he thought I was going to enquire about Shiv and Garrett.

'All living their best lives.' He threw me a wry glance. 'Winning. At everything. Tennis. Happy marriages. Career trajectories.'

I wondered about asking if I could 'reach out' to them, then settled for saying, 'Give them my love.'

Quin nodded at my empty glass. 'Another?'

Oh. I looked at him with curiosity. Was I imagining that he was holding his breath? That *I* was?

There was a mood, as if a match were poised against flint, waiting to be struck. A moment passed. Then another. I exhaled. 'No. Thanks. Work in the morning.'

He watched me, his expression hinting at something. 'If I texted you in a few days, could we get a coffee?'

He was so confident, so persuasive, already certain I'd agree.

'Quin. What about you and Golden? Was it a one-off . . . ?'

My voice trailed away as I watched him flush. With an awkward laugh, he said, 'We're, ah—look, I don't . . . She sometimes . . . Hey, you remember Prosser? How he and she . . . ? Well, that's still in play.'

'And you too? You're Golden's *sidepiece*?'

'. . . Ah, yeah. No.'

Fascinated, I watched his internal tussle: the consequences of a confession could be awkward, but he so *badly* wanted to boast.

'It's, as they say, complicated.'

As understanding dawned, I began to laugh. 'Oh, Quin. Who is she? Not Shiv?'

'Shiv?' He rolled his eyes. '*No.* You don't know her. Valeria is her name.'

Valeria? Where had I heard that . . . ?

'She works at the airport, at the private terminal.'

'I've met her! One morning when I came to pick you up! She's absolutely gorgeous. Young, though. Oh Quin, don't treat her badly—'

'I'm lovely to her.' He gave me a longer look. As if to remind me of just how lovely he could be. 'And she's . . . great. Calls me Mr Quinlivan. When we're—' Abruptly he stopped.

Mother of God. 'Look, it's none of my business, but I'm not sure how "lovely" you're actually being, if you're still porking Golden on the sly.'

'"Porking Golden on the sly"?' he mused, then sighed. 'And this is why I miss you so much.'

'You don't miss me. Not even a tiny amount.' Affectionately, I added, 'You great big eejit. Bye, Quin.'

*

'You bumped into him "by accident"?' Nola asked. 'Girl, do you think I came down in the last shower?'

I shrugged.

'Last night, at twenty to nine, was the first Monday you went there for your weekly shop?'

'. . . No.'

'How often? Recently?'

'. . . I went last week too. But it wasn't *exactly* a conscious thing.'

Nola took a sip of tea from her bone-china cup and gave a smug little smile. 'So? Did you find out what you needed to know?'

I took a breath. 'There's no going back to Quin.' A mix of sadness and relief came with the admission. 'I feel a lot of affection for him. But as a life partner? Not any more.'

Nola took another sip of tea.

'And *he's* okay.' That's what I'd really needed to know. 'He's doing fine.'

'I see. And how do you feel about *Luke* these days?'

I waited, trying to sort it all out, but 'Besotted' jumped from my mouth. 'Obsessed? No, forget I said that. It's just nostalgia. With strong physical attraction. It's bad. But it will pass.'

'Will it, though?'

Startled, I asked, 'What does that mean?'

'It's been four months and you've only got more gooey-eyed about him. Maybe you and he should have a conversation? Like adults. He might feel the same way.'

'No. The Luke I loved wouldn't have slept with me. Not while he had a partner. He's not that man any longer.'

'Do you know he was still with Kallie when he slept with you? As an actual fact?'

'Not, I guess, as an actual fact . . .'

'For the love of God, would you fecking well ask him!'

That's what Claire said, that's what Yara said. Maybe I should.

'Give me a day or so and I'll have a think.' I was exhausted from my incessant wondering and worrying about Luke. Then last night's mini-summit with Quin had depleted me entirely.

'Right now, I have to get some rest.'

93

I tumbled into bed and was deep in sleep when my phone jolted me awake—it was Claire.

'Has someone died?' She was the one who'd mocked Luke for making an actual phone call.

'No. No one. Sorry for ringing, but this is *big*. Have you seen her stories?'

'Who? Kallie?' I was still trying to get my head to work. 'No.'

'Her thoughts and prayers stuff? She's got her big break. Well, *a* break. One of her songs will be on a new TV show. Something on Hulu. From her carry-on, you'd swear she was being inducted into the Rock and Roll Hall of Fame.'

I was clicking on my iPad. And there was Kallie, bursting with excitement. Yes, it was real—a song she'd written and sung would be featured on Season One, Episode Four of *Widow Spider*, which would air in October on Hulu.

'Guys.' Now Kallie was tearful. 'You don't know how many times I almost gave up. I've made a lot of sacrifices to keep my dream alive. A lot, a *lot*.'

And you know what, I had to hand it to her. She'd done what she'd needed to do to live her life while continuing to keep faith in herself and her talent.

Okay, trying to swizz Kate out of money was fairly shoddy stuff. And if she was with Luke, I was horribly jealous of her. Despite all of this, I admired her determination.

There was also a strange relief. Although life didn't tend to dispense consolation prizes, my guilt about sleeping with Luke had been assuaged by Kallie's good fortune. She deserved a break.

She was still talking away, exhorting us to hold fast to our own dreams. 'Never, ever, *ever* give up.'

But not every dream comes true.

Many times it was better to walk away. Often a person was better off letting go of an unachievable goal than wasting their life.

'Listen to her.' Claire was so scornful. 'Like she's won the Nobel Prize for Taylor Swift Impersonators. Anyway! *That* was her big news. Not getting married or whatever to Luke.'

But Luke was still moving house. Probably—okay, well *possibly*—in with Kallie. And I was so worn down from the torment of not-knowing that maybe I didn't mind any longer?

Was I sensing a change in me, some sort of progress? Perhaps I really was letting go of him? Perhaps being *forced* to let go?

'Thanks, Claire, we'll talk tomorrow.'

'Oh. Okay.' She sounded deflated that I hadn't been more excited.

I expected that there wasn't a hope of getting back to sleep but when my phone rang again, I was once more fathoms down. Fighting my way to consciousness I was thinking that if this was Claire with some *more* fecking news about Kallie, I'd—Oh! It wasn't Claire, it was Helen.

It was thirteen minutes past one—a funny time to be checking in on me. 'Howya,' she said. 'Look. Something's . . . I don't know, but I'm bleeding.'

Horror-struck, I sat up. 'Where's Artie?'

'Geneva. That's why I'm ringing you.'

'Is it heavy?' I was out of bed, pulling sweats from a drawer, grabbing my keys and looking for my phone before I realized it was in my hand. 'Do you need an ambulance?'

'I . . .' Suddenly she sounded terrified. 'Rachel, I don't know.'

'Are you haemorrhaging?'

'No. It's like the start of a period. Not heavy. But it's there.'

'Okay. I'm coming to get you.' Would an ambulance be better? I had no clue. But the only person I trusted to do this was me. 'Be dressed, be ready to leave. I'll be with you in twenty minutes.'

Lit by a streetlamp, she was outside her home, looking pale and scared. I put her in the passenger seat and then drove to the hospital. Trying to be gentle, I hustled her inside.

'She's sixteen weeks!' I told the receptionist. 'She's bleeding.'

It was hard to not scream, *See her now. Right away! Make this terrible thing stop!*

Gratifyingly quickly, Helen was whisked off for a scan. Then my relief collapsed into horror—what if the baby's heartbeat had stopped?

Immediately, I wanted Luke.

Breathing in for four and out for seven, I talked to Yara, begging her to make this be okay. *In for four, out for seven.* Telling myself that Helen would be fine. *In for four, out for seven, in for four, out for seven.* On and on and on.

It had been ages now, over an hour, was that a good thing? A terrible thing? *In for four, out for seven. In for four, out for seven.*

And here came a nurse. I leapt up.

'She's fine, baby's fine. It was just spotting. It's frightening, but it happens. She spoke to her partner, reassured him. We'll keep her in overnight, just to be on the safe side, but she can go home in the morning.'

'Can I stay with her?'

'She needs to rest.'

I blurted, 'Were there two heartbeats on the monitor?'

'Yes.'

'You're sure?'

'. . . Yes.' Politely, 'You need to leave now.'

No. I needed to keep watch. It was where I'd gone wrong with Yara.

You're insane, I told myself.

I can't help it, I replied.

Outside in the night, I got into my car, but it was impossible to leave. Not yet anyway. So I breathed in for four seconds and out for seven seconds, then I did it again, then again, and the moments ticked by, one by one by one.

Every so often a taxi passed. At some stage two women walked by, then a man on his own, but the city was quiet. Still breathing in for four and out for seven, I stayed awake, on guard. At some stage there was a noise that sounded like a bird chirping. I waited, listening hard. I heard it again. It *was* a bird. Above the rooftops, a muddy glow appeared in the sky.

Another bird chirped, then more. The overhead glow became a radiant brown, then gleaming ochre.

It was tomorrow.

But I was still trapped in last night's horror.

I returned to the hospital. Helen's bleeding had stopped, she was ready to be discharged and the mood was upbeat. I drove her home, arriving just as Artie got in from Geneva.

After a shower and coffee at their place, I went to work. It was a busy day, a productive one, where a long-awaited breakthrough with one of my most stubborn ducklings finally happened.

There were times I was *really* good at my job. About once a year, I actually impressed myself and today was one of those days.

But it was all taking place a long way away, as if I were watching everything from a small, dark room.

After work, I went to an NA meeting and tried to explain my dread. Then I visited poor Nola and talked in rambling circles until I'd exhausted her. After going to a second meeting, a late-night one, I went home, managed to have a chat with Kate and Devin where I must have appeared normal, and went to bed.

But I couldn't sleep, still trapped in a place where I'd just experienced the most appalling loss.

Nola's instructions were to keep coming back to the facts. And the facts were that it was seven years later, I'd survived and my life was good.

Even so, I'd ended up back in this long-forgotten, liminal place where nothing felt real but everything felt terrible.

Finally I slept. Two and a half hours of blissful nothingness were mine, but at around 5 a.m., a jolt of adrenaline thrust me back into my waking hell.

When the birds began to announce the day, I knew I couldn't go to work. I could wing it on one sleepless night but not two.

In quiet despair, I thought—again—about calling Luke, but it was probably too late, it was one in the morning his time.

Unexpectedly, I felt a pang for Mum and Dad. I wanted to be minded even though I knew that they—that no one—could fix anything. But being in the family home might soothe me? It was worth a try.

Parking outside, their bedroom curtains were still pulled. Nine a.m. and they weren't up yet. No judgement from me. I let myself in, went to the kitchen and automatically began boiling the kettle. I'd try a mug of mint tea.

'What are you doing here!' Mum had appeared, impressively spectral in her rollers and pale billowing nightdress.

'Nothing. Just, I can't sleep.'

'You gave your poor father the fright of his life!'

'Sorry, Mum.'

After treating me to a good, long stare, she said, 'Why can't you sleep? Did Helen give you a scare? Are you thinking about your baby?'

Too exhausted to pretend, I said, 'I feel as horrific as I felt back then. Like it's just happened.'

'Would you like a biscuit?'

'No—'

'Would you like a sleeping tablet?'

'Wh-aat?'

She began rummaging through her fruit bowl. 'There's a load somewhere. For when we thought we'd have jet lag, but we didn't. Here they are!' She slung a small, familiar white box at me. 'Take a couple of them with a glass of water, then get some sleep. Your old room has the bed made up. I'm going to get dressed.'

As soon as she left, I slid the card of pills from the box. With trembling hands, I began popping them through their tinfoil, then I turned towards the kitchen tap.

94

Being in my teenage bed made no difference, I still couldn't sleep. I down-loaded an audiobook about the battle of Waterloo because I thought it would be boring, but it was actually fascinating.

I'd just googled 'extremely boring books' when Nola rang.

'People make fun of the word, but you've been "triggered",' she said. 'Helen's scare has brought it all back.'

She was right. And something else, I knew. After Yara's loss, I hadn't been taking those pills to sleep, I was taking them to escape. There was a differ-ence—subtle but, for an addict, it was huge.

Because I felt it now. I wanted to sleep. But I also wanted blank nothing-ness. They were not the same.

At some stage Dad came in with a Danish pastry and four chocolate Kimberleys on a plate. He showed his love by offering sweet things. About an hour later Mum arrived. 'I thought you'd be dead to the world,' she declared. 'Maybe the tablets were out of date? Come down and we'll watch *Escape to the Chateau*, it's hilarious.'

'No, thanks.'

'Do you mind if I do?'

Alone once again, I talked in my head with Yara, asking her to help me, to take away the fear, and if that wasn't possible, to help me bear it.

Why don't you call Luke?

But I couldn't differentiate between Yara and me. Was this real advice? Or was I just telling myself what I wanted to hear?

Dad had returned. 'Will you come down for Telly Bingo? We got you a card.'

'Oh, Dad. Thank you, but . . .'

'No bother. I'll do yours for you but if you win, you can claim it.'

'Thanks, Dad.'

You should ring Luke.

I, so badly, wanted to see him, to hear his voice. He was so kind. But it wasn't even six in the morning in Denver, he'd probably be asleep. And if Kallie was there, I didn't think I could cope.

'You didn't win.' Mum was back. 'On the Telly Bingo. None of us got anything. We're an unlucky family, we always were. Will you come down and eat something? There's quiche. Your father walked down to SuperValu by himself and bought it specially. There might be a small bit of ham in it, by accident. He says he's sorry.'

'Maybe later, Mum.'

After she'd departed, I stared helplessly at my iPad, overtaken by what I decided to call 'restraint fatigue'. I'd run out of the stamina to resist Face-Timing Luke. Anyway, it was nearly seven in the morning in Denver, he might be up.

'Rachel?' He was still in bed, the artificial light bleaching his face as pale as his bedsheets. 'Everything okay?'

'Sorry for waking you. Are you alone—'

'Hey, take a breath.' The camera steadied and there he was, in his dishevelled beauty. 'It's okay,' he insisted, sitting upright, pulling a sheet chest high. 'No one else is here. Tell me.'

'Helen, you know she's pregnant? Two nights ago she started bleeding—'

'*God.*' His alarm was visible.

'She's fine. But I was the one she called—Artie was away. I took her to the hospital and even though it wasn't what we went through—you and I—it's really affected me.'

'Yes. Like, of *course.*'

'She's back home, the bleeding has stopped, it wasn't the terrible thing I first thought but I still feel . . . in the middle of some horrible, horrible nightmare. The way I did in the hospital when you and I realized there was only one heartbeat.'

'*Angel.*' His voice was soft. 'Rachel. I'm guessing this is normal, after what we went through?'

'I know. Probably. Yes. Can I ask you a question?'

'Work away.'

'Luke.' I took a breath. 'Did you tell Kallie about us? About that night?'

'No.'

My heart sank to the centre of the earth.

'. . . Why would I?'

'Do you mean that you and Kallie are just carrying on, without her knowing?'

449

'Wha—No!' He gave a short, startled laugh. 'She and I were done before I even left Ireland.'

Thank you.

Thank you, thank you, thank you.

Sounding astonished, he said, 'I thought you knew.'

'How would I?'

'But . . . you know what I'm like,' he said. 'Mr By-the-Book. That night, outside your house, you asked if I'd like to come in and . . . yeah.' He sighed softly. 'That was it—me and Kallie were done. I had to tell her.'

'Right.' My voice was faint.

'And our night together? I would hardly have . . . Rachel!'

'Okay . . .'

'It was . . .' He paused. '. . . *hard* having to hurt Kallie. But what took place with you and me, I'm . . .' Again, he hesitated over the right word. '. . . grateful. So grateful for it.'

'You and Kallie still go horse-riding together?'

'Our horses are stabled at the same ranch. Our paths sometimes cross. We're, you know, friendly to each other. But no.'

'Quin and I broke up.'

'Yeah.' He half sighed. 'I kinda guessed.'

'How?'

'I'm an optimist.' Then he laughed. 'Okay, I'm not proud of this but I, ah . . . Quin's Instagram? He used to post a lot of photos of you . . . Are you okay? About the break-up?'

'Fine. He is too. But, Luke, I can't sleep. Not since the night with Helen. I mean, I can, slightly. It's not as if I've been wide awake since Helen rang. I'm just managing a couple of hours here and there—'

'Wait.' Suddenly he was urgent. 'Have you any access to pills?'

'I'm in Mum's, she gave me a whole box, this house is like a pharmacy—'

'Get rid of them!'

'I already have.' Speaking quickly, I said, 'Luke, listen to me, it's okay, I threw them down the sink. I didn't want them, not at *all*. But it was better to be safe—although Mum will probably kill me when she finds out. I've been to meetings, I had an epic session with Nola, I'm doing the breathing and meditation, I'm asking Yara for help, but I still feel so . . . *nightmare-y*. I could ring some helpline but . . .' I had to swallow hard. 'The only person I wanted to talk to is you. I'm so sorry.'

'Rachel.' His voice was so soft. So *lovely*. 'Why are you sorry? This is okay. It would always be okay.'

'Your kindness.' My voice shook. 'It's just so . . . Can you talk to me for a while? Until I feel slightly less . . . scared?'

'Of *course*. Is there anything that might help? If you were counselling a person who was upset, the way you are, what might you say?'

'. . . It's not my specialty, but I'd ask if they had memories of feeling calm or at peace.'

'Got it. So can you remember a time you felt calm? At peace?'

Something immediately came to mind and I discounted it.

'Maybe when you were a kid?'

'Let me have a . . .' I found another memory. 'I was about six or seven. Anna and I had draped a blue bedspread over a table. We were underneath, there were seashells on the floor, like we were under the ocean. The light was dim and blue, I remember feeling serene. Anna and I were the only ones who could breathe underwater. It was just us. I felt strong. Calm.'

'Any other memories? Places? People? Who made you feel that?'

'Luke.' My voice broke. 'I feel like that with you.'

'When?'

'Kind of . . .' I gulped. 'All of the time.'

'Okay.' He was thoughtful. 'Okay.' Then, 'So why don't I come and see you?'

'. . . What do you mean?'

'I mean, get on a plane and come to your house and, you know, *see* you?'

After a long silence, I asked, 'When?'

'Now. Well, as soon as I can catch a flight.'

'Are you . . . is this a joke?'

'Not a joke.'

'Would you really do that?'

'I really would.'

'. . . Why?'

'Can that wait? We can talk when I get there.'

'I have to ask, are you a Republican now? A Trump supporter?'

'Wha—No! Rachel, why would you think that?'

'Because people change.'

'How different did I seem that night? Because it felt to me as if nothing had changed.'

'That was just sex. We were always good at it.'

'It wasn't "just" anything, Rachel.' He paused. He frowned. 'It was *everything.*'

It was certainly how *I* had felt. But . . . 'You go horse-riding now. You're a bit holy. You're not a vegetarian.'

'These days you're a gardener, I was always slightly holy and even though there are times I eat meat, I'm mostly vegetarian. But the fundamentals of who you are or I am, they haven't changed. You always made me feel safe. Since we reconnected, it's been the same.'

About an hour later, he called. 'Are you still at your mum and dad's?'

'Yes. Where are you?'

'In my car. Heading to the airport.'

'Seriously?'

'If you could go home to your house? Take tomorrow off work?'

'Luke! Is this really——?'

'Layover in O'Hare, then landing in Dublin, just before five in the morning your time.'

Stunned, I said, 'I could come and pick you——'

'No. Thank you. I'd prefer privacy for . . . Yeah, a taxi is fine. Rachel, go home. Wait for me. I'll be there in the morning.'

At my house, Kate and Devin were *all action.* A large shopping bag stood on the kitchen table and they seemed to be emptying the contents of the fridge into it. Wildness was in the air, a sense of last-minute lawless looting.

Crunchie was clicking about, looking very concerned.

Devin looked up. 'Uncle Luke called.' Overlapping him, Kate said, 'We have to go to Devin's parents. Like, *now.*'

'Okaaay. Are you leaving me anything? Some chocolate? Apples?'

Ignoring my request, Kate asked, 'When can we come back?'

'I don't know. Maybe in a week?' I laughed slightly too much. 'I'll text you.' Then began laughing again.

I rang work, booked time off, then took a look in my fridge. It was almost empty, so I went to the fancy grocer's in Greystones and every ridiculous thing that caught my eye, I threw into my basket: truffled honey; small yellow tomatoes; things I thought were plums but were actually more tomatoes, purple this time. Crozier Blue cheese; abnormally big strawberries; attractively packaged mushroom soup even though mushrooms tasted to me like death; bananas, because you can't go wrong with bananas, unless of course, they're plantains (as three days later I discovered they were); chocolates from the Skelligs; smoked almonds; a large bouquet of white peonies; and finally, ice-cream, lots of it, and four pizzas—probably the only practical purchases.

Returning home, I put the flowers in a jug, then changed my bedsheets, had a bath, washed my hair, covered myself in Crème de Corps, painted my toenails and scouted out my shortie satin pyjamas from the back of a drawer. An impractical gift from Claire, I'd been saving the slippery, slidey top and shorts for a special occasion. Which—unless I'd misunderstood something fundamental here—seemed to have arrived.

I was woken by a text—which meant I'd been asleep! In a taxi. Be with you by 5.30am. L x

He was here, in the country, less than half an hour away. I set up sentry by the living-room window, content to do nothing but wait.

Outside, the sky was pitch black—my house was far enough from the city to escape the ever-present purple glow. After a while, a faint disturbance occurred in the darkness, a diffused yellowness, which grew into car head-lights. Then came the sound of an engine. A taxi pulled up in the road—curved and humming, looking like the only car on earth.

A man got out—tall, longish hair, leather jacket. He was carrying a bag. An exchange of low voices took place with the driver. Then the man turned from the car and came towards my house.

As he reached the door, I opened it.

'Babe.' Luke laughed in delight. 'Hello.'

I pulled him into the hall, patting his shoulders through his jacket, having to convince myself that he was real.

'You're really here,' I told him.

'I'm really here.' He dropped his bag.

'You've come all this way.'

'I've come all this way.' He slid his arms around my waist, his hands on my slippery pyjamas.

'But *why*, Luke?'

'Because . . .' he said, 'and I really need you to listen to this, Rachel Walsh.'

'I'm listening.'

'Because. I. Love. You.'

'Oh, thank God,' I blurted in a sharp exhale of relief.

'You're saying this is . . . good news?'

I gave him a look.

'Anything to say to me . . . ?'

'I love you too, Luke Costello.'

His smile was so wide, so happy. Taking my face in his hands, he moved his thumbs across the lilac circles under my eyes. 'Have you slept?'

'About three hours.'

'Not enough.' As his body stirred to life, he grimaced. 'Rachel, ignore it. It's got a mind of its own around you. I apologize for it. Come on, up those stairs, you need to sleep.'

'But—'

'Shhh. There's gonna be plenty of time for that.'

In the bedroom, with efficient speed, he cast off his jacket, whipped his T-shirt over his head and kicked away his boots. Briefly shy, he turned from me to tug at his belt, before unbuttoning himself, removing his jeans and underwear, then he reached for me. His fingers slid and slithered around my pyjama buttonholes and still he had the top open and off with commendable speed. Then he hooked his index fingers inside the waistband, laughed softly and shook the shorts. They shivered their way to the floor where I stepped easily out of them.

Lifting me as if I were a precious object, he placed me in the centre of the bed, then climbed in himself. Already I was curling and twisting my arms and legs around him, the familiar feel of his body and the beautiful smell of his skin calming any residual anxiety. This was how we'd always gone to sleep together, night after night, when we'd lived in New York.

'I love you,' he whispered.

'And I love you.' Dreamily, I admitted, 'This was what I thought of when you asked me to remember a time I'd felt at peace. This, just going to sleep with you on a random regular night.'

'You can do it again any time you want. Every night for the rest of your life, if you like.'

Somehow I already knew that. 'You live in Ireland now?'

'Soon.'

Sleep was pulling me deep into its delicious slipstream. 'Best news of all time. Luke, would you do me a favour?'

'Anything.'

'When we wake up, could you ask me something?'

'Of course.'

'Can you say, "I suppose a ride is out of the question?"'

With a jolt of unexpected laughter, he said, 'Done.'

He settled the duvet over us both, then turned out the light.

Skin against skin, his lips in my hair, my hand on his thigh, his arm across my body. My tight chest loosened and eased, every individual breath slow and calm. His exhales lengthened until, without even trying, we were keeping time with each other.

Together, we tumbled off the edge of the world into a deep, sweet sleep.

Acknowledgements

I've addressed some very painful life events in this book. If you've been affected by any of them, I offer you my sincere compassion. I didn't do formal research for the various addiction storylines because, as a recovering alcoholic, I know the condition well. If you're concerned that you might need help, your first port of call should probably be your GP.

If Trassa's story happens to be yours, RAINN and the Canadian Centre for Child Protection offer help in the US and Canada respectively.

Writing about Yara was a challenge and something that was extremely important to get right. I'm profoundly grateful to Clare Parker for, so generously, sharing her tragic loss with me. I've read and listened to other people's stories, and I hope I've adequately conveyed the enormity of such a devastating loss. If you've been affected by this part of the book, there are resources to follow that offer help.

Writing a book is a great privilege and a pleasure, but also a challenge—it's very hard to know when I'm doing it right. And especially so with *Again, Rachel* because so many readers (thank you!) cared about Rachel from the first time round and I *really* didn't want to let you down. There were a million times I doubted myself and without the support and hard work of all the people listed below, this book wouldn't exist.

My heartfelt thanks to the entire team at Michael Joseph, for working so hard and so generously on this book and all of my books over the past twenty-five years.

My career and life would have been so different if I hadn't been lucky enough, twenty-six years ago, to meet Louise Moore, my visionary publisher. From the word go, she has trusted me to write what I need to write, and I trust her to edit me as she sees fit. (Admittedly, I usually spend three days raging around the house when the notes first arrive, but then I calm down and acknowledge that she's right.) As well as publishing me with such sensitivity and verve, she's given me the courage and the space to take risks with my writing, something I appreciate deeply. I'm incredibly lucky to have her.

May I offer boundless gratitude also to Liz 'Lizzie McSmith' Smith for bringing so much enthusiasm, imagination and fun to every publication. Working with her and her fabulously creative team, including Lucy Upton, Jen Breslin and Colin Brush, is lovely!

Heartfelt thanks to the formidable Grace Long for her skilled editorial input; Christina Ellicott, Deirdre O'Connell and the entire sales team; Lee Motley for designing such a great jacket; Nick Lowndes for his heroic proofing and copy-setting; and Roy McMillan for his painstaking coaching and devotion to the audiobook—*and* for making it such fun.

At home, in Ireland, it's *lovely* being published by Penguin Ireland. It's a great team and especial thanks goes to my beloved Cliona Lewis, and Brian Walker and Carrie Anderson in sales. GRMMA!

I *love* Gemma Correll's cover illustration of Rachel and Crunchie—thank you.

Jonathan Lloyd has been my agent for twenty-seven years and, as with Louise, the day my path crossed with his was one of the great ones. Always supportive, always on top of the fine print and always, *always* great fun. I owe him so much.

Indeed, thank you to everyone at Curtis Brown, from the foreign rights department to TV & films, for taking such great care of my books.

Enormous thanks to the truly *terrifying* (although only when necessary . . .) Kealey Rigden for all the publicity and events work. As well as Fiona McMorrough and all at FMCM.

I'm so grateful to the people who read this book, in lumps and chunks, as I wrote it and who gave me all kinds of helpful feedback along the way: Jenny Boland, Róisín Ingle, Caitríona Keyes, Ema Keyes, Ljiljana Keyes, Mammy Keyes, Rita-Anne Keyes, Liz Nugent and Eileen Prendergast.

Special thanks goes to Louise O'Neill who, in November 2019, was the person who convinced me that I should try to write this book and who then encouraged me every step of the way.

And where would I be without my long-time bestie, 'Posh' Kate Beaufoy? She must have read this book at least twenty times, offering absolutely great editorial advice and always, always, love and encouragement.

I'm very grateful to Sarah Moore Fitzgerald who did an eleventh-hour pass of the manuscript just to put my mind at rest. Then Sophie White and Vicki

Notora, my first readers of the 'actual' book, who promised me it was okay.

My sobriety is the foundation stone that the rest of my life is balanced on; without it I'd have nothing. Every person at every meeting I've ever gone to has shored this up. v I want to thank two special women who have held my hand, given me strength and enabled me to stay safe: my own Nola, the angel-in-human-form that is Judy McLoughlin and my stalwart AK.

There aren't adequate words to thank my beloved husband. Always in my corner, he's the perfect first reader, somehow managing to be both honest and entirely encouraging. Endlessly patient, calm, proactive, hard-working and *very, very kind*. None of this would be possible without him.

Booksellers up and down the land have supported my writing since day one. I'd like to thank them for their generosity, enthusiasm, kindness and support.

Likewise, the many book bloggers and reviewers who've taken the time and trouble to read my books and report on them with such positivity, please accept my delighted gratitude.

Over the years countless other writers have recommended my books, given me cover quotes and provided a community that's supportive, funny and warm. There are too many to list individually, but thank you to every single one of them! Yizzer great!

I write (and never shut up talking . . .) about families. I fecken LOVE mine—Mammy Keyes, my brothers, my sisters, their spouses and my FAB-ALISS nieces and my nephews. Spending time with them is what makes me happiest in life.

One of my nephews is called Luka, and you may have noticed that Claire's son is also called Luka. That's because, several Walsh books ago, when Luka Keyes was only a babbie, I thought it would be cute. But I hadn't bargained on so much time passing and it's important that the two characters aren't confused. Luka Keyes is *nothing* like Claire's Luka: Luka Keyes is *not* earnest and no-craic, on the contrary he is charm itself and a right laugh. I just needed to say that . . .

Charlotte Mendlesson's beautiful book *Rhapsody in Green* arrived in the post at a time when I was struggling to find Rachel's 'missing piece'—and it turned out to be *gardening*! (No one was more surprised than me, but this is one example of the several serendipitous things that helped me to keep writing.)

You probably noticed I set this book in 2018. I'd already started writing *Again, Rachel* before the pandemic, and I didn't want to incorporate it into the story.

Finally, you, my beloved readers, I'm so grateful for how you've loved Rachel since she first appeared in print. Your fondness for her, for the Walshes (and Luke ;)) has filled me with delight. I honestly feel that you and I are friends, even though we might not have actually met (yet, like). I *sincerely* hope I didn't let you down.

Every day in North America, a number of families are faced with the devastation of the death of their baby. If you have been affected by Rachel, Luke and Yara's story, and would like to talk to someone, there are several organizations in Canada and the United States available for resources and support.

CANADA
Baby's Breath (www.babysbreathcanada.ca)
National: (800) 363-7437
Local: 905-688-8884
Email: info@babysbreathcanada.ca

UNITED STATES
The Compassionate Friends (https://www.compassionatefriends.org/)
National office: 877-969-0010
Email: nationaloffice@compassionatefriends.org